I0599765

Best FOR Last

BALEIGH JAYNE

Copyright © 2025 by Baleigh Jayne

All rights reserved.

No part of this book may be used or reproduced in any form or by any means, electronic or mechanical, including photocopying, recording, or by any information storage and retrieval system without prior written consent of the author except for the use of brief quotations in a book review.

The characters are events depicted in this book are fictitious. Any similarity to real persons, living or dead, is coincidental and not intended by the author.

Published by Baleigh Jayne

Edited by Kristen Hamilton

Cover Design by Ink and Laurel

Playlist

Best Friend's Brother (feat. Victoria Justice) - Victorious Cast
Nothing New (feat. Phoebe Bridgers) (Taylor's Version) (From the
Vault) - Taylor Swift
mirrorball - Taylor Swift
BIRDS OF A FEATHER - Billie Eilish
SUBJECT TO CHANGE - Kelsea Ballerini
Untouchable (Taylor's Version) - Taylor Swift
Delicate - Taylor Swift
Bejeweled - Taylor Swift
Paper Rings - Taylor Swift
Packing it Up - Gracie Abrams
Fix You - Cold Play
Little Bit Better - Caleb Hearn, ROSIE
The Alchemy - Taylor Swift
Anywhere But Here - Hillary Duff
Carry You home - Alex Warren
Close To You - Gracie Abrams
boyfriend (with Social House) - Ariana Grande, Social House
I Think I Like You - The Band CAMINO
Sally, When the Wine Runs Out - ROLE MODEL

Moonlight - Ariana Grande
Star - Bazzi
Family Line - Conan Gray
Friends - Chase Atlantic
you're all i ever dreamed of - Chelsea Cutler
Iris - The Goo Goo Dolls
As It Was - Harry Styles
Like Real People Do - Hozier
First Time - Hozier
Someday, someone - Kenzie Cait
Supercut - Lorde
Ribs - Lorde
Black and White - Niall Horan
Mess - Noah Kahan
Everywhere, Everything (with Gracie Abrams) - Noah Kahan,
Gracie Abrams
warm - Ariana Grande
Strong - One Direction
Bloom - Bonus Track - The Paper Kites
Look At That Woman - ROLE MODEL
Listen to the playlist on Spotify.

To the people who haven't quite found their place, you are worthy as you are. As the great Hannah Montana once said, "life is just a party so come as you are."

Author's Note

Best for Last is a story about overcoming challenges and facing fears, and naturally that includes some themes that might be upsetting for some readers. Don't you worry, there is a happy ending, but there are some things along the way that you might want to be aware of.

Some elements of this story might be triggering to some readers, such as: controlling parents, high school bullying, panic attacks, and parental neglect in childhood and adulthood. Please take care of yourself, and if any of these are triggering for you read with caution.

I hope you love Cami and Charlie. This story was one of discovery and fun for me, and I am extremely proud of it. These two leapt off the page for me and I hope you have the same experience reading it as I did writing it.

Grab your knitting needles and let's go.

With the most love,

Baleigh

November

CHAPTER 1
Charlie

"Bottom line, you're going to get traded if you don't make the people love you. You're a storm cloud of grumpy and mysterious, and while that was intriguing to the public for the first few years, they've forgotten about you now."

Sophie is the best agent money can buy, and trust me there's a lot of money involved, but right now I want to wring her neck. I'm coming up on a contract year with the New York Rangers and she seems to think the only way I'll stay with them through the end of my career is if I fix my public image.

She isn't wrong, I guess. I would say the state of my image right now is...nonexistent. I don't have one. I don't go out, I don't have friends besides my sister and Cami, I don't join the team for post-game bar crawls, and I don't date. If I can stay out of the media, I'm happy. There's nothing to talk about because I do nothing. It's easier that way.

Except now, if I want to be a part of the elite group of players in the National Hockey League who stay with the same team their entire career I need to step it up. Not being traded at some point within a player's career is not the norm, but when I signed on with the New York Rangers in my senior year of college, I knew I had to defy the odds.

I had found a solid organization with a solid coaching team and from what I experienced, the guys weren't bad. I wanted to get comfortable there, but not too comfortable, and do what I needed to in order to stay under the radar. Not only from the media, but from my team as well. The last time I got close with my teammates, it didn't end well. I promised myself I would never put myself in that position ever again. If I get traded, I might get stuck with teammates like *them*, and that can't happen.

So as much as I wish what Sophie was saying wasn't true, I know it is.

"And how do you suppose I do that, Soph? I don't like *the people*." I use my hands to put quotations around the words and she rolls her eyes, done with my drama.

"We both know you aren't this grumpy, surly, mean man that you present to the world. Underneath it all you're just a giant teddy bear." She reaches up and squeezes my arms. I swat her hands away. "To the world you're just another big scary hockey player with a nice face, and we have to change that. We need to make you one of *the* faces of the Rangers, so there's no way to separate you from them. When people think of the Rangers, they think of you."

She's not wrong, I don't let anyone see the softer side. I used to, but once someone takes advantage of your kindness and vulnerability and uses it against you...it's hard to come back from that.

Sophie is one of the few people who get this version of me, this more open and lively version, and she's earned that place in my life. When I graduated college I had lots of men in their forties and fifties wanting to work with me as my agent, but the barely five foot blonde in a kick ass pantsuit caught my attention immediately. She's young, in her thirties, and the way she held herself and spoke about her craft showed confidence and maturity. Plus she was a woman in a male dominated field. That in and of itself was impressive.

"I guess you're right."

"My two favorite words," she says with a wink. I scoff.

"So what do I do?"

"You need to start dating someone."

Excuse me?

"*No*. Dating someone? How is that the first solution you jumped to?"

"Charlie, come on." She says the words like it's ridiculous that she needs to explain it to me. "Love sells, I mean look at Taylor and Travis. If the media starts to see you with a girl that's charismatic and spunky on your arm, you are sure to catch their attention. Especially because you never date. It'll be front page news and then, once they're hooked, you can keep showing them the softer side of you. They'll love you."

That is my problem. I don't want anyone else to see the softer side of me. My soft side is reserved for a very small group of people and the media is nowhere on that list.

"I don't think this is the best solution. Plus, you know I don't date. I don't even know where I'd start with trying to find someone to date."

"Okay, so I'll make you a few profiles on dating sites," she says, completely ignoring my first comment. "*Honey Love* apparently is doing really well right now. Their success rate is a solid thirty percent."

"You do hear yourself, right?" She smacks my shoulder with the back of her hand. "*Honey Love*? A success rate of thirty percent?"

"Well, it's better than *Grab n' Go*," she scoffs.

"There's a dating app called *Grab n' Go*?" She nods her head solemnly. "I don't even want to know what that is referring to."

"Don't go to their website. You don't want to know."

"You don't have to tell me twice."

I run my fingers through my hair and swipe my palm down my face, releasing a frustrated groan. It's irritating that this is my current reality, but I guess I'm not surprised. I've been with the Rangers for seven years now, which is really unheard of. Hockey players don't stay in one place for long. There are only around 120 guys that have stayed with the same team their whole career and I'm determined to be one of them.

Not only do I want to stay with teammates I've grown comfortable with and somewhat trust not to turn their backs on me, I don't want to leave my sister. Alana and I had an interesting childhood with parents who did the bare minimum when it came to loving us. They showed their love to me far more than they did to my sister, and the more they showed me favor the more I resented them. Now, she's the only close family I have and it's the same for her. If I move away from the Rangers, I'd also be moving away from her.

I groan realizing that, with those things in mind, I know I need to do this. Sophie is the expert and if she thinks a girlfriend will keep me in New York, then I need to do whatever she says.

"Okay. I'll do it." I breathe in deeply and let it out. Sophie starts bouncing up and down on her toes and clapping. "But I'm not dating someone for real, just until I get another contract. And she's going to know it's for show from the start. I don't want to loop someone into this and have them think it's something that it's not. I'm not doing this to get into a long-term relationship and I don't want someone expecting that."

"Aww." She reaches over and playfully pinches my cheeks. I pull my head back and push her hands away with a laugh. Sophie has turned into family in the seven years we've been working together. She's not as close as a sister, but I'd say she's definitely in cousin territory. "You're such a good guy. Some woman is going to be very lucky to fake date you."

"Whatever. You're just saying that because you're my agent. You have to."

"Not true, you're a stellar guy. Once you let someone see every side of you and you let them all the way in, they don't have any other choice but to love you."

I smile at her placatingly, but she's wrong. No one knows every side of me—and no one ever will—not even my sister. But I can smile and keep up appearances while I fake date someone. Once I get signed again everything will go back to normal.

"I'll find someone, I don't need to get on a dating app."

"Have you seen the current dating scene?" I just stare at her. She knows how long it's been since I've tried to date. "Here look at this."

She shoves her phone at me, a screenshot of a guy's profile lighting it up. The man is in his late thirties and standing in one of the dirtiest bathrooms I've ever seen. There are stains all over part of the countertop and behind him the sheetrock in the wall is completely torn apart, so there is a gaping hole in the wall. The shower curtain is pulled back to reveal a grimy tiled tub and a broken shelf. The guy himself has one arm out of his shirt, leaving that side bunched up around his shoulder. He's flexing his (imaginary) muscle, but really it just looks like he got caught in the middle of taking off his shirt.

His bio says he's married.

"Married? What the hell?"

"I know. If men have anything, it's the audacity. You haven't even seen the worst of it, this was the second photo on his profile."

She scrolls up and shows me a photo of the guy in his bedroom. His disgusting bedroom. He has *Among Us!* sheets on his twin sized bunk bed—he's in his thirties—and there's trash everywhere. Without saying anything, she reaches over and zooms in on a box sticking out from the top of the bed. A box that absolutely should have stayed in his side table drawer where no one would have ever seen it. I want to puke.

"Did this guy like you?" I ask, alarm clear in my voice. I have to cover my mouth to keep from gagging. My mind immediately goes to my younger sister and our best friend, Cami.

Cami was Alana's friend first, the two of them becoming close when Cami's family moved into a house next to ours in Celebration, Florida when my sister was just entering high school. Over the years, the three of us have grown close, and if they are having to field off these kinds of people on these apps, I think I may need to have a conversation with them about deleting them.

"Just one of many. You're sure you don't need any help?"

"I'll figure something out."

"Whatever you say, boss man."

This whole thing is extremely overwhelming and makes me uncomfortable, but I don't have a choice. I have three months to work on my public image and while I don't want to pretend to date someone just for some bogus media stunt, I know I need to. I just need to figure out who.

CHAPTER 2

Cami

ME

If I ever get married, I only want you at the dress shopping

BESTIE FRIEND

Oh, come on. You'd want your mom and sister there. Enjoy today. You only get to go wedding dress shopping with your sister once.

ME

You're right, but who knows maybe we'll be doing this again

BESTIE FRIEND

With Colette, I think we both know she's a one and done kind of girl.

BEING BURIED IN LAYERS AND LAYERS OF TAFFETA, organza, and satin in various shades of white and cream is not how I would typically start my Saturday mornings, but here I am. The tiny bridal boutique I've found myself in this morning is making me claustrophobic for more reasons than one. Drowning in wedding dresses is never a state I thought I'd find myself, but thankfully I'm not here for me today.

"Ooo bring that one here, Cam, I love the pearls." My sister makes grabby hands at the dress that is currently half draped over my arm and right shoulder. She pulls it off of me, thankfully, and hands it to the attendant who is helping us today.

She's tried on more gowns than I can count and none of them have been "the one" so we're still looking. I don't blame her for wanting to get it right, it's a big deal.

I can't imagine picking one single dress for the biggest day of your life, but that tracks because I can't ever seem to love something enough for it to be *the one*. I usually end up picking the *two* or *three*, then switch back and forth between them until I figure out what feels right in the moment.

Shoes, clothes, boys, favorite sodas, coffee order, lunch spot. I can't ever stick with one thing for too long. It's my mother's least favorite trait about me and possibly one of the things I love most about myself. It keeps people guessing.

My best friends, Alana and Charlie, and my job are the only two permanent things in my life that I feel secure in. They keep me grounded. Right now though, Alana is preparing for a business trip to Paris with our coworker, Alex. She's been so busy that it almost feels like she's already gone, but we still have a little over a week before she officially leaves.

I'm losing precious hours with my bestie this weekend because my sister and mom insisted I come to Florida to help with wedding planning. My baby sister, Colette, who is twenty years old, is getting married in February and I've been roped into helping out. Not that I don't want to, I love my sister and I'm happy for her, but she's so young and my parents keep reminding me that *I* should be the one getting married first, that *I* need to be settling down. Why can't I be more like their precious Coco who stayed close to home? It's just a reminder of how I never lived up to my parents' expectations for me.

I try to stay in the moment though. These are memories with her I won't ever get back and I don't want anything clouding them.

She walks out in a dress that I swear looks like a cupcake. It has a tight bodice and a full skirt that I know I could balance a glass of wine on if I wanted to. The skirt has sparkles all throughout, which remind me of sprinkles, and fabric draping in wide U shapes all around the top of it. I can tell by the look on her face that she hates it.

"Oh, sweetie, just look at you. This one is my pick, I knew it would be beautiful on you." My mom stands and walks until she's behind Colette, then pulls her hair back and looks at her through the mirror. "What do you think?"

My mom, Miranda Slate, is the picture of perfection. She's put together, poised and charming. I love her to death, but she and I have had a tumultuous relationship as I've grown up. She's never been quite satisfied with the way I live my life, and it's caused tension.

There are a few moments of silence while the attendant watches on from the corner. Colette and I make eye contact in the mirror and I narrow my eyes just slightly, hopefully communicating *Don't censor yourself, this is your wedding* and I think I get through to her.

"Um..." She picks at the skirt nervously. "I like it, we can keep it as a maybe while I try on the others."

My sister, ever the people pleaser. She gets her desired effect though as my mom smiles happily and steps back, allowing the attendant to take her back into the changing room.

We repeat this over and over until finally Colette steps out in the most beautiful dress I've ever seen. A dress that, if I was wearing it, might cure my commitment-phobia.

It's a strapless satin ivory dress and the fabric is bunched just so that it looks like it ties in the middle of her chest. The skirt drapes down from her waist and an overlay flows down around it. The best part, though, are the pearls fixed to the tulle skirt. They rain down around her in an unpredictable, yet even, pattern from her waist to the ground. This dress screams romance and fairytale and it's absolute perfection for my sister.

The attendant has gathered her hair into a makeshift updo and fasted a pearl clip into it, then added a veil overtop. She looks radiant and the smile on her face reveals what I already know. This is the one.

"Do you like it?" she asks timidly, glancing at me out of the corner of her eye. Of course she checks with everyone else before sharing her opinion. I cut in quickly before my mom can get a word out.

"What do *you* think about it, Coco?"

She looks at herself in the mirror, her hands brushing reverently over the fabric.

"I love it." There are tears in her eyes and as soon as I notice them, they appear in mine as well. I stand and walk over to her, enveloping her in a hug. It hits me now that my little sister is getting married. Starting her own life with a partner who isn't me. We've always been close, and I know that won't change, but adding someone to your life is a huge change.

"I think you look stunning. You have to get it, this is absolutely the one. Derrick is going to freak when he sees you."

"You think?"

"I know." I realize I've completely forgotten my mom behind me, and I brace as I turn to hear her comments. Where I expect to find a critical eye, I instead find her with tears streaming down her face. She stands and joins us, hugging us both tight.

"You look absolutely beautiful, sweetheart. This dress is perfect."

I sigh in relief.

After our emotional group hug, Colette gets changed and my mom heads to the front of the store to handle the ordering and payment. We meet her up there and walk out, my sister and I hand in hand.

"Cami, Joan told me her son is looking for a girl. I could set you two up."

I tense and I think Colette can feel it through my grip. I was waiting all day for this conversation, but I stupidly thought I had made it out of the danger zone. Guess I was wrong.

"That's nice of you to think of me, Mom, but I'm good. He lives here and I'm in New York, it wouldn't work."

"He actually lives in New York, I think she said Scarsdale?"

Scarsdale is one of the wealthiest towns in the country. Not to mention it's an hour and a half away from where I live.

"Wow, what does Joan's son do for a living?"

"He's a lawyer. He'd be a great option for you, honey. He can provide for you and you could bring him to the wedding. It would be so fun to have a date, wouldn't it?"

My sister squeezes my hand in a show of support. This is probably the hundredth time my mom has pressed me to bring a date to my sister's wedding and I have told her every single time that I don't want to, but clearly that isn't working. She doesn't let me speak before continuing.

"I just think it would be good for you to settle down. You can't keep flitting from boy to boy and expect someone to take you seriously. You do all those silly little hobbies and can't ever seem to stick to one thing. Men don't see that as an attractive trait, sweetheart, they see it as immature and flighty."

I take a deep breath, trying not to go off on her. I've done it before and it doesn't help. The sad thing is, she thinks she's being loving and helpful right now by giving me advice, but it's anything but. I don't know why I can't seem to stick with any one thing or person for longer than a few weeks, but I just can't. Nothing feels like staying material.

I just want her to stop, and before I can even think about what

I'm doing I blurt out an excuse. "I can't date Joan's son and I don't need a date to the wedding because I already have one."

I feel Colette tense beside me as we approach our car. I turn and she looks at me with wide, confused eyes. I know I'm mirroring her expression, because I have no idea what possessed me to say that but I can't take it back now.

"You have a boyfriend? Someone you plan to bring to the wedding in three months?"

"Mmhmm," I say as I climb into the back seat.

"Oh, honey, that is the best news. I can't wait to meet him."

I am so screwed.

CHAPTER 3
Charlie

Angel's—Cami, Alana, and I's favorite Mexican restaurant—is busy for a Tuesday night, but I'm not complaining. The noise and buzz of conversations surrounding me make it easier to slip into the crowd with less chance of being noticed. I wouldn't say I'm a celebrity, I try to stay out of the spotlight as much as possible, but there are people who recognize me in public. I love that the Rangers' fans are so supportive, but I hate making a scene.

There was a time in my life when I'd loved being the center of attention. I was always itching for the popular position in school. Quarterback, captain, student body president, you name it and I was gunning for it. But that was before. Now I prefer to sit in the booth in the back corner alone with my people and not be bothered.

I notice as soon as Cami walks in, because it's impossible not to. Her personality fills up a room and forces everyone to turn their heads, as evidenced by the fact that the four tables closest to the front door all turn at her entrance. She speaks loudly, a smile splitting her face as she says hello to the hostess, Sierra, and after exchanging a few words she makes her way back to our booth.

"Charles," she says as she slides in across from me. We started this silly little nickname game a few years ago. I have no idea why, but one day she walked up to me and called me Charles. I grumbled at her that it wasn't my name, and in true Cami fashion she decided she would stick with it after realizing it annoyed me. I've gotten used to it, it would feel weird not doing it now.

"Cassandra. No Alana today?" Not only did Alana not make the walk with her after work, but she also typically sits across from me in the booth, where Cami is currently sitting.

She and Alana work together. We became a trio in high school when I needed a soft place to land, and we've been inseparable ever since.

"Nah, she said she had too much to do to get ready for Paris. You know her, perfectionist control freak and all that jazz."

She reaches toward the middle of the table and snags a chip from the basket, then dips it into the queso and takes a bite, moaning in pleasure as she chews.

"That is so forking good."

"Forking?" I ask, wondering if maybe I misheard her. She tends to have a bit of a potty mouth. She doesn't care what others think of her, so she just lets it fly. It's something I admire about her.

"Trying not to cuss as much. They say it on *The Good Place*."

"Incredible TV show, but why are you cutting back on the cussing?"

She shrugs and I don't push it. That's another thing about her, she doesn't always have elaborate reasons behind the things she does. Sometimes she just feels like cussing less, so she does it.

"So, how was work? And your trip?" I ask.

"Work was good. Just getting settled in after being away on Friday and making sure everything is ready to go for the next issue. The trip was fine. Colette found her dress so that's good."

She keeps eating without meeting my eyes and I know that means it must've been a bit of a hard trip. I've known Cami for awhile, so I know spending time with her mom can be hard for her sometimes. Her relationship with her mom is a good one all things considered, nothing like mine with my parents, but she can be critical of her and I know that's hard for Cami.

"How was your mom?" I say after debating whether or not to ask the question, then ultimately deciding to.

"Oh you know, same song, different verse. She had plenty to say about me "flitting" from hobby to hobby and my lack of settling down being seen as "immature" to men. Other than that, peachy." She says the two words with air quotes and I try not to let my unhappiness show on my face. Cami is a different kind of girl. She's in her late twenties, and has a beautiful figure and gorgeous blonde locks that flow down to her back. She's petite at just about five foot two, has a quirky and bright personality, and you always know when she enters a room because her signature pineapple and vanilla scent follows her.

"I'm sorry, Cam. You know none of that stuff is true." I reach over and touch her hand, bringing her attention back to me. I think I notice a watery sheen to her hazel eyes when she looks up at me, but it's gone as soon as it appears. She clears her throat and a wobbly smile touches her lips.

"I'm over it." She waves her hand in the air in a dismissive gesture. "Tell me about your weekend. I watched the game, looked like it went well."

She doesn't understand much about hockey, but she's always been to every game she can attend with Alana right by her side. This weekend we played the New Jersey Devils and won three to one. It was a solid game.

"Yeah it did, I think we've figured out our stride. How to work together and all that."

"You still refusing to be friends with anyone on the team?"

Now it's my turn to shrug, not really wanting to talk about it, but of course she pushes anyway.

"You would probably hit an even better stride if you hung out with the guys off of the ice. I know you're hesitant after what happened in high school." My eyes shoot up to her, suddenly afraid she knows. But I can tell she doesn't; she's just making a general reference. I take a deep breath and force the panic in my chest to ease as she keeps talking. "But these are good guys. You've been around them for seven years at this point. You have to trust them and let them in sometime."

"Don't remind me it's been seven years, Sophie is doing that enough these days," I say, trying to guide the conversation away from making friends. I didn't think, though, about the topic I was bringing up. This is another one I'd rather not touch right now, but I'm the one who mentioned it.

"What do you mean? Is she talking about your contract?"

I sigh, not wanting to talk about this.

"Yeah, she thinks I need to work on my public image if I want to stay in New York."

"Your public image? What do you mean? You don't have one."

"That seems to be the problem."

We pause briefly to place our orders, then continue.

"So she wants you to put yourself out there more?" I can tell she's determined to help me by the look on her face, and I need to shut it down quickly. I don't want her help and I don't even know if I'm going to actually go through with operation *make the people love you*.

"Amongst other things, but I'll figure it out. I've got it."

"Well, sure but I can—"

"I said I've got it, Cami," I say firmly, but she needs to understand that this is my problem to fix. I've never liked going to others to ask for help and I don't want to now. It's a last resort, and one that I'm already coming to terms with in regards to having a fake girlfriend.

I almost tell her about that, too, but then decide not to. I don't want her dragged into it. I can see the rejection sting in her eyes, but she recovers just as quickly, moving on to another topic. If there's anyone in the world I would share this with besides my sister, it would be our best friend. I just don't want her to have to carry my burdens.

"So, how are you feeling about your sister leaving?" she asks as our waiter brings our food. I'm grateful for a topic change as I dig in.

"I'm a little nervous for her if I'm honest. And I don't know how I feel about that Alex guy."

"Alex is great, and I think they'll work well together. I also think he has a thing for her, but she disagrees."

The protective nature within me rises and makes me want to go and meet this guy, then threaten him with serious harm if he does anything to hurt my sister, but I know that isn't my place. They haven't even established anything beyond a friendship, so I force the feeling down.

"Well, if you think he's great then he must be."

"I can't tell if you're joking or serious."

"A little of both."

She throws a chip at me and we laugh and talk through the rest of our dinner. When we finish, I walk with her a few blocks to her apartment building and make sure she gets inside, then I head back to my car.

CHAPTER 4

Cami

BESTIE FRIEND
You coming?

ME
Running two seconds late

BESTIE FRIEND
Not surprised!

ME
Sorry, shoe situation. Will explain

I'M STUMBLING THROUGH MY DOOR AT 7:05 A.M., exactly five minutes after I'm supposed to meet Alana in the hallway to walk to work. Her and I have lived in the same apartment building, just a few doors down from one another, for a while now. It's another level of friendship when you work *and* live together in the same apartment building. I can't ever get rid of the girl, and I wouldn't want to.

We became friends when I moved into the pastel yellow house next to their baby blue one. It was the summer before our freshman year of high school and our family had just moved to the small Florida town of Celebration. I was incredibly grateful for the girl next door who was welcoming and kind, and the way she took me under her wing and showed me the ropes of the town.

We entered high school together after hanging out over the summer, and from that moment on we were inseparable. It was always just the two of us, with little glimpses of Alana's older brother as he passed through the kitchen or left to hang out with his friends, but all of that changed during his junior year.

I remember the day almost vividly, Alana and I were sitting on the floor in her bedroom making friendship bracelets and she shared with me that her brother had become very withdrawn and stopped hanging out with his friends. She told me her parents hardly paid attention or cared, but she was worried.

He came in that night and sat down with us on the carpet, messing around on his phone and pretending not to care about whatever we were talking about, but chiming in regardless. He never really stopped spending time with us after that night, and I was happy to have him tag along.

He never got his sparkle back, but we got to know the new, more quiet version of him and that's who he's been ever since.

Thankfully I thought to text Alana this morning that I was running a little late so she didn't end up standing in the hallway knocking and waiting for me to get myself together. I tend to always be a little late, a little disorganized, a little *immature* as my mother would say. I think it's charming.

"I am so sorry, Lan, I was hurrying but then I got distracted trying to pick out shoes. I ended up finding those midnight blue ones that I wore to the gala last winter, remember those?" She nods her head as we walk. "Anyways I had to try them on because I missed them and then I realized I was running behind."

"No worries, girl. Finding a missing pair of shoes is worthy of a five minute delay."

This is what I love about her. She doesn't ever make me feel silly for my type B chaos. She embraces it and loves me because of it, and that's not something I have a lot of in my life. Most people want to fix me. They think my disorganization and general flightiness is a negative trait, and it can be, but I try to make sure I show up when I commit to something.

I love our apartment building for a lot of reasons, but one of the main ones is the proximity to our office. It's only a few blocks away, and after a few short minutes of chit chat as we walk, we've arrived in front of it.

The *Impress Magazine* building stands tall amongst the other skyscrapers on Fifth Avenue. The large glass doors swing open, courtesy of the doormen, as we approach. Our shoes click clack on the marble floors as we make our way past the receptionist and towards the elevators.

Impress is one of the top fashion magazines in the country and I've been working here for five years now as a beauty assistant editor. I got this job right after I graduated from New York University and was convinced I was in some sort of simulation. It wasn't normal to land a job this huge right out of college but Heather, the editor-in-chief, said she saw something in me and took a chance on me. It's been an incredible five years.

The elevator doors slide open when we reach the twentieth floor and we head to our cubicles. Thankfully our desks are right next to each other, so I can bother her whenever I want.

Our work spaces reflect our personalities well. While Alana keeps her office in tip top shape every day and color coordinates her sticky notes and highlighters, my space looks like a tornado flew through it. I know where everything is, though.

I get settled into my desk for the day and look over my calendar. Only the permanent things make it on to the calendar, which means *Angel's* dinner dates, work meetings, and knitting club. Everything else is just floating inside my brain.

I have a meeting with Olivia, an editorial assistant, in half an hour to go over the details for a shoot happening this week. We're preparing for the spring issue, so while the world around me is buried in a foot of snow and bundled up in coats and mittens, I'm surrounded by flowers and pastels.

I make my way down to the conference room we're using for our meeting today and stop by the break room to grab a coffee. I pop it into the machine and push the button, watching it slowly stream down into my mug. I'm in a trance staring at the steam coming up from the brewing coffee when someone catches my attention.

"How's it going, Cami?"

Alex, an editor at the magazine and one of Alana and I's friends, has just slipped into the breakroom likely to grab he and Alana's morning beverages.

"Good, just fueling up for another grueling day talking about makeup and hair."

"Grueling, indeed. Need anything from the fridge?" He pauses, the door ajar, his sparkling water tucked into his elbow and a Diet Coke in one hand. I love this about Alex. He is constantly taking care of the people around him in all of the small ways. He'd be so good for Alana and I know he's into her, he just needs to admit it to himself and to her. Maybe something will happen while they're together in Paris on this business trip they're being sent on.

"No, I'm good. Thanks though."

"Anytime, have a great day."

"You too."

I follow him out, coffee in hand, and head the opposite direction towards the conference room. Olivia is already inside, jotting things down in her notebook. I pull out the chair next to her and take a seat, pulling out my materials.

"What's the coffee today?" she asks. Coffee is yet another thing that changes daily for me. I never like to land on any one flavor or type, so I change it up and pick something different depending on my mood.

"It's brown sugar cinnamon. I wanted something a little spicy and a little sweet."

"Just like you," she says with a wink.

"Exactly."

We turn to our computers and get to work coordinating and making sure we have all of our ducks in a row. It's a lot to manage and I'm thankful I have Olivia to help me make sure nothing slips through the cracks. If you're coordinating a shoot and forget to schedule hair or makeup, or give the model the wrong venue or date, you've wasted a lot of money and a lot of time. It's never a good look.

My phone buzzes on the table, distracting me from what Olivia is saying, but I see the name Charles on my screen and I can't ignore it.

CHARLES

Thought you might be interested in this.

Attached is a link to a TikTok about different knitting stitches, which showed up on my feed earlier this morning. It makes me smile thinking he gets knitting videos on his page just because he's started sending them to me. I know he doesn't care at all about knitting, but knowing he watches them through to see if they might be useful to me makes me smile.

ME

I'll be sure to show the ladies this week, thanks Charles. Having a good day?

CHARLES

Good enough. Practice later.

Some might be turned off by his to-the-point style of communicating, but it's just Charlie to me. This is how he is, how he's always been since that day in high school when he changed. I still to this day don't know what happened, he keeps it close to the chest, but I can only imagine it was pretty rough considering the way it changed and morphed him into the closed off version of himself.

ME

Be safe. Can't have you wiping out and
breaking something

CHARLES

You know I wear a ton of padding. Plus I've
been doing this my entire life.

ME

I know, just messing with you. See you later?

CHARLES

Yep. Have a good day Cassandra.

ME

"All set?" Olivia's voice takes me out of my own head and
reminds me I'm in the middle of a meeting.

"Oh, yes. I'm sorry, where were we?"

I bring my attention back to what we're discussing. Everything
for the shoot this week is in order and prepped. I'll feel better once
it's done, but I always feel that way. There's this weird nervous
anticipation that comes along with events and shoots like this for
work.

The rest of the day moves by quickly. We have a meeting with
all of the editors at the magazine, one we have once a month to
make sure we're all on the same page, then Alana and I had lunch
together at a local bistro. In the afternoon, I make sure I have the
layout for the beauty sections of the spring issue, or at least an early
mock up of them. The day passes quickly, and I'm thankful at the
end of it to head home, arm in arm with one of my besties.

CHAPTER 5
Charlie

I SLIP THE SKATES OVER MY FEET AND PRESS MY WEIGHT down onto them, settling into the comfortable routine of lacing them up and preparing for practice. After growing up in the sport, I could do this in my sleep.

My teammates race past me, headed to the ice. I shift subtly, angling my body so I can see better out of the corner of my left eye as I lace up my skates. The position allows me to see what's coming and I recognize that it's a response to what happened in the past, but I don't correct myself or force myself to relax. These instincts are there for a reason, and it doesn't hurt to be aware of what's going on around me.

I don't think anyone close to me is aware of how jumpy I can be. I always feel like I'm looking around the corner, always waiting for the other shoe to drop. I've been on the Rangers for a long time now, and these guys have proven themselves mostly trustworthy, but I still can't seem to relax.

I was tempted to completely quit after...we'll just call it *The Event*. There was no way my dad would have let me, though. My hockey career was and is everything to him, not *me*.

I used to be loud and goofy and the life of the party, but I retreated after everything that happened. I didn't ever go to a therapist, but I'm sure I was experiencing some sort of depression. I've mostly figured out how to deal with it at this point in life, and I'm far enough away from the past that I can manage. I know those close to me noticed the shift in my personality, but no one pushed and I wasn't about to open up my deepest wounds if I didn't have to.

I stand and walk towards the ice, hopping the boards and skating a few slow laps to warm up. I observe my teammates as I stretch a little and for the first time in a while I feel a pang of jealousy. It's probably because of all this talk of being more liked, but I find myself feeling bitter at their easy conversation and laughter. The way they trust one another on and off the ice.

I trust most of these guys on the ice, they're good at what they do and they love it, which makes them pretty well qualified. Off the ice is another story. Not because they've done anything to prove that they aren't deserving of trust, but because I haven't even given them the opportunity to earn it.

That has to change though, because along with Sophie's desire for me to make the public like me, she also wants me to improve my relationships on the team. Fake dating someone sounds easier than making friends with these guys, if I'm being honest.

I spend the entire practice thinking about the best way to strike up a conversation with Soren Wright, a left winger on the first line with me. He's a few years younger than me and started his contract with the Rangers last year. From what I've observed, he seems like a good guy. He's always offering to stay after practice and help other players on the team if they're struggling with a skill or offering to stay back and help our equipment managers if things get crazy. I keep reminding myself that just because I speak to him and try to make friends, doesn't mean I have to give him my trust.

We do a few drills and I feel good today. Coach calls out orders and critiques as we play and I get lost in the feel of the ice beneath my feet. Despite the fact that I resented this sport at one time in my life because of the pressure from my dad, it really has become a place for me to release all of my stress. My thoughts and worries disappear when I'm on the ice, and the game is the only thing that exists.

As we wrap up, I place a heavy hand on Soren's shoulder.

"Nice job out there today, Wright." I hold my hand up for a first bump and it lingers there in the air for a second. The shock on Soren's face is evident and he clearly is so stunned that I'm speaking to him that he doesn't register the gesture. When he doesn't raise his fist to meet mine, I go ahead and use mine to tap his shoulder.

"Sorry, man, you too. You're always great on the ice."

The compliment makes me uncomfortable, something within me trained to not accept it, but I push past it and try to continue the conversation. I just keep reminding myself that casual conversation is a small price to pay for another few years here.

"You got any big plans this weekend?" I ask.

Soren hesitates again, but recovers quicker this time.

"Not much, hanging out with a few buddies." He reaches his hand back and rubs his neck. "A couple of the guys and I are going to Teddy's for beers after this. You wanna join?"

I should say yes, but the interaction itself was enough of a stretch for me today. I'm supposed to be making friends, and I am trying. After this conversation, I'm going to say that mission is accomplished for today.

"Thanks for the offer, but I've got plans tonight." I don't. "Maybe next time." I'm lying.

"No problem, have a good night." He slaps me on the back and we both head into the locker room. I shower and change quickly, making an effort to be sure I don't end up alone in here, and gather my things before heading out and climbing into my Lexus.

The door closes behind me and the silence feels like a weighted blanket. It's comforting and I lean my head back against the headrest, close my eyes, and take a deep breath. Sometimes if I think too much about how my personality has changed over the years I get sad. I used to be such a people person, and now it takes so much effort just to be in a small group. That's why I stick with Cami and Alana now.

I pull my phone out of my bag and find a few texts from my sister and best friend discussing plans for the next few weeks. Alana is leaving soon for her business trip and will be gone for a full month, so we're trying to pack in lots of time together before then. I don't really do any of the planning, I just show up wherever they tell me to be.

I drive home in silence and after twenty minutes I pull into the garage of the building I live in. I use the private penthouse elevator and make my way up to my place. It's big, way too big, and was furnished when I moved in so it feels sterile. I haven't added anything to liven it up or bring any warmth and it shows.

I grab the dinner my chef prepared that is sitting in the microwave and stand as I eat it, swallowing it down in a few minutes. Walking up the stairs, my feet feel incredibly heavy. I am going to sleep well tonight.

After changing, washing my face, and brushing my teeth, I sink into my California King mattress and sigh deeply. The cold sheets feel nice against my skin and bring me into a state of relaxation almost immediately.

I close my eyes and wait for sleep to take me, except it never does. I just lie there, eyes closed, listening to the sound of my own breathing and the silence of my home. Over the last few months it's started to feel more and more empty. Lonely.

I open my eyes and groan in frustration. I bet the guys are still out right now, laughing and drinking and enjoying one another's company. I run my hands through my hair and pull a little at the roots in frustration. I wish it was easier for me to just make friends.

I can't start and carry conversations like a normal person and that is infuriating, especially because I used to be able to.

Eventually I give up and climb out of bed, throwing on swim trunks and grabbing a towel. I head out the door and up to the indoor pool to loosen my muscles and wear myself out enough that sleep comes easily.

CHAPTER 6

COCO
Which plates do you like?

ME
The ones on the left are sort of grandma-ish

COCO
So, right?

ME
I guess

COCO
Super helpful, thanks

ME
You're welcome!

I HOP OFF THE SUBWAY AND WEAVE THROUGH THE throng of people crossing this way and that on the way to their destinations. Everyone is in a hurry in New York City and no one has any time for pleasantries. That was something I had to get used to when moving from Florida to here. No one really stops to say *excuse me* when they bump into you. If you're lucky, they won't curse at you while telling you to watch where you're going.

I've mastered the weave and walk at this point. I head up from the subway and back onto the streets, then start the three block walk to Brookdale Retirement Living. I pull my bag closer to my body and shove down the colorful yarn that has made its way up and is now peeking out of my bag. I brought a new chunkier yarn today, hoping Gladys might help me out with it.

About a year ago, I was looking for the next hobby I might pick up and was scrolling on a website where people can advertise local groups or clubs for people to join. I saw something about knitting, grabbed the information, and made my way there the very next Tuesday afternoon. I should have looked a little closer at the details, though, because it turns out it is a knitting club specifically for the people who live in this retirement community.

Thankfully, the ladies allowed me one session as a trial run and apparently liked my personality enough that they deemed me acceptable to keep coming back. Now they all just feel like bonus grandmas to me. This is the one hobby I've actually found myself staying interested in for more than a month, so I'm calling that a win. It's probably because of the women that I get to hang out with, but don't tell them that. They already think everything is about them.

I push through the rotating door and sigh in relief as the heat hits my cheeks. Turning left, I pass the front desk and wave hello to Shauna, one of the receptionists. Everyone who works here is extremely kind.

I press the button in the elevator for the fifth floor, stepping off and heading down the hallway. I pass a few recreation rooms, the swimming pool, and a fitness studio before finally reaching my destination. This is one of the nicest retirement homes I've ever been in, and it is definitely a luxury.

The room where knitting club takes place is technically called the community room, but it's really like a big living room for the residents to spend time in. It's a wide open space with lots of windows and natural light. The center of the room is marked with three large floral print couches in the shape of the letter U. Absolutely something you would find in your grandma's living room.

In front of the couches is an electric fireplace that is currently lit and filling the room with a beautiful glow and warmth. On either side of the couches there are bunches of round tables and chairs set up, a place where residents can play cards or have a meal together.

As I enter the room, four pairs of eyes—I guess I should say eight, because they all wear glasses—look up at me. They all crinkle at the edges as they smile and it warms something deep inside.

"Well, it's about time you showed up," Gladys says, rolling her eyes in feigned outrage.

"It isn't even five past. Lighten up, old lady," I tease as I make my way over to the couch and plop down in my unofficial assigned spot.

"Two minutes late is still late, young lady."

"I love you too," I say back, and blow her a kiss. She huffs a laugh in my direction and smiles over at me.

The women in this group are an interesting bunch. Gladys is the snarkiest of them, but I like that about her. She has been living at Brookdale since her husband passed away a few years ago. She doesn't talk about him much, but I can tell when she's thinking about him. Her eyes go unfocused and it's like she isn't in the room anymore.

Emery and Rhonda are sisters. They're a funny duo and clearly grew up spending lots of time together. Their mannerisms and the way they talk are so similar to each other, it reminds me of Colette and I, or even Alana and I. She is essentially my sister, and we have that bond, even if we don't share DNA.

Then there's Linda. She is clearly the mother of the group, always keeping track of the projects we're all working on and what the logistics are for each meeting, even though in the last year we've only changed up where and when we meet maybe three times. She's quiet but extremely kind and likes everything in order. She reminds me of Alana, and I think that might be why I love her so much.

I never really expected to find myself as a regular member of any club, definitely not a knitting club, and definitely not a knitting club with only women over sixty. I have found that I really enjoy my time with them, though. They have a level of wisdom that I don't get from any of my friends and they aren't nearly as worried about my marital status as my family is. It's refreshing.

"What is everyone working on this week?" Linda asks, getting straight to business.

"I'm still working on the strawberry cardigan I started last week. I got a new chunkier yarn I was hoping you four could help me work with."

"I'll let Emery help you," Rhonda says with a wink. Emery shoves her in the shoulder playfully and Rhonda rolls her eyes. "I'm working on a blanket for the grandson," she says, holding up a small rectangle made of different shades of blue. It looks cozy and like something a toddler would love to curl up in.

"And I'm working on a matching hat," Emery says, holding up what looks like a bundle of yarn and not a hat. It will get there, though.

"A blanket for me," Linda says.

We all turn to Gladys in anticipation of her answer.

"Did you really think I would have an idea of where I was going today?" she asks, eyebrows raised. I snicker a laugh and the other women shake their heads and roll their eyes. "I'm just going to let the yarn speak to me."

"I like it," I say before settling into my spot on the couch. I grab a blanket and cozy up, taking a deep breath as I begin to work on my project. The repetition of making the stitches over and over again is soothing and somewhat mindless, allowing me to unplug my brain for a moment.

I appreciate knitting for a lot of reasons, but I love that it doesn't require a ton of supplies or any specific dedicated workspace. I can curl up on my couch, grab my yarn and my knitting needles and that's all I need. It's simple and I like that about it.

"What's going on in the world of Cami?" Rhonda asks. "We all know way too much about each other being stuck in here."

I laugh at her comment as I continue to work, not looking up.

"Aw, come on, Rhon. I know you all love spending time together," I tease and she shrugs. "Not a whole lot going on. Alana is about to leave on her big fancy work trip to Paris, so we're trying to spend a lot of time together before she's gone. My mom and Colette are in wedding planning mode and they pull me in to help every once in a while."

"Planning weddings has gotten way out of hand," Gladys pipes in. "Back when Roy and I got married, it was the two of us in the church with our parents and the pastor and that's it. Didn't need all that fancy crap everyone insists on having now."

"It has definitely changed," I say.

"I'll say," she replies.

I hesitate before speaking again, but these ladies tend to give the best advice, so I say what's been on my mind since my visit with my mom and sister. "I'm a bit worried about the actual wedding though."

"Now why would you be worried about that?" Rhonda asks, clear confusion in her voice. "Weddings are an exciting time. Plus, once you get to the event there isn't much else to worry about. You just sit back and enjoy a glass of wine while everything happens in front of you."

"I don't think she'll be doing much wine sipping as the Maid of Honor, Rhon," Emery says. "What's got you worried, sweetheart?"

Man, I love them.

"Well, it's probably stupid," I say, suddenly feeling self conscious about my fears.

"It most certainly is not. Now out with it." Linda's tone is no-nonsense.

"My mom and sister, my whole family honestly, is really layering on the pressure when it comes to my dating life. I think Colette's wedding is bringing my unmarried status to the forefront of their minds. Everyone wants to know if I'm bringing a date, and every time I say I'm not they want to know why I haven't settled down."

"Well you haven't settled down because you haven't found the right fella yet," Emery says, matter-of-factly.

"And I tried to say that, but they're convinced it's because I can't pick something permanent. That I'm being immature by not settling down and choosing someone long term. The term I think my mom used was flighty," I trail off, embarrassment creeping up my cheeks.

"She called you flighty?" Linda asks, shock in her tone.

I nod and shrug, then realize I've started biting my nails, an anxious habit I picked up when I was a kid. I mentally scold myself and get back to my project in an effort to keep my hands busy.

"That's absolutely ridiculous. You are not flighty and you make commitments when you feel like they're worth your time. I can't believe she said that to you."

I smile at Gladys's words.

"I think they're just scared that I won't ever find love. They see it as this ultimate thing, but for me it's not something I'm too concerned about right now. I mean I don't mind having a little fun here and there, but I just don't feel the need to settle down yet. I'm only twenty-seven, it's not like I'm past child-bearing age or something."

"You're right, you have your entire life ahead of you. Trust us, you just live your life right now, sweetie. You don't need a man to make that life complete." Three heads nod in agreement with Emery.

"I agree, so I did something really stupid."

"Oh, now it's getting good," Rhonda says with a smirk. "Whatdya do?"

"I told them I had a date."

"Oh, well then problem solved," Linda says, not picking up on the problem. "I didn't know you were dating anyone. What's his name?"

"That's the thing...I'm not. Dating anyone, I mean."

"So you lied?" Linda asks.

"I lied," I say in confirmation. "What do I do?"

"Well, you obviously need to bring a date," Emery replies, clearly deep in thought. "Do you have any ideas of who you could bring? Who could you take that you could tell them the situation and it wouldn't be weird?"

"I'd really rather not explain this situation to anyone." I sigh in frustration. "I don't even know who I'd ask."

"What about that young man you're friends with? What's his name, Charles?"

I laugh at the incorrect name, old habits die hard.

"Charlie, Alana's brother, but I doubt he'd do that. He'd help me with just about anything, but he likes his privacy and stays to himself. He wouldn't want to be in the middle of all of that."

"I bet he would if you asked. Doesn't hurt."

"I don't know, Rhon. This whole thing is embarrassing as it is. If I ask, I'm going to have to explain why I need a fake date and I'm not sure I want to do that."

"Well, you're going to have to explain it to whoever you convince to help you out. Might as well be someone you can trust not to judge," she says.

"That's not a bad point. I'll think about it."

We continue working on our projects and the women tell me all about their week. They have their fair share of drama here, surprisingly enough. There was a plant stolen off of Linda's front step and apparently George is trying to get Gladys to have dinner with him. It's all very intriguing.

I leave feeling happy and less stressed. The two hours I spend with these ladies always leaves me feeling refreshed and I think it's because I don't have to think about all of the other things happening in my life, and if I do they almost always help me solve whatever problem there is.

I mull over Charlie being my fake date the entire way home. I'm almost certain he'd turn me down if I asked. I'm his little sister's best friend, and while we are very close I don't think he'd be comfortable with something like this.

I push the idea out of my mind and resolve to try and figure out who else I could ask. Pulling out my phone, I scroll the dating app Hinge while I sit on the subway. After about five minutes of absolutely nothing, I lock it in frustration and throw it back into my purse. I lean my head back against the car and close my eyes; this is a problem for future Cami to solve.

CHAPTER 7
Charlie

WE PLAY THE RED WINGS TONIGHT AND I'M CURRENTLY trying to get in the zone. I have game days on lockdown after years and years of perfecting them. Typically I don't talk much to anyone—although I guess that isn't much different from the day to day for me—and I have a strict routine I follow.

I'm up before sunrise for a workout, something that warms my body up like swimming or a light jog, then I eat breakfast. My private chef prepares the same thing for me before every game— pancakes topped with Greek yogurt and berries, turkey bacon, and a protein shake. Then I head to the rink for pregame skate and practice.

There's this thing about hockey players and superstitions, the two go hand in hand. Even though I don't necessarily buy into all of that, I've done this routine for so long that I'm not sure I want to know what would happen if I switched it up.

I climb into my car and navigate past the random daylist that Spotify created for me titled "Sleepy Weepy Depress Sesh" and turn on my game day playlist. It's a mix of artists like the Lumineers, Bastille, and a few others. I need something calming to put me in the right headspace. The familiar music relaxes me and I drop my shoulders, breathing deeply. The Red Wings are a good team and their record so far this season has been solid, but then again so has ours.

As I arrive at Madison Square Garden, I park my car and climb out, grab my gear, and then head inside. Most of the guys tend to arrive two to three hours before the game, but I like to be here earlier. We have about five hours until go time, and being in the building helps me turn off the outside noise and get in the zone.

I get settled in the locker room and make sure I have everything I need, then visit one of the physical therapists down in the gym. I had an MCL injury about a year ago and they've been working on helping me heal it ever since. Grayson pats the table and I hop up, allowing him to feel around on my left knee.

"Having any pain?" he asks as he works.

"Nothing that's any different from normal usage strain."

"Any swelling or increased instability?" He pulls my leg out straight, then bends it back again.

"Nope."

"Good. Lay back for me."

I do as he asks and he continues working on my knee, bending and stretching it.

"Any plans this weekend?"

I cringe a little at his effort to engage in small talk. It's a toss up on whether or not he'll want to chat while we work, and while I appreciate his desire to get to know me and build a relationship, I don't want to wade through a conversation right now. But I'm not a jerk, so I indulge him.

"Nothing special. I'll probably just hang out at home, watch a movie or something. My sister and I are hanging out this weekend. She's about to leave on a work trip to Paris."

"Oh, no way? What does she do for work?"

I breathe a sigh of relief. I could brag on Alana for days. "She's an editor for *Impress* magazine."

"Seriously? My girlfriend loves that magazine."

I smile and swell with pride for my sister. "Yeah, they're headed to Paris to assist the European branch of the magazine. Should be a pretty cool trip."

"Sounds like it."

He helps me off the table and leads me through a few strengthening exercises. I thank him afterwards and head to the treadmill to walk and warm up a bit. I don't go too fast, being sure not to push it or exert myself, but I keep it at a brisk walk in order to get my muscles moving.

After about an hour there, I head back to the locker room. Guys are starting to arrive for the game and as the typical locker room banter begins, I find myself trying to find a spot to interject. I need to be trying to make friends, but the thought of interrupting and chiming it makes my skin crawl.

Turns out I don't have to worry about that, because Soren addresses me a few minutes later.

"How was your night at home, Cade?" He doesn't say it in a condescending way in order to shame me for staying in, but he asks like he's genuinely curious. I'm still a bit skeptical he isn't trying to make fun of me so I decide to answer like he's seriously asking.

"It was nice. Watched a movie and drank a beer in silence."

"Sounds nice, man. These guys were the opposite of silence."

"I'm not sure you guys know the definition of silence."

No one speaks and it's awkward. I start to frantically search back through my words to find where I went wrong when Theo Adams, one of the goalies, interrupts my overthinking.

"Cade. Did you just make a joke?"

They're freaking out...because I made a joke? Am I seriously that cold around these guys that they were shocked because I tried to be funny? *Damn.*

"Uh, yeah, I guess I was."

The room breaks out in loud laughter, so loud that it causes me to jump, and I find myself smiling at my successful attempt to make friends. This isn't going horribly.

"Why don't you come with us tonight after the game?" Soren asks. The temptation to turn him down is strong, but I resist. I can't get closer to these guys by staying at home and never going out with them.

"I'll think about it."

"That's what I'm talking about," Theo says, punching me in the shoulder. "Let's go kick some Red Wing ass!" The shouts around us fire me up and I turn, getting my gear on. Maybe this isn't as impossible as I thought it was.

CHAPTER 8
Cami

BESTIE FRIEND
Please cheer for me.

ME
I will. It's so weird that you aren't here

BESTIE FRIEND
I know, work is so stupid.

ME
But you get to hang out with Alex 😒

BESTIE FRIEND
Shut up.

I push my way through the crowds of people in red, white, and blue, and find my seat. Madison Square Garden is huge and the first few times I came here I was extremely overwhelmed. Thankfully, I'm more comfortable now.

I make my way into the arena and down to our row. We always sit pretty close to the ice. Charlie has these seats reserved for us every home game, just five rows from the glass. The one on my left is empty and it makes me sad. Alana never misses one of her brother's games, but she has a late meeting with Alex tonight in order to prepare for their trip to Paris, so she can't be here.

I pull my phone out and turn the camera around so it's facing me. I hold up the sign I made for tonight's game and snap a picture, then send it to her.

ME

Do you think he'll like this one?

BESTIE FRIEND

Oh my gosh he's going to lose it.

Each game, I make a different sign. I typically put some ridiculous phrase on it or something that I know will annoy Charlie. It's impossible not to mess with him.

Tonight's focus is on number thirteen, Josh Murphy, a rookie on the third line. Charlie despises the guy and hasn't shut up about how annoying he is lately. The red and blue letters on the sign say "Murphy, can I get your number?" I covered it in little "#13" stickers and topped it with glitter paint. He's going to hate it. It's perfect.

I sit down and scroll on my phone as I wait for the guys to come out. About half an hour before opening face-off they skate onto the rink to warm up. The crowd stands and cheers, excitement building. I wait until I see number nine skate around towards where I always sit, and then I hold up my sign.

I see him pause and focus on me, then shake his head in disappointment. He flips me off as he turns and skates away and I laugh. The crowd eventually settles back down as the guys warm up and I settle into my seat, pulling out my phone again. I've been coming to these games for a long time, so the hum of the crowd has turned into a familiar background noise. After a few minutes, someone nudges my shoulder and motions out to the ice.

"I think someone wants your attention."

I look in the direction they are pointing and see that Charlie has made his way to the glass and is motioning for me to come down. I'm only a few rows from the front, so it only takes a few seconds to get down there, but my cheeks heat at the unwanted attention from those around me. Being beckoned down to the rink by a player isn't exactly casual.

"Is everything okay?" I ask. He nods his head yes.

"Meet me in the suite after?" he asks. He sort of pantomimes, pointing to himself and then in the general direction of the friends and family suite. I can read his lips somewhat and sort of hear his voice, but with the crowd and the thick glass in between us it's quite muffled.

"Yes, weirdo. Now go before your coach takes your head and mine." He looks back at said coach and winces, then turns back to me.

"Nice sign. Can't wait to destroy it after."

"Play well and I might let you."

He rolls his eyes and turns back to the ice, getting back to his stretches. I head back to my seat and soon after, the game starts. When Charlie first started hanging out with Alana and I, I knew nothing about hockey besides the fact that it was played in an ice rink. I still don't know everything, but I've learned a lot since then, and now I enjoy every game. The adrenaline of the game and the crowd is like a high.

It's a tight game, but the Rangers end up winning with a score of three to two. I gather all of my things, including the sign I made, and head out. I make my way up to the friends and family suite and grab a Coke while I wait.

There are plenty of wives, girlfriends, and children running around the room waiting on their players and I sit back off to the side observing. They all seem to know one another, but Charlie is pretty closed off. He doesn't make friends very easily after whatever happened in high school, so it makes sense that he doesn't have many guy friends to introduce to his people.

After a while the guys file in. They're showered and changed into streetwear and most of them look absolutely wrecked, but happy with a job well done and another game won.

Charlie walks through the door and his eyes immediately find mine. I smile at him and he returns it with a small one of his own as he makes his way over. He's about halfway to me when he gets intercepted by a younger looking guy in a blue short-sleeved button down and jeans. His smile slips and the light in his eyes dies as his gaze moves away from me, and I try not to let it bother me.

I've been worried about him for a while now. I understood when he needed to lean on us in high school after whatever happened, and I liked that we stayed close through college and into adulthood, but I worry about him not having any other friends besides us. He doesn't even seem to have the desire or energy for them, and that worries me.

I like that Charlie only shows the real him when he's around me. I like that I get the version of him that's cheesy and funny and openly happy, but I know he deserves more people he can open up to like that.

I see him gesture towards me, and the guy with him turns to look at me. I wave and smile, and he returns it. Charlie walks him over and I'm trying not to freak out that he's about to introduce me to someone. This man has been on this team for seven years and not once has he personally introduced me or Alana to a teammate. Sure, we've gone to family skates and picnics for the team, but we always keep to ourselves.

"Cam, this is Soren. He's a left winger on the team." I can tell Charlie is a little uncomfortable, but I love seeing him trying. I put my hand out towards Soren and he takes it, shaking it lightly and smiling at me.

"Hi Soren, I'm Cami. It's nice to meet you."

"Right back at you." He looks over at Charlie. "You should bring her out tonight. Tell me you've decided to come with us."

Charlie looks back and forth between Soren and I, and I try to gauge how he's feeling about this offer to go out. He doesn't seem too opposed to the idea, and he isn't doing that scowly look with his eyebrows that he does when he is feeling particularly antisocial, so I decide to go for it.

"I'd love that, as long as it's good with Charlie."

"We're going to Teddy's," Soren says. "See you both there."

Charlie nods in affirmation. "Sounds good."

Soren slaps him on the back and moves back to his family, leaving us alone.

"Oh my gosh, do you have a friend?" I whisper-yell.

"Shut up. He's been my friend."

"Yeah, but you don't ever go out with them. Are you okay with going? I tried to read your body language. You weren't doing that thing with your eyebrows."

"What thing?"

"That thing you do with the—" I scrunch my face up in order to try and mimic the look I'm referring to.

"Stop it," he says, reaching forward and smoothing out the scowl on my face. "You're going to hurt yourself."

"Come on, you know what I'm talking about," I say, swatting his hands away. He rolls his eyes and chuckles at my antics.

"We don't have to stay long."

"Whatever you want."

"Okay, let's go. I'll drive."

CHAPTER 9

Cami

THE BEACH BOYS ARE PLAYING SOFTLY IN CHARLIE'S car as he drives us to the bar. Might seem like an odd choice for a drive to the bar, but that's Charlie. A walking contradiction at times.

I was surprised he actually took me up on my offer to come tonight, considering he is usually home and in bed as soon as possible after a game. Regardless of the reason, I'm glad he's going out and spending time with his teammates. After seven years it's about time he tried to make some lasting relationships. I wonder what it was that happened all those years ago that caused him to pull away as severely as he did—it's not the first time I've been curious about it.

We haven't talked much, just embraced the comfortable silence. This is one of the things I love best about my friendships with Alana and Charlie: the ability to feel comfortable while not speaking at all. It's a special level of a relationship to be able to be with someone and not feel the need to fill the quiet moments with noise.

The song is interrupted when a call comes through the speakers. George Cade—his dad—flashes on the screen, and he

46

hits ignore before it can ring a second time. Charlie's dad calls him after every single game, and he declines the call every single time. Their relationship is extremely strained, pretty much nonexistent, and his contact name in Charlie's phone is evidence of that.

"You okay?" I don't know why I ask it. I know Alana's relationship with their parents is strained, and with how close he is with his sister I know that affects him.

"M'fine." His clipped response tells me he's anything but, but I don't push it.

We drive in silence for a little longer before I speak again, trying to steer us into better territory.

"You were great tonight. Like always." He looks over at me and I wink, causing him to laugh and shake his head in annoyance at my praise.

"Wright's goal at the end was epic."

It *was* epic. He weaved around the opposing team and it was like the puck floated and followed his stick, sailing right past the goalie and into the net. It was unreal, and judging by the crowd's reaction, totally unexpected. But Charlie's response is so typical of him, never taking a compliment or wanting any spotlight on himself.

"It was. The crowd went crazy."

"He's really good, Wright. Seems like a good guy too."

"Do you know much about him?" I ask.

"Not really. He has one more year in his contract, but I wouldn't be surprised if they re-sign. He's got a lot of talent and fits in well with the team. He has a girlfriend I'm pretty sure. I think I saw her tonight."

"Maybe she'll be at the bar. I'd love to recruit a friend to sit with me while Alana is gone."

"Yeah, clearly we can't leave you alone." His comment reminds me of the situation that happened before the game started and I can't help but ask.

"What was that about? Calling me down to the glass was a little much."

"Just wanted to talk to you. Make sure you were coming up to the suite after." He shrugs and stares forward like it was nothing, meanwhile I'm confused. He knew I would be at the suite, we always go after the game. I don't have time to address it further, though, because just as I start to respond we pull up to the bar.

Charlie steps out of the car at the valet, then comes around to my door to get it for me. I take his hand as I step out, then straighten my jersey. I'm wearing light wash jeans with holes in the knees and a red, white, and blue jersey. The number nine and the name "Cade" feel like a claiming, and they should. I'm here for Charlie and I'm honored that I get to support him.

We make our way inside and move towards the back of the bar where the rest of the guys are. There's about twenty of them here, some with girlfriends and some without, and it's busy. I don't mind it, but I can tell Charlie is struggling to get comfortable.

We make our way towards the bar and after pushing forward there isn't enough room for us to stand side by side, so he stands behind me. I feel his front press up against my back as he leans forward to yell his order to the bartender and can't help the shiver that passes through my body at the contact.

That was weird.

My body has never once recognized his as anything more than a friend, so I chalk the reaction up to the fact that we're pressed up against each other like we haven't ever been before. I can't even see his face like this, and my body would react that way to any man pressed up against me...right? Right.

I turn around to try and remind myself that this is *Charlie* behind me, not some 6'4" hockey player (same diff, my brain supplies), and find him looking down at me.

"Thanks for coming with me tonight." His eyes warm as he smiles down at me and I return it. I love getting to see these glimpses of him that he doesn't show anyone else, and getting them in a crowded bar feels like a whole different level of intimate.

The bartender gives us our drinks, an old fashioned for him and a margarita for me, and we turn to make our way back towards the tall tables where the guys are standing. I spot Soren first, standing with a woman next to him. She's beautiful, with long chestnut hair and a small frame. Her jeans and cropped Rangers tee make her look effortlessly sexy.

"Hey, man," Soren says to Charlie as we approach. They clasp hands and slam their bodies against each other in a sort of bro-hug. He then turns to me and smiles.

"Good to see you again, Cami. This is my girlfriend, Mia."

Mia steps forward and pulls me into a tight hug, one that lasts a little longer than a normal hello hug would last, but it feels welcoming and not awkward.

"It is so nice to meet you. The more women around here, the better. I get tired of being the only one," she says and we both giggle.

"This is Theo," Charlie says as he motions to the other man at the table. "He's a goalie on the team."

"Pleasure to meet you, ma'am," he says as he reaches out to shake my hand.

I do my best not to freak out at being introduced to not one, but two, of his teammates in one night.

Theo steps back to his spot around the table and Mia tucks herself into Soren's side. He pulls her close as the guys start talking about the game, but I'm not paying attention to what's being said. I'm stuck staring at Soren's hand resting on Mia's hip and the look in her eyes when she looks up at him.

Her smile looks confident, like she's sure of her place next to him. I want to ask her, *How did you know it was him? That he was the one you wanted to stick with?* I don't, of course, but my thoughts stick there.

What is it within me that doesn't want to settle down? Why

can't I find anyone that I want for more than a few days or weeks? My family's comments roll through my head and I don't realize someone is speaking to me until Charlie nudges me with his shoulder.

"Cam?" He looks over at me and can tell I spaced, so he thankfully repeats the question for me. "Soren was asking what you thought of the game tonight."

"Right, sorry." I clear my throat. "It was a great game, close one until the end, that goal was incredible."

"Total luck that no one stole the puck."

"Nah, that was skill, my man," Theo says from across the table.

"I agree. You handled it effortlessly."

"It was a miracle Cade here stayed out of the penalty box tonight," Soren says with a laugh. Charlie takes a drink of his old fashioned and shakes his head in disappointment.

"I do know how to control myself, unlike some of you."

I'm honestly so impressed with his ability to carry this conversation with his teammates. It's not like it's anything groundbreaking, they're just discussing the game, but Charlie doesn't do this. He doesn't go out to bars and debrief with his teammates. He goes home to the solitude and the safety of his apartment.

It feels like a tiny glimpse of the old him from high school. The one that had more friends than I could count and was the one every girl wanted. He used to know how to work a crowd like a pro, and I was afraid after everything that happened that version of him was gone. I smile at the fact that perhaps it isn't entirely.

The conversation continues to flow easily, and I find myself enjoying the back and forth banter with his teammates. Charlie seems to settle into himself the longer we spend time with the guys and hope this might be the start of new friendships for him.

CHAPTER 10
Charlie

We've been at Teddy's for a little over an hour now and I'm shocked I don't want to leave. I figured we would make an appearance, enough for me to tell Sophie I tried, and then head out after having one drink.

I stopped after my first because I'm driving tonight, but Cami is on her second and I love watching her confidently work the room. She's been talking with Mia, Soren's girlfriend, for the last half hour and I try to listen in on their conversation as I talk with the guys.

Mia is telling Cami how she and Soren met—apparently they were friends first and someone made the first move—and Cami is listening intently. She hums and nods her head at all the right moments and I find myself jealous of her easy ability to make friends and carry on conversation. She just met this woman an hour ago and they're hitting it off. I've known most of these guys for many years and this is the first time I've gone out with them.

Watching her interact with the group and effortlessly participate in their banter has a thought floating in my mind, one that is absolutely insane. So insane that I decide to think about something else, except that doesn't seem to be possible.

Whoever I fake date needs to be able to help me get the fans, and my teammates, to love me and see me in a different light. They need to see me as essential and part of the culture, and if Cami is *this* good at a night out with the team I wonder if she might be up to the job. She wins everyone over with her easy charm and funny personality, and that is exactly the type of person Sophie would tell me I need.

She would never go for it, though, so I actually do put it out of my mind this time and go back to focusing on my teammates. Theo is talking about how his one year old daughter started saying "Da-Da" a few weeks ago and passes his phone around, showing her off. I watch when it reaches me and smile at her sweet little voice.

"That's awesome, Adams, she's adorable. How long have you and your wife been together?"

I know I've said something I shouldn't have as soon as it leaves my mouth, because the entire table goes silent besides the girls, who quickly join in when they realize they're the only ones talking. I'm not sure what happened with Adams, but it's clear he is not married and now I feel like the biggest jerk.

"No woman in the picture. Just me and Chloe," he says and swallows hard. I start to feel my fingers tingle, and my face grows hot.

"Sorry, man, I didn't know."

"No worries. I'm gonna go to the restroom." He sets his drink down and storms off, clearly tense after that whole interaction.

"Don't feel too bad," Soren says, placing his hand on my shoulder and giving it a squeeze. "Adams is a private person and you two aren't close, so it would make sense you didn't know. Chloe's mom cheated on him about six months after she was born. Ran off with her new guy and left a letter and papers signing custody of Chloe over to him."

"What a nightmare," I say, releasing the breath I was holding. I suddenly feel like the biggest jerk for not being involved in these guys' lives. I should know that my teammate is caring for his daughter alone so I can help him pick up the slack. Instead I've been hiding in my own little bubble, where it's safe and I don't have to take any risks.

Suddenly this mission to plant roots in the community and with this team becomes about more than just staying with the Rangers for my own selfish comfort. These men deserve a teammate that is there for them on and off the ice, and I need to step up. If that means getting comfortable being out of my comfort zone, and placing myself at risk of someone stabbing me in the back, that might just be what I have to do.

The night continues on after my slip up and Adams is composed when he returns to the table. I check in with him silently and he nods his head in my direction, letting me know we're okay. Cami continues to thread herself into the conversation easily, including me where she can and helping me when I get a little too awkward. The longer the night goes on, the more she seems to be the right person for the fake dating job.

After another hour, she tugs on the hem of my shirt to get my attention.

"I think I may grab an Uber, I'm falling asleep standing up." She smiles sheepishly up at me.

"No way you're getting an Uber this late at night. I'm ready to go too."

"You don't have to do that. I don't want to cut off your time with the guys."

I ignore her protests and turn to the table. "We're going to head out. Thanks for inviting us." We say our goodbyes and Cami hugs Mia after exchanging phone numbers. I place my hand on her lower back and lead her out of the bar, then hand the valet my ticket.

The burst of the cold air outside feels refreshing after being inside the crowded bar and I take a deep breath, feeling good about my successful attempt at making friends tonight. The drive to her apartment is quiet, because she falls asleep about five minutes in. Once I pull up, I reach over and brush the hair that's fallen in front of her face, behind her shoulder.

"Hey, Cam, we're home," I whisper, softly nudging her shoulder.

"Huh?" she says groggily. After a few seconds, she realizes where she is and sits up, stretching her arms out. "Thanks for the ride and for tonight. It was fun."

"Right back at you. Thanks for coming."

She gets out and I watch her enter the building before pulling away.

CHAPTER 11

Cami

I STRETCH OUT IN MY QUEEN SIZE BED AND ROLL OVER, looking at the clock on my side table. My eyes widen at the numbers flashing back at me. I can't remember the last time I slept in until eleven thirty in the morning. The margaritas from last night are giving me a mild headache, and the pounding is a reminder that I can't drink like I used to in college. Back then I could down three drinks and a few shots without being too terribly hungover, and now I max out at two drinks.

I love Saturdays when I don't have any plans because it feels like a blank slate. Nothing to do, no one counting on me, and no one needing my attention. Alana is about to leave on her business trip so she's busy getting things together, and I just hung out with Charlie last night, so I'm solo for the day.

Most people would use the weekend to plan out their weeks. Meal plan, grocery shop, clean the baseboards, and such. I don't really roll that way, I much prefer to just do those things when I'm forced to.

I run out of food? Time to grocery shop.

The fridge starts to smell funky? Could probably use a clean out.

Cobwebs on the baseboards? Wait three weeks, *then* clean them.

I do keep my space tidy, though. I don't think I could function if the house wasn't picked up and put together. I do not, however, complete a full top to bottom clean every weekend. Weekends are for relaxing and a deep clean is the farthest thing from relaxing, in my opinion.

Eventually I amble out of bed and brush my teeth, then make my way into the kitchen for a coffee. I pop an espresso pod into the machine, set a mug underneath it, and press the button. It roars to life and the constant stream of straight energy into the mug hypnotizes me. I'm sure if someone were to walk into the kitchen right now and saw the way I was staring at this inanimate object like it was the key to life, they might think I was unwell.

Once it's finished, I go about steaming the milk, adding the vanilla syrup and putting my latte together. My apartment is your traditional NYC apartment, extremely small and outrageously expensive, but I love it. The size makes it charming and cozy, and my decorations make it feel like mine. Growing up with a family who wanted to be involved in everything made it hard to find space for something that was just for me. Back at home I shared a room with Colette, and in college I had a roommate, so I never got to decorate a space exactly like I wanted.

The large array of plants and colors strewn about could be seen as chaotic to some, like my mother, but to me it feels perfect. I climb up onto the small couch and face the window, tucking my knees up to my chest and covering up with a blanket.

I love spending my mornings watching the people walk around on the streets of New York City. There are all kinds of people in a hurry to get to their destination, or leisurely strolling despite the cold weather. Some in work clothes, others in more comfortable outfits, and some in workout gear. A few are pulling children by the hand, some have their dogs walking beside them on leashes, and many have headphones on to keep the noise out.

My parents have always said they think I was drawn to New York City because they think it's a place where people stop on the way to where they settle for the rest of their lives. Neither of them actually know anything in relation to how many people stay in New York for their whole lives (which is many people, thank you very much) but they like to bring attention to my chaotic personality as often as they can.

There was more than one reason why I wanted to move here. Sure, my best friends were going to be here so I'd want to come, but there's more to it than that. My mind has always felt like a hamster wheel, always running and always going, never stopping. However, when I sit here in my quiet apartment and stare down at the chaos below, something about it allows me to still my thoughts and focus on what's in front of me. It's like the chaos of the city around me quiets the chaos inside of me. Quite the opposite of what my parents believe, but I'd never tell them that.

I sip my coffee and giggle at the woman trying to get her mini dachshund to stop sniffing the grass and follow her, when my phone begins to ring. Glancing down, I see my sister's name light up the screen and swipe to answer the video call.

"Hey, Coco."

"Hi, Cami, how's your morning?"

"Just starting, what about you?" She laughs and it makes me miss her. I just saw her the other weekend, but it's hard being away from her when we grew up so close. While sharing a room with her was irritating, the late night conversations and uncontrollable giggles over the stupidest things made it worth it.

"I will never understand how you can sleep in so late," she says. Her fiancé, Derrick, pops his head into the screen to say hello and asks her if she wants lunch. "My morning is going well, just getting a few wedding things crossed off the list."

"Anything I can help with?" I ask, anticipating that was the reason for her call.

"Yes, actually. I just needed to bounce some ideas off of you, is now an okay time?"

"Sure, go ahead."

"So I'm trying to decide on a caterer. The venue has someone they work with, but it's just your traditional chicken or beef with a salad to start, and that just feels boring to me. They'd serve everyone, so that's fancy and a nice addition, but I sort of think people like to serve themselves these days."

"I do feel like every wedding I've been to with plated service ends up with so many half eaten meals, there seems to be so much waste," I reply. I like that she comes to me to talk through these things, it feels nice to be involved.

"Exactly. Derrick, did you hear that? Cam agrees with me." I see Derrick approach her from behind and wrap his hands around her middle. He leans down and whispers something into Colette's ear that causes her to giggle and a blush to creep up her cheeks. The picture of the two of them warms my heart and sends a pang of jealousy through me.

"Don't start making out, it'll burn my eyes," I joke. She laughs and pushes him away from her. He plants a sweet kiss on her cheek before leaving and I smile at the way her eyes light up.

"Okay, thanks for helping me convince him. I think we're going to have a Mexican buffet."

"That sounds perfect, can't wait."

"Okay, well I'll let you get back to your morning. Love you, Cam."

"Love you, Coco."

The screen goes black and I set it face down on the couch. For the first time maybe ever, these feelings of desire are swimming inside my gut. I hate to admit it, because then it might prove my parents right, but I think I may be getting to a point in life where it might be nice to settle down.

Maybe *"settle down"* isn't the right way to word it, maybe I am just starting to feel like it would be nice to have someone that's there for me like Derrick is there for my sister. The term "settling down" makes it sound like I would be dimming my light in order to find a future with someone, but I don't think that's how it has to be. Your partner should illuminate the best parts of you, even if those parts are a little chaotic and messy.

The longing in my chest grows each time I see people I love with the people *they* love, but the process of actually finding someone I want to keep around long term feels impossible. The only people I can tolerate for extended periods of time are my sister, Alana, and Charlie.

Thinking of Charlie brings me back to last night and the feeling of him pressed against me at the bar. I shake my head to clear it of the thought, because going anywhere with that is not something I can do. He's my best friend's brother, and my best friend. That isn't what our relationship is.

Despite the fact that he is strictly off limits, I can't help but think about what Rhonda said at knitting club, her suggestion to ask him to be my date to the wedding. I haven't gathered the courage to bring it up to him, and I'm still not completely convinced he's the best option, but it sits in the back of my mind like a heavy weight.

I take a deep breath and another drink of my latte, then do what I do every time I want to turn my brain off. I grab the remote and turn on *The Vampire Diaries*. It's likely that I've rewatched this show at least twenty times over the years, but it never gets old. The predictability of multiple characters dying and coming back to life is easy to disassociate with. Grabbing my knitting needles and current project, I lose myself to the show and the motion of my hands. I'll save all of these thoughts for some other day.

CHAPTER 12
Charlie

SOREN

Had a good time last night. Thanks for joining us.

I GROAN AS I CLIMB OUT OF BED, MUSCLES SORE AND body groggy from spending more time out than I usually do. I move through my morning routine of washing my face, brushing my teeth, making my bed, and heading downstairs for my coffee and breakfast.

My chef, Giovanna, has a plate sitting at my place on the island. It's hot, like she just finished preparing it, but she's nowhere in sight. I will never understand how she does it, how she times these meals perfectly even when I'm a few minutes off of my regular schedule.

The omelet and fruit are delicious and my black coffee burns going down in the best way. I pull up my texts from my sister and scroll social media as I eat.

On Instagram, I see Soren posted a few photos from last night and I take time flipping through them. The second to last photo has me freezing, looking at a smiling Mia and Cami staring back at me. They're bunched up close together, Mia's arm over Cami's shoulder, and they look like they've been best friends for decades. Cami looks happy, her eyes sparkling, and it makes me happy to see her happy. I like the photo, then lock my phone and finish eating.

The first floor of the penthouse is open concept, so from the island I can see the living room and dining room. The far wall is lined with floor to ceiling windows that let in tons of natural light and are optimal for people watching. Everything is gray and black, which to some might be boring, but I don't really care. It lacks personality, but I guess so do I sort of. No one else would see this place aside from Alana and Cami *if* we ever came here, and the occasional girl I might bring back, although that hasn't happened in a long time.

I place my dishes in the sink and make my way into the gym, where I start my usual every day workout. I'm halfway through the stretches and exercises the physical therapist has me do for my MCL when my phone rings. I answer and put it on speakerphone.

"Hey, Soph."

"Good game last night."

I grimace. "You know I don't like taking compliments."

"And that's exactly why I continue to give them." I roll my eyes, even though she can't see it. "Just wanted to check in. Find someone to fake date you yet?"

"Right to the point I see."

"Would you rather me talk your ear off about unimportant things?" she asks as I drop into a side lunge, breath picking up as I move through the exercises. "Are you working out? Seriously?"

"Oh *today* you decide not to have small talk?"

"You're lucky I don't drop you when you sass me like that."

"You wouldn't, we're family."

"Unfortunately you're right. So, got an update for me?"

I sigh deeply, realizing that we really are going to do this.

"I have someone in mind, but I haven't asked her yet."

"Why not? Who is it?"

I hesitate before I answer her, afraid that once I speak it out loud Cami will jump out from around a corner and laugh at the notion of dating me.

"Uh...my best friend, Cami. She lives here in New York City, works for a fashion magazine. We can trust her."

"Okay that sounds great. Why haven't you asked her yet?"

"I don't really know how to approach the topic..." I trail off.

"You need to just come out and ask her. We don't have time to wait for you to find the exact right moment. Conversations are starting soon about trades and you've been with the Rangers for longer than anyone expected. If this is going to work we need to get moving."

I sigh deeply, trying to calm my nerves surrounding the whole situation. I really cannot be traded. Just thinking about it causes my breathing to pick up and my heart rate to accelerate. I have had seven really good years with the Rangers and I don't want to play anywhere else. Whatever I need to do to make that happen, I'm going to do.

"I'll ask her. This week, I'll ask her."

"Good. And how is making friends going?"

"Actually pretty good. I went out with the guys last night after the game."

"No way?" I hear the surprise in Sophie's voice. She doesn't know what exactly went down back in high school, no one does, but she knows it was bad enough to cause me to withdraw. "I'm proud of you."

She understands why I'm closed off and hearing her pride at my attempt to socialize feels good. I know this is a long time coming, and even if the possible trade is stressful, I'm glad it's pushing me to try and build relationships.

"Wasn't groundbreaking, just had a drink with them."

"Well, still. That's a big deal when you normally would rather die than go out with a group of guys." I hear someone ask her a question in the background, meaning she must be in the office on a Saturday. "I gotta go. Let me know when you ask Cami about the dating situation. I'll get an NDA sent over."

She hangs up before I can tell her she doesn't need to have her sign an NDA, she isn't going to tell anyone. I move back into my workout routine and let it soothe the anxieties within me. I know staying with the Rangers for another contract is a long shot, but I have to try.

I start thinking through how I might approach this topic with her, but just thinking about it stresses me out even more, so I push it out of my mind. I'll figure it out at some point before Monday. I just want to get it over with.

I'm also only about half way confident that she will accept and actually agree to help me with this. Without having something in it for her, I'm honestly not sure why she would say yes, but I have to try something.

CHAPTER 13
Cami

THE OFFICE IS A MESS THIS MORNING. THERE ARE people running around left and right, and after I almost ran into a guy from finance I retreated to my cubicle for solace. Unfortunately, there isn't much peace here either. I stare angrily down at my phone and the multiple calls I've placed to the people we hired for makeup for today's shoot. They didn't show up, and I've been scrambling for the past hour trying to find someone to replace them.

Mistakes happen, I get it, but they can't happen when it's for something like this. If just one thing is off, just one person doesn't show up, the whole thing is a waste. We can't have a shoot if models don't have makeup, so I'm thankful when the fifth person I try finally answers my call and says they can fill in. Now they are only a half hour behind, and I can breathe a little easier, despite the fact that I want to drop kick the people who didn't show up in the first place.

I try to do some busy work to calm myself down, but nothing is really working. Normally, I would roll over to Alana's cubicle at times like this and talk to her about something random until I calmed down, but she's in Paris so I can't exactly do that. I miss her, but I don't want to make it harder for her by telling her that over and over. I replied to her one text telling me she missed me, but I'm practicing restraint. I know she's likely having anxiety over this trip, and I don't need to add to it.

After trying to distract myself to no avail, I stand and make my way to the breakroom in search of some kind of snack or drink. I grab a Dr. Pepper from the fridge and plop down in one of the comfortable chairs. The TV in the corner is playing an episode of *Gilmore Girls*, as usual, and I watch for a few minutes before glancing down when my phone buzzes.

CHARLES

Can I stop by later?

I smile seeing his name. We haven't talked since the bar last week and I missed him over the weekend. It's a little harder to hang out without Alana around, but not weird.

ME

If you bring me a coffee

CHARLES

Are you kidding? I know I'm not allowed in empty handed. I wouldn't dream of coming without a gift for the troll.

ME

Did you just call me a troll?!

CHARLES

No, of course not.

ME

Whatever, weirdo. See you tonight

Feeling lighter after that conversation, I make my way back to my desk and settle in. I get an email a few minutes later from the shoot organizer with raw, unedited photos and they are beautiful. I sigh in relief at another shoot in the books and get back to work.

When I get home from work, I give in and FaceTime Alana. It feels good to see her face and be able to physically see how she's doing. This trip is a big stretch for her, and I am so proud of the steps she's taking to get out of her comfort zone.

Unfortunately, her ex is trying to rain on her parade.

"He is so into you," I say, after she explains how Alex answered her phone for her when Brad, her ex, continued calling, despite being told to stop.

"No, he is not. He just saw a problem and tried to fix it. He's a fixer."

"Yeah, a fixer who is into you."

"Whatever."

Alana is so delusional it's funny, but I'll let her discover this on her own and have fun watching it all unfold. Alex is a good guy and she deserves someone good after that *jerkwad* Brad.

Sometimes cuss words are way more satisfactory than some made up word.

I fill her in on what's going on at the office and get fired up venting about the missing makeup crew at this morning's shoot. She affirms my frustrations and offers to send a strongly worded email for me, which I decline.

I'm halfway through giving her an update on Ian, our managing editor, and his move when the door opens behind me. I jump, afraid someone is breaking in, but see Charlie enter with two coffees in hand and remember he had asked to come over. He doesn't speak, seeing me on the phone, but Alana must be able to hear him enter because she asks about it.

"Who's that?" she asks, eyes looking around the screen to try and see who it might be.

I don't want to lie to her, but I don't want her to be sad if she sees her brother and I hanging out without her. I also really don't want her getting the wrong idea. I would never make a move on him—he's my friend—but I don't want her to even start thinking in that direction.

"Oh, no one," I lie.

She pauses and scrunches her brows like she's confused. I'm clearly not very skilled at lying. Even Charlie gives me a confused look and rolls his eyes.

"Well, it's obviously someone. Wait, are you seeing someone?" Charlie's eyes widen and I quickly shake my head no.

"Trust me if I was seeing someone you'd know. It's just the neighbor bringing some dog food and treats. They asked me to watch their dog for them this week."

"Okay...I guess I'll let you go and talk to that neighbor."

"Love you, Lan," I say, trying to get off the phone.

"Love you too."

I hang up before she even finishes the sentence, and I feel bad but I'll make it up to her later. I glance over at Charlie, who is sort of just standing awkwardly in the kitchen, and nod my head toward the coffee on the counter.

"One of those for me?"

"Oh...yeah." He grabs my latte and walks it over to me. I take it and he sits down on the couch next to me. "Why didn't you tell her it was me?"

I suddenly feel embarrassed that I hid him from his own sister, but I try not to let that show.

"I just didn't want her to get sad seeing us together. She just left, I figured it would just make things harder."

"Makes sense," he says, nodding his head.

"How was your day?" I ask, taking a sip of my coffee and humming in happiness.

"Not bad, just practiced and worked out."

"Another day in the life of a hockey superstar."

He rolls his eyes at me and takes a drink of his own coffee. I stare at him while he focuses his attention on a nonexistent speck of dust on the couch. He picks at it and is so far into his own thoughts that he doesn't hear me when I clear my throat in order to get his attention.

I place my hand on his shoulder, and he jerks his head up to meet my eyes.

"What?" he asks.

"Why did you want to stop by?"

CHAPTER 14
Charlie

Cami's question hangs in the air. I'm well aware that I've been staring at her for far too long without actually answering, but she waits patiently and doesn't push. After a few long seconds, she speaks again.

"Is everything okay?"

She says it softly, like she can tell I'm seconds away from running out the door and she doesn't want to spook me. I'm worried that asking this question is going to change everything between us, and she's a good friend. I don't want that to change.

Regardless, I really need her to do this for me.

"Everything is okay, sort of."

"Explain that to me."

"So you know I'm up for a contract renewal this year." She nods, her eyes going a bit dark. Neither Alana nor Cami like when contract renewal years come around, because it means I could be moving and no one wants that, least of all me.

"Well Sophie had some suggestions on what might help me stay with the Rangers."

"Okay?" She looks confused, trying to place what her role is in this.

"She wants me to win over the fans. To let them in on the *'loner life of Charlie Cade.'* She thinks boosting my image will make me valuable to the Rangers brand."

"You've stayed with the Rangers for seven years and she hasn't wanted you to do anything differently. Why does she want you to change now?"

"I think she's been hearing more than she's letting on in regards to a trade. Clearly my position is vulnerable this year." I don't realize I've started to bounce my knee nervously until she reaches over and stills it with the press of her hand. She rubs back and forth for a second in a gesture of comfort before pulling away.

"Okay, what does she want you to do?"

"That's where it gets complicated," I say, deciding to start with the easiest one first. "She wants me to make better relationships with the team. Start hanging out with them more and build friendships."

"I think that's a great idea. Is that why you went out after the game?"

"Yeah," I say as I reach back and rub the back of my neck. "That one isn't going to be too difficult, I don't think, but there's something else..."

"Spit it out already."

"She wants me to date someone." I look up now, and meet her eyes. She has a blank look on her face and I can't read her at all.

"Is that something you want to do?"

"Well, I don't really think that matters much. I don't have a choice."

"Why don't you have a choice? I know you want to stay with this team because Alana and I are here, but it wouldn't be the end of the world if you had to move. We'd be sad, but we would figure it out."

My pulse quickens at the thought of having to move teams. The palms of my hands get sweaty and I wipe them on my jeans. I think she can tell I'm getting antsy, because she speaks again.

"What makes you so nervous to leave? Is it what happened in high school?"

I shrug, because I can't talk about this. I don't want to share this part of me with her or anyone else. It's embarrassing and no one needs to bear witness to my past humiliations. All we need to do now is find a solution.

"What happened back then?"

"I can't, Cam."

"You don't have to, but you know I'm here for you. I won't judge you, and I'll listen."

"I know."

She nods and seems placated enough to not press me further, thankfully.

"Okay, so you need to date someone. Easy, you're hot. We can find someone to date you no problem." I'm stuck on the *you're hot* comment, a bit taken aback that she thinks that of me. I mean, I know I'm not bad looking, but to hear your best friend say it is a bit strange.

"Oh don't read into it you big idiot," she says and shoves me. "Objectively, you're nice-ish looking."

"How'd I go from hot to nice-ish?"

"You were being mean. Staring at me like I was stupid for calling you hot."

"I was not—"

"Whatever, not the point. Give me your phone, I'll set you up with a dating profile and start swiping. I can help you start conversations too. Don't worry, I'm an expert." She reaches out and takes my phone from my hand, punches in the password, and navigates to the app store.

"Woah there, tiger, not so fast." I take it out of her hands.

"Well, how do you expect to get someone to date you if you aren't on apps? People don't just pick people up at bars anymore."

I hesitate again, taking a sip of my coffee, and clearing my throat. I think she can tell I'm nervous because she gets quiet and doesn't make a move to take my phone from me again. Finally I get enough courage to ask.

"Sophie suggested I find someone to fake date, and I was thinking that person might be you."

She chokes on her coffee, and begins to violently cough. I reach out and pat her back, but she jerks away quickly and stands up.

"You"—she points at me dramatically—"Want me"—and then to herself—"To pretend to date you? So the fans like you more? I'm sorry there are so many issues with that."

"Okay, let's talk through them."

"You're serious?"

"I am."

"Oh my gosh," she groans and falls down onto the couch dramatically. "You're my friend. How am I supposed to fake date you? That would be so weird."

"Not really. Because we're friends we're comfortable around one another. It would probably be easier with you than with some stranger."

"Well what about Alana? What are we going to tell her?"

"She doesn't have to know right now. She's in Paris and the tabloids there won't be reporting on some American hockey team. We can wait and tell her before she comes back, when it isn't such a big deal."

She stands again and starts to pace the room back and forth, back and forth. I trace her movement with my eyes and wait for her to bring up another reason why this won't work.

"Why would the public like me?" she asks eventually, a nervous look on her face. "I'm nothing special."

I stand and cross the room to her, then place my hands on her face forcing her to look at me.

"Cam, you are extraordinary. You helped me gain my footing with the team last week and helped me start conversations. You're charismatic and charming and win everyone over within seconds.

They'll love you, and in turn hopefully me." She looks so deeply into my eyes it makes me want to squirm.

"And you're just okay with this?" she asks.

"It might be a little weird, the PDA and stuff but—" Her groan cuts me off. "What? What's wrong?"

"PDA? I didn't even think about that."

"Well, we're going to have to make them believe it somehow."

She nods her head in understanding, then breaks away from my hold and goes back to the couch. She pulls a blanket from behind her and hugs it to her small frame, then suddenly pulls it up over her head. I cock my head to the side as she disappears underneath it.

"Cami?" I ask.

"Mmhmm," she hums under the blanket. It's muffled, of course, because she's speaking to me through the fabric.

"Why are you under a blanket?"

"I'm not sure I can look at you while we have this conversation."

"Okay..." I trail off, trying to decide if I should wait for her to emerge or just keep going. Eventually, I decide to push forward. "Well, I was just going to say I feel a bit bad that you won't be getting anything out of this."

She doesn't say anything for a moment, and I can tell she's thinking. Eventually I see the blanket pull down just slightly, so all I can see are her eyes. I can tell she wants to say something, but she still isn't talking. "What is it?" I ask.

"It's probably stupid..."

"No, tell me. If there's something I can do to repay you, I would be happy to." She hesitates another moment, then pulls the blanket back up over her head. I sigh in disappointment, finding myself much preferring to look at her eyes than this blob of blanket.

"You know my sister is getting married in February," she says.

"Yes, in Florida, right?"

"Yeah. Well the other weekend when I was with them, my mom would not get off my case. She kept going on and on about how I needed to settle down and be more responsible and maybe then a man will love me."

"Cami, that's not—"

"No, I know, that's not what I'm saying. I accidentally told them I was bringing a date." She pauses then and I can't take it any longer, I reach forward and pull the blanket down from her face gently. There's vulnerability in her eyes. "I didn't know what to say, but I just wanted them to stop pushing me and it felt like the only thing that would get them off my back."

"So I'll be your wedding date."

She looks stunned. "Just like that?"

"Just like that."

CHAPTER 15
Cami

I AM FREAKING OUT. CHARLIE JUST ASKED ME TO BE HIS girlfriend, well his fake girlfriend, and then agreed to be my date to my sister's wedding.

What in the Hades is happening?

"We need to set some ground rules," I blurt out, trying desperately to be the voice of reason when I typically am not. Normally I'm the go with the flow, have fun, and fork the consequences kind of gal.

"Ground rules?"

"Yeah, like only brief kissing and hand holding, no making out, and only when we're in public."

"Well, of course. Why would I kiss you if we weren't in public?"

"I don't know. I'm just trying to be responsible here," I shout it at him and immediately feel bad. "Ugh, I'm sorry. I'm just freaking out a little and I'm trying to make sure our friendship is still intact at the end of all of this."

"Hey." He reaches out and squeezes my hand. "I'm freaking out, too, even though it might not seem like it. You're important to me and I don't want our friendship to change so whatever you need us to do to make sure it doesn't, I will do."

"Okay." I nod. "That's good. I also think we need to set an end date to this whole thing. When is our fake break up?"

"That's a good call." He worries his lip a little as he thinks and my eyes snag on the movement. "The trade deadline is in March, so let's say after that."

"Okay, that sounds good."

"And if you need me to come to any other family stuff so they don't think my showing up is weird, I can. As long as I don't have a game or practice."

"They won't think it's weird. They've been telling me I need to make a move on you for years now." I straighten and snap my lips shut as soon as the words leave them. My family has always suspected I have a crush on Charlie, but admitting that now is just going to make this even more awkward.

If I was honest with myself, I know I've had a small tiny baby crush on him for a while now. Who wouldn't? My best friend's brother who is a charming, huge, gorgeous hockey player? Doesn't take much to feel the butterflies. Plus, it isn't like I've known him since we were in elementary school. We met in high school when I moved into the house next to his and didn't even really become friends until whatever happened in high school took place, and he pulled away from his friend group and started hanging out with Alana and I.

Basically what I'm trying to say is, I don't view him like a brother. A best friend? Yes, but not a brother. I've resolved to push all of those teenage crush thoughts away, though, and chalked them up to childish fantasies. Nothing was ever going to happen between us.

Except now it is, I guess. Even if it's fake, I'm still going to have to hold his hand and touch him in public and kiss him. I take a deep breath, not feeling very confident that I'm going to make it out of this in one piece.

"Tell me what you're thinking," he says, and I laugh. I can't possibly tell him what I'm thinking. If I do that, this will be way more awkward than it already is.

"It's just a lot."

"If it's too much we don't have to do it. I'll figure something else out, I can try the dating apps. I don't want to make you uncomfortable."

"You don't make me uncomfortable. This situation is a little uncomfortable, but I don't think there's a world in which it *would* be comfortable for someone to fake date their best friend."

"So, you're in?" He looks so unsure, but at the same time full of hope. I know this means a lot to him and it's extremely important for him to stay on with the Rangers. I want that for him too.

"I'm in." He lunges forward and scoops me into a hug. "But no touching or kissing unless it's in public and we need to discuss how we're going to tell Alana about this. I don't want it to affect my friendship with her."

"Deal."

"Did Sophie say anything else she wanted you to do?" I ask.

"Nope. Just make the fans like me, so I guess we need to try to be out and about doing community stuff or whatever."

"*'Community stuff or whatever?'* Listen to you. We have some work to do," I say and laugh at his lack of seriousness.

"What did you have in mind?"

"That's for me to know and you to find out."

"Why am I scared?"

I narrow my eyes at him and lower my voice as I say, "You should be."

He rolls his eyes and looks around before standing.

"I'm sorry, I have to head out. We have an away game this weekend and Coach wants us for another early practice tomorrow before we leave." I can tell he doesn't want to go after dropping this bomb, but I know he has to.

"Where are you headed?"

"Predators in Nashville. Should be a pretty good game, they're solid this year."

"I'll watch."

"You don't have to," he says, running his hand through his dark brown hair.

"Sure, I do. My fake boyfriend is playing." He meets my eyes abruptly and a blush creeps up his cheeks. I wink at him and he rolls his eyes before heading towards the door.

"Thank you for agreeing to do this. You're a lifesaver."

"We don't have that contract just yet, big guy. Thank me when we do."

He squeezes me tightly around the waist and then makes his way down the hall and away from me. I take a deep breath as I shut the door and lean back against it. What in the world just happened?

I can't believe that I am going to fake date Charlie Cade, my best friend, and the media is going to report on it. I don't even want to begin to imagine all the ways this is going to throw a wrench into my life.

I can't help but be thankful, though. This is going to solve my problem with my family and will hopefully get them off of my case for a while. It'll be a nice reprieve from their constant nagging.

As I climb into bed that night, all I can think about is how I can't wait to tell the ladies at knitting club about this.

December

CHAPTER 16

Charlie

My stomach still feels unsettled the next day as I board the plane for our game in Nashville. We've officially reached the month of December, and while that adds another level to the pressure for a re-sign, that isn't the reason why I'm feeling uneasy.

I should have timed things better, because leaving Cami after dropping a bomb like that didn't feel right. I know she says she's okay with everything, but this is going to be a lot. Changing our friendship to be something *more* in front of the world is not an easy task, physically or mentally. I pull out my phone and type a text to her, because she never was one to keep her feelings from me, and our relationship isn't one of tip-toeing around a problem.

ME

> I feel bad leaving you last night after our conversation. We didn't even really get to talk about logistics or about how you were feeling. I'm glad you agreed, but are you sure you're good with this?

CAMI

> Aw, are you worried about my feelings Charles?

ME

You know I always am Cam. You're my friend.

CAMI

I know, me too. I'm good, really. I mean it'll be weird, but we will figure it out like we always do

ME

And you know there's going to be media all over you 24/7?

CAMI

I know that

ME

And we're going to have to hold hands and kiss and stuff.

CAMI

Are you trying to talk me out of it?

ME

No, of course not. I'm grateful you're willing to help. I just want to make sure you know what you're getting yourself into.

ME

What if none of this even works?

CAMI

Wow, a double text. Someone's anxious today

CAMI

Don't worry, superstar. I'm working on a list right now of things we can do to help your image, and I can handle the craziness. It'll probably be exciting

ME

You promise to tell me if it's too much? We'll call the whole thing off.

CAMI

I promise. Now get on the plane, get your head in game mode, and stop worrying about me. Go kick some booty

ME

I won't ever get used to the no cussing thing.

CAMI

👍

ME

How does that not count?

She doesn't reply, but she doesn't need to. I make my way toward the back of the plane to the last row and my unofficial assigned seat, but as I go Soren's hand on my wrist stops me.

"Hey, man, want to sit up here with us?" I look around to the guys in the aisles around him. Soren is in the window seat, leaving the middle open and the aisle for me. In the aisle across from us is Adams and in the row in front of him, Murphy. I could do without being in close proximity to Murphy, I hate the guy. He's constantly making the most misogynistic and gross comments and is overall just an annoying rookie. He gets on my nerves, but I need to be making friends and at least he's in front of Adams and not Soren and I. I shrug and plop down in the aisle seat next to him.

"Have a good night last night?" I ask Soren as I get settled in my seat. Our flight today is just under three hours, so it won't be too long.

"Yeah, not bad. Just hung out with Mia. We usually try to spend the evening together before I travel."

"We all know what you mean by *spend the evening together*, right, boys?" Murphy laughs at his own joke even though no one else does.

I ignore him. This is exactly what I mean; he's arrogant, crude, annoying and doesn't know when to stop. A few weeks ago we won a shutout and he started messing with the other team after the game, taunting them about how they didn't score. He got himself in a fight and ended up with a broken nose.

"How long have you two been together?" I ask, ignoring Murphy.

"About four years now. We started dating before I was drafted, so she's been with me the whole way."

"That's nice, it's scary dating now." Adams rubs the back of his neck. "I never know if a woman is in it for me or for fame. And now that I have Chloe, it's really important that I know the difference."

"Yeah, man, I bet that's tough," Soren replies. "Charlie, you dating anyone?"

I tense up. My first instinct is to say no, but I know that these guys are going to start seeing Cami around more often, and after meeting her at the bar they would be curious why I didn't say anything.

"Um, yeah actually. The girl from the bar the other night, Cami. We just started seeing each other."

"I knew it! You owe me," Adams says, making eye contact with Soren.

"Damnit," he groans. He reaches into his bag and grabs a few folded bills before handing them over.

"What's going on here?" I ask, confused.

"I bet Soren something was going on between you two. I could tell there was something there."

I don't know what he was picking up, because there wasn't *anything there*, but I don't question him. It just makes our story that much more believable.

"Ah, well it's new. We've been friends for a long time, but just started making things a bit more serious."

"Dating friends is dangerous waters," Murphy chimes in. "You screw it up and you lose more than just someone to warm your bed, you lose a friend too." I clench my fists at his words. They annoy me because he's right. Thankfully Soren speaks before I say something to him I'll regret.

"Maybe, but friends can make the best romantic partners too. Mia and I were best friends before we became more and I think she knows me better than anyone because of that."

Murphy huffs a laugh and turns around before pulling his noise-canceling headphones over his head, dismissing himself from the conversation.

"What's that guy's problem?" Soren asks.

"He's just an ass."

Murphy holds his middle finger in the air at my comment.

"Don't let him get to you. I'm serious, I think our friendship is why we've lasted for so long."

"Chloe's mom and I were not friends and you saw how that turned out. Data suggests you are set up for success, Cade."

"I'm sorry about Chloe's mom," I say, not quite sure how to broach this topic of his family after so many years of running from friendships. "How is life with a one year old?"

"No worries, man, it's in the past. Sucked, but what can you do?" He takes a deep breath and slowly releases it. "Life is insane. Being a single dad to a new toddler is...I don't even know what it is. Easily the most difficult thing I've ever done. I just hired a new nanny though, so hopefully that will help lighten the load a little."

"Good call hiring help," Soren says. "It'll get easier. I mean I don't know that for sure, but from what I've heard parents say, it should get easier."

"Fingers crossed."

We talk for a bit longer about Adams's daughter and her new nanny before settling in for the remainder of our flight. I close my eyes to try and gain an hour or so of extra sleep, and before I know it flight attendants are coming around asking us to prepare for landing.

The Nashville Predators's arena is pretty large and can fit 17,500 people. In comparison, Madison Square Garden can hold a little over 18,000. Getting into game mode in a stadium that isn't ours is a bit harder, but after so many years I have it down pretty solid.

I stick to my same breakfast if possible, depending on how early the flight is, and once we get about half an hour to landing I plug my headphones in and turn on my game day playlist. I move through my routine of getting things put in my locker, stretching and working on my PT exercises, and getting dressed for the game.

I'm about to head out to the ice when my phone buzzes in my locker.

> **CAMI**
>
> Good luck, superstar. I'll be wearing number 9 and shouting for you from the couch

> **ME**
>
> Number 9 and not number 13, right?

> **CAMI**
>
> I'll send proof

Cami's picture comes through and I open it and smile. It's a picture of her, standing in her living room with her red, white, and blue jersey on. It hangs low, past her knees, and it looks like she's wearing it as a dress. I know better though, she absolutely has on a pair of sweat shorts under there. Her curly blonde hair is thrown up into a messy bun, tendrils falling and framing her face. Her cheeks are flushed and her face is clean of makeup. She's sticking her tongue out at me and motioning toward the big number 9 in the center of her jersey.

A pang goes through my chest and I realize I'm missing her. I wish I could reach through the phone screen and pull the tie holding her hair up, then sink my fingers into it.

Where did that come from?

CAMI

I might tease, but I'd never wear another number, Charles

ME

Good. I don't want to see another number on the back of my girl.

I panic a little after I hit send. Was that too much? I can't unsend it, but she isn't responding and I need to put my phone away. Reluctantly, I put it back in my locker and head out to the ice.

After the game, I make my way back to the locker room. I've been on edge the entire three hours wishing I knew what her response was and freaking out that I had freaked *her* out. The message wasn't outwardly flirty, but I called her mine and I don't want her to take that the wrong way.

Despite my distraction, I played pretty well and only visited the penalty box twice. I walk straight into the locker room and to my locker, pulling my phone out to see a text from Cami, along with other unimportant notifications. My stomach is in knots as I unlock it.

CAMI

9 til the end of time, superstar

CHAPTER 17

Cami

I'VE BEEN CURLED UP ON THE COUCH ALL NIGHT watching Charlie's game and staring at his last text to me. I know I'm reading into it, and he likely did not intend to sound flirty, but that's how I read it. He called me his girl, and while that is absolutely true, there's something about that possessive word *my*.

I struggle with my response, but eventually I decide to stop overthinking and type out an equally flirty-but-not-flirty message and send it. *9 til the end of time, superstar.* I'm not sure where it came from, but calling him superstar just feels right. Plus, it gets on his nerves which is a bonus.

He's played well tonight, despite the fact that he seems a little distracted. Earlier in the game he got into it with one of the Predators's first line men. He got a good punch in before the refs split them up and he was given five minutes in the penalty box.

When he texted me on the plane to check in that I was still good with our arrangement, it got me thinking about all of the things we could do to help his image. I've been making a list while I watch the game.

The truth is, even though he has his own reasons for wanting to stay in New York, I have my reasons for wanting him to stay too.

He is one of my best friends and our lives have intersected so much over the last few years. We transitioned from high school to college together, and then from college into adulthood. I've seen him when his teenage boy acne flared up and he's seen me during my PMDD mood swings. He knows me on a level that only one other person in the world, his sister, does. It would suck if he had to move across the country.

Sure cozying up with him sounds weird in theory, but in reality I don't think it'll be too difficult. I feel comfortable around him and we've fallen asleep snuggled under a blanket together before. Plus, he's not *not* attractive. I guess it wouldn't hurt if I had to hold his hand or sit close to him.

I shake my head to bring my thoughts back to the current task at hand, getting the fans to love Charlie enough that the Rangers have no choice but to sign him again. I start to think through the things that make men likable and immediately wish Alana were here to talk through this with me.

I'm glad she isn't home right now. If she was, she would make this her problem to solve and throw herself into fixing this for her brother, so I'm glad she's away from it all. I don't mind stepping in to help this time.

Regardless, this would be more fun if I had someone to brainstorm with. I check the time, a little past seven thirty in the evening, and do the math. It's one forty five in the morning in Paris, but sometimes Alana is up late working. I text her instead of calling so I don't wake her.

ME

R u up?

BESTIE FRIEND

Is this a booty call? I'm a little far for that, don't you think?

ME

You better pick up the phone

It rings once before she answers. "This better be good, I was almost asleep."

I let out an involuntary sigh of happiness once I hear her voice. The annoyance in it is reminiscent of countless days when I was running late or got us in trouble for something stupid. The way it gets a little higher at the end tells me she isn't actually mad, just a little irritated. It's a little scratchy, and it only gets that way when she stays up too late working. It's a special kind of thing to be able to know everything about someone's current state of being, just by hearing them speak a few words. "I miss you."

"Same." I hear her yawn. "What's going on? Is everything okay?"

I push back the desire to pester her about why she's still awake, knowing the reason is likely just work, and get to the point of my call. As I take a breath to begin speaking, I quickly realize I hadn't really thought out my game plan. I don't want her to know about her brother's contract issues and I *really* don't want her to know about the whole fake girlfriend thing.

"Um...yeah everything's great! I just—" Come on, *think*.

"Please move at a glacial pace. You know how that thrills me," she says, quoting *The Devil Wears Prada*. I smile at the familiarity. She hasn't even been gone that long but it feels like it's been forever.

"Sorry, got distracted. I was just working on an idea for the magazine and I needed some help brainstorming. Got any brain power left for your bestie?"

"No."

"Great, so I am trying to come up with a list of things that men do that make them likable."

"That feels like a weird spread topic."

Shoot.

"Yeah, I know. Angela pitched it and you know how she is."

She hums in understanding and I take a deep breath of relief.

"Okay well." I hear her shift and can almost imagine her sitting up in bed. "Men with dogs are pretty cute. I think most people swoon when they see a big guy holding a tiny puppy in their arms."

"Oh that's a good one. Remember that one time they were hosting dog adoptions on the quad in college? Everyone was drooling over Zach Ford."

"I rest my case."

"What about a hobby? Guys with hobbies are generally considered a green flag," I suggest.

"Total green flag, especially if they're actually into it and not just doing it because they're being forced to."

Well, Charlie will be forced into all of this but that's besides the point.

"So true. I'm writing it down in my notes and *now* I will let you get some sleep because it is way too late for you to be up."

"It's okay, I never mind hearing from you, Cam."

"What's got you up so late?" I say, losing the battle to not prod.

"Just the normal racing thoughts and anxieties. I'm good, I just can't get my brain to shut off long enough to fall asleep."

Don't love that, but there's not a ton I can do for her from here.

"Been there done that. How's Alex?"

"He's good. He's Alex."

"What does that mean?" I smile as I wait for her answer. These two are totally made for each other.

"You know, generally perfect in every way."

"What a shame you have to live with him."

"I know, It's a hardship." She yawns and I take the hint.

"Okay, get some sleep. I'll talk to you tomorrow."

"Wait, isn't Charlie playing tonight?" I smile at her ability to keep up with his schedule even while being so far away. We did some research on how she might be able to watch the games from Paris, but weren't really able to decipher any of the instructions. So I just give her a play by play the next day usually.

"Yep he is. They're playing the Predators tonight and it's going well."

"Okay, good. I'm so tired I can't keep my eyes open. I love you."

"Love you more."

I hang up the phone and look down at my list I've started. The game is entering the second period and Charlie is on the bench, so I go back to scribbling on my notepad and jot down my ideas. Ultimately this list will have to be cleared by him and Sophie, but I feel pretty good about it.

The hours pass quickly, and even though Charlie had some bumps early on in the game he did pretty well overall and only ended up in the penalty box one more time. That's a pretty good outcome if you ask me.

It's just after eleven now, and the game finished up about twenty minutes ago. I'm not expecting a text back from him tonight. With the way our last conversation ended, a response isn't really needed. Plus, the guys have to get showered and get all of their stuff together before boarding the plane and heading back home. I'll see him tomorrow when we go over the game plan and the list I made.

I go through the nightly routine of shutting down my tiny apartment. I start at the door and triple check that the dead bolt and the handle are both locked, then I head to the kitchen and put away the few dishes I took out today. After filling up my water bottle, I shut off all of the lights and head to my bedroom.

I wash my face and brush my teeth, then climb into bed and sink into the mattress with a sigh. There must be some kind of science to explain the burst of happiness one feels when they get into bed after a long day. All of the happy endorphins travel through me as I cuddle into the cold sheets and wrap myself up in my comforter.

I build a sort of cocoon around myself, only the glow of my phone lighting up the room. I scroll through social media for way too long before finally setting my phone down and closing my eyes around one in the morning. The events of the last few days run through my head and I find it difficult to settle, some of Alana's anxiety passing through to me, but eventually I drift off thinking about seeing Charlie tomorrow.

CHAPTER 18

Cami

THE TEAM'S PLANE LANDED IN THE MIDDLE OF THE night and Charlie must've been feeling the effects of a long day, because he texted around five in the morning and pushed our afternoon hangout to the evening.

I was thankful for the extra time to reset my space a little bit. I'm in the mood to clean today and that doesn't happen often, so when the itch sets in it's best to scratch it. Never know how long it'll be before it comes around again.

About half an hour before he's supposed to be at my place, I run down to our favorite deli a few blocks over and grab our regulars. The walk there is brisk in an effort to spend less time in the cold, and when I get to the small shop I barely fit inside. Some would call this a bodega, but others would say it doesn't fit in that category considering they only sell deli products and nothing else like milk and eggs. I just call it by its name out front: Waverly.

The same man who is always behind the counter stands there now, taking orders and throwing together sandwiches. He's not friendly, but that's never scared me. Once I make it to the front of the line, I place my order and he grunts back at me, so I know he heard me correctly.

Charlie always gets the grilled chicken classic deli sandwich with no tomatoes, and I rotate between three or four "regulars" because I can't ever pick. Today I order the honey glazed turkey sandwich, and as I watch him prepare it I know I made the right choice.

He hands the two rolled up sandwiches to me over the glass deli counter, and I take them before giving him a smile he doesn't return. I make my way down to the equally unfriendly man at the cash wrap, pay, and head back to my place.

Waverly was a little busier than usual today, so I'm not surprised to find Charlie manspreading on my tiny couch when I walk back into my apartment.

"I was about to call and put in a missing persons report," he says.

"Sorry, Waverly was busy and it took a little longer."

"You should've texted."

"Do you want to argue about it or come and eat your sandwich?"

"Fair point."

He walks into the kitchen and grabs two paper plates from the cabinet as I unwrap the sandwiches. As I set each of them on our plates, he turns to the pantry and grabs each of our favorite chips, Cheetos for him and Ruffles for me, and carries our plates to the small bistro table in the corner while I grab strawberries from the fridge. We move like a well-oiled machine at this point in our friendship. It takes no effort to be around one another.

"How was the flight?" I ask as he takes the biggest bite of his sub. He chews for a second before he speaks, thankfully.

"Wasn't awful. I was wiped after, so I slept for most of it."

"How'd you feel about the outcome of the game?"

"It was a good one. The Predators are a solid team this year, so they gave us a strong fight." He takes another huge bite and I take the opportunity to approach the task at hand.

"So...I thought up a few items for your list."

"I can't wait to hear them, but can we talk it through after we eat? I have been surrounded by nothing but hockey for the last twenty-four hours and I just want to breathe for a second."

His comment catches me slightly off guard. His life is hockey and while I know anyone can hit burnout after too much time doing one thing, he is usually up for talking about it all the time. Even if he's just spent multiple back to back days on the road.

"Sure, that's fine." I search my brain for something else to talk about. It's not like it's difficult to talk to him, but now that there's this new fake relationship at play things feel a little more serious than they did before. "I spoke with Alana last night."

"How is she? That guy treating her right?"

"*Alex* is treating her just fine. He's sweet. I think you'll really like him."

"We'll see about that," he scoffs as he shoves a handful of, like, seven chips in his mouth at once. I roll my eyes. *Men*.

"Did she say how things were going?"

"She just said she was having trouble falling asleep and that work was a little crazy. She sounded good, though."

"I'm glad. She deserves that trip."

"Agreed."

By the time we finish talking about Alana, he has scarfed his whole meal down and I have half of my sandwich left. I wrap it up and put it in the fridge for tomorrow's lunch, then we make our way into the living room and sit close together on the couch.

My living room is cozy, mostly because it's small, but also because I've tried to make it that way. The loveseat, where he and I are now, is an old piece of furniture I got at a thrift store when I first moved in here. It's worn and I've had to sew patches of different patterned cloth in places, but I think it gives it character. It sits in the somewhat center of the room facing the television. It's enough distance that you wouldn't have to strain your neck looking up at the TV, but it's still pretty close. The joys of living in NYC.

I have a small window to the left of the couch that doesn't have much of a view, but it does let in natural light which I love. On the wall I have two TV trays that I use for almost every meal, and a picture hangs above it of Charlie, Alana, and I.

After we get settled on the loveseat, I speak. "Can we talk business now?"

"Yes, I'm ready," he says as a serious expression takes over his face. I stare at him for a few seconds before laughter bursts out of me without my permission.

He scowls. "What?"

"I'm sorry you just looked so serious and this whole situation feels unreal. I can't believe we're actually doing this." I sigh deeply and drop my head onto the back of the couch.

"Cam, if this is too much please tell me. The last thing I want to do is mess with our friendship. It means too much to me to risk it."

The worry in his voice is apparent, and I have the strongest desire to do whatever I can to assuage it. I reach over and place my hand on his knee.

"It's going to be fine. I want this to work as much as you do. If you leave, it'll wreck Alana"—and me—"and she needs her people around her just as much as you do. No more worrying about if this is going to mess things up between us. I'm telling you now that it won't and I need you to trust me."

"I do trust you."

"Okay, great. Then let me go over the things I think we could do to make the world like you more."

"Harsh much?"

"You know what I mean."

"So you made a list while I was gone? Of like...activities I can do?" He looks so unsure of himself, which is totally not like him. He normally has this easy calm about him that makes him seem like the most confident guy in the room, even in social situations that make him antsy and quiet. He's always been that way.

"Yeah, I came up with a few ideas. But you have to have an open mind."

"Oh, great. I don't know if I'm going to like this."

"I can guarantee you won't," I say. "But it'll be good for you and it will help your image. Plus, I'll do them with you so it will be fun."

"Okay, lay it on me."

I hand him the list and watch as his eyes roll down it. They widen in places and narrow in others and judging by the look on his face I know this is going to be fun.

How To Keep Charlie on the Rangers

1. Find a hobby, like knitting
2. Volunteer at a retirement home
3. Get involved with a charity
4. Library Story Time
5. Volunteer at an animal shelter
6. Fake date someone (me?)

"Cami, I am not going to your knitting club. Those ladies are going to eat me alive. I'm terrified of them." He genuinely looks a little scared and it takes everything in me to hold in my laughter this time, but I'm successful thankfully.

"They aren't scary at all, don't worry. They already love you."

"Wait, how do they know me?"

Whoops.

"I've mentioned you before. They're excited to meet you. Plus, if you don't want to go to knitting club we can just knit here and I'll set you up to volunteer at the retirement home." He looks at me quizzically, so I move on to the next item so he doesn't keep going down that line of questioning. "What charity do you think would be good to get involved in?"

He thinks about this for a few minutes, scrolling on his phone and googling things before giving me his answer.

"This isn't really a charity, but it's an outreach program for guys in high school…" he trails off and I know this has something to do with his past. Whatever happened that he hasn't and won't reveal to anyone, not even his sister. This doesn't feel like the time to press, so I don't. "It's a twice a month mentorship program. I'd get assigned a kid and then meet with them and like…help them and stuff I guess."

"That sounds like fun. How do we get in contact with them to sign you up?"

"Looks like I just need to fill out this form." His fingers fly over the phone screen as he types and I can tell he's excited, even though he won't show it. "Done."

"Nice. I can't wait to hear about the student they pair you up with. Now, onto one of my favorite ones."

"What is library story time?"

"Only the most magical thirty minutes ever."

"I think I'm scared."

"You don't need to be. The public library has story time every week and people can volunteer to go and read to the kids. If you went and we snapped a few pictures of you for social media everyone would go crazy."

"I'm not sure." He reaches up and rubs the back of his neck. "This all feels like a lot. Won't everyone catch on when all of a sudden I'm just out doing all of these things? Especially if Sophie is calling reporters ahead of time."

"Not if we don't use reporters."

"How do you expect this to work if no one sees me doing all of the things we're saying people need to see me doing?"

"We'll post it on social media. I can add it to my stories and tag you, like any girlfriend would do, and you can repost it on your page. Fans will see it and a few reporters are bound to pick it up naturally that way."

"Okay..."

"The next two are easy. If you volunteer at the retirement home and meet the ladies we can mark off two in one."

"Sure, I don't mind doing that."

"And then volunteering at an animal shelter. Playing with animals all day hardly sounds difficult."

"Agreed." His eyes scan the list one more time, landing on the last item, *fake date your best friend.* "Looks like you saved the best for last."

He says it with no hesitation, no question that I am the best thing on that list, and it causes my stomach to flip. It's not uncommon for him to cheer me on or say nice things about me, but in this context it feels completely different. I look down to try and hide my blush, but I'm not sure I'm successful.

"I would hardly say *the best*."

The comment is kind, but it's an unfamiliar feeling to be considered someone's best. I've never been able to make my mom proud enough to be her best, always falling behind my sister. I certainly haven't ever been another man's best, considering the fact that none of them lasted longer than a month or two. I have to admit, I think I'm afraid to fully feel what it might be like to be someone's best.

"Well, then you and I must have different definitions of the term. Dating you will be easy."

"*Fake* dating," I remind him.

"Right."

"Perfect," I say, eager to move on. "By the time we've completed all of those things the Rangers fans won't be able to let you go and you'll stay here for the rest of your career."

"I really hope this works," he says as he anxiously pulls at a thread on his shorts. He's wearing a white Rangers tee that hangs off of him, and a pair of black Lululemon shorts. Every bit casual and handsome.

"It will. It has to."

"Okay, so when are we taking this relationship out on the town and making our public debut?" I ask. He continues to fidget nervously for a few minutes before clearing his throat and squaring his shoulders.

"I was thinking about the Nutcracker. We were already going to go, so we can just make it a little more cozy and post about it. Does that sound okay?"

"Sounds great to me. We can take a few pictures and that should do the trick."

By the time we're done talking logistics for everything it's around eleven, so we decide to move into the bedroom to watch a movie. The next thing I know, my phone buzzing wakes me up and the screen tells me it's just after one in the morning. Alana's name scrolls at the top and I startle as I realize her brother is in bed with me. *Not the best look.*

I press answer anyway, concerned at her calling at this time of night even with the time change.

"There better be a good reason why you're calling me. I just fell asleep," I whisper, trying not to wake Charlie.

"Oh thank you baby Jesus."

"What's going on?"

"I think I want to jump into bed with Alex and I need you to remind me why I decided not to."

"I'm not going to do that. And why are you whispering?"

"Because I don't want him to hear me. Just be a good friend and go get the letter I put in your junk drawer in the kitchen."

"You've got to be kidding me." I groan and slowly pull the covers back, then tip toe into the living room and close the bedroom door quietly behind me. Opening the kitchen drawer, I find a piece of pink notebook paper, Alana's signature, folded neatly inside. "When did you even put this in here?"

"That's not important. Just read it."

"Alana, it's Alana Cade from *Impress Magazine* speaking to you through Cami, friend and beautiful editor," I read. "Wait, is this from *Parks and Rec*?"

"Just keep reading. Leslie Knope won the presidential election for a reason."

"Do not do anything with Alex. Be responsible, no matter how cute his mouth is. Your job is on the line."

"Great delivery. You're exactly right, thank you," she says and I huff a laugh. As much as I'm annoyed that she just woke me up, I miss her. Even though I literally just spoke to her.

"You're forgetting Leslie and Ben end up together and become arguably one of television's biggest power couples."

"I need you to help me stay strong. I just put myself back together, Cami."

The conversation continues and I help soothe her fears about her feelings for her coworker. Personally I think they would be a really great match, and I've seen the way he looks at her when they're just hanging around the office.

I head back into the bedroom as I say my goodbyes to Alana and cringe when Charlie speaks.

"Cam? What's going on? What time is it?" I slice my hand across my neck to try and communicate that he needs to stop talking, but I'm not sure he understands in his delirious state. I need to get off of the phone with his sister and I need to do it now. If she finds out he's slept over...I don't know how she's going to take that. And nothing even happened.

"I'm extremely tired so I should probably get back to sleep," I say into the phone. "I want you to just take it slow, but don't completely close yourself off. You deserve love more than anyone I know, Lan."

"I'll try."

"Good. I love you."

"Love you, too, Cam. Thanks for picking up."

"Always."

I hang up the phone and take a deep breath, thankful she didn't ask any questions even though I'm sure she heard her brother and just didn't realize it was him.

"Who was that?" he asks as he rubs the sleep from his eyes and yawns.

"Your sister. She thankfully didn't catch on that it was you who was over in the middle of the night, but in the future we need to be more careful." He's tense all of a sudden and I wish I could take back the seriousness in my voice and replace it with humor, but I can't.

"You're right, but I won't be staying here again. This was just an accident." He stands and starts to put his shoes on quickly, bumping into things left and right because we're sitting in darkness.

"You don't need to leave. It's the middle of the night, just stay and go home in the morning."

"No, I really should go." He moves towards the bedroom door and hesitates with his hand on the knob. He turns back towards me, takes the two steps to the bed and leans down before placing a soft kiss on the top of my head. He pauses, three inches away from my head, eyes wide. I don't dare breathe.

"Sleep well. I'll lock up," he says quickly before turning and darting out of the room.

He turns and leaves, closing my bedroom door behind him,

and a few seconds later I hear the lock fall into place on the front door. I stare up at the ceiling, grab the pillow next to me that smells like him, and scream into it. What in the world just happened? Why did he kiss my forehead? I can't help but think how thankful I am for the darkness of the room so he didn't see my blush.

I snuggle back down into the sheets and as I fall asleep I can't shake the thought that I wish he'd stayed.

CHAPTER 19
Charlie

"We're going to catch you, Cade, no sense in running. You're just making it more fun for us." The voice echoes off of the locker room walls as I run from it. I look down each row of lockers and search for a place to hide, coming up empty.

The showers. I'll run and hide in the showers and hopefully Troy and the others won't find me there. I turn the corner and head towards them. I run back to the farthest stall and push past the tiny shower curtain, then tug it in place behind me.

I sit in the far corner and pull my legs up, bending my knees. My breathing has picked up significantly, but I'm trying to calm it so I don't clue them in as to where I am. The more I try to quiet it though, the harder and louder it seems to get. I hear their laughter and sneering get closer and their footsteps bound toward me. I bury my head in my knees and pray they won't find me.

I'm startled by the sound of the plastic rings scraping on the metal rod as the shower curtain is pulled back.

"Found ya."

I jerk awake, panting heavily and covered in sweat, and a chill passes through me at the memory of Troy Price's sneering voice.

Looking over at the clock I see it's ten minutes past eight in the morning and I sigh deeply as I realize I'm at home and not back in high school. I'm safe. I remind myself of it over and over as I work to regulate my breathing.

It's still pitch black in my room considering the early hour and my blackout curtains, but the sounds of the city help to ground me and bring me back into my body. The nightmares don't happen often, but I notice they get worse when I get less sleep. Sleeping on an airplane after an exhausting game doesn't usually trigger it, but that on top of falling asleep at Cami's and leaving to come here in the middle of the night created the perfect storm.

I can't believe I fell asleep at her house last night. I mean, I guess I can. Her bed is insanely comfortable and I felt relaxed for the first time in days after being with the guys and performing on the ice.

Cami's presence is soothing for me, something I am just noticing now that my sister is gone. Alana has always been a safe place for me to land, and I just figured Cami was along for the ride because they were always together. But now that I'm spending more time with her alone, I realize she provides that same kind of comfort that Alana does.

Regardless of the fact that it was innocent, I know it isn't a good idea to get in the habit of staying over. Plus, that damn kiss. Why did I kiss her when I left? I wasn't thinking, and she is not the kind of woman I can be thoughtless with. She deserves more than that.

We have to keep clear boundaries if this whole fake dating thing is ever going to work and she has told me more than once how she's scared it will ruin our friendship. I've promised it won't, and I intend to keep that promise, which means no sleepovers.

Come to think of it, maybe we need some rules. I grab my phone and pull up my texts with Cami, then type one out and press send.

ME

I think we need to establish some rules.

CAMI

Oh come on. I hate rules

CAMI

Wait, rules for what?

ME

For our relationship.

CAMI

What relationship?

I hesitate, because what does she mean? She knows what relationship, we just spent the whole prior evening discussing it. I type and delete, then type and delete, over and over trying to figure out what to say. Then my phone buzzes as another text from her comes in.

CAMI

Just kidding

ME

You're annoying. Anyone ever told you that?

CAMI

Yep. Why do we need rules?

ME

You don't want this to mess with our friendship, and neither do I. I think we probably should set some boundaries to make sure that doesn't happen.

She takes a little while to respond to that one. I would like to pretend that I'm not staring at my phone waiting to see what she says, but that would be a lie because I am. Finally, it buzzes.

CAMI

Okay that's probably not a bad idea. What were you thinking?

ME

For one, no sleepovers.

CAMI

I really don't think these rules are necessary, but if you feel like they are, then okay. No sleepovers. What else?

ME

No touching.

CAMI

Like, ever? I think you'll need to touch me if we're going to convince anyone that we're dating.

ME

Okay no touching unless we're in public.

CAMI

I assume the same rule applies to kissing?

Suddenly the room is hot and I'm sweating again. Just thinking about kissing her is causing my breathing to quicken for some reason. Probably because it's weird to think about kissing her, considering we're such good friends. I know, though, that at some point we likely will have to kiss. I breathe deeply and reply.

ME

Yes.

CAMI

A man of many words

ME

We'll edit and adjust the rules as needed.

CAMI

Sounds good, captain. What time are you picking me up for the nutcracker tomorrow?

ME

Is six okay? The ballet starts at seven.

CAMI

Yep. I'm going to wear a pink dress if you want to coordinate colors. Not sure if Sophie is planning on having press there for pictures for our first night out or if we're just doing social media, but either way it would look better if we match

I'm reminded of how grateful I am that I chose her to do this with me. She's constantly looking out for me and is smart when it comes to the world of public opinion.

ME

Pink. Got it. I'll coordinate, thanks.

CAMI

Sure, see you tomorrow

I crawl out of bed and shuffle into the kitchen to make myself a cup of coffee. Pressing the button to brew, I stand and watch the coffee drip into my mug as I think through what I'm going to wear. I'll likely choose mostly black, and let her color be the show-stopper. I'd rather blend into the background anyways.

I move through the morning slowly, getting dressed and scrolling on my phone until I gather enough motivation to head down to the gym where I do some weightlifting and walking on the treadmill.

Our outing to The Nutcracker is one that we do every year, but this year it's different because Alana isn't around. That and the fact that Cami and I will be pretending to date, a fact I am trying not to overthink even though that seems impossible.

I shake the thoughts from my mind and head back to my room to shower.

CHAPTER 20

Cami

IT'S AN ACT OF SACRIFICE TO HOLD YOUR ARMS IN THE same position for many minutes in a row in order to achieve the perfect curls. The cramps and the shoulder pains are all worth it though as I stare back at my reflection in the mirror.

I slicked back an inch or so on either side of my hair, tucking them behind my ears and giving the illusion of a headband. The rest of my hair hangs in big loose Hollywood waves, cascading over my shoulders. The hairstyle pulls the front section of hair away from my face, making my gold earrings stand out.

I stayed true to my word and am wearing pink tonight. The dress is a soft pink with a fitted, but modest, top. It flares out at my hips and floats down to mid-calf. It's silky and shiny and pretty much every girly girl's dream dress. As much as I'd love to wear something a little more show-stopping, I figured our first public appearance should be a bit safer. I've paired it with a pair of black kitten heels and a small black clutch. Something tells me Charlie will be wearing black tonight, so hopefully we pair together well.

I've been getting ready all afternoon, making sure there isn't a hair out of place, and I am fully prepared to play hockey star girlfriend. Charlie called me earlier today and let me know that Sophie wants some press photos of us tonight so she can make sure our relationship is "officially announced" and that I should expect cameras. The phone call made everything even more real, so I've been distracting myself with tasks all day.

This morning I walked to the coffee shop down the block from my apartment. It's become one of the places I frequent and has that classic New York charm about it. It doesn't have an actual name, the word "Coffee" above the door is the only marking, so Alana and I have started referring to it as *coffeecoffeecoffee*. Very Lorelai Gilmore-esque. I went with a dirty chai, double shot of espresso obviously. A dirty chai in the winter always feels like a solid choice.

After I grabbed coffee, I hopped on the subway and got off at W 94th street, then walked the five minutes to Central Park. I don't normally go there often, but for some reason I felt like I needed a walk in a pretty park, so that's where I ended up. Normally, I would drag Alana with me for coffee and a walk, but I couldn't because she's thousands of miles away. The pang of missing her is growing all too familiar and it proves to me that I wouldn't want to live anywhere she wasn't. Of course, life throws you unexpected things sometimes, but if I have any say in it I will live within driving distance of Alana for my entire life.

Unable to stop the heartsick feeling, I pulled out my phone and sent her a text.

ME

I got coffeecoffeecoffee

BESTIE FRIEND

Noooo. I miss it. What did you get?

ME

Dirty chai

BESTIE FRIEND

YUM. Take a sip for me. Miss you!

ME

Miss you more

I walked around for an hour or so before heading home, and I have been home since then. Getting ready for my first date with Charlie Cade.

Cheese and crackers this is insane.

I'm still standing in the bathroom, working on clasping my necklace, when I hear the door to the apartment open and shut.

"Cam?" Charlie shouts.

"Back here."

I hear his footsteps as he approaches and while I was prepared for him to look good tonight, I was not prepared for him to look *this* good. My eyes start at his feet and make a slow ascent up his body. He's wearing a pair of black Oxford dress shoes and black dress pants that are tailored specifically for him. They fit his hips and backside like a hug and taper down at the ends perfectly. He's got a white button up tucked into them and a black jacket thrown on top. As my eyes meet his chest, I see the light pink pocket square that matches my dress exactly.

My eyes meet his and he smiles at me, then suddenly breaks eye contact. He looks down in what seems to be shyness, but it does little to hide his blush. Not that I care, because my cheeks are heated as well. I step forward and wrap him in a hug. It takes him half a second, but he wraps his big long arms around me and squeezes. We stand there like that for what seems like forever, before he finally pulls back to look at me.

"You look stunning," he says as his eyes slowly drink me in.

"Not so bad yourself," I reply, reaching up and shoving his shoulder playfully. "I just need to put my necklace on and I'll be ready to go."

I turn and move back towards my vanity where my jewelry sits. I pick the simple gold chain back up and start to reach behind me, but his hand on my wrist stills my movement.

"Here, let me," he says as he reaches around me and grabs both ends of the necklace from my hands. I reach back and pull my hair away from my neck, so he has room to clasp the ends together. I feel his hands softly brush the back of my neck and I shiver. Glancing up, I see the slight lift of his lips in the mirror and curse my body for reacting to his.

This whole thing is not real, I remind myself.

I feel the cool metal rest on my skin, and a second later he takes my hair from my hands and lightly lets it down, then smooths it gently. I look at us now in the mirror, him towering over me from behind, and we look good together. For just a second, I imagine what this might be like if it were real, but am quickly humbled by the jarring noise of his phone ringing in his pocket.

Serves me right. I shouldn't be thinking things like that.

"Thanks," I mouth to him while he presses the answer button. He nods his head in acknowledgement.

"Hey, Soph." I watch as he listens and nods his head in understanding a few times. "Yeah, we're about to head out. The car is downstairs." A few more nods. "Yes we should arrive around half past six. We'll be ready."

After a few goodbyes, they end the call and he turns back to me.

"Ready for this?"

"As ready as I'll ever be."

He reaches down and grabs my hand, weaving his fingers through mine.

"I thought you said no touching unless we were in public," I say, referring to our texts from yesterday.

"I figured we could use a little practice before we're out in front of the cameras."

"Not a bad idea, I guess."

We leave my apartment and head down to the car. He opens the door and ushers me in first and then slides in next to me. The driver confirms the address and we're off. Being out with Charlie while he is being a perfect gentleman is a completely different feeling than being out with him as one of my friends. He's always cared for me and opened my door or let me go first when stepping out of an elevator, stuff like that. But being cared for like I'm *his*... that is a whole new ballgame. Holding hands, putting on necklaces, and the hand he rests on my knee when we sit in the back of the car has me sweating just a bit. So much for rules, that lasted less than twenty-four hours.

I look down at his hand on my knee, then pointedly up to him. I repeat the path with my eyes a few times until he gets the hint.

"Just practicing," he says with a rub of his thumb back and forth on my knee. He seems confident, but the way his hand shakes gives him away.

"Okay," I reply, feeling stiff and awkward. This doesn't feel uncomfortable, which is probably *not* a good thing, but the fact that our relationship has changed so quickly makes me jumpy and self conscious in a way I haven't felt before.

I watch the city outside the window as we drive the half hour to the theater, staring at the people walking by and trying to calm my nerves. It isn't far from my apartment, but it takes twice as long to get anywhere in the city. We don't say much on the ride over, both too in our heads.

As we pull closer, I see at least ten men with cameras just hanging out on the sidewalk. People walk into the building, but they don't care much for any of them. They seem content to lean against the side of the building, until they see our car pull up. Suddenly the sides of the car are swarmed with men and their camera lenses are pressed to the window. Sophie must've really called the most enthusiastic reporters she knows, because while I'm sure people care about hockey I don't think they care *this* much about hockey. Charlie takes a deep breath beside me.

"Ready?" he asks.

"I guess. Let's do this."

He opens the door and slides out, then turns around to block my body from the cameras as I get out and smooth down my dress. Once I have my footing, he steps back so we can shut the door and takes my hand in his, then leads me towards the door of the theater.

"Don't let go of my hand," he whispers sternly in my ear. He doesn't have to tell me twice, I am counting on his body to make a path for me to get through. I nod up at him and we continue forward.

Everyone on the street has stopped to watch us, and I take a deep breath before forcing a confident and sexy smile on my face. I am dating this man, I remind myself. I am here so the fans fall in love with us. I can do this.

I press the side of my body into his as we walk. Flashes go off in every direction and I have to work hard not to squint at the bright lights. People are shouting all around us.

Charlie, who's this hottie?

Charlie, are you two dating? When did this happen?

Miss, can I have your number?

Come on Charlie, move your hand a little south for a photo!

He stops in his tracks at that last one and turns to glare at the photographer that said it. I didn't realize it, but the driver stepped out of the car and is following behind us, keeping reporters from crowding too close. Once he pinpoints the sleazy man in the crowd, he turns his serious face to our driver.

"I want his credentials," he says in the lowest voice I've ever heard from him. It causes a shiver to roll through me. The driver nods and turns, heading for the guy.

He pulls me closer into him in a protective gesture and pushes through the front doors to the theater. As they close behind us, the sounds of the shouting outside ceases and I take a deep breath. Charlie turns towards me, so I'm facing him, and pinches my chin between his thumb and pointer finger, tilting my head up so he can look me in the eye.

"Are you okay? I'm so sorry that guy said that. I promise I'll take care of it." He seems so worried and I can't help but let out a little laugh. He furrows his brow in confusion.

"I'm okay, I promise. I've heard worse being catcalled on my way to work. Trust me."

"Maybe I need to walk you to work from now on." I laugh at his outrageous comment, but he seems completely serious.

"It's just par for the course. Being a woman in society is a dangerous sport. Occupational hazard. Seriously, I'm okay. I want to enjoy the ballet."

He pauses a moment and his hands flinch by his side, but he doesn't move them.

"You're sure you're okay?"

"Positive."

"Okay." He reaches down and slides his hand into mine again. I ignore the way it comforts me. "Let's go find our seats."

CHAPTER 21

Charlie

CAMI IS STUNNING TONIGHT. I'M NOT SURE WHY I expected anything less, but it's a strange feeling when your little sister's best friend starts to look like a woman you might be interested in. Strange, and also startling, because Cami Slate is not a woman I'm allowed to want.

Back at her apartment, I didn't properly prepare myself to see her all dressed up. I didn't think I *needed* to prepare myself, but it affected me more than I was expecting. Maybe there's something about the fact that she dressed up for me that made it more special, I'm not sure. What I am sure about, though, is that I need to get through this evening and somehow convince a multitude of media outlets that she and I are madly in love. Little do they know, I was freaking out over chastly placing my hand on her knee in the car.

Then when we arrived at the New York City Ballet, the overwhelming feeling of anger and possession that came over me when that reporter started making nasty comments about her was surprising even to me. My emotions are all over the place tonight. I can tell Cami was shocked by how aggressive I got, but I wasn't about to let that man make that comment and not have any consequences. I had Greg, our driver, send his information to Sophie and she's working on getting his credentials stripped. Sophie keeps a list of photographers and media people that she calls for events like this when we want press. I needed to ensure that he would no longer be on it.

As we make our way to our private box, it's impossible to ignore the many eyes on us. If the commotion outside wasn't enough, people do tend to recognize me when I'm in public. Especially when I'm dressed up and in the city.

I place my hand on her lower back and feel her warmth through the satin material, willing my hands to calm as they make contact with her. I lead her onto the elevator and another couple, a man and a woman, steps inside with us. We step towards the back corner of the elevator and they settle towards the front. The woman turns and looks over her shoulder at the two of us, then leans over and whispers in her partner's ear. He then looks back at us before turning fully and giving me a wide smile.

"Hey, man, are you Charlie Cade? New York Rangers?"

I usually hate getting recognized in public, but I paste on a smile. The whole point of all of this is to get the fans to love me and want me to stick around. I wouldn't be off to a good start if I ignored this perfectly kind stranger in the elevator, no matter how much I would like to.

"That's me."

"I knew it, you're awesome on the ice. Do you mind if we get a picture?"

"Not at all."

The man hands Cami his phone and she moves towards the front of the elevator car, while the man and woman come and stand on either side of me. I keep my arms clasped in front of me— I know the tricks people pull—and smile for the camera. The elevator dings just as the flash goes off and she hands the phone back to him.

"Thanks for the picture. Enjoy the ballet."

"You too. Thanks for supporting the team."

They walk out and head in the opposite direction from us. Cami is looking up at me with wide eyes and I look down at her in confusion.

"What?"

"It's so crazy to me when people recognize you. Like, you're just a normal fixture in my life but to these people you're a celebrity."

"I've always wanted to be described as a 'normal fixture' by my fake girlfriend."

"Oh, come on." She swats my shoulder. "You know how much you mean to me."

I continue to lead her to our box, the hand splayed across her back our only point of connection. There are people everywhere and each time we have to squeeze between two groups her body is pressed close to mine. She sucks in a breath each time we make contact, and I try not to press *too* close, but sometimes it's unavoidable. Thankfully we make it to our seats rather quickly and we both have some room to breathe.

Our box is a few levels up above the stage and just a few to the left of the center. There are two chairs placed in the center of it, and they look a bit odd just sitting in the large space. This box could accommodate six, but the attendants fit it to however many people are assigned to it for any given show.

While the box is private, it's open to the space around us, so anyone can see us from where they're sitting if they are on the same level as us. I don't know that anyone in here will recognize me from so far away, but I pull Cami's chair close to mine just in case, and place my arm around her back. My hand grazes her shoulder and I feel awkward with it just hanging there, so I reach up to play with the blonde strands of hair that brush across her collarbone. She shivers.

"So." She clears her throat. "How much longer do we have before it starts?"

"Um." I shake my wrist in order to move my jacket sleeve out of the way enough to look at the watch face. "About ten minutes. Do you need anything?"

"Nope. I'm good." She fidgets with a thread on her dress and it feels awkward. It never felt awkward with her before all of this, and I start wracking my brain for things to say to get us out of this tension.

"Oh," she says as she reaches into her purse and pulls out her phone. "We need to take a picture and send it to Lan. I know she'll be sad she isn't here, but I think she'd be equally as sad if we don't send her one."

Cami, Alana, and I usually go to the ballet together every Christmas. It's a part of our list of traditions we do together, but this year with her gone she encouraged us to still go together. She doesn't know that the occasion is doubling as our first fake date, but what she doesn't know won't hurt her.

I do remove my arm from around Cami's shoulder, so there isn't any suspicion, and she awkwardly smiles at me. I lean in next to her as she takes the photo, then watch over her shoulder as she sends it in our group chat with my sister.

CAMI

We miss you!

BESTIE FRIEND

Noooo I'm sad!!

CAMI

Don't be sad. We aren't having any fun right Charles?

She looks up at me, then at my jacket pocket, then back at me, and then back at my pocket. Finally, I give in and pull out my phone.

ME

No fun at all. Your friend is a bit of a meanie.

SIS

You take that back right this second.

CAMI

You heard her

ME

I will do no such thing.

The lights dim a few moments later, and we both put our phones away and resume our earlier positions. The longer we sit through the ballet, the more comfortable both of our bodies become. She leans her weight into me and I let my hand relax on her shoulder, brushing my knuckles back and forth over her arm. When the lights rise for intermission, it's like a spell breaks. We both straighten and look around as if we have no idea where we are.

"I think I want a glass of wine," she says while standing and smoothing down her dress.

"Yeah, a beer sounds good."

We stand and awkwardly both go for the exit of the box at the same time. She steps behind me as I also step back to let her go ahead, then we both step forward and bump shoulders, before we look at each other and break out in laughter.

"This is—" she says through laughter.

"It's a lot," I finish for her through my own chuckle.

"It's fine, we're not doing an awful job."

"Not at all, come on let's go." I usher her forward when I pull open the door and she goes out ahead of me, much more graceful than moments before.

We make our way out into the crowd and, as expected, everyone takes this opportunity to grab drinks or a snack. Thankfully, the boxes have their own lines for concessions, but even those are hectic.

"Why don't you stay here and I'll get the drinks? That way you don't have to mess with the crowd."

"Are you sure?"

"Positive." I lean forward and brush a kiss over her temple, then turn away and head for the line. I curse under my breath as I do, because that felt all too natural. Much like that kiss I gave her when I left her house the other night. I cannot get used to giving this woman meaningless kisses. I absolutely cannot.

I give myself a pep talk as I wait in the line. I remind myself that this isn't real. She's just helping me out and being a good friend and I cannot let the lines get blurry. The more I do that, the more it'll hurt in the end. The goal is for no one to be hurting when this is all over.

I grab our drinks after about a ten minute wait and turn to head back to Cami. Intermission is only fifteen minutes, so we don't have much time to get back to the box.

As I approach her, I notice a man standing across from her. He's speaking and she has something like a smile on her face, but her arms are crossed around her body like she's giving herself a hug. She looks uncomfortable and annoyed and it doesn't seem like this guy is taking the hint. I quicken my pace and slide up next to her, holding her wine out in front of her.

"Here you go, sweetheart." She looks up at me and I immediately see relief in her eyes. I slide a hand around her waist and pull her back to my front, wincing at the way she stiffens before melting into me. We have never been close like this before. "Hey, man, I'm Charlie, her boyfriend. Who are you?"

"Whoa, I'm sorry." He holds his hands up in surrender. "She didn't say anything about a boyfriend."

"Not like you'd listen if I had."

He looks taken aback at the fact that she would interject. He seems like the kind of guy who would tell his wife to *be quiet honey, the men are talking.*' I settle in behind her, offering my silent support.

"It's not my job to tell you I have a boyfriend within the first five seconds of you speaking to me, but it is your job to take a hint when it's extremely obvious I don't want to speak to you."

"Whatever, bitch," the man says under his breath as he turns. At that, I decide that while she can absolutely handle this on her own I wouldn't mind providing some physical reinforcement, but she stops me by placing her hand on my chest and applying a bit of pressure.

"Don't, he isn't worth it. Let's go back up and watch the rest of the ballet. This is too good of a night to let someone like that ruin it."

"Fine, but for the record I am dying to kick that guy's ass."

"I know you are. Down boy."

She turns and takes my hand, leading me back to our box.

CHAPTER 22
Cami

ON THE RIDE BACK TO MY APARTMENT I CAN'T STOP replaying the night's events in my mind. The paparazzi lining the walkway, the photo we sent to Alana, the annoying creep who wouldn't stop talking to me, and the way Charlie just slipped right in like he belongs by my side, calling himself my boyfriend. I'm reeling and I absolutely need to rein it in because it was all fake.

That was only evidenced by the fact that, once we got back to our seats and the lights went down, he dropped his hand from my knee and settled next to me in his own chair. Not in an unkind way, but in a way that clearly communicated what we were and what this relationship was intended to be. And it was a good reminder.

He isn't touching me as we ride home in the back of the car, and thankfully we didn't get ambushed by any reporters as we left the theater. I've had enough public interaction for one night, and I was beginning to wonder if I might have signed myself up for too much by agreeing to do this.

My thoughts drifted to the text I got from Alana while we were at the ballet. I looked while I was in the bathroom, because I knew there was a reason why she was texting me separately and not with Charlie included.

BESTIE FRIEND

You two look awful cozy in that pic Cam.

ME

He got close for the picture, what do you mean?

BESTIE FRIEND

I'm just saying, looks a little closer than he needed to be.

ME

Whatever. Stop trying to meddle in my love life and suggest I'm cozy with your brother when your love life is up in flames

BESTIE FRIEND

Hey. Not nice.

ME

I'm sorry, I didn't mean it that way. I'm just saying I'm as much of a mess as you are. There's nothing going on

BESTIE FRIEND

Okay. But if there was, you know you could tell me.

ME

I have to go, I'm missing the ballet

BESTIE FRIEND

Okaaaay goodbye.

ME

Love you

BESTIE FRIEND

Me too.

I felt bad lying to her, but no matter how much she says she would be okay if we were dating, I know it would be weird and I can't risk losing our friendship. Alana and Charlie feel like some of the only permanent things in my life. Them and my job are two areas where I have never felt the need to give into my desire to constantly switch it up and try something new.

I'm deep in my own thoughts when I feel a warm pressure on my shoulder. I turn towards Charlie, who is looking at me with concern.

"You okay?"

"I'm good. Just a lot tonight, but I'm okay."

He stares at me a beat longer, maybe trying to determine if I'm being truthful, then turns to look out his side of the car. A while later, the car comes to a stop.

"Let me walk you up." He nods his head in the direction of my building, which we've just pulled up at. I spent the whole car ride so deep in my thoughts I hadn't even realized we were already here.

I hesitate, but ultimately decide to decline, feeling the need to reinforce the boundaries we've set. Tonight was fantastic, and I have no doubt we were able to convince those around us of our relationship to one another, but I need to remind myself of what this is. This relationship is not real.

"I'm okay," I say, taking in the confused look on his face. "Thanks for tonight, it was fun."

I turn and open the door, sliding out before he has the chance to come to my side and open it for me. I see his face as I shut it, feeling a twist in my stomach at the slight hurt I see there.

I turn and make my way into the building, riding up the elevator to my floor and unlocking my door. Tonight was fun, yes, but it also showed me a picture of something that I don't think I will ever have and I'm not so sure how I feel about all of that.

The chemistry with Charlie, while awkward and stilted at times, is almost too easy. It feels too comfortable. Maybe that's because we've been friends for so long, or maybe it's some other reason, either way I cannot get used to it. No matter how good it felt to have someone solid by my side all night.

I peel off my dress and swipe a makeup wipe over my face, feeling suddenly drained and heavy. I climb into bed and set my phone on the nightstand, choosing not to doom scroll.

I click off the lamp and the room descends into darkness. I sigh deeply and wait for sleep to come.

CHAPTER 23

Charlie

SOPHIE

Look...

ME

Is that what I think it is?

SOPHIE

Do you think it's the article announcing your relationship? Because if so, then yes!

I SLEPT LIKE SHIT LAST NIGHT, FOR PROBABLY MORE reasons than one. I couldn't stop thinking about everything that happened at the ballet, and if that's how I feel after one fake date with Cami, I'm not sure I'm going to come out of this unscathed. I promised her we would remain friends on the other side of all of this, and I have to keep that promise.

My feelings after just one night out with her are scaring me, if I'm being honest. I know I have to maintain the boundaries we have set in place, but I was slightly disappointed when she declined my offer to walk her up last night.

Nothing would have happened, obviously, but I wasn't ready to leave her just yet. I just wanted to be around her, and that is so confusing to me that it's frustrating. I had to spend an hour on the treadmill when I got home just to wear myself out enough to sleep.

I mindlessly scroll through the press releases on my phone, looking at the pictures of the two of us. I am shocked when I see the first one. We are about half way from the car to the door, and Cami is a few steps ahead of me. My hand is on her lower back as I lead her forward into the building, but she has her head turned and she's looking back at me. It's a stunning photo of her. Her big blonde waves swish as she turns, and her eyes are wide and looking right at me. The smile on her face is eager and bright. She looks like she's smitten with me, and I'm blown away at how good she is at all of this.

Cami is someone who goes on dates often, but never has a boyfriend. She can't seem to find someone she likes enough to make things official, so it's a bit of a revolving door with her when it comes to men. There's nothing wrong with that, and I've hopefully never given off the impression that I ever judged her for it. It's paying off now, though.

I roll my eyes at the headline *"Mysterious Hockey Hottie Charlie Cade Spotted with a Gorgeous Woman."* At least they got one thing right, she did look gorgeous last night. I scroll through the article, skimming the words for the third time, and take a deep breath. This is really happening; we're really doing this. My phone buzzes with an incoming text.

SOPHIE

> Good work last night. Things are looking good so far, lots of positive press. Keep it up.

ME

> I don't really have a choice at this point, do I?

SOPHIE

> You can't tell me you didn't enjoy yourself. It's written all over your face in these pictures.
> Hers too.

ME

We were faking.

SOPHIE

Riiiight.

I toss my phone down on the side table and slowly sit up in bed, stretching my arms and groaning as I do. I won't be playing hockey much longer if my aches and pains have anything to say about it. I'm nearing the end of my time in the sport, approaching my thirties, and depending on how long my body will let me play determines when I retire. If I could guess, I think I have another two years, maybe three. The length of this one last contract hopefully, if I can swing it.

I shower and throw on some sweats before making my way into the kitchen to eat breakfast. We play Seattle tonight, and I have to meet with Coach before the pregame skate, so I need to head out pretty soon if I'm going to get to physical therapy and the gym before that meeting.

"Here's your breakfast, just like you like it." Giovanna places the plate down in front of me, then turns her back to me as she goes back to cleaning up.

"You don't have to do that."

"Who else is going to do it?" she asks as she gives me a look, raising one eyebrow. Giovanna is a woman in her sixties who has been my chef for the last few years. She's a pain in my butt, always nagging me about this and that, but she means well.

"I don't know, I can see if cleaners can come by today. I just feel bad making you do it when you do so much."

"Charlie, caro mio, cleaners do not need to come to wash the one pan and few dishes we used for breakfast," she says in her thick Italian accent. "I will clean it. It's no trouble for me. You just eat and get focused on your game tonight."

I shake my head in defeat and eat quickly, then take a few

moments to drink my protein shake while I scroll through the photos again. I just can't help myself.

"Oh, why are people taking photos of you and Ms. Cami?" Giovanna asks, peeking over my shoulder. "That is not normal?"

"It's not, you're right. Cami is um—" I rub the back of my neck anxiously as I wrack my brain for words to describe what's happening, then decide to just come straight out with it. "She is pretending to be my girlfriend."

"Scusi?"

"Sophie thought it would help my public image if I was dating someone who was charming and beautiful. I asked her. It's not a big deal." I stand and start to gather my things so I can head out, but she stops me with a hand on my arm.

"What do you mean not a big deal? This is a big deal. She is your best friend and you better not hurt that sweet girl. Do you hear me?" My eyes widen at the passion behind her voice. I understand her concerns, I have them myself, but I didn't expect her to be this outspoken about it.

"I promise I won't hurt her. She knows what this is and has agreed to help me if I help her in return. It's all going to be okay, but I really do have to go, I'm sorry." I lean down and kiss both of her cheeks before turning and heading out the door.

A little while later, I pull up to the stadium and make my way inside. As I approach the doors, my phone begins ringing in my hand. Glancing down, I see it's my dad and hit ignore. He normally doesn't call before a game, only after to critique me, but whatever he has to say I don't want to hear it. It still baffles me how my parents remember to call me multiple times a week, but can't seem to pick the phone up for my sister. Granted, all they want to talk about is hockey, but still.

I make my way to Coach Smith's office, and knock twice on his open door before heading inside.

Richard Smith had a stunning record in high school—250 goals and 65 assists—and the Toronto Maple Leafs snatched him up when he was eighteen. He played for them for the majority of his career before being traded to the Rangers and finishing out his time playing there. After he retired he took a few years off, but got a call when the previous Rangers coach retired. He took the spot after him and has been coaching for seven years now. His first year was my first year, and I think that's created an unspoken bond between us.

"Come on in, Cade, take a seat." He gestures to the chair sitting in front of his desk. I sit and place my bag down next to me.

"How are you, sir?"

"I'm doin' well. How about you?" He leans back in his chair and places his ankle on his opposite knee, the picture of relaxation. I'm not exactly sure why he called this meeting, although I can speculate it has something to do with the press release considering it showed up on my calendar just this morning.

"Good. Going to hit up physical therapy before the game tonight so I should be good to go."

"I heard you went out with the boys a few games ago. I was glad to hear it."

He has talked to me before about how I need to be more involved with the team, so this is probably a long time coming for him.

"It was nice. I'm trying to get to know them a little better."

"It's about damn time. You've been a part of this family for seven years now, son."

"I know." I look down at my feet, unable to hold eye contact as I speak the sentence. "I have a hard time connecting and trusting people but...I'm trying to change that."

He just stares at me for a beat. The silence goes on so long, I eventually look up at him to see if he's waiting on me to say more.

"Well, I'm glad to hear that," he eventually says. "Was also glad to hear you seem to have yourself a girl."

My cheeks grow warm and I take a deep breath in, trying to ease the churning in my stomach. Lying to the world? I can handle that. Lying to my coach? That feels a lot different. He is like a dad to me, especially since mine is so shitty. It feels like a huge act of betrayal to lie to him, but I don't really have a choice.

"Yeah, you remember Cami? She's usually around. My sister's best friend." He nods his head in understanding and sits forward, placing his elbows on the desk and steepling his fingers.

"I remember her, nice girl. I'm proud of you, kid. This is good for ya. I always worry you're too isolated out there in that big apartment with no one to share it with. You hanging out with the boys and going out with your girl makes me happy. As long as you keep your head in the game."

"Yes, sir. Don't worry about that, I promise my game won't suffer."

"That's what I like to hear. You go get ready for tonight, and I'll see you out there."

"Thank you, sir."

I breathe a sigh of relief as I stand and make my way back to the locker room, thankful that the meeting went well enough. This entire situation is a lot, but so far, so good.

CHAPTER 24
Cami

BROOKDALE RETIREMENT HOME IS BUZZING WITH activity, the monthly family day coming to a close. I weave through the families in the lobby and make my way to the community room. I made sure to be five minutes early this time, so no one has any excuse to make any comments about my tardiness today.

When I enter, only Linda is sitting on the couch. Her basket of yarn is placed next to her and she has the beginnings of something in her lap. I can't quite tell what it is just yet.

"Hey there, you. Long time no see, get over here so I can squeeze your neck."

I walk over and lean down, wrapping my arms around her. It's been a little while since I've come to knitting. The last couple of weeks have been busy with helping Charlie and getting work settled with Alex and Alana gone. I haven't been able to make it and I always feel bad when that happens.

"I'm sorry, but I promise to make it up to you. I have lots of personal drama."

"Oh, you know how I love hearing about the drama. Take a seat." She pats the space next to her and I sit down before pulling out my materials. "Rhonda and Emery had family come in, but they should be here soon. I think Gladys too."

Sure enough, a moment later all three make their way into the room.

"Oh, she's decided to grace us with her presence," Gladys says in a dramatic tone.

"Leave the girl alone, she said she has drama to share."

"Oh, well then let me just get comfortable."

As the three women make their way to the couches and get settled, I contemplate how much I want to share with them. Even though they encouraged me to ask Charlie to be my date to the wedding, they know nothing about the fake dating for his hockey career thing. That information is on a tight lock down, because if anyone found out we were faking this it would ruin everything. As I mull it over, I decide that these ladies are probably some of the only women I could tell this secret to. I'm not able to talk about this with anyone, and they are some of the most trustworthy people in my life as they're essentially my chosen grandmothers. Not only that, but they don't know anyone in the media, nor do they follow professional hockey. I'm not even sure they know he plays hockey.

I decide to go ahead and just tell them, thinking they're going to be seeing more of him if we follow through on all of the items on the list, and I trust them not to share with anyone.

"Okay, what happened?" Rhonda asks, not even picking up her knitting materials. Everyone in the room is staring at me and I suddenly feel shy, a feeling I'm not familiar with in the slightest. I'm lost in thought, trying to decipher what about this situation feels particularly sensitive, when Rhonda speaks again.

"You don't have to share if you don't want to, sweetie."

"No, I want to. I just...it's a lot is all. I think I'm starting to come to terms with how overwhelming this whole situation is. I need to talk about it though." I play with the yarn in my lap, gathering the words I want to say. "But before I tell you, I need you to promise me you won't talk to anyone about this. It has to stay a secret."

I glance around the room to see four pairs of wide eyes all staring at me and nodding slowly.

"I have to say, you've got me a little spooked," Linda says as she picks up her needles and begins to knit slowly. "Go on."

The rest of the women pick their projects up, too, and start to knit as they wait to hear what I have to say. The normalcy of it calms me, so I pick my materials up and start knitting as I speak.

"So remember how last time I was here, you all told me to ask Charlie if he would be my fake date to Colette's wedding?"

"Oh, did you ask?" Emery asks, perking up in her seat.

"I did. But there's more to it than that. So, he plays hockey."

"That's hot."

"It is, Rhon. It totally is. So he's played for the New York Rangers for his whole career, which is essentially unheard of in the professional hockey world. Only a handful of players have stayed with the same team their entire career."

"Wow, they must really like him if they've kept him this long," Gladys chimes in.

"I think his coaches see his value. He's coming up on a contract year, though, and his manager wanted him to do some work to up his public image. She thinks this will be one of his last contracts before he retires, and if he wants to stay with the Rangers he needs to do an overhaul on how the public views him."

"What do you mean?" Linda asks.

"Well, he's a closed off guy. He doesn't let very many people in and he likes to put his head down and get his work done. He isn't one for public appearances or getting photographed, so a lot of the time he isn't what people think of when they think of the New York Rangers. Sophie, his manager, wants him to put himself out there so fans start to consider him a part of the Rangers brand. That way the team wouldn't consider a trade and they'd re-sign him."

"I see. So what does that have to do with you?" Emery asks.

"One of the ways his manager suggested he up his image is by publicly dating someone."

The room is bathed in silence for a few moments as the words land. Each of the women have stopped knitting and are staring up at me.

"And he asked you," Emery concludes.

"He did."

"And you said yes?" Rhonda asks.

"I did. And then I asked him to be my date to the wedding in exchange."

"Well, that sure sounds fun. So are you two official yet? To the public I mean." Gladys leans forward as she asks. Her easy acceptance surprises me, but I answer her question.

"We had our first date last night. We went to the Nutcracker Ballet, which we do every year, we just don't typically do it alone or with the presence of cameras and media."

And I don't usually freak out over my best friend touching my knee.

"How did it go?" Linda asks quietly at my side. I notice she hasn't said much in this conversation so far.

"It wasn't bad. I think it hit me how real this all is. There were a lot of cameras and intrusive questions. The article went live this morning. Here." I hand over my phone to Linda and let her scroll through the photos, then pass the phone around.

When I saw the headline this morning it made me giggle. I was flattered they referred to me as 'gorgeous' and the photos were surreal. We looked famous and important and weirdly comfortable. I guess that comes from years of being best friends, but to see his hand on my lower back and the shot someone got when he leaned in to whisper in my ear was shocking. Just seeing the photos caused a phantom heat at my back, like I could feel his hand there all over again.

"Oh, she's smitten," I hear Gladys say.

"What? No I'm not," I insist, panicked.

"Considering you just went all melty eyes and transported to another world, I would say you're full of bullshit."

"No, I promise you we are just friends. We're best friends. He promised me we wouldn't let this arrangement mess that up. I don't know what I'd do if things ended badly." I worry my bottom lip and feel Linda's warm hand land on my knee.

"Just be careful. Even the nicest of boys can lead us astray sometimes, and this seems like quite the whirlwind with all of the media attention. I think I can speak for us all when I say we worry."

"I know and I appreciate that. I will be careful."

"We love you, sweetheart," Rhonda says and they all nod their heads in agreement.

"Thanks, I love you too. Now, how do you feel about having an extra attendee at the next meeting? Because one of the things on our list to make Charlie more lovable is him having a hobby, and I think I know one that might fit well."

"You know we can make room for anyone. And we won't ask too many questions," Emery says with a wink.

"Hell yeah we can," Gladys says.

"Gladys," I exclaim and playfully nudge her shoulder. "You know I'm trying not to swear. The more you do the more it'll wear off on me."

"I'm an old lady, I can say what I want."

I laugh at her brashness and shake my head.

"So, what are we going to teach him ladies?" Rhonda asks with a conspiratorial smile on her face.

"We could try to teach him a lace stitch," Gladys says.

"If we teach him a lace stitch first we'll ensure he never tries again," I joke.

The lace stitch is one of the more difficult knittings. It creates fabric that looks like lace, including all the small holes. It can be difficult to create stable holes while also making sure the whole thing doesn't unravel. I tried it once, and it ended with an emergency slice of cheesecake and a trip to my therapist.

"Don't worry, honey," Linda says. "I won't let these three give him too much trouble."

"And, Gladys, no naughty pictures in your projects the day he comes," Emery says.

"Please," I say as I turn to Gladys and flash her my puppy dog eyes. "I don't think I'll be able to handle an interrogation *and* embarrassing pictures."

"We'll see about all that," Gladys says with an eye roll.

Over the next hour and a half together we laugh and knit, and the more time I spend with them the more I feel grateful I shared this with them. I didn't realize how much I needed to just tell someone about what was going on, and although I'm still overwhelmed with the whole thing I do feel lighter.

CHAPTER 25
Charlie

I USHER CAMI THROUGH THE FRONT DOOR TO THE small and intimate Italian restaurant we have reservations at tonight. We were able to walk to dinner, and my hand hasn't left her lower back since we stepped out of her building. Good thing, because as we've gotten closer to the restaurant we've run into a few photographers. It's been about a week since our first date, and with Cami posting on her social media about the two of us there has been no shortage of attention.

They don't even need to be tipped off as to where we are anymore, they're just constantly lurking. I have a suspicion they know the area in which I live and have a car tailing me, otherwise I'm not sure how they'd know where we are. I feel uncomfortable with them knowing exactly where Cami lives, but they haven't photographed her building at this point so I take solace in that.

As far as I know, they still haven't pinpointed exactly where my penthouse is, just the general location where my car usually pulls out of. I'm thankful for our back entrance to the building, which is set apart from major traffic flow and somewhat hidden. Worst case scenario, we have a safe hideaway there.

The hostess walks us to our table, which is tucked away in the far corner of the restaurant. The lights are dimmed throughout the space and candles are placed on each table, giving it an intimate feel. I pull Cami's chair out first, allowing her to slide in, then take my seat across from her. She delicately places her napkin in her lap and smiles over at me. The candlelight dances across her face and I find myself smiling back.

"A smile from *the* Charlie Cade. Someone buy me a lottery ticket."

"I smile."

"Not randomly like that. I usually have to work pretty hard to get you to smile at me."

"Well, maybe I'm just happy."

Her smile grows at that, as does the blush on her cheeks. She glances down at her lap and pulls at a thread on the tablecloth. A flash from a few feet away startles us both and I notice her smile fall and her body stiffen. A manager rushes over to the table and I assume asks them not to take photos of other patrons enjoying their dinner. It irritates me. I just want Cami to be comfortable and to enjoy this dinner with her, but I guess that was the purpose of all of this.

Glancing back at her, I can tell she still feels a little uncomfortable. I reach my hand across the table and cover hers with it, giving it a little squeeze.

"You okay?"

"Yeah, totally good. Just took me by surprise is all. I should start getting used to it at this point."

"You know we can stop at any time. This gets to be too much? Say the word and we'll stop."

I know that the effects of "stopping" and all that that entails would be far more complicated than just saying we're done, but I wouldn't dare keep doing this if I knew she was struggling. That's the last thing I want.

"I promise, I'm okay. Let's talk about the list."

I groan and let go of her hand, making a big show of throwing my head back in defeat.

"I am appreciative of the list, really I am, but I don't want to do that stuff."

"I know, but it'll be fun. Trust me."

"I do. Implicitly. But more than half of the things on that list sound very far from fun to me."

"Well, let's tackle one of the more fun ones first. I have a plan for finding you a hobby."

"I have hobbies, Cam."

She raises her eyebrows at me as if to say, "*What hobbies?*"

"I go to the gym."

"And..."

"I...like to watch movies?"

"You need a hobby that isn't a part of your job or normal daily life. Something you do with your hands to get your mind off of everything else going on around you."

My mind is drawn to the ball of yarn and knitting needles that sit in a basket in Cami's apartment. She started knitting about a year ago, and I've noticed her picking the materials up on more than one occasion when she seems particularly stressed out. It's not a bad idea.

"Okay, so what are you suggesting?"

"Hobby day." She brings her hands to her chest and taps her fingers together manically. It's honestly a little unsettling, but it makes me laugh all the same. "I have a list of hobbies and a very well thought out and specific schedule for us to follow. We're going to try a bunch on hobby day and I'm going to document the whole thing on social media. I've already gained like twenty thousand followers in the last week."

"Seriously?"

"Yeah, one of the writers put my Instagram handle in their article and my phone almost blew up. But it's good because now we can post and that will help things along. Actually—" She reaches into her bag and pulls her phone out, bringing it low almost to the table but not quite. "Hold my hand, let me snap a pic for my story."

I oblige, not bothering with asking her what she's doing. She knows her stuff and I trust her to know what will work best in this area. She snaps the picture and turns it around so I can see. It's dark and grainy, but in an artistic sort of way. The photo feels cozy. My face isn't in it, but you can see our hands clasped together on the table, the candlelight flickering in the center. Only the right side of my torso is showing, up to my shoulder. She's written "Dinner with him" on it and placed a heart emoji next to the words. Something swirls in my stomach, and I do my best to ignore it.

"That's a great photo," I say, wiping my palms on my jeans as they've suddenly become sweaty. "Won't Alana see it, though?"

"One step ahead of you. I've blocked her on my stories for the day. This will help with the PR for now, but I'll wait to post you to the feed until she's back and we've told her about everything."

I nod my head in understanding and push back the feelings of nervousness where telling my sister is concerned. I'm afraid of what she'll say, but I'm hopeful she will be supportive. I am doing this to stay close to her, after all. Amongst other things.

"So what are we doing during this hobby day?"

"Come on now, I can't spoil the surprise."

"Give me something," I say.

"Fine I will tell you two things we're going to try, but that's all."

"Let me guess one."

"Go ahead," she replies.

"Knitting."

"Hey, how'd you know?"

"I figured we'd do something you are familiar with and I know you knit."

She smiles shyly and glances down at her lap, a blush creeping up on her cheeks. "Yes, knitting is one of them. Do you want me to tell you another one, or do you want to guess?"

"Tell me."

"Competitive dog grooming." A smile creeps up her lips. She starts to giggle and I hope it's because she's joking, even though I think she is probably telling the truth.

"Is that a joke?"

"Nope," she says as she shakes her head and her laughter grows. "Sorry, I'm just imagining you wrestling a poodle under a hose. It's going to be great."

"Cam, I don't need to try out professional dog grooming. I can tell you right now I'm not going to enjoy that."

"Don't knock it 'till you've tried it. You never know."

"If that's one of the ones you'll let me in on, I'm scared to find out what else you have up your sleeve."

"Don't worry, it'll be fun."

The waiter brings our dinner and we continue to chat as we eat. Eventually, we make our way out of the restaurant and into the swarm of reporters waiting for us at the entrance. I'm not sure when all of this will die down. The attention we've gotten so far has already been surprising to me, but I know I need it.

Without thinking about it, I lean down and gently press my lips against her temple. She sucks in a sharp breath, looking up at me with wide eyes, but quickly remembers we're supposed to look comfortable with public affection and replaces her shocked eyes with warm and gooey ones.

I'm not sure why I did it. I can blame it on the cameras, because that's what I was supposed to do, but I know it was more than that. My appreciation for her has grown more and more each day as she's taken all of this on effortlessly. She's finding ways to help me and is allowing her life to be cracked open by strangers on the internet, and I am so grateful.

I'm realizing now, that even though spending time together

isn't new, something has changed. We haven't been keeping up this charade for very long, but I can already tell that the sneaky kisses and easy affection is bonding the two of us in a way. It's opening my eyes to what it might be like if this *was* real, and the more time I spend with her, the more I crave her presence.

I might be in trouble here.

CHAPTER 26
Cami

I'M BENT OVER MY NOTEBOOK, PLANNING LIKE MY LIFE depends on it. It's just a few days before our scheduled day to find Charlie a hobby and I think I have our every breath scheduled at this point. I want to make sure we can get in as many hobbies as possible. It's hard to get an entire day from him where he doesn't have another team obligation, practice or a game, so I'm taking advantage of his day off.

I'm also trying to ignore the butterflies in my stomach, which have only grown since we started all of this, and it's the strangest feeling. I don't usually experience this when I spend time with him. He's a friend, there's no place for these feelings where he's concerned. In fact, I can't remember the last time spending time with a man gave me butterflies. It's like this has just all of a sudden gone from something I was reluctantly agreeing to, to something I look forward to and I'm not sure when the switch flipped. Maybe it's the way he seems to know me so well or how he provided silent support at the ballet. Maybe it's the way I felt when he kissed me, like electricity was coursing through my body, or the way all of it has felt so natural, if not a little awkward at times. The longer we pretend, the less it feels like we're pretending, and that's what I was afraid of.

Knowing that I can't go any further down that line of thinking, I chalk it up to our friendship getting stronger and decide to put it out of my mind for now. I scribble out the last few ideas I have to fill our afternoon and look down at my list. Arguably the one I'm most excited about is competitive dog grooming. I had no idea this was even a thing that people did. I mean I knew there were dog shows, but I didn't consider that there was an entire portion strictly for dog grooming. The only problem is, I need to borrow a dog.

I've always wanted a dog, because they're cute and cuddly and the best companion when you feel lonely. However, living in a teeny tiny New York apartment doesn't make for a whole lot of space to house a four legged animal. It hasn't ever felt right to bring one to live with me when they wouldn't get a backyard, or at the very least space to experience the zoomies. If they had the zoomies in my little one bedroom they would certainly break something.

I call a few different groomers in the city before finally finding one that will let us come and help them with one of their clients. I smile as I cross the item off of my list, feeling proud of myself. My mom always poked fun at my inability to be organized, but I'm proving her wrong with every bit of planning I do. I consider sending this perfectly timed out day to her with a note that says "In your face, Mom!" but that seems a bit juvenile so I toss that idea and keep moving.

Today better go well because I deserve an award for the amount of planning I've done. I've been up almost all night preparing. A banner is hung in the living room that says "Happy Hobby Day!"

and I have a schedule printed of our plans hour by hour, starting promptly at eight this morning. I used the same brown butcher paper I'm using for wrapping Christmas presents for the sign, and I grabbed some red, white, and blue craft paint from the store in order to give it some New York Rangers spirit. I know Charlie is going to freak when he sees how serious I've taken this, but I can't find it in myself to be sorry. Not only is this going to be so much fun, it's going to be great for social media content.

Which is what this is all about. *Right*? Right.

All around the tiny apartment I have set up stations for each hobby we're going to attempt. Everything but the dog grooming and flower arranging is going to take place here in this shoebox. I have three tables set up in the living room for painting, calligraphy, and soap carving, and a scrapbooking station at the small table in the kitchen. The knitting station is in the bedroom, because you have to curl up in bed while you knit. It's a requirement to be comfy for that one.

Each station has the materials needed laid out, along with any tools we might need. Smocks, carving knives, paint brushes, scrapbook paper, the list is endless.

I place our printed and laminated schedules on the coffee table in the living room, then sit down on the loveseat with a deep sigh. I did it. Now I just need to wait for him to arrive.

"Hey, Cam."

I feel a pressure on my shoulder, a hand I realize, and I try to peel my eyes open but they feel impossibly heavy. The hand shakes me a little and I reach up to rub the sleep away, blinking rapidly to clear my vision. Charlie's tall broad form stands above me, his dirty blond hair covering his forehead, and he reaches down to brush my hair out of my face.

All of a sudden, I realize that I've been asleep when I should have been awake. I didn't even hear him knock on the door, or unlock it and come in for that matter. I shoot up to sitting, looking around frantically for the schedule. He jolts back in surprise and carefully sits down next to me like I might jump him at any given minute.

"What time is it?" I ask, panic clear in my voice. He gently places his hand on my knee and begins rubbing soothing circles with his thumb.

"You looked like you needed the sleep so I waited a little bit before waking you. It's not been that long, maybe forty-five minutes."

"What?" I grab my phone frantically, see that the time reads eight fifty in the morning, and stare down at my hands. My moms voice is suddenly playing on a loop in my mind.

You've always been the disorganized one.

We should let your sister handle the planning for this one, Cam.

A girl your age should be working off of a calendar, honey.

You're never going to find someone who wants to marry you if you can't remember when and where the date was supposed to be.

"I can't believe I did this."

"Did what?" he asks. I had practically forgotten he was there, lost in my own thoughts.

"I can't ever seem to do anything right. I plan this whole day out and I can't even execute it on time. I freaking fall asleep and it all goes to shit. What is wrong with me?"

Charlie startles, I guess at my outburst, and I slump further in my seat.

"You cussed," he whispers.

"Oh." I close my eyes and cringe. "Of course I did. I didn't even realize I was doing it." And if that isn't a paradigm of my life.

I am constantly disappointing people without even trying. Making mistakes I don't even see coming.

He reaches out and places his hands on either side of my face, turning it to look straight into his sapphire eyes. I startle at the sudden unexpected contact. The calluses on his hands from days of handling a hockey stick should feel rough and uncomfortable, but they don't.

"Cami, there is absolutely nothing wrong with you. You are perfect. Your hair is perfect." He reaches up and takes a strand of blonde hair between his thumb and pointer finger, rubbing it between his fingers, twirling it, then placing it carefully back behind my ear. "Your brain is perfect," he says as he leans forward and places a gentle kiss to the middle of my forehead. "It comes up with the best jokes and the smartest ideas."

I look up at him, stunned by his words and the physical contact.

"Your eyes are perfect." He brushes his thumbs under my eyes as they flutter. "These lips are far too perfect." His thumb presses into the middle of my bottom lip and swipes. A shiver escapes me as I desperately try to not let his touch affect me. "But most importantly." He cups my face with his palm. "Your heart is perfect. It's kind and loving and sees the good in people. It seeks for ways to help others and meets needs. I could care less about your ability to plan something down to the very second when you have a heart like this."

I have no idea how to respond, so I take a deep breath and nod.

"Now, let's look at your schedule and see what we can move around to make this work, okay?"

"Okay."

"So, we're a little more than a half hour behind. It looks like you have an hour for lunch. What if we grab sandwiches and eat them while we walk to our after lunch spot? That should make up the time."

"That...should work."

"Good. Now, I'm not so sure about all of this," his eyes slowly slide from the top of the page to the bottom, reading all of the things I have planned for the day. Watching the way he takes it all in, and the way the corner of his mouth ticks up about halfway down the sheet, takes me out the self deprecating spiral I had been in and brings me back to the moment.

"We're really doing this professional dog groom thing, huh?"

I nod hesitantly, still feeling a little off, and he smiles at me. I've seen Charlie smile many times over the years, but seeing that smile directed at me? Because of something I've done? I'm a goner. I lunge forward and wrap my arms around his large body, burying my head against his chest.

He seems a little shocked for a moment, but quickly recovers and starts rubbing his hand up and down my spine soothingly.

"Thanks for doing all of this. I appreciate it more than you know. Means a lot," he says into my hair.

"Thanks for telling me I'm perfect."

"Anytime."

"I'm going to quote you on that. Next time Alana and I are trying to plan where to eat and you're the tie-breaker, you have to vote for me. If I'm perfect, then so are my dinner choices."

His chest moves beneath me when he chuckles softly and I pull back to look at him. His eyes twinkle in a way I don't think I've seen in the over ten years that I've known him.

"Okay, well we might as well get started then, I brought you a coffee." He hands it to me, then nods his head towards where the sign I made hangs. "The banner was a nice touch."

"Ugh, I wanted to see your reaction when you walked in." I scrub my hands down my face and reach out for the coffee he places gently in my hands. "Thanks." I pick up the laminated card with our schedule and make my way to the station for our first activity.

"So, painting is first. I was planning on posting everything we're doing today on my Instagram story and tagging you so you can repost it. Does that work?"

"Do you think Alana will see?"

"She's still blocked from my stories but not yours, hand me your phone." I take his cell from his hand and navigate to the Instagram app and block his sister from viewing his stories. "There, now she won't be able to see them. Once they're expired I'll fix it so she can see them again and won't suspect anything. She's not on social media that much right now with how busy they've been, but better safe than sorry."

He nods and takes the phone from my hands.

"You're going to have to show me how to repost."

"I'll help you, grandpa," I say and pat his back a few times. He rolls his eyes and scoffs at me.

I hand him a plain white smock to protect his clothes, and he pulls it over his head. Despite the fact that I bought him an extra large, it still looks comically small on him. I spin him around, tying the straps in a bow on the center of his back, and work hard to hold in my laughter. He looks so out of place in this too small smock in my too small apartment. It's endearing.

I grab my own smock, pink with hearts obviously, and turn so he can tie mine for me. Then I reach for my phone and open the app, clicking on the plus sign to add a story. I move so I'm in the path of sunlight streaming in from the window and hold down the button to record.

"Hi everyone." My voice is an octave higher than it normally is and Charlie chuckles next to me out of frame. "Today we are helping my favorite guy find his new favorite hobby."

I turn a little to get him in the frame with me, and instead of just standing there he slides up behind me and wraps his arms around my middle. He rests his head on my shoulder and turns his face towards me, placing a loud kiss on my cheek.

I giggle, forgetting for a second that I'm recording a video, but recover quickly.

"We're starting with painting, so naturally he had to suit up. Give us a spin, Charles." I double tap to switch to the back camera on my iPhone and point it at him. He gives me an exasperated look, but turns regardless.

"My name is not Charles."

"Yeah, yeah, yeah." I flip the camera back to me. "We'll keep you updated on how it goes. For now, drop any hobby suggestions in the box on the screen. Maybe we'll give them a go."

I end the video, then type to add Charlie's handle and a box for people to drop their ideas in before posting. He hands me his phone wordlessly, and I go through the motions of showing him how to repost on his stories.

Then, we get to work.

CHAPTER 27
Charlie

SOREN

A smock with a little bow on the back?

ME

Shut up.

SOREN

It's okay, Picasso. No need to hide your passions from us.

ME

I'm deleting your number.

SOREN

Sure you are.

WE'VE BEEN AT IT FOR THE LAST FEW HOURS. CAMI DID A phenomenal job getting this entire day together, and she's been posting on social media like a trained expert. I have no idea what she's doing most of the time, or how she gets the photos edited the perfect way or adds little funny icons. I just let her do her thing and order me around.

I've been her friend for a long time now, and I've seen her in many life stages. Through the awkward high school years, into the transitional time in college, and now in adulthood. She is a free spirit, always doing whatever makes her happy in that moment, and it's admirable. Her family doesn't understand her, and it's frustrating for me.

When she essentially closed in on herself this morning after realizing she had fallen asleep I wanted to pick up the phone and talk some sense into her mom. I knew she had been thinking over what she's been told many times before—that she's too in the clouds, too silly, too immature, too unstable. But everything that Miranda finds lacking in her daughter, I find charming. I'll work hard to show Cami the beauty I see in her personality and try to undo all the damage her mom has done.

Which started with me telling her a few things I love about her this morning, and has continued as we've executed her plans. I knew that the words I spoke to her were needed in the moment, but I can't help but feel a sense of dread that perhaps I went too far. Holding her face in my hands, kissing her on the forehead when it was just the two of us and there was no need for it, and swiping my thumb across her lips. It was a mistake and I vow to myself to be more careful when it comes to showing her affection in private. It was one of the rules, and I need to try to stick to them, no matter how increasingly difficult that is becoming.

I will admit, when I walked into the apartment and found the over the top banner in New York Rangers colors and the different hobby stations set up all around the place, I was apprehensive. I know what she is doing is going to help me, but part of me doesn't want to change my closed off persona. It's easier this way and safer, but I also acknowledge that by closing myself off I might be missing out on some relationships and memories with the people around me. I know it's my trauma speaking, and it's always been difficult for me to put the incident from my past behind me, but with her by my side I guess it might be possible.

I glance over at her and smile. She's in her own world, hardly paying any attention to me. She has pink and white paint smudged over her cheek, and a scrap of patterned paper is wedged between her curls where her golden hair is thrown up and off of her shoulders. She's a vision and I feel lucky to be able to take it in.

We've done painting, scrapbooking, and are finishing up soap carving now. I have found myself to be pretty good at this one, surprisingly. The painting and scrapbooking, not so much. I don't have many creative bones in my body, so taking a blank canvas or page and turning it into something was difficult.

Cami, however, is a natural. She painted a beautiful picture of abstract lines and shapes, in different shades of pink and red. I told her I want to keep it to hang inside my house, and she agreed. Maybe it'll bring a little life into the space.

During scrapbooking, she had printed out various photos of Alana, her, and myself through the years. She also had some photos of my sister and I growing up, which I was sure she stole by logging into Alana's Google photos. Not the first time she's done that.

She had blocks and blocks of different colored soaps for us to cut into, and showed me multiple different videos of people creating little designs in theirs. I found the methodic cutting to be calming, and I didn't notice her snickering at my side until her laughs grew louder. I glanced over, trying to determine what was making her hysterical, and found the soap in her hands depicting something not very PG.

I rolled my eyes and she remarked that she would be sure to put this in my bag so I could use it in the shower.

Now, we're finishing up our third soap design. Mine has the New York Rangers symbol carved into it. My first thought was it would be too detailed, but carving out the square symbol was easier than I thought. It's rounded at the bottom corners and comes to a point in the center. The top sort of flares out and has two divots on either side of the middle. The words "NEW YORK" are written across the top, with the word "RANGERS" diagonal from left to right. I sit back, pleased with my work.

Cami has carved a rose that has lots of ridges and dips, making the petals look three dimensional. She chose a pink soap to start, so the design looks quite realistic. She looks over at mine and gasps.

"Charles Cade." Her hand shoots up to her chest as if she's taken aback. "You really are so good at this." She pulls her phone out and I gear up for another video. "Everyone, look at what Charlie made."

I hold up the bar of soap proudly, smirking at the camera. "And to think, you all probably counted me out for this one."

"I never counted you out, babe."

I blush hearing the pet name, then remind myself that it's all for show. I lean forward and place a loud kiss on her cheek, knowing the camera won't see it but will be able to hear it. She laughs as she stops the video, tagging me and closing out. I repost it, like I've been doing all day, and we start to clean up.

"Okay, so we're grabbing sandwiches at Waverly and heading to the groomer. We made up some time with the scrapbooking since you were so terrible at it"—I roll my eyes—"so we have about forty-five minutes until we're supposed to be there."

"Sounds good. You want to pick up this mess before we go?"

"Nah, we'll deal with it later."

Classic Cami.

We each put our shoes on, pull on coats, and head out into the crisp city air.

"So, you're going to take the curved shears and lightly carve out the shape you want the face to be in. Nala's owner likes her hair around her face cut into a teddy bear shape."

Nala, the teacup Goldendoodle, stares at us like we bore her. She's just been freshly groomed and her body has already had a trim, one that I hesitantly did with lots of help, and now we're onto her face. Thankfully, they chose a calm dog for Cami and I to work on.

"A teddy bear shape? What does that mean?" I ask.

"A teddy bear shape is basically when we trim her coat to about one or two inches long. It'll be a rounded face trim, which makes her look like a teddy bear plush," the groomer says. "I'll show you with this one, and if you come back for another try we'll let you give it a go."

I hand over the shears happily and watch her work her magic on this sweet pup. Eventually, Nala is all fixed up and looks beautiful. Our grooming was uneventful, and while I didn't hate it I certainly wasn't a big fan. I couldn't drown out the constant barking and whining of the dogs in crates waiting for their turn. The staff was extremely friendly, and even allowed dogs with high anxiety out of the crate to roam or lay by their feet while they worked on other dogs, but I know I couldn't do this every day.

Once we finish and Cami has taken and posted videos of the whole process, we make our way back out onto the street. She tucks her arm through my elbow and stays close as we head to our next spot, a local florist. We stop for coffee before getting on the subway and taking a short ride to 5th Ave, close to The Empire State Building.

It's started snowing, a light blanket covering the ground, and the hustle and bustle of everyone around us warms my heart. Even though I like to be alone and stay to myself, the city provides a weird sort of opposition to that part of me.

The door dings as we step through the small entryway of the florist. There are bouquets of all different kinds of flowers surrounding the shop and the smell is intense. It's an amalgamation of lots of different floral smells, and it's a bit overwhelming at first.

"Hi, my name is Cami. We have an appointment to make our own bouquets," she says as she greets the shop clerk. They speak for a few moments, getting details arranged, and Cami reaches for her card. I interject before she slides it over the counter and hand the woman mine.

"I planned on covering it," Cami says.

"I'm not letting you pay for your own flowers." I turn before she can argue and look at the various flowers behind us. The clerk joins us on the other side of the counter and talks us through arranging our own bouquets. She shows us which flowers we can choose from—ranunculus, peonies, roses, amaranths, carnations, poinsettias, and orchids—and demonstrates how to gather them onto the paper we'll use to wrap them up.

After a few minutes of instructions, we get to work and start gathering different flowers and bunching them together. Cami goes for a few white roses, then takes a pinkish purple peony and places it in the center. She chews on her bottom lip as she surveys it, determining how she should proceed.

I turn away and begin collecting my own flowers, not really putting much thought into the task. My mind is wandering, specifically back to the fact that she tried to pay for our appointment. I realize then, that she must have dropped a pretty penny on just this one single day.

"Cam, send me the bill for all of the stuff we did today. I'm paying for all of it, you did it for me."

"It really wasn't much."

"You had to have spent a fortune. Between all of the materials and the appointments for the dog and the flowers, it couldn't have been cheap."

"I had all of the materials. I've done my fair share of hobbying through the years."

I guess that makes sense. She is constantly trying new things and I admire that about her. She follows the things that bring her joy, like a flower to sunlight. Her constant hobbying has made our day much smoother because of her detailed knowledge of all of the tasks.

"And the dog grooming?"

"They didn't charge us for that. They said they were happy to have our help."

"Well, that was nice."

"Yep."

She grows quiet as she continues gathering her flowers into the perfect bouquet. I wonder what she's thinking about, but after a few moments of us working silently, she speaks in a soft voice.

"How are you feeling about...everything?"

"You mean like us, everything?" I whisper, looking around and making sure the shop clerk is not in earshot. She nods her head yes, still keeping her eyes trained down on the flowers.

"I'm feeling okay about it. I think things are going well." I gather a few roses and add them to the bunch of peonies in front of me. "What about you?"

"I feel good. The response on social media has been good so far."

She's right. Ever since the first article dropped we have had an overwhelmingly positive response, not to mention all of the comments and likes our stories have had today. Seemingly reminded of it, she picks up her phone and holds it up. I grab a rose and hold it up to her, staring beyond the camera and into her eyes. She snaps the picture, looking at me and not the screen, and hesitates a moment before looking down at her phone to edit and post the photo.

My phone pings as the notification of her mention comes in, and she stares in the direction of my back pocket waiting for me to pull it out and repost.

"My hands are busy. Help me out?"

Her eyes flit from my face, to my waist, and back again. Without breaking eye contact, she reaches her hand around me and into my back pocket, grabbing my phone and pulling it out. I work hard not to react to her touch, but relish in the small smirk that plays on her lips.

She messes with my phone, unlocking it and navigating to the app where she reposts. After that we continue working in silence, only a Taylor Swift song playing softly over the store's speakers. After an hour, we leave with two beautiful arrangements in hand and head back to the apartment.

The amount of ink covering my hands is a little concerning. Is there such a thing as ink poisoning? How much ink does one's skin have to absorb before succumbing? I'm pondering these questions as Cami cleans up the calligraphy materials around me.

When we got back to her apartment, we made a quick dinner —grilled cheese and tomato soup—and sat down to watch countless tutorials on how to achieve the perfect handwriting. I didn't realize how technical calligraphy was. There is special ink, specific paper, and fancy pens and brushes needed. After a few too many attempts and lots of fits of laughter, we've decided to give up and move on to our last hobby of the day.

I'm going to admit, I am wiped. This has been the most exhausting day in the best way. I don't think I've had someone put this much effort into something just for me in, well, ever. I'm touched at Cami's attention to detail and planning, when that isn't usually her thing. It communicates that she really cared about this day, and about me.

She carries an arm full of materials into the kitchen and I tidy up the small living room while she puts everything away. I fluff the pillows on the couch and pick up the throw blanket, fold it, and drape it over the corner of the loveseat. I think, not for the first time, about how much cozier her place feels than mine. I'm glad she did all of this here. It would have felt wrong in my huge penthouse.

"Okay, so for the last one we're taking it to the bedroom."

I pause, running her words over in my head trying to make sense of them. I know she doesn't mean what my brain thinks, and maybe hopes, she means.

"What?"

"Charlie Cade." Her hand flies out and hits me square in the chest. "Get your mind out of the gutter. I meant knitting. Knitting is the last hobby of the day, and I always do it while cuddled up in bed. It's a requirement to be cozy and comfy while you knit, so bedroom it is."

I see her roll her eyes as she walks ahead of me into the room and it sounds like she mutters "men" under her breath. Following behind her, I step into her room and take in the scene. There are lots of different colored bundles of yarn piled on the bed and two pairs of needles sitting near them. She plops down on one side and pulls a blanket onto her lap, then pats the spot next to her.

"So, there are three basic things you need to know when knitting. The first is something called cast on, which is basically how you start the project. The next is the knit stitch, and then cast off which is how you get the stitching off of the needles."

I nod my head as I get comfortable next to her, feeling confident that those steps sound simple enough. We both pick out our colors, and she shows me how to get the yarn on the stick thing, which she tells me is called a needle. After a series of loops, she's created a perfect set of stitches that sit right up against the needle, readying it for the rest of the project.

Once we both have done the cast on step and have about twelve stitches, she tells me that we're ready for the knit stitch.

"This is the most basic stitch for knitting. First, you push your free needle through the first loop here," she reaches over and points to the spot she's mentioning, then guides my hands to complete the step. "Good. Then you wrap your yarn around the back, and pull it down between the two. Yep, exactly like that."

I smile to myself, feeling a sense of pride at my ability to get my large calloused hands to do something so delicate and detailed. It's satisfying.

"When did you start doing this?"

"Knitting?"

"Yeah. I knew you did it because I've seen the balls of yarn lying around, but what got you into it?"

"Well, I've been doing it for about a year. I saw an ad for a knitting group online and joined on a whim."

"Not surprising," I say and she huffs a laugh.

"No, I guess not. Anyways, when I showed up I realized it was at a retirement home. I went in anyway and ended up really liking the ladies there. They meet weekly, and I go as often as I can now."

"That's sweet, Cam. How did I not know you were doing that if you've been going for a year? Kinda sounds like something we'd discuss."

"Yeah, I don't know." I can sense her starting to close off. She looks down and focuses on what her hands are doing. I give her the space to determine if she wants to elaborate further, and eventually she does. "I kinda stopped mentioning things like that to people. I don't normally stick to things for very long, so it's easier to just not talk about them."

"That doesn't sound like the Cami I know," I say and she looks over at me quizzically.

"What do you mean?"

"The Cami I know can't shut up about the stuff she enjoys spending her time on. She's bubbly and sunshine personified. She doesn't care if something is around for a day or a year, she's going to be excited about it. It's one of my favorite qualities about her."

"You like that I can't make my mind up and waste money and time on random things?"

"Is it a waste if you're enjoying it? Even for a moment?"

Her hands have stopped their motion and her gaze has left mine. I can tell she's thinking about what I said, so I wait for her to speak.

"No. It isn't a waste."

I nod, happy she's come to that conclusion. She looks like she's been in a fog and it's just now clearing.

"Who made you feel like the things that bring you joy were wasteful?" I ask quietly.

"Um, I guess my mom. I told you the stuff she said about me never finding a man to settle down with." Anger blooms in my chest and I take a deep breath in an effort to tamp it down. This isn't about me avenging her right now, I'm just here to listen. "She's said stuff like that for a long time about pretty much everything I choose to do. So eventually I just stopped sharing in an effort to spare myself the embarrassing comments. I guess that bled into my friendships as well."

"You don't have to censor yourself for me. I want to know all of you, every stitch," I say as I hold up the knitting in my hands and smirk. She laughs, and even though it sounds weak I know it lightened the mood a little. "Sorry about my dad jokes, but I'm serious. You don't need to hide parts of yourself from me. I've seen almost all of them and you haven't scared me away yet."

She blushes and looks down in an effort to hide it. Before thinking better of it, I reach out and catch her chin in my hand, drawing her eyes back to mine. They're wide as she looks up at me, surprised by the sudden contact.

"Tell me you understand. I don't want you to pretend with me."

"I understand," she whispers.

I lean forward and place a soft kiss in the center of her forehead, smiling into her skin at the little gasp that escapes her lips. "Good."

I feel something change between us in this moment, and while I know it isn't smart, I can't find it in me to draw back. To close off. Not after everything she did for me today and the sacrifices she's been making to help me stay on a team that I love. She knows this is important to me, and she has gone to great lengths to ensure my spot on the team. That, plus all of the things she's done today have snapped whatever control I had around her and have shown me just how much I care about her.

We silently go back to knitting, and after a long time we settle under the covers to watch a movie. I wake up the next morning early, before the sun has risen, and slide out of bed, quietly closing the door behind me. I vaguely remember a rule we made for no more sleepovers, but just as easily decide to forget it, and I think I'm okay with that.

CHAPTER 28
Cami

CHARLES

So...I have our next mission.

ME

Is it sneaking out of a girl's apartment in the wee hours of the morning?

CHARLES

No. Sorry about that, didn't want to wake you.

ME

No worries, just messing with you. Whatcha got?

CHARLES

There's a charity ball coming up that I have to attend. Sophie wants us to go together.

ME

Okay when is it?

CHARLES

That's the thing...

ME

☺

CHARLES

It's tomorrow night.

ME

TOMORROW?!

CHARLES

I know. I'm sorry. But I can pay for whatever dress you need to get and I'll send people to the apartment to do your hair and makeup.

ME

Why don't you just have them come to your place and I'll get ready there? Then you won't have to pick me up and maybe we can save a little bit of time

CHARLES

Okay, sure. I'll have them here at 5 so they're here when you get off of work.

ME

Got it

CHARLES

Thank you Cam. You're a saint.

ME

😇

SITTING AT MY DESK, I CHEW ON MY THUMBNAIL AND stare down at the calendar in front of me. I'm in the middle of reviewing dates for the upcoming beauty shoots. We have two scheduled at the studio in the office for some close up staged makeup products. We're doing winter trends this issue, so it's lots of icy blues and silvers.

There's an email open on my laptop that I've written to confirm dates with the shoot managers and models involved, but I haven't hit send. My brain has been so occupied with everything Charlie lately, and I'm so afraid I'm going to let something slip with *Impress*. I might not be very detail oriented in my everyday life, but I pride myself on being good at my job.

Computer on the left, and my text thread with Charlie on the right, I stare back and forth at each. I push my phone to the side and take a deep breath, forcing myself to focus on work while I'm *at* work. I make sure the email looks good, hit send, then pick up my phone again and stare at the messages.

I guess I'm attending a charity ball tomorrow, and I have no idea what I'm going to wear. I'm grateful he is setting up hair and makeup for me, but the problem is I have no time to get an outfit before tomorrow evening. I'm thinking over how to make this happen when I hear a knock on the wall of my cubicle.

"Hey, hey," Kaitlyn, one of the editors on staff, says in her cheery tone. "Are you planning on going out for lunch? I could use a buddy. I'm thinking sweetgreen."

"Yum, that sounds so good. Are you going now?"

"Yeah, in a few. Are you at a stopping point?"

"Yep, just let me close things down here and I'll be ready to go."

I close my laptop and reset my desk space so it's nice and tidy, then grab my wallet and throw it into the purse I keep here and head out with Kaitlyn.

"So...Charlie Cade," she says hesitantly. I huff an uncomfortable laugh and roll the hem of my sweater in between my fingers.

"Yeah, I guess we should talk about that."

"I'd like the 4-1-1 if you're willing to give it. Kind of a big deal."

"I mean, not that big of a deal."

"One day you're single, and the next you're all over news articles dating a famous hockey player. And not just any famous hockey player, the brother of our coworker."

"Well, when you put it that way..." We turn the corner and

head towards sweetgreen. "It just kind of happened. With Alana gone we've been spending more time just the two of us and we've been friends for so long. One thing led to another and..." I trail off, not wanting to give too many specific details.

We haven't discussed what we'll tell people when they ask how this started between us. I think this excuse is the one that makes the most sense. We step into the restaurant and join the line, gathering behind every other person in this part of the city who frequents this place. Sweetgreen is a popular chain restaurant, and they have an incredible kale Caesar salad, which is what I'm going for today. I love a burger and fries as much as the next girl, but sometimes I just want a Caesar salad. A sentiment Alana's ex, Brad, couldn't get on board with. She broke up with him after he made one too many comments about her eating choices, and now she's enjoying croissants with a way hotter guy in the city of love. Sucks to suck, Brad.

We place our orders, putting our conversation on pause until we pay, and make it to a table.

"Does Alana know?" she asks.

"Not yet. We didn't want to distract her while she's in Paris and trying to do a good job there, so we decided we'll tell her when she comes back."

"I'd honestly be surprised if she doesn't see it on some kind of social media. You should get ahead of it and tell her before she stumbles across it by accident."

"You're probably right. We've been lucky she's been so busy. I think it's keeping her off of news sites and Instagram, but it is sort of inevitable that she'll find out."

"You'll figure it out," she says as she pushes her quinoa around on her plate. "So enough about his sister, tell me about him. How has everything been between the two of you?"

This was not something I thought much about when we decided we were going to do this whole fake dating thing. Showing off for paparazzi and faking at events is one thing, but lying to friends and family is an entirely different beast. It feels weird and icky, so I focus on the truths I can share.

"He's great. He's kind and caring and lets me be myself. I feel lucky, to be honest. I've been with plenty of guys that are the exact opposite of that."

"You could say that again. That's great, Cam. He sounds like a keeper."

I think about her words. He *does* sound like a keeper. Why does that not scare me? Probably because it isn't real, so I don't even have the option to keep him.

"Yeah, absolutely. Although he is like every other man in the fact that he plans so last minute. He just texted me this morning about a charity ball we're going to. Guess when it is."

"Tonight."

"Thankfully, no. Tomorrow night, and I have not a single thing prepared. I need to shave and paint my toenails and self-tan. I also need a dress, but I have no time to go shopping after work." I groan in frustration and take a long sip of my lemonade, wishing it had vodka in it.

"Ugh, men. But you should just look at the sample closet. They just added new stuff and there was a really gorgeous champagne dress in there this morning when I was poking around. No one will care if you take something out for the night and bring it back the next day."

"That's actually not a bad idea. I'll do that, thanks, Kait."

"My pleasure. I'll come with you. Maybe I want to go out for a fancy night on the town too."

"Your curves would look incredible in this." Something shimmery comes flying at my head and I reach my hands up to catch it in my arms and block it from hitting my face. It's the gorgeous champagne dress Kaitlyn mentioned at lunch.

We're in the sample closet, which is basically a big closet of different designer clothing items that editors use to put outfits together for shoots. The space is filled wall to wall with the current season's trends and designs. It's heaven, and rare that I make my way inside. *Impress* is less uppity about the sample closet as some other magazines I've heard of, but they're still careful with who they let in and for what reason.

I stopped by Heather's office on the way in from lunch and explained the situation. She told me I could borrow a dress for the night if I mentioned the magazine when I'm asked about what I'm wearing. I agreed, knowing I likely won't take any interviews anyways, and if I do they will mostly be Charlie talking.

I flip through the countless dresses and let out an unhappy sigh. It's hard to enjoy time in the sample closet without my bestie with me. Kaitlyn is great, but I miss Alana something fierce and she would kill to do this with me. Not to mention, I'm shopping for a dress for a date with her brother.

I push thoughts of my best friend aside and try to focus on the task at hand. I have a few dresses draped over my arm to try on, and after searching through what I can I head into the dressing room at the back of the closet to slip into the few options.

I put on a little fashion show for Kaitlyn, walking an imaginary runway. The first option is a Prada embroidered organza mini dress. It's beautiful, but a little too plain. It's black, with an organza overlay that looks almost like a button up dress shirt. It's different and interesting, but not what I'm going for.

The next option is a silk satin black Chanel dress. It has narrow straps that rest on my shoulders, and the top portion hugs close to my body like a corset. It has a drop waist, and the skirt flows down to my ankles. It's iconic, but still doesn't feel right.

The last option is a white Versace mini dress that has geometric satin covered embroideries on the neckline. It's sleek and professional, definitely something the partner of a hockey player might wear if they wanted to look beautiful on his arm, but not draw too much attention.

It's the perfect mix of fun and different, with the shorter length and funky neckline, but still modest and appropriate for the occasion. Kaitlyn agrees with me and we pick out some silver Versace kitten heels to complete the outfit.

I breathe a sigh of relief feeling a little bit more prepared for tomorrow, and ignore the nervousness that creeps in at the thought of another public event. I don't know when we're going to have to start getting a little more handsy in public, but I do know I'm not sure I'm ready for it. Or maybe I'm a little *too* ready for it.

CHAPTER 29
Charlie

SOPHIE

You two good for tonight?

ME

Yes.

SOPHIE

Wow. Super enthusiastic.

ME

?

SOPHIE

Nevermind. Be ready for the car at seven.

THE DOORBELL RINGS AND I STAND ABRUPTLY FROM THE couch and rush to let Cami in. She hasn't been here before, and it feels like a big deal to invite her in now for some reason. I was living in a different building before this one, and moved here about a year ago. She had been to my old place a few times, but I never really want to spend time here, so any time we hang out we always do it at either her or Alana's apartment.

The "glam squad," as they call themselves, arrived about fifteen minutes ago and got everything set up. She is earlier than I was expecting, but I'm glad she'll have a little extra time. I open the door and she smiles up at me. It's the first time I've seen her since hobby day, which was earlier this week. It's Friday now, and it feels like it's been way too long. The more time I spend with her, the more it feels like something is missing when we aren't together.

I pull her bag from her hand and set it on the floor, then tug her into me and wrap my arms around her. She freezes, perhaps taken aback by my sudden physical affection, but a moment later she melts into my chest and breathes me in. I kiss her head and pull back a little, not letting her go but meeting her eyes.

"Makeup and hair are here," I say, nodding my head in the direction of where their station is in the living room. Her eyes dart their way, then she looks back at me with something that looks like disappointment, but it's gone as fast as it arrived and I think I must have imagined it.

"Great." She looks over her shoulder, then raises up on her tiptoes to whisper in my ear. "Will you give me a tour? I've never been here and I need to seem like I have."

I grab her hand and pull her behind me shouting over my shoulder, "We'll be right back." They snicker and probably think we're headed off to do something much more intimate than touring my home. Good, let them think that. Helps the illusion.

I pull her up the stairs behind me to the second floor. The hallway extends forward from the stairs and there are four rooms, two on either side.

"This is my office." I open the door on the left and let her peek inside. "Doesn't get a lot of action, but it's here if I need it."

I expect her to look in from the doorway, but instead she goes inside the room and walks behind my desk. Her hands roam the top of the leather office chair, to the candle on the desk, then the stack of papers sitting in the corner.

"No pictures in here?" she asks. I shrug. "Hmm...this could use a little decorating."

She circles back around to the front and places her hands on the desk behind her, then hops up and sits on the top of it. I don't even realize I'm moving, but I cross the room to her like a man possessed. She widens her legs on instinct and I step between them.

Lately, it's been a lot easier to be physically affectionate with her. I'm getting dangerously close to crossing a line I know isn't smart to cross, but I'm not sure I care all that much. The only thing stopping me is my sister. Something tells me she wouldn't care much about Cami and I being together, fake or real, but the fact that she isn't aware of what's going on eats at me.

We share everything with one another, we always have, and it feels all kinds of wrong to stop now. She's the only person I've ever even come close to telling about what happened in high school, and after everything we've been through with our parents we are each other's rock. I hate keeping things from her.

I let my hands rest on the tops of Cami's thighs. She's wearing black trousers with a red flowy top tucked into the waistband. The color of her shirt brings out the warmth in her hair, and before I can stop myself I've placed a strand in between my fingers, stroking its softness.

"How was work today?" I ask as I place her hair behind her shoulders. My hand returns to her leg and I rub up towards her hip, and back down to her knee. Up, and down. Up, and down. I can tell she doesn't mind the soothing motion, because she looks like she's going to fall asleep any second now.

"Long," she says on a sigh. She leans forward and presses her forehead to my shoulder. "That feels so good. I'm so tired."

"Do you want to cancel tonight? We can have a night in. Watch a movie and order pizza?" I move my hands from her legs to her back and gently massage in circles. She groans and I shift on my feet at the sound.

"No, we need to go. It's important."

"You're important." I don't stop my movements, but I feel her take in a sharp breath. I expect her to look up at me, but she doesn't. "Why do you always put yourself last?"

"I don't," she says, still not looking up at me. I cup her face with my hands and bring her eyes up to meet mine.

"Yes you do. You have needs too. You're just as important as anyone else. You're more important than anyone else, to me."

Her eyes shine with tears, and I catch one with my thumb as it spills over.

"I don't think anyone has ever told me I was important. I think it's just second nature for me to think about myself last. Other people have things they need done, so I do those first and worry about myself later."

"If you don't take care of you, who's going to? You gotta look out for yourself. Plus, you can't pour from an empty cup." She chuckles at this and I finally get a smile out of her.

"You sound like a therapist."

"Well, I'm tired of you saving the best for last."

"Oh, shut up. I am not the best." She puts gentle pressure on my chest, silently asking me to move away. I step back and she hops down, then turns to look at the space again.

"You most definitely are. And I never lie, so you have to believe me."

"Whatever. You know what I believe, I believe you need something to make this space feel more homey. It's like a model home in here."

"Wait until you get to the bedroom."

I show her the rest of the penthouse and she continues making the same remarks about the state of the decor and the home. I agree with her wholeheartedly, but I'm not sure what to do to fix it and we don't have the time now anyways. After seeing my bedroom and guest rooms upstairs, and the gym, kitchen, and dining room downstairs, we head back to the living room and Cami settles in to get her hair and makeup done. I make myself scarce, even though I just want to sit by her side, and head back up to the office.

I sit in my chair and think about how it felt to have my hands on her, to have her trust me enough with her feelings and thoughts. I think I could get used to that.

"Okay, you can come down," Cami shouts from downstairs. They wouldn't let me come back until she was fully ready, something about the surprise factor. I stayed up in my room and got ready by myself, then sat down on my bed and watched hockey tapes. I'm wearing a classic black wool Giorgio Armani suit that Sophie picked out for me. She said it was classy and would go well with anything, and I didn't argue.

I head down the stairs to a vision in white, and immediately I picture walking towards her in another white dress, then scold myself internally. *What the hell?*

Cami is standing at the bottom of the stairs in a short white mini dress that has these gem-like embellishments at the neckline. Her hair is curled in soft looking waves down her back, and she has a thick white satin headband in her hair that matches the dress perfectly. She does a little spin, then looks up at me through her thick lashes.

"Do you like it?" she asks in a quiet voice.

"We were feeling a little Jackie Kennedy inspired," one of the makeup artists says. "That dress is absolutely something she would've worn."

"Thank you for your help." I smile over at them. Then, I step forward and put all of my attention on my girl in front of me. "You look absolutely stunning."

I place my hands on her hips, then slide them to her back. The urge to lean down and kiss her is strong, and I know I could play it off as performing for the people here, but I resist and place a kiss on her cheek instead.

"Thanks, superstar. You're not so bad yourself."

I wink at her and get a notification that the car has arrived, so we gather our things and head out. It's a sleek black town car tonight, and we cuddle close in the backseat. I don't even realize I have my hand placed casually on her leg until a few minutes into the drive, but decide not to pull away.

"I don't even know what this charity is for. That is probably information I should be aware of," she says as she looks down at her phone.

"It's for childhood cancer. I started donating to them a few years ago, and they invite me to their ball every year. I've skipped a few years, but with everything going on Sophie felt like it was important."

Somewhere in that sentence she put her phone down and gave me her undivided attention.

"Is there a reason why you chose childhood cancer?"

"A buddy in high school had a brother with leukemia. He battled it for a while and is cancer free now, but when I started making the big bucks I knew I wanted to donate a lot of it. I had Sophie pull some different charities and ended up settling on this one."

"I love that. I'm glad you connected with it and aren't just giving them your money. I mean not that donating is a bad thing, but having a reason is special."

"Thanks," I say, smiling softly at her.

A few moments later, we arrive at the venue and I help her out of the car. There are lots of photographers at this event and a red carpet I forgot to warn her about. It's usually never too invasive. A few photos, a kind question or two, and then they send you on your way. I look down at her, afraid she might spook at all of the attention, but she just squares her shoulders and slips her dainty hand in the crook of my elbow.

I smile down at her and lead her towards the carpet, where we pose together for a few shots. When we move to the reporter at the end of the line, she holds a microphone out to us and I take it from her.

"Charlie, it's great to see you again this year. Who do we have here? I don't think you've ever brought a date with you to one of these events."

"This is my girlfriend, Cami."

She looks up at me with so much warm affection in her eyes, it almost feels real. I'm caught in her gaze and don't notice when the reporter starts to ask her a question. She asks the usual about her dress, and Cami rattles off the name Versace like it's no big thing. She mentions the magazine she works for, and then the reporter thanks us for our time before we turn and make our way into the building.

"Versace?"

"Don't worry, superstar, I didn't put it on your credit card. Work let me borrow it."

"You could have. I wouldn't have been upset, you can get whatever you need. What's mine is yours."

"Well, I'll remember that the next time I get a craving for a new Chanel bag."

I laugh at her teasing and lead her into the large ballroom. There are people all around us in conversation, grabbing drinks from the bar, or finding their seats. I get a glass of champagne for each of us, then lead her toward our table.

"Mia!" Cami passes me her champagne glass and I just barely have it in my grasp before she's dropping it to pull Mia into a hug. "I didn't know you were going to be here. I feel so much better now that I have a friend."

"What am I, chopped liver?" I say under my breath.

"Charlie didn't tell you we were coming?"

"He didn't, but I'm glad you're here."

The girls sit next to one another and Soren and I sit on either side of them. There are two other couples at this table, and we make polite conversation with them both. After dinner is served, a speaker takes the stage and shares how the charity changed their life when they were suffering from a brain tumor at a young age. It's a powerful story and makes me thankful to be involved with a charity doing this kind of work.

After the speech, the dance floor opens and I stand, holding my hand out towards Cami.

"Come on, babe. Let's show Soren who the better dancers are," I say, pulling her behind me.

She turns and gives Soren a cheeky wink, then takes my hand and lets me whisk her off to the dance floor.

CHAPTER 30

Cami

MIA

You two look so good out there.

MIA

Seriously, where did Charlie learn to dance like that?

MIA

I'm guessing it comes from the time on the ice, but Soren looks like a baby giraffe when he dances so IDK.

MIA

GIRL. That man adores you. The way he's looking at you right now. Wait, let me take a pic.

MIA

one attachment Seeeee what I mean!!!

MIA

I'm so happy for the both of you. Okay I'll stop blowing up your phone that is sitting right by me at the table.

CHARLIE IS SURPRISINGLY A PHENOMENAL DANCER. HE'S moving around this dance floor like it's second nature to him, and I'm enjoying letting him lead. Pressed up close to him with my head on his shoulder is right where I want to be tonight, and I'm not going to dig deeper into why that is. I'm just going to enjoy it.

I was so thrilled to see Mia here. We exchanged numbers after that night at the bar and have been texting on and off ever since. *Us WAGs need to stick together,* she told me. I always knew what a WAG was, wives and girlfriends, because Charlie has been playing professional hockey for years, but I never thought I would be considered one. It was good to see a familiar warm face in a large room of strangers.

We've been swirling around other couples for a few songs, and he hasn't let go of me once. I appreciate his steady presence, and the way he never wavers. He feels so secure, like he will always be here no matter what, and that feels like a drastic opposite to most of my life.

"How you feelin', Cam?" he asks softly.

"Mmm I'm good."

"Getting tired?"

"I'm always tired." I pull my head back so I can look up at him as we talk.

"You need to take a break. You work too hard." He reaches his hand up and tucks a strand of hair that's escaped the headband behind my ear. His touch is gentle and his soft blue eyes hold such warmth and affection, I want to get lost in them.

We just stare at each other for a few long seconds, no longer moving to the music but stuck in an undefined moment together. The silence is broken when he whispers four words I never thought I would ever hear Charlie Cade say to me.

"Can I kiss you?"

I'm taken aback at the way he comes right out with it. He's straightforward in a way that's charming and not awkward. I forget for a moment that this is all an act. He's probably seen someone around us that he knows and wants to reinforce our lies, but I don't give that much thought. I can't get the idea of his lips on mine out of my head, and I need to know what it feels like.

"Yes," I whisper, looking up at him with an expression that I hope isn't too eager.

He brings his hand from my hip to cradle the back of my head. His fingers sink into my hair and he tugs on it just enough to control the direction of my head when he leans down and places the softest kiss I've ever received on my lips.

I've been a participant in many a kiss over the last few years, but pretty much all of them were passionate in a desperate way. There was no longing or care or thought behind the action, we were both just doing it to feel good. I mean, sure I had affection for other boyfriends I've had over the years, but I was never with anyone long enough for that affection to grow into anything past the physical.

With Charlie, it's like our entire friendship is pouring into this connection between the two of us. He reads me like a book and knows exactly when to slow down or when to push further, and exactly how much. He pulls away for a fraction of a second before diving back in for more and I am fully lost to the kiss, until I hear the click of a camera in the distance. It startles me enough to bring me out of the moment and back to reality.

We part, but he doesn't let me go far. His forehead is pressed to mine, and I'm not sure if his eyes are open but I don't open mine. I want to stay suspended in this embrace for a few more seconds before I crash back into the fake reality we're painting.

"I guess we shouldn't get too handsy in front of Mr. and Mrs. Martin," he says as he arches his eyebrows and looks to our left, where an older couple keeps sneaking looks at us. They look positively shocked and if the woman was wearing pearls, she'd likely be clutching them.

"Probably the most action they've seen this year," I say with a laugh, thankful for the way he so easily took the pressure off.

Joking for us is second nature, and definitely an area where we feel most comfortable. That felt way too real for me, even though I know he only did it for the benefit of the cameras and the crowd.

"Nah, I bet they get more action than you'd think."

"Ugh, gross."

"Ready to head back home? You've had a long day and we've been here long enough."

"Are you sure? I don't want to leave too early. I'm good to stay if you need to."

"I'd rather get you home and in bed. Let's go." He clasps my hand in his and pulls me towards our table. We say goodbye to Soren and Mia, and head out into the cold December air.

The car ride to my apartment is short in theory, but with New York City traffic it takes ten times longer than it should. The energy in the enclosed space is tense, but I don't dare bring up the kiss. We talk about his upcoming game schedule and the shoots I have this week, and before I even realize we're pulling up to my building.

It's very possible the reason I don't realize it's my building is because there are paparazzi swarming the entrance. The car starts to pull up to let us out and I go still, not putting all of the pieces together but sensing the unsettling situation.

"What is—"

"Take us to my place," he says to our driver, cutting me off.

"Wait, why are we going to your place? What's going on?"

"If you think I'm letting you go stay alone in your apartment with barely any security when the paparazzi clearly know where you're living now, you're crazy."

"So, what? You're just kidnapping me and making me stay at your place?"

"Do you have another option?"

"I don't know, let me think."

My mind is racing as our car crawls forward. I'm overcome by the anxiety of knowing my address is known to many strangers who want nothing more than to get a photo of me doing something damning like walking out with my shirt inside out or talking sternly on the phone with my mom. These reporters can take anything and spin it to be something big. Not to mention, my safety. I don't want tons of people I don't know, knowing where I live.

Despite all of that, I love my tiny apartment. I can walk to work, it's cozy, all of my hobby supplies are there, and it's mine. I know this is just one night and it might seem dramatic, but I was really looking forward to climbing into my bed at the end of the night and scrolling on my phone for an hour.

"If you're uncomfortable coming to my place, I can get you a hotel. But, Cam, I won't have you going there without security. So you either stay somewhere else for a while, or let me hire you private security."

I know he can sense my discomfort with the entire situation. I'm not speaking, not looking at him, and likely not showing any emotion on my face but stress and anxiety. I'm trying to make some kind of decision, but I can't quiet the thoughts in my mind long enough to land on one.

The warmth of his hand on my knee is startling, but I don't pull away. He squeezes in a pulsing motion, once, twice, three times. It clears away enough of the clouds for me to get it together and I look up into his eyes.

Tears are spilling over before I even decide I'm going to cry. I don't even know why I'm crying. This is stupid. There is no immediate danger, everything is going to be okay, and I have a really great friend looking after me. But it's like the emotions of the last few weeks are all of a sudden crashing in on me and the only way I can release the pressure is by crying it out. Charlie groans an unhappy noise, and wraps his arm around me before pulling me into him. I wrap my arms around his waist and cry into his chest.

"I hate this, Cam, hate seeing you like this. The last thing I want to do is make you cry, baby." We stay there for a few more minutes, the car moving at a glacial pace and the driver pretending he is anywhere but here. Once my sobs have quieted, Charlie brushes the hair from my face.

"Look at me." I do. "If this is too much we'll stop. We can go back to being friends and if I get traded, I get traded. It won't be the end of the world, but it will be if you're unhappy."

"It would make me unhappy to go back," I say in a quiet whisper.

"Yeah?"

"Mmhmm," I say before burying my face back into his chest. I'm sure I'm getting makeup all over his suit, but he doesn't seem to care. "Take me to your place."

Later that night, once I've settled into his guest room and have calmed myself enough to feel drowsy, I finally take my phone out of my bag. Scrolling through the texts from Mia makes me laugh, a welcomed reprieve to the highly emotional night I've had, but the photo she sent makes my heart skip a beat.

If the photo from our first date was shocking, this one is devastating. He has his hand on my lower back, pressing my body into his. The angle Mia took it from shows his face, but only the back of my head. The way he's looking at me...he looks like he wants me. Nothing about that photo looks strained, or forced, or fake. He looks perfectly at ease and his eyes communicate a want that I didn't realize was there before now.

I lock my phone and collapse down onto the bed. The thought of Charlie wanting me for real not scaring me nearly as much as I thought it would.

CHAPTER 31

Cami

SUNLIGHT STREAMS ACROSS MY FACE AND WAKES ME from the deepest sleep I've had in a while. I groan as I stretch, and roll to the left to feel around for my phone on my nightstand, only when I reach out my hand doesn't hit my phone. I touch something that feels like a glass of water, which is confusing because I don't remember getting water before going to bed last night.

In a few seconds, everything comes flooding back to me. The charity ball, Mia and Soren, the paparazzi at my apartment, and the kiss. Sitting up, I slowly take in my surroundings. I am in a bed that looks like a fluffy white cloud. It has white sheets, white pillows and a white comforter that is fluffier than any comforter I've ever seen before. It looks like no one has ever slept in it, which is probably the truth knowing Charlie.

His guest room is just as devoid of personality as the rest of his home is, and it makes me sad. I need to liven this place up, especially if I'm going to be staying here for a while. I run my hand down my face and sigh in frustration. This whole situation with people knowing where I live is annoying. I'm sure it'll die down at some point, and as long as they aren't there 24/7 I should be okay to go home soon without a bodyguard.

I know Charlie though, and he protects what's his. I know he cares about me deeply and this probably shook him, especially after I emotionally unloaded on him last night.

I could tell I was nearing a breakdown earlier in the evening when the bartender told me they didn't have Diet Coke, only Diet Pepsi, and I wanted to cry. I don't normally drink Diet Coke, but I was missing Alana and that's her drink of choice. That was the first sign that I was working myself a little too hard this week and not taking enough time to rest.

I had planned to stick it out through the evening, then do the whole crying hysterically part at home alone in my bed, but Charlie's fame status had other plans. I turn and sit on the side of the bed, finding my slippers sitting there, pink ones with little bows all over them, and I wonder how they got here. I slip my feet in and head to the bathroom to make myself look a little less like I just woke up.

Charlie gave me one of his T-shirts last night, and it swallows me and hangs down to just above my knees. As a hockey player, he spends a lot of time in the gym and that means he's a pretty big guy. Behind all the muscle, though, is a big teddy bear.

I brush my teeth and my hair, then grab my phone and make my way downstairs. I check the time and see that it's a little after ten. I'm grateful I got to sleep in some. I haven't had that luxury for a few weekends now because we've had the craziest schedule at work. Normally I don't have to work on the weekends outside of a scheduling conflict with a model or a photographer, but with the holidays coming up there have been additions and changes left, right, and center.

"Good morning, Ms. Cami," Giovanna, Charlie's chef, says in greeting as I enter the kitchen. The smells of waffles and bacon greet me and I sigh happily. Her cooking is exquisite, but it's been awhile since I've had the pleasure of indulging. I haven't been over to his place since he moved, so it's been some time.

"Good morning, this smells amazing." I take a seat at the island as she places a plate in front of me. "Have you seen Charlie this morning?"

"He is in the gym. They have a game tomorrow and then are off for a few days to celebrate Christmas. He said he would join us soon."

I nod as I chew and think through the upcoming week. His game tomorrow is an away game in Seattle against the Kraken, and with everything happening with my apartment I'm not sure what the game plan is here. Thankfully, he walks in a few minutes later and silences my swirling thoughts with his presence alone. Not to mention, his light gray T-shirt clings to him, his skin glistening and his hair damp with sweat. He smiles brightly when he sees me, nothing like the closed off Charlie the world knows, but instead the softer version only I get.

"Hey, Cam," he says as he crosses the room, leans down, and places the quickest kiss on my lips. I'm so shocked I don't even think I kiss him back. "Gonna go take a quick shower, then I'll join you."

I nod my head at his retreating form and continue nodding it until Giovanna clears her throat.

"You okay, Ms. Cami?" she asks.

"I don't know. You saw that right? You saw him kiss me?" I know she knows about our arrangement, because he told me when he told her. He said he wanted to be honest and make sure I knew everyone who was in on the situation, which as of now is Sophie, his chef, and the knitting club ladies.

"I saw."

"Okay. Well...I guess I'll just sit here and wait for him."

For the next ten minutes I sit and ponder everything I know about this situation. I know we are best friends. I know I would take a bullet for him and he would do the same for me. I know what I saw in that photo from last night, and I know there is an insane physical attraction between the two of us—an attraction that I ignored for years. I know we kissed for the first time last night, and I know all of this is *supposed* to be fake. So then why did he just kiss me with no one around to pretend for?

He waltzes back into the room like nothing is amiss, smelling like his santal body wash I got him for Christmas last year. It came with a huge carton of refill soap, and I'm glad to know it's lasted him the year. I make a mental note to grab some for him soon, because I'm sure he's almost out.

Giovanna has been cleaning the kitchen, but finishes up now and turns to go into her workstation, muttering something about grocery lists and meal planning. I'm sure she sees the need for privacy, and I'm thankful because I am beyond confused.

"How'd you sleep?" he asks as he grabs my fork and stabs a bite of waffle, stealing it from my plate.

"Um, good. Really good, actually."

"Good, I'm glad. I did too. Felt good knowing where you were, that you were safe."

"I probably would have been totally safe at home, superstar."

"Probably isn't good enough for me. Are you going to eat any more of this?" he gestures to my plate with the fork he stole. I shake my head no and he pulls it towards himself.

"Charlie, what is going on?"

"Well, I have an away game tomorrow so we're flying out tonight. You can stay here since I'll be out of your hair."

"That's not what I mean."

"What do you mean?" he asks, quizzically.

"You just kissed me. On the lips. In your home."

"I did," he says, shoveling more of my leftovers into his mouth.

"We have rules, things in place to keep this from getting messy."

"I know. I think we should change the rules."

"What?" I ask, shocked how he just came right out and said it.

"I care about you."

"I know you do," I say.

"And I could see this going somewhere good."

"What do you mean?" I ask.

"I mean, what if this wasn't fake?"

The room is silent as he stares back at me. I can see the vulnerability in his eyes, the way he's taking a risk by saying this to me. I don't want to shut him down, but I don't know that I'm ready for this conversation.

"Can we press pause?"

"What?"

"You're about to go away for the game and I'm going to be at home—"

"You're staying here, Cam."

"I don't need to stay here, I have my own place. I'll be fine there, I promise."

"It would really make me feel better if you stayed here while I was gone. I know it probably doesn't seem like a big deal, but if I don't know you're safe I won't be able to focus on anything else."

I knew he cares for me and he cares about my safety, but to hear him put it out there so plainly is a shock to the system. I don't know if I've ever had anyone care about me like that. Sure, Alana loves me and would absolutely be concerned if she thought I was in danger, but she has been so busy in Paris, so we've barely had time to talk. The most I got was a FaceTime while she got dressed for a fancy Christmas party she's going to with Alex.

Speaking of Alex, those two have finally stopped ignoring their feelings for each other and I am thrilled for Lana. She deserves someone who loves her like he does, and I just know he's going to treat her right. Charlie seems pretty happy about it too. The two of them have been talking more often and I'm glad for him to have another guy friend.

"If it means that much to you, I'll stay." He sighs in relief. "But can we finish this conversation when you get back? I'm just not sure I'm ready."

I look down at my lap, feeling bad about shutting him down so quickly, but I know I need to get my head on straight before we discuss this. Our relationship is too precious to me to handle it carelessly.

"Sure, we can talk when I get back." He pauses, thinking. "Speaking of me coming home..."

"What now?"

"Well, Alex called me a few weeks ago wanting to set up a surprise for Lana. I wasn't sure it was going to work out, so I waited to tell you, but it looks like everything is set to go. He wants me to fly to Paris and surprise her for Christmas. I'm going to have to fly to Paris from Seattle, then I'll leave Christmas night."

"Wow, short trip. But I guess you can't stay any longer because you have games next weekend."

"Yeah. And I know Alana is about to come home, but Alex is completing this list of hers, and spending Christmas with me is on it."

"Alex never does anything halfway."

"Apparently not."

"Okay, so good. Then I'll stay here while you're there. Anything else?"

"One more thing...and don't freak out." Telling a girl not to freak out is a sure fire way to make her freak out. "I want to tell Alana."

"You want to tell her...what?"

"About us."

"Us?" I ask, my eyes wide.

"Yeah, us. Our relationship."

"Okay," I say, thoughts running through my head about what this means.

"I know it's big, but she's coming back in about a week and I don't want her to be bombarded and surprised by it when she gets here. She deserves some time to process."

"I agree. I wish I could be there with you, but maybe it'll be good for me not to be there."

"I know she'd want you there, but yeah it might give her a second to collect her thoughts before she says anything."

"And you're going to tell her about the arrangement? That this isn't real?"

There's that look in his eyes again, like I've hurt him.

"Yeah, I'll tell her everything."

"Okay. So you're leaving tomorrow for most of the week, telling your sister you're fake dating her best friend, and I'm staying here alone in this huge penthouse."

"You're *my* best friend too. And you'll have Giovanna."

"Giovanna needs some time off for Christmas. Hey, Gi," I shout in the direction of the door she escaped behind. She pops her head through the opening. "You're off for the week. You can head home any time. Merry Christmas."

"Thank you, Ms. Cami."

Charlie huffs a laugh next to me and I turn to look at his bewildered expression.

"What?"

"You haven't even been here twenty-four hours and you're already running the ship."

I shrug and he laughs again.

"Gonna go pack, you good here?" I nod. "I went over to your place last night after you fell asleep and grabbed some things. They're upstairs in your room, but if you need more please take Greg with you. He can act as driver and security and escort you into and out of the building."

"Yes, sir," I say and salute him. "Thanks for going to grab some stuff. Sorry for the trouble."

"No trouble at all. Wouldn't want you anywhere else." He stands and starts to lean forward, but catches himself and jerks back. I wince slightly at the awkwardness, but appreciate him maintaining the rules once again. He turns, walks up to his room, and leaves me to think about his words and the *somewhere good* this is going.

CHAPTER 32
Charlie

ME

ME

Taking off, should land this evening. Shoot me the address to the building.

ALEX

No need. Marco will pick you up when you arrive. He'll be at baggage claim with a sign with your name on it.

ME

How romantic.

ALEX

Be safe, see you soon.

ALEX WENT ALL OUT AND PURCHASED FIRST CLASS SEATS for me. I was grateful, because after our game against Seattle I needed to sleep. The game started out okay, we had a few shots on goal, but nothing made it in. In the second quarter though, things took a turn and we started sucking.

I really couldn't tell you exactly what happened, but my guess is we all got a bit shaken when a rookie on their team got a breakaway at the end of the first and our defense struggled after that.

A bad game is a bad game, it happens, but with my contract hanging in the balance I feel them a little more than I have in the past.

I was grateful to be able to stretch out and get better sleep than I would have if I had been in coach, and I cling to that gratefulness as I talk on the phone with a guy who I liked five minutes ago, but it's possible I hate him now. I called to tell him I landed, and he's just dropped the bomb that my sister left.

"What do you mean she left? What did you do?"

"Well." He sounds absolutely wrecked. "You know there's a promotion available at the magazine?"

"Yeah," I say, not liking where this is going.

"A few hours ago Heather called and let me know I was being offered a promotion."

"So she found out you got the promotion she's been working so hard for and that upset her?"

"No, no. The promotion is for me to stay in Paris. They want me to stay here and be managing editor. Heather told me to take the day to think about it and she'd send over the offer letter. I knew immediately I didn't want it—I want to be with Alana."

"Okay, that's great. So what's the issue?"

At this point, I'm maneuvering my bag with one hand and have my phone pressed to my ear in the other. I walk up to a line of greeters, and see a man with the last name Cade on it, so I walk up and nod my head at him in hello.

He does a little half bow and takes my bag from my hand, then motions for me to follow him.

"I went out to grab a gift for my mom and left my phone at the apartment. It must have gone off with the email notification and Alana must have seen the beginning of it because she wrote me this note and told me she needed time."

"What does the note say?"

"She told me she saw the notification and promised she wasn't snooping, which I believe, and said she needed time. She left me the hotel she's going to and asked me not to follow or call. I want to honor that, but I'm going to have Marco take you to her instead of here."

"I'm sorry, man, that's tough. She probably got scared thinking you were leaving her and needed to process away from you."

"Yeah, I get it. I just want to be sure she's okay. She'll be glad to see you."

"Thanks for getting me here. I'll go see what I can do."

"Thanks. Text me if you need me. Marco knows where to go."

We hang up and I look up at the rearview mirror.

"I'm guessing you're Marco," I say to the driver.

"That's me. I'm taking you to Ms. Cade."

"Perfect, thank you."

I settle back into the leather seats and watch as we drive. It's chilly here and the sun is going down, painting the city in a golden glow. A golden that reminds me of a certain blonde's hair. That's been happening more often lately, Cami just popping into my thoughts. I pull my phone out and shoot her a text.

ME

I landed and am in the car on the way to a hotel. Alana and Alex had a bit of a fight and she left, but I'm heading to her now.

CAMI

Oh no, and on Christmas Eve? That sucks. Give her a big hug for me

ME

Can do. You burn the building down yet?

CAMI

You'll have to wait and find out 🐷

ME

> I bet you're sitting all cuddled up on the couch watching a Hallmark movie.

CAMI

Do you have cameras set up in here?

I chuckle to myself and slip my phone into my backpack as we pull up to a very fancy looking hotel. Leave it to my sister to choose a place like this to escape to.

Marco helps me with my bags and speaks to the front desk before telling me Alana's room number. I head up the elevator and find my way to the room, knocking on the door. When she pulls it open, she looks like an absolute mess. She has on a pair of pink silk pajamas with bows all over them, her face is blotchy and swollen, and her hair hangs past her shoulders in half dry waves.

As soon as she realizes it's me at the door, she starts to sob. It breaks my heart to hear the broken noises coming from her, so I step forward and wrap her in my arms, shutting the door behind us and walking her to sit on the bed, rubbing her back until she can get control of her breathing again.

"How are you here?" she asks.

"There's this thing, it's really cool. You get inside and it flies you anywhere you want to go."

She swats me with the back of her hand, and my goal is accomplished when a small smile pushes past her lips. I sigh a little in relief.

"Your boyfriend flew me here."

"What do you mean he flew you here? All of this only just happened."

"The trip has been planned for a few weeks. He wanted to complete the last thing on your list."

Realization blooms on her face and I can tell she's already feeling better, despite the fact that there are still unresolved issues and conversations that need to be had. She wraps her arms around my waist and buries her face in my shoulder.

"I can't believe you're here," she says. "I missed you so much."

"I missed you too, Lan. It's really good to see you," I reply, pushing some of her damp hair off of her face. "You gonna tell me what's got you looking like that?"

"I saw something on Alex's phone and got scared." I nod my head in understanding.

"Did he tell you?"

"He did."

"What did he say?"

"Well I think you might have a few things twisted up since you don't have the full story, but I want to hear what's going on in that head of yours. Then we can talk about what he said if you want. I'm here for you, not him. If you decide you want to talk to him about the situation, he needs to be the one to explain it to you."

"I'm just scared. I don't want to have to come back from heart-break again. I'm worried about him taking this promotion and staying here while I'm in New York. It would be awful. Plus he didn't tell me about it."

I stroke her hair, trying to bring her comfort as she speaks her fears out loud. Alana has had such a bad experience with trusting people who are supposed to love her and be there for her. I don't blame her for having a hard time not running at the first sign of abandonment.

"Lan, I think you're maybe getting ahead of yourself here. Did he keep information from you? Yes. Should he have told you when he found out? Maybe. I also think he deserves a little time to download that information before sharing it. It's not like he kept it a secret for months."

"I guess you're right. I just don't want to jump into something if he's not fully in it either."

"I think you and I both know Alex is in this."

She nods her head, and I know she knows I'm right. I can tell, even from the short interactions I've had with him over the last few weeks. Hell, Cami can tell.

"It's so frustrating. I just want to stop being scared and throw caution to the wind, but then when I try, something like this happens."

I chuckle at her. "You can stop being scared, while still being cautious. Those two things are not synonymous. I admire the way you look out for yourself and think before you make moves, it keeps you safe. Sometimes the right decision is the scary one, and you can step into that while still being aware of what is going on around you."

"I hadn't ever thought about it that way before. I was committed to just doing it even though I was afraid, but part of my fear was because it felt reckless."

"I think that's a common misunderstanding, but think about how much you'd get to experience if you stopped being scared. Or you let yourself be scared, but you did it anyway. You didn't let the fear win."

As I say the words, I feel a little hypocritical. I have this big life changing trauma that I won't tell a single soul about, and it's because I'm terrified. I know it's keeping me from living a life that is free of fear, stress, and anxiety in relation to this specific situation. I know it affects my relationship with my sister and with Cami, but I'm just not quite there yet.

"How do you do that?"

"I'm not totally sure. I think it looks different in every situation. What do you think it looks like in this one?"

She pauses for a few moments to think.

"I think it would be giving this relationship my all, even though I know I might lose it one day. Diving in head first, even though I know it might end up hurting in the end."

"What would happen if you ended up hurting in the end?" I ask, trying to bring forth all of the possible excuses running through her mind.

"If I ended up hurt, it would probably suck for a while."

"Uh huh, and what else?"

"I might have to find a place to live if we moved in together and that would be weird."

"Sure, anything else?"

"Work might be weird for a while, but Alex and I are mature so it would probably be okay."

"Good. Then after all that, what would happen to you?"

"I'd be okay."

I smile at her, proud of her for getting to that conclusion. It's one I know I need to come to as well. If I share my trauma, it will be scary, but even if I end up getting hurt I'll still be okay.

"I'd be okay and I would have had an incredible experience with an incredible person and we would have great memories," she says.

"You would."

"I think I need to go home."

I laugh and toss a pillow at her. "I think you do too. But first let's hang out for a little bit. I stopped downstairs and asked them to send a pizza up."

"Oh, and I ordered chocolate cake."

As if on cue, a knock sounds at the door and I open it to a man with a cart with wheels. He removes the covers sitting on the plates to reveal a seven layer chocolate cake and a large pizza with mozzarella and basil.

"That looks incredible," Alana says, already standing and making her way to the cart. I join her and we dig in.

"So, I want to talk to you about something."

It's been a few hours, and we've eaten dinner and watched a

movie. She seems to have come to a conclusion on the whole conflict with Alex and has settled into spending time with me. It's been long enough, and I know she's going to leave soon, so I need to talk to her about Cami.

"Okay," she says and scoots to face me. "That sounds a little scary."

"Only a little," I say and wink. She waits, looking nervous for whatever I'm about to say.

"So you know my contract is up this year."

"Oh, are you being traded?" The question comes out desperate and sad and it only furthers my resolve to continue this thing with Cami. "I really can't take any more life changing news tonight."

"No. Well, at least not that I know of."

"What does that mean?"

"Well, last month, Sophie came to me and told me she thought I needed to work on my public image. She said the fans didn't know me well enough, and I needed to create some buzz in order to make me a household name when it comes to the New York Rangers. She thinks if I do that, the team will be less likely to trade me."

"Okay, I'm still not sure where this is going."

"She wanted me to publicly date someone. She said if I dated someone who was bubbly and charming, fans would enjoy hearing about our relationship and it would boost popularity. She also encouraged me to get closer to the guys, and I've been trying to do that."

I throw that last bit in because I know it'll make her happy. She's been pushing me to build more relationships and make more friends besides her and Cam, and it's always been something I was resistant to. But with the threat of a trade I am willing to do anything, and this particular thing *has* been good for me. I can admit that.

"Well, I'm glad to hear you've been working on your relationship with your teammates. Has that been going well?"

"Yeah. I've been going out with them after games for drinks and I've been texting with Soren."

"Soren Wright? Left winger on your line?"

"Yeah, that's the one." Her knowledge of my team and the game makes me smile. She's always put the effort in to know me and she's the Rangers biggest fan. She does her best to not miss a game, even if she's watching online, and if she does miss she always catches the highlights.

"Okay, that's all great. Now let's go back to the dating. So did you find someone? Did Sophie set you up?"

"She offered but I turned her down. I did end up finding someone, but the arrangement is just that, it's an arrangement. She knows it isn't real and has agreed to help me in order to get my last contract before retirement. We'll end things in March, after trades are finalized."

"Who is it?" She seems awfully suspicious now, and I wonder if she's putting puzzle pieces together. She's called on more than one occasion when Cam and I are together, and she acts so suspicious every time. I take a deep breath, and decide to just rip the Band-Aid off.

"It's Cami."

She doesn't move, doesn't blink, doesn't say a word. I wait, terrified this is about to turn into more drama for me to resolve. We should have told her before now. We should have just been honest and made the damn phone call and not blindsided her like this.

"Cami, as in my best friend Cami?" I nod and wince.

"Our best friend, yeah. But it's not real and we have an agreement. She's helping me and I'm helping her. I'm going with her to Collette's wedding next year to get her family off of her back."

"I kind of suspected something might be happening, but I wasn't sure." She stands and starts pacing the room, running her hand through her hair. "Then Kaitlyn from work said something weird in an email, but I chalked it up to her being confused. It makes sense now."

"Are you mad?"

"I don't know, I'm a little surprised. Has it been working? The dating, I mean."

"Yeah, it's working, Lan. She is so good at social media and any time we go out she posts the best pictures. She came up with this whole list of stuff we can do to bring more positive attention my way. It's been great, but..." I trail off, not sure how to say this next part. I decide it's better to just state it plainly, so I do. "When you get home there are going to be articles and pictures. And you're going to see us holding hands, and cuddling up next to each other, and probably kissing."

"You kissed her!" she yells. "Oh my—EW." She makes a gagging noise, and I let out a self deprecating laugh.

"Yeah, we kinda had to. And also the media knows where she lives, so she's staying with me for the time being. I don't want her there alone."

"That's smart and nice of you, but that's also where I live."

She continues pacing, not meeting my eye. I can tell she's freaking out just a little bit, so I say whatever I can to calm her down.

"Yeah, I'm working on getting security for you both, at least until all of this dies down. She's staying with me now, but she's said she wants to go home. I don't blame her, my place isn't the most homey environment."

"Well, we can change that."

"Yeah, I guess. I just never felt like putting the effort in."

She rolls her eyes at me.

"I have to be honest, I'm a little frustrated you didn't tell me sooner. I don't love that you two have been keeping things from me. It feels pretty shitty."

"I know, I'm sorry. We just didn't want to distract you while you were out here trying to work. I knew you missed us and I was afraid we'd make it worse, plus you've been so busy and we both know how important it was for you to do a good job here. We didn't want to add to your stress."

"I understand that, I do. Can you give me just a minute?"

She crosses the room to the bathroom, then shuts the door behind her. I stare at the spot she just vacated, praying I didn't just drive a wedge between my sister and I. She is the only family I feel close to at this point in my life, and if I lost her I don't know what I'd do. The hockey contract doesn't even matter if I don't have her.

I pull out my phone to text Cami while I wait.

> **ME**
>
> I told her. She said she needed a minute and left the room. I don't know what to do.

> **CAMI**
>
> OMG go after her

> **ME**
>
> She said she needed a minute. I want to give her time to process.

> **CAMI**
>
> But not too much time

> **ME**
>
> How much time is too much time?

> **CAMI**
>
> Just feel it out but don't wait too long. She's probably just feeling weird about the fact that she's been gone for a month and not only has life continued without her, but now her brother and best friend are dating. Fake or not, that's a lot

> **ME**
>
> You're right. I'll go check on her.

I stand outside the bathroom door, trying to get the nerve to knock. Hearing my sister's quiet sniffle pushes me over the edge, and I skip straight past knocking and just push open the door. She's sitting on the edge of the bathtub, her head in her hands and softly crying. I move to sit down next to her and drape my arm over her back, pulling her into my side.

"I'm sorry, Lan, I didn't mean to make you cry. It's Christmas Eve."

"No, it's okay. I think I'm just having a lot of emotions and I get that this whole thing isn't real right now, but you two are perfect for each other. I've been sitting here for the past ten minutes thinking about how if I could pick someone for you it would be her, and vice versa. I hear you that it's fake, but imagining you together is...magic."

"Magic?"

"Mmhmm. And If I can see that, I guarantee you it isn't long before one of you does, if you haven't already. Then what happens when you become each other's person and I'm left on the sidelines?"

"You would never be left on the sidelines. We might find and explore a new side to our friendship, which is not happening by the way," I say as I give her a stern look. She doesn't look convinced. "But we will both always need you. I don't know what I'd do without you."

She gives me a watery smile and leans her head on my shoulder.

"Are you mad?" I ask again, hoping to get an honest answer this time.

"It stings a little, but I understand why you didn't say anything. Work has been crazy and it would have added to that. I want you to know, though, if this changes course and it turns into something more than faking, I approve."

"Alana, you were just sitting here crying and stressing about Cami and I *fake* dating. Are you sure you'd approve of it being real?"

"I just needed a minute to freak out, but I'm good now. The

more I think about it, the more I see how well you compliment each other. Cami needs a little grounding in her life, and you could use some fun. Plus, you're both phenomenal people."

I stare at her, confused how we're now considering this thing between Cami and I to be something real.

"I'm just saying, if either of you ever decides to make this more, you have my blessing, but if it does go that direction, please just tell me, okay? Don't keep it from me."

I sit there, staring down at her for longer than is considered polite, until she laughs at me and shakes her head.

"Um, okay. Okay I will."

"Good."

A little while later, she gathers her things and heads back to their apartment. I decide to stay here for the night to give them time to make up, because I certainly don't want to be there for that, and I'll go and join them in the morning.

I lay in bed for hours thinking about my sister's words.

If either of you ever decides to make this more...

CHAPTER 33
Cami

BESTIE FRIEND

You have a lot of explaining to do.

ME

Do you hate me?

BESTIE FRIEND

Never. But I am a liiiittle confused why you didn't just tell me.

ME

IDK it felt like if we did we would be distracting you and I knew how important Paris was to you. And then everything with Alex was happening and I didn't want to bring down the mood

BESTIE FRIEND

I get that, but you never bring down the mood. I'm grateful you're helping him. We can talk more about the kissing and the hand holding when I get home though, because that shit is weird.

ME

I know, it's absolutely so weird

BESTIE FRIEND

Also, I got into a huge fight with Alex. But it's fine now.

ME

Well, let's talk about your drama and not mine

CHRISTMAS ALONE IS DEPRESSING, SO I'VE MADE IT MY mission to spruce the place up. Charlie didn't tell me I could, but he did leave me his credit card, so I'll take that as permission. Everything I'm buying is for his own benefit, so it's only right he'd foot the bill. I guess it's for my benefit as well because I'm staying here for the time being. Not only that, but the retail therapy has helped distract me from my thoughts when it comes to the owner of this penthouse.

Earlier this week I had photos printed and framed, then started placing them all around the apartment. I added a big canvas of Charlie, Alana, and I in the living room, put some framed 4x6s in the office on the bookshelves, and added one of he and I by his bedside. Don't ask me why.

I took a risk and printed a team photo from when the Rangers won the Stanley Cup a few years ago and hung that in the gym, then added a picture I found on Soren's Facebook of him, Charlie, and Theo Adams in there as well. Their arms are slung around one another and Charlie is sporting a rare grin. It was taken pretty recently, and it makes me smile to know that his efforts in building relationships on the team are paying off. It's good for him.

I went to Target and got a few throw pillows and blankets, and that alone has also made a huge difference. I didn't go for any crazy colors, no pinks or purples, but I kept it neutral with a few cream colored ones and some deep blues. It looks sophisticated and like Charlie.

I went to a tree farm nearby, picked one out, and had it delivered here last night. It's Christmas Eve now and Mia is about to be here. Soren was away with the guys for the game, then his family had some kind of emergency so he had to fly to them in Michigan. It isn't looking like he'll be back for the holidays, so I found myself a buddy.

I'm glad I won't be alone, but I haven't been able to escape the calls from my mom. She is pretty frustrated with me deciding not to come home this year, but I really can't deal with the constant judgmental comments and comparisons. I know she doesn't mean to do it, but I know if I go she will and I don't trust myself not to snap back. I don't want to make my mom cry on a holiday, so I'd rather make her mad and just not attend.

I ordered take out from one of the Chinese restaurants that is open, and started a fire in the gas fireplace. That, plus the glow of the tree in the corner have created a cozy home whereas the place I walked into a few days ago was sterile and cold. I hope he likes it when he gets back, but worst case scenario I'll send everything back.

Giovanna has been off for the week and with her family, so she hasn't seen it either. I'm probably more excited to hear her opinions than I am to hear Charlie's, but that's because men walk in and don't even realize there was a change while women notice when you've had an inch taken off of your hair.

I'm just finishing lighting the pine and spruce candle I purchased today when a knock sounds at the door. I head towards it and open it up, revealing a flushed Mia in red, green, and pink striped pajamas and fuzzy red slippers.

"Merry Christmas!" she shouts as she comes towards me. She hugs me with one arm, wine cradled in the other, and squeezes me tight. I'm happy she's in such a good mood. Alana and I usually get into the holiday spirit—she's really good at planning fun things for us to do—but with her in Paris, and Charlie and I so focused on this fake dating thing we just haven't had the time.

"Merry Christmas. What do you have there?"

"Oh, just a Pinot Grigio. Just in case we need it," she says with a wink.

"Takeout should be here shortly. I queued up a few Hallmark movies to choose from and we can eat in the living room. I'll put this in the cooler," I say as I take the wine from her and she makes her way into the living room. She's staying the night tonight, so I grab her bag and take it to the guest room across from the one I've been staying in. I moved all of my stuff into Charlie's room earlier today, knowing it would look strange if I was staying in a room that wasn't his. I can't tell if I'm excited or anxious to be sleeping in a bed that smells like him tonight.

I walk into his bedroom, just to be sure the painting I spotted earlier is still there and I wasn't imaging it. My painting from hobby day is hung in his closet, tucked away where I wouldn't have seen it the first time he showed me around. When I moved my things in here earlier I came across it while I was hanging up a few shirts. I smile and turn, leaving the room.

As I'm heading back to Mia our dinner arrives, so I grab that, take it to the living room, and sit down on the couch next to her. We dig into our boxes of sweet and sour pork and kung pao chicken and chat briefly about the guys' game earlier in the week.

"Charlie seems more solid lately. I mean, not that he wasn't solid before, but it seems like something has shifted in the last few weeks."

"You think?" I ask, biting my bottom lip nervously.

"Yeah. He's killing it."

"He's doing a pretty good job this year. Soren too."

"Aw, I know. I'm so proud of him."

"How did you know Soren was who you wanted to be with? What made it worth it to take the risk of possibly messing up your friendship?" I ask. It's possibly an illuminating question, but she doesn't seem surprised by it.

Mia is so much like me. She has a bubbly and outgoing personality, she's a little chaotic and wild but can be serious when she needs to be. I love Alana like a sister, I'd die for the girl, but she's always been the Type A of the two of us. As much as she sympathizes with my disorganized and impulsive lifestyle, she can't understand it. I feel like Mia might, though.

"It was really scary, I'll admit. It's weird going from someone being your friend to someone being your partner. They were there for you in a lot of ways before, but when you decide to take it a step further the relationship changes and that's weird.

"Soren and I had been friends since elementary school. He moved into my neighborhood in the sixth grade and we were in the same homeroom. He pulled on my braids one day and I called him an asshole, and we were immediate friends. I did get a folder sign for the curse word, but it was worth it."

I laugh, pouring some of the wine I retrieved from the cooler a little ways into our meal, and take a sip.

"You would cuss at school, I can totally see that."

"Don't tell me you didn't get in trouble for language in school?"

"Oh, I totally did. More than once."

She shakes her head in feigned disappointment.

"Anyway, after high school he got a scholarship to play hockey at Michigan, which is where we were living and grew up, so it was perfect. I applied, got in, and about three months into our freshman year we were out to dinner and he just kissed me."

"No way."

"Yeah, the psycho. Totally just leaned forward and planted one on me. I was shocked, it was probably the worst kiss ever because I was unresponsive, and he immediately pulled back and was like 'oh no, what have I done?' He completely freaked."

"Poor thing. What did you do?"

"We talked about it and he told me he had been thinking about doing it for a while and I looked so beautiful sitting across from him that his body just took over. It was romantic and sweet, but I was too scared to start anything. I told him thanks but no thanks and we stayed friends for like two more years."

"Seriously? I did not think the story was going in that direction."

"Hah, yeah. I was scared of commitment and I thought more time would help. Spoiler alert, it didn't. We were just in this limbo of uncomfortable physical attraction and sexual tension, but I had put a stop on all things romantic and he respected that. My refusal alone almost ripped us apart a few times, but eventually I came to my senses."

"How did you get over the fear?" I hesitate, then decide to be a little bit transparent. "I am so terrified of commitment. I can't stick to one thing for longer than like a month. I am constantly switching body washes, hobbies, favorite TV shows, music, OBGYNs."

"Woah, switching OBGYNs? Those are hard to find too."

"I know, but I keep thinking there might be a better one out there."

"I get it. Listen, life is always full of options and that makes things hard. Wanting things to go well isn't a crime, but when you are always on the go and never staying put in the areas that matter, it's hard to feel settled and fulfilled. Switching body washes and coffee orders is absolutely fine, you do what makes you happy, but I can tell you that taking the leap to commit to someone is worth it. You just need to do the work to determine how you feel about committing to that person. When you think about Charlie, can you picture yourself on a porch with him when you're old? Sipping coffee and bitching about your kids making stupid decisions?"

I smile at the picture that pops up in my mind.

"I can totally see us doing that."

"And can you see the two of you in the in-between? Stressing over finances, working hard to put your kids through college, taking anniversary trips, building a home together, and fighting over the remote?"

"Yes," I say in a small voice. "And that is terrifying because I have never been able to picture that before."

"It doesn't have to be terrifying, let it be exciting. It means you've found the right one."

Yeah, except he's my best friend's brother and this whole thing is supposed to be fake.

"That's good advice. Thanks Mia, you and Soren are lucky."

"I know he sure is."

We cozy up and watch a movie about two sisters, one who loves Christmas movies and one who hates them, who end up stuck in a Christmas movie. It's cheesy and cute and romantic and the perfect thing to get my mind off of my conversation with Mia.

Eventually, we make our way upstairs and I crawl into Charlie's bed, breathing in his woody and spicy scent. It makes me miss him, so I grab my phone and text him to tell him just that.

ME

Merry Christmas

CHARLES

Merry Christmas.

ME

How's Lana?

CHARLES

She's good. It's early here, which means it's pretty late there. You okay? Mia come over?

ME

Yeah. Missing you

CHARLES

Me too.

ME

Gonna go to sleep, just wanted to tell you that

CHARLES

Thanks for telling me. Sweet dreams.

I fall asleep thinking about porches and children and coffee with my fake boyfriend.

January

CHAPTER 34
Cami

AFTER CHRISTMAS, CHARLIE CAME HOME AND FREAKED when he saw the apartment. Well, I say freaked, but his version of that is probably a little more tame than most. He came in and didn't say a word for a solid five minutes, just walked around the house looking at all of the pictures and little touches I added. I was honestly scared he was mad, but I knew I was safe when he turned to me with glassy eyes and pulled me into his arms. He squeezed so tight I struggled to breathe, then kissed the top of my head and whispered a quiet "thanks" before letting me go and going into his room to change his clothes.

While there might have been a version of him in the past who would have shown his excitement in a much louder way, this version doesn't do that. He's quieter with his gratefulness and enthusiasm, but it almost means more to get those small moments from him now. I could tell he was really happy, and over the last few days he's been asking me about the details I added and why I chose them.

Now, we're headed to my apartment, because I need to grab a few things and Alex and Alana are going to be home any minute now. I'm thankful when we show up to the building and there are no photographers out in the front. I say as much to Charlie, but he isn't as positive as I am.

"Just because they aren't here now doesn't mean this is a safe place for you."

"Well, it seems pretty safe to me."

"They've only stopped coming because you stopped going inside. I'm sure they have people watching the building to alert them once you've started coming back. It's actually pretty crazy how they seem to know everything."

"I can't stay at your place forever."

"We'll see about that."

I roll my eyes at him, which he ignores, and we walk inside the building and head up to my apartment. We've decided that, in order to avoid paparazzi, Alana and I will stay with our male counterparts. I refuse to say boyfriends, because technically I don't have one. Mine is fake, and I am trying to remind myself of that, even though I think I'm failing miserably.

We make it to my doorstep and I unlock the door and push inside, smiling at the comforting smells of my home. It smells like me in here and I miss that. I miss the way this shoebox makes me feel secure, and while Charlie's place is starting to be that for me, being here now makes me miss it.

"Can we go lay down in the bedroom for just a few minutes? When will Alex and Alana be here?" I ask, moving towards my bedroom door. Charlie looks at me quizzically.

"We have about forty-five minutes. We could lay down for maybe fifteen, but then we need to get to packing up some of the stuff you want to bring." He follows behind me. "Why do you even want to lay down? And why do you need me for it?"

"Because"—I reach up and tug on his hand until he falls down next to me—"I miss my bed and my house and the way it smells and feels, and I get why I can't stay here, but I want to be here for a few minutes and be comfy. With you."

"With me."

We haven't picked the conversation back up from before he left for his away game, but things have been pretty cozy between the two of us ever since he's been back. Easy affection and sneaky touches that have made things feel a lot more real than they should, and after my conversation with Mia on Christmas I've resigned to not stress so much about it, but to instead enjoy the way it feels to be comfortable with someone.

"Mmhmm. Now shut up and hold me." I lay on my side, facing away from him, then reach back for his wrist, wrapping it around me and scooting back into him so he's the big spoon and I'm the little one. I sigh in contentment and close my eyes.

We have cuddled in bed before when he's accidentally stayed over, but it's always been just that, an accident. This time I am asking him outright to cuddle with me, and I really can't bring myself to be bashful about it. I've been feeling out of place the last few weeks and here in this place with him I feel grounded, so I'm asking for what I want.

He doesn't fight me, and instead pulls me even closer against him. My eyes close and I drift off, only to be awoken by soft touches on my face. I'm confused for a second before I remember where I am and who I'm with, but his whispering helps everything click back into place.

"Hey, Cam, time to get up, baby. Alana is going to be here any minute." I reach my arms above my head and stretch, loving the feeling of my striped forest green comforter wrapped around me.

"I thought you said fifteen minutes?"

"You were sleeping so well, so I let you go a little longer. We can pack while we talk to Alana."

"Mmkay. Thanks, I needed that, I think."

"You're welcome," he says as he presses a kiss to my temple. Every time he shows affection when we are in private, I get more and more comfortable with it.

I'm pulling the comforter back up my bed and he must see the longing on my face, because he asks, "What is it?"

"Oh, it's nothing. It's silly."

"Nothing you need or want or are worried about is silly. What is it?"

"Um...I just miss my house. I miss my bedding and how cozy it is and I was just feeling a little sad about leaving it again." He stares at me for a beat, then nods decisively before exiting the bedroom. I feel a little frustrated at his dismissal, but turn back to my task of making the bed instead of going after him, not wanting to start a fight right before his sister gets here.

A second later, he is waltzing into the room with trash bags. He snaps one in the air a few times so it opens up, then starts pulling on the comforter and messing up my just made bed.

"Hey, what are you doing? I just made that," I say, trying to grab it back from him.

"I'm packing it for you," he says as he starts to roll it up into something that looks like a large version of a sleeping bag. He then begins to shove it into the trash bag, then grabs my pillows and throws those in a second one.

"Why don't you grab your sheets?"

"Charlie, stop. What are you doing?" He stops, his hands holding onto the edges of the, now stuffed, trash bag.

"You said you missed home, so let's bring it to my place. It's safer for you to be there right now, and I'm not budging on that, but I know what it's like to be uncomfortable, and I don't want you to feel uncomfortable or out of place in my home, so let's make it ours. What else do you need to feel at home?"

I stare at this giant six foot four man standing in my tiny room, clutching my forest green and pink pillows in his arms, and want to cry. I can tell how serious he is and how much he genuinely wants to help, so instead of crying I do what he asks and think about what else might make me feel at home.

The additions I made while he was in Paris have helped a ton, but it wouldn't hurt to have a few more items. I grab a few knitting supplies, a fuzzy blanket, a few more clothing items, and some trinkets from my night stand and around the room. We compile it all into a few bags and are putting them by the front door when Alana bursts through it.

"Cam!" she shouts, and throws herself at me. Those tears I held at bay earlier come back tenfold now as I hold my best friend and sink into the familiar feeling of being with her. She was gone for a full month, the longest we've ever been apart, and every day sucked. Eventually we got into a rhythm of quick FaceTime calls and texting, but the time change and her busy schedule made it hard. It feels so good to have her home.

"I missed you so much, Lan."

"I missed you more."

"Not possible," I say as I pull back to look at her face. She's crying, too, and we both smile and laugh at our hysterics. "We're pathetic."

"I know, but it's fine."

"It's so fine."

I notice that Alex has stepped into my apartment and is looking around hesitantly, like he isn't totally sure what to do with himself.

"Ashford, get over here and say hi to Cami. She isn't a stranger and no one is going to bite."

Alex laughs and shakes his head at his girlfriend before coming over and giving me a one armed hug. He clasps Charlie's hand in his and then sorta slams against him in some kind of bro greeting.

The men take a seat in the living room and I pull Alana back into my bedroom, closing the door for a few minutes of privacy. I really haven't had a chance to talk to her about this whole situation and I know we need to.

"Wait, where's your bedding and stuff? This room looks weird," she asks and she walks around before sitting on the bare mattress.

"Your brother is determined to make me feel at home in his

penthouse, so he insisted we take some of my stuff there. It was actually really sweet."

"Yeah, he is pretty sweet," she says and smiles at me. "So, should we talk about it then?"

"Yeah we probably should."

"He explained to me how it all started, or at least why he needed your help. But he said you also needed his?"

"Ugh yes," I groan and sit down next to her. "I told my mom and sister I was bringing a date to the wedding because I was so tired of hearing them ask me over and over if I was, then giving me advice on why no one wanted me when I said I wasn't. So I just said "I have a date" and they were both freaking out and then I was freaking out and then Charlie came to me with his proposition and it just ended up working."

"Well, let's not call it a proposition. Sounds scandalous."

"I guess it kind of is scandalous," I say with a laugh.

"But there's no sex involved in your...contract?"

"Oh my word, no. No sex involved. I really don't feel comfortable discussing physical encounters I might have with your brother with you."

"I know it's weird," she says as she breaks out in an uncomfortable giggle. We make eye contact and soon I'm also laughing. Once we've settled down, she speaks again.

"I don't love hearing about it either, but I feel like we need to talk about it. Otherwise, things will get bad-weird and not just uncomfortable-weird."

"You're probably right," I say with a sigh. "Um, well we've agreed on no kissing or touching unless it's in public and for show."

"Okay, and have you held to that?"

How does she know? Can she read minds?

"Mostly. He's started kissing me on the forehead and temple. Calling me baby, which isn't against the rules but feels like it is."

"Okaaaay," she says, drawing out the word. "And how does that make you feel?"

"I don't know. It's complicated. This is all supposed to be for show, so it doesn't really matter how I feel."

"That's not true, Cam. You know he cares about how you feel." She reaches over and places her hand on top of mine and squeezes. "Do you have feelings for him? Feelings that are more than friends."

"I don't know. I don't want to say no, but I'm not sure if I'm ready to say yes. I think he's physically attractive and oh my gosh this is such a weird conversation."

"I know it is, but keep going. I'm good."

"You're sure?"

"Yep. Hit me with it, bestie friend."

"Okay um." I clear my throat. "I think he's attractive, but I'm not sure if it's more than that. I know I love him as a friend, but I haven't let myself explore what that would be if he was something more than a friend."

"That makes sense. Are you open to that?"

"It terrifies me, to be honest. I've never been able to envision myself staying with someone long term, and I can't start something with Charlie if I don't see it going in that direction. He's going to be around for a long time no matter what, and I'm scared I'll screw that up if I take it to a different level."

"Yeah, I get that. You don't want to put that friendship at risk."

"Exactly. So I'm a bit stuck there right now. We're just trying to make sure he gets signed with the Rangers for another contract and then I guess we'll go from there."

"That's good, but I want you to know that if this does go anywhere that is in the more-than-friends territory, I'm okay with it."

"Really?" I ask. I didn't think she'd be upset about the

prospect of Charlie and I being a couple, but I did think there would be at least some push back.

"Yeah." She shrugs her shoulders as if to say why not? "I've had some time to process since that conversation in Paris and I love you both. Having you as a sister-in-law would be a dream come true."

I burst out in laughter, the thought of getting married sounding comical.

"Let's not go too fast there, Lan. I'd love to be your sister-in-law, but your brother and I are still playing pretend. I will let you know if that changes though."

"That's all I ask, just don't keep it from me."

"You got it, girlfriend. I love you. Thanks for being so cool about all of this."

"I love you. I'm glad to be home, I missed you so much."

"Same. Now, do you need help getting your stuff together so you can go stay at your hot coworkers house?"

"Oh shut up."

CHAPTER 35

Cami

BESTIE FRIEND

I cannot believe you got him to do this.

ME

You underestimate my abilities

BESTIE FRIEND

He looks so cute! They're all so small.

ME

I know. My ovaries are going to explode

WALKING A FEW STEPS TO THE LEFT, I MOVE THE ANGLE of my phone and snap another photo of Charlie. He's sitting at the front of the room, a book about a boy who wanted white mittens in his hands, and a group of kids sitting at his feet. Many are dressed in red, white, and blue, and some are even sporting a Cade jersey.

Back when I came up with the list for bringing Charlie's media persona back to life, we agreed a story time at the library would be great for socials. Well, *I* agreed and when he sent it to Sophie she was really excited about it. She is standing next to me at the back of the room, smiling as he changes his voice to match the characters. I hadn't met her before today. Usually I'm not involved in anything that has to do with his hockey career, so I hadn't had a reason to meet his agent before.

She's short, but her three inch heels help her some. Her blonde hair is pulled back away from her face in a low ponytail and she's wearing a deep plum pants suit. I would have immediately been intimidated by her if she hadn't walked up to us and pulled me into a hug before even saying hello.

"He looks like a natural up there. Totally opposite of what anyone would have thought, I'm sure," she whispers as she leans over towards me.

"I know. The kids love him and how is he so good at the voices?"

"I don't get it. It's honestly kind of scary. Did he practice these with you at home?"

As soon as she says it, he changes yet again to a new voice for a character that's just been introduced. Both of our eyes go wide at the change and I throw my hand over my mouth in an effort to hide the snicker. The back of her hand smacks my shoulder at the same time as Charlie gives me a subtle glare and I quickly try to gather myself.

"I'm sorry, I've just never seen him like this. We definitely did not practice at home."

"It's okay, I get it. I just don't want him to stop and he will if you laugh."

"You're right. I'll keep it together."

The parents at the back of the room are all holding up cell phones and taking videos and photos as he moves through the story, eventually coming to the end, and asking the children to raise their hands to share what they thought of the story.

One child says they liked the part where the grandma made the mittens, another said they liked the animals in the story, and one took off on a story about how his grandma was old and fell down the stairs but she's okay now. Watching Charlie try to break into the kid's story so he can close the book and move forward with the event, but not hurt his feelings, is comical.

He's so gentle with them and I wonder if things like this are some of the reasons why I can see a future with him that goes beyond the next few months. He's so endearing and each day I am struggling more with the inability to resist falling into something real with him.

My phone buzzes in my pocket and I take it out, smiling at the texts from Alana responding to the pictures and videos I sent her of her brother reading.

BESTIE FRIEND

Okay I don't want to know about your ovaries when my brother is involved.

ME

It's just a saying. You know when you see a hot guy do something with kids?

BESTIE FRIEND

Pretending you didn't call my brother hot.

ME

Too much?

BESTIE FRIEND

Just weird. But I'll get used to it!

I heart her message and switch over to Instagram to reply to the few fans who have commented on my story of his reading. Most people have been really kind to me and welcomed me into the Rangers fandom, but there have of course been some who aren't so kind. I choose to ignore those people and focus on the positive.

As I type, I see Charlie talking with the two reporters Sophie invited to come today. She didn't want to bring a ton of people in, not wanting to communicate this was purely for press, even though that was one of the main driving factors. He smiles demurely and speaks in a quiet voice into their microphones. I admire him from my place in the back, the feelings of fondness and warmth swirling in my chest. Over the last few weeks he has become something different to me than he was before.

Before he was my best friend, and that's still true, but things have changed in subtle ways. When something happens, he's the one I want to tell. When I can't decide what coffee I want or if I should buy something or not, I want to text him and ask for his opinion. When my family drives me nuts and I want to rip my hair out, my first instinct is to pick up the phone and dial his number. He's quickly becoming my person in more ways than just how I spend my time and while that's terrifying, it's also exciting.

He finishes up with the interview and makes his way over to me. Once he reaches me, he slides his hand from my hip to my back, then presses his palm into my lower back and pulls me forward to press into him. He leans down and places a soft and slow kiss to my lips, then pulls back and smiles down at me.

The action sends butterflies through my chest and I have to take a deep breath to calm myself. I know we're in public, but the way he's been making me feel lately is all too real.

"How'd you like the story?" he asks with a smirk playing on his lips.

"Loved it. No notes, except can you talk to me in those voices?"

"Nah, that's a little too out there for me, Cam."

"Oh, I didn't mean it like that," I say as I laugh and swat his chest.

"Hey, you said it, not me."

I roll my eyes at him and pull him back into me for a hug. My head fits perfectly under his chin and it's quickly turned into one of my favorite places to be. He holds me there for a few moments, then removes one of his arms, reaching back to pull his phone out of his back pocket.

"Ugh," he groans. "Did you send a video of me doing the voices to my sister? Seriously, Cam?"

"What? She would have seen it on Instagram eventually, she isn't blocked from our stories anymore."

"I am never going to hear the end of this."

I snicker into his chest and squeeze him one more time before letting go and turning to face the room. He gives me another kiss before going back over to the table they have set up for him to sign autographs. The turnout today says enough about his growing popularity. The event is free, but people had to sign up in order to attend and the spots were gone within just a few minutes. It makes me happy to see him getting some love from fans, and I hope he sees how much they genuinely love seeing more from his life.

Sophie manages the line and the news people take photos while fans shuffle forward for their turn to meet Charlie. Young children get their jerseys signed and some even bring in hockey sticks. I hear one little boy tell him that he joined the squirt team, which is just a term for his age range of 9-10, and was inspired by seeing him on the ice.

It's touching and I find that I could be content doing events like this again. I don't think I mind being a WAG for a professional hockey player nearly as much as I thought I would, and I might even be interested in being promoted to permanent WAG status, that is if my fake boyfriend is at all interested in being not-so-fake.

CHAPTER 36
Charlie

SOREN

Will you bring a side dish or something?

ME

Yeah, what do you want me to bring?

SOREN

IDK something with cheese

ME

Okay...that was oddly specific yet also very vague

SOREN

I know what I like

A FEW DAYS AGO, THE GUYS AND I WERE ON THE ICE AT practice and they invited me to this game night. I haven't ever been to a game night, but it sounded sort of fun and I knew Cami would go with me. Any time she's around I have a good time, so I figured it wouldn't hurt.

I'd like to say I'm working on my relationships with my teammates because Sophie told me I had to, but that wouldn't be the full truth. That *is* how this all started, but I'm starting to enjoy having actual friends on the team. I'm starting to enjoy knowing that I have guys who have my back, even though I can't help but think it won't last.

I can't quite shake the instinct to brace myself for something, even though that something isn't real. Yet. We have our game against the Carolina Hurricanes coming up, and I know that isn't helping with my efforts to overcome my high school trauma. I'm going to have to face Troy Price, center forward on the Hurricanes and the source of a lot of my issues currently, yet again.

We played together in high school and I thought we were friends, until everything happened and I learned how wrong I was. I've had to play against him often during my years in professional hockey, and you'd think over time the rage and embarrassment would simmer down, but it hasn't. I don't know how to break out of the cycle, and that almost makes it all worse.

I shake my head to clear it as I cross around the back of the car to open Cami's door for her. She's been purposefully ignoring that conversation we need to have about my feelings for her, but I know she'll get there eventually. For now, I've been trying to show her in small ways how good we could be together. Slowly breaking some of the rules and showing her affection in public *and* in private. I'm hoping that will help whenever we *do* finally have that conversation.

She's holding the queso and a bag of chips in her lap. The game night is being held at Soren's townhome, which is literally steps from Central Park. It's a five story townhome that was built in the 1890s but has been completely gutted and redone. This is my first time hanging out here, but I'm already in awe from just the outside of it and the proximity to the park. I can tell Cami feels the same by the way her jaw dropped as we got closer and never returned back to normal.

She clutches the closed crock pot in her hands and I hold the bag of chips as we make our way up the steps to the front door. A few moments later, someone pulls it open.

"Hey, so glad you could make it," Mia says cheerfully as she stands in the doorway.

"Girl, you did not tell me you lived in a place like this," Cami says as she widens her eyes and steps inside.

"Well, you didn't really ask," she replies with a laugh. "But thank you. It's a privilege to live here."

"Thanks for having us," I say in greeting as we enter.

We make our way through the entryway hallway and into the kitchen. The cabinets are all white and the countertops are made out of a white marble. The space is clean, yet homey and cozy, sort of how Cami has made my penthouse feel.

"Hey, man, good to see you," Soren says as he grabs my hand in his and pulls me to him for a bro hug. I hug him back and when I pull away I catch Cami smiling over at us affectionately. I know she's been pleased by my growing relationships with my teammates, but especially Soren. I think it's just because she likes Mia, but regardless I'm glad we have another couple we can spend time with.

"You can make a plate and we'll gather in the living room. Theo is already in there," Mia says before grabbing her plate full of appetizers and leaving the kitchen. Soren sticks around, adding queso to his plate and grabbing chips.

"You go ahead, babe, I'll get your plate," I tell Cami as I press a kiss to her head. She smiles up at me.

"You sure you know what I want?"

"I think I can make a good guess. Give me a shot and I'll come back and switch things out if I don't get it right."

"Okay, you got it, superstar." She leans up on her tiptoes and pops a quick kiss to my lips before turning and heading into the living room behind Mia.

"She's got you good there, bud."

"I could say the same thing about you."

"You totally could, and I would happily admit it."

We smile at each other, sharing a moment of camaraderie before I pile Cami's plate with some veggies, ranch, chips, queso, and a few slices of salami from the charcuterie board. Walking into the living room, I find Adams sitting in a large chair at one narrow end of the coffee table in the center of the room. There are loveseats on either side of it and the two women have taken their spots on either one, leaving room for Soren and I next to each one of them. I place the plate in front of Cami and settle in next to her.

"Look okay?"

"It's perfect, thanks," she says, smiling softly at me.

We start off playing a game called Chameleon. Everyone in the group gets a card, and one person is deemed the chameleon. The goal is not to let on to anyone that you are the chameleon, but it's tricky because everyone else gets a code on their cards that tells them a specific word. Then you go around one at a time and have to say a word that relates to that word without hesitating.

So, for example, if the word was bread you might say dough or bagel or toast. But if you're the chameleon you don't know that the word is bread. You have to figure it out and try not expose yourself as having no idea what the word is. It's tricky, but really fun, and I can immediately tell that Cami is the first chameleon because she's put her left hand under her thigh. It's a nervous tick she's had for as long as I've known her, and I debate whether or not I'm going to call her out on it.

At the end of each round, the group goes around and votes who they think the chameleon is. Although I know who my guess would be, I decide to pick on Soren instead and let her survive another round.

When he flips his card around, we all see we were wrong and it's revealed that Cami was in fact the chameleon. She becomes the dealer for the next round and we go again. We play countless rounds before switching over to Monopoly, which everyone knows takes forever to play to completion. We do it though, staying out until the early hours of the morning sipping on wine and moving our metal pieces around the board.

Watching her effortlessly fit in with this group of my teammates and friends isn't a surprise to me, but it's another reminder that this could work. She fits into my life seamlessly and I love having her in it, in this role. She balances me out and makes me better and I don't want that to end when I get my next contract.

I mull over my thoughts as we finish up our game and say our goodbyes, following after Cami to the car. We make our way back to my place, because she still hasn't left, and she reaches over the console of the car to grab ahold of my hand. I smile to myself at her initiation of physical contact.

"How are you feeling about the game tomorrow?" she asks.

"I'm feeling fine." I know my tone is short, but I really don't feel like discussing it after such a good night.

"It's the Hurricanes..." she trails off, not needing to finish the thought or question. I know what she's asking. She doesn't know exactly what happened back in high school that turned my entire personality from charismatic and lively, to quiet and reserved, but she knows it has something to do with Troy.

"Yeah, it is. It's okay, Cam, I'm good."

"You're sure? I'll be there in the stands. If you need me, I'll come straight to you."

"Thanks, baby. I promise I'm okay. As long as he doesn't come chirping at me and I stay away from him, everything should be fine."

"What if he does? Chirp at you I mean," she asks. Chirping is a hockey term for when someone on the opposing team trash talks you or the team. It's annoying, and used to get people out of the game and into their heads, but it usually doesn't work on me.

"I'll ignore it. He's just insecure and I've moved on." I know even as I'm saying it that it isn't entirely the truth. I haven't moved past it, because I still can't even talk about it. It seems so silly, like it wasn't even that big of a deal, but I just can't get myself to open up and be vulnerable when it comes to this.

"Okay, but just be careful out there."

"Always."

She smiles over at me, then pulls her phone out when she hears it ring. It's really late, or early I guess, so her getting a phone call at this time is weird.

"Who is that?" I ask.

"It's Collette," she replies as she swipes to answer the call. "Hey, Coco. You okay?"

I hear her sister's muffled voice as she replies, and watch Cami's face go from worried, to relieved, then to frustrated.

"You're lucky I'm awake right now. If I had been asleep and you had woken me up to talk about the groomsmens' tuxedo colors, I would not be a happy sister."

I roll my eyes, laughing a little at her sister's antics. She's been pretty frenzied planning this wedding, but I can tell they're a good match from what I've gathered. Cami likes the guy and I'm glad; I just wish they could be a little more respectful of my girl and how she lives her life.

"I think you should just go with black. It's classy and simple and won't cause anyone's eyes to be off of you two." She pauses. "I know I'm right. Now I need to go, we're just getting home and I want to wash my face and go to bed." Another pause. "I told you I was dating someone, Coco, remember I said I was bringing him to the wedding." She turns away from me so I can't see her expression at all. "Yes, I was being serious. Are you kidding? I'm bringing a plus one, so if you didn't factor that in you're going to need to. I don't have time to help you with this right now. I love you, bye."

She presses a button to hang up the call and throws the phone forcefully back into her purse, then pulls her hand back into her lap.

"I don't want to talk about it."

"Okay, we don't have to talk about it then."

It's like the words release the tension within her and she takes a deep breath, then sulks against the seat of the car and closes her eyes.

"Thank you."

"You're welcome. You don't ever have to talk about anything you aren't ready to talk about yet. But, if you'll let me, I'd like to hold your hand." She opens her eyes and turns her head so she's looking at me, no doubt trying to figure out why I'm asking her to give me her hand back when she just took it away. "You can feel whatever you're feeling, but you need to know you aren't alone. I'd like to sit with you in it and hold your hand and remind you I'm here."

She just stares at me for a few seconds, then wordlessly flips her palm up and holds it out to me. I take it in mine and begin rubbing circles on the heel of her hand with my thumb. She shivers, but I ignore it and just continue to drive.

"Thank you," she whispers as we pull into the parking garage.

CHAPTER 37
Cami

"Lan, where's my jersey?" Alex yells from down the hall. "I thought you put it in the wash."

"Seriously, Ashford?" She walks toward the bedroom that they share and I follow, because I want to see how this turns out. She grabs the jersey, which is laid out on the bed, and holds it up for him to see as he walks back in the room. "If it was a snake it would have bit you."

"Well, good thing it wasn't a snake then."

He squishes the jersey between the two of them as he winds his hands from her hips to her lower back, pulling her into him. He kisses her softly and looks down at her lovingly. I look away, feeling like I'm intruding on a private moment.

"You look beautiful," I hear him whisper.

"Not so bad yourself," she replies.

I look back up in time to see him grab the jersey from her hands and exit the room, heading back to the bathroom where he was freshening up for the game tonight. I came over to Alex's, now Alex and Alana's, place to get ready for the game because we're all going together. I am so happy to have her back, things finally feel somewhat normal.

We're all sporting Cade jerseys tonight, as usual, but instead of pairing mine with my normal leggings, I grabbed a new one that is one size bigger and am wearing it with a pair of knee high boots. It's a little shorter than I'd normally wear, but I made sure to put some shorts underneath just in case. I know Charlie is going to love it and that's really all that matters.

I have been increasingly worried about the game tonight, because I know they're going up against the Hurricanes, which means Troy, and while they usually don't have any major issues besides a short penalty box visit for one or both of them, something just feels different tonight. I can't quite put my finger on it, but I'm hoping it's just paranoia.

"Cam, you good?" Alana asks, placing her hand on my shoulder and giving it a squeeze.

"Yeah, just a little nervous. Hurricanes and all."

She nods knowingly. "He'll be okay. He's got this and you'll be there if anything happens. We'll all be there."

"Thanks, bestie friend. I'm glad you're home."

"I'm glad too," she says and throws her arm over my shoulder to give me a side hug.

"And I'm glad too," I hear from behind as Alex wraps both of his arms around us both. "Group hug."

"I love a group hug," I say, patting him on the arm. It's been interesting getting to know Alex in this way. He is Alana and I's coworker at *Impress*, so I knew him before they got together, but now they're living together and he is spending a lot more time with us, and it's fun.

We disperse and start collecting our bags, then head out and down to the subway. The journey to Madison Square Garden isn't too long and before I know it we're walking into the arena and heading to our seats. They're close to the glass, courtesy of the tickets Charlie provided us, and the fans start to file in around us. They're all wearing different colors of red, white, and blue, and some are wearing various designs of face paint.

About half an hour before the game starts, the guys come out for a warm up skate. We watch them stretching and skating, and Alex heads out to grab some snacks for the three of us. Fans watch from their seats and the excitement in the building only grows as we get nearer to game time.

"I'm really glad he's had you these last few weeks," Alana says out of nowhere.

"He's always had me, Lan."

"Not like he's had you recently. Even if the kissing and hand holding and touching only happens in public, which I'm not convinced of by the way, he's been able to have that closer connection with you and I'm glad. He needs it."

I'm not sure what to say, so I just smile over at her and she pulls me into a quick hug. I'm saved from having to discuss this further when Mia comes up behind us.

"Oh my gosh, what are you doing here? Did you switch your seats?"

"I didn't know, but it looks like the boys switched us so we were together."

"Yay," I exclaim as I pull her into a hug. Lots of hugs tonight. "Mia, you know Alana."

"It's good to see you again," she says, hugging her as well. "How was your trip?"

"Really great, thanks for asking."

About that time, Alex returns with our snacks and passes the soft pretzel and Diet Coke to Alana. I take my popcorn and Dr. Pepper from him, then settle into my seat.

"Are you nervous?" Mia asks from my right.

"A little. The Hurricanes are hard for Charlie. An old rival."

"That makes things tough for sure. Soren will swear left, right, and center that he doesn't have any teams that are that way for him, but don't look too closely when they play Seattle."

I laugh at her, thankful the joking has brought a little lividity to the tension I'm feeling. I haven't been able to shake this all week and it's frustrating. I just want to be able to support Charlie and not worry so much about his time on the ice. It's his job and he does it effortlessly, so I have nothing to worry about. I keep reminding myself of that as the guys take their places for the start of the game.

CHAPTER 38
Charlie

THINGS HAVE GONE PRETTY WELL SO FAR. I'VE BEEN ignoring Troy as much as I can, even though he seems to be trying his hardest to engage with me, and we're about to start the last period. I can tell Cami is getting more and more relaxed the closer we get to the end of the game. She tried to put on a brave face for me, but I know she's nervous about the conflict between Troy and I even though she doesn't know exactly what happened between us.

Usually when we play against the Hurricanes, Troy and I don't have many issues. We're both center forwards, so we do get a good amount of interaction, but we always keep it mostly professional. It still gets on my nerves to be on the ice with him, even if he is on an opposing team, but he ignores me and I ignore him. Tonight, though, it feels a bit like he's a shark circling his prey. Nothing has happened so far, but I can't help but feel like he's biding his time.

I take the ice for the face-off, and Troy and I get low right on top of the face off dot. Soren is to my left, and just knowing he's there feels good. It makes me frustrated with myself that I didn't make friends sooner, because knowing I have support makes things a lot less stressful.

The ref is getting ready to drop the puck, but before he does Troy takes his shot.

"Got a hot new piece, Cade," he says in a low mocking voice.

"Don't go there, Troy. We're here to play a game."

"I wonder what kind of games she'd like to play. Back in high school she loved playing games," he draws out the word loved. I wonder why the ref isn't dropping the puck because if this guy keeps on I'm afraid of what I'll do.

"Shut up, man."

"She did look so pretty underneath me back in high school. You think she compares us now that she's with you?"

I don't consciously make the decision to drop my stick and grab him by the jersey, but before I know it I'm doing it. He's surprised by my attack, probably because I'm usually a gentle giant and I haven't snapped back at him ever, and it's an advantage for me because I have him down on the ice before he can even retaliate. I use the palm of my hand to push his helmet off, then get one good punch in before someone is pulling me off of him and I realize two seconds later that it's Soren and not a ref.

"You don't ever speak about Cami like that, you understand me?" Soren yells as he straddles Troy and throws two solid punches. The referees are trying to break up the fighting, but I'm not about to help as I watch Soren stand up for my girl. He's holding Troy down by pushing on his chest. "I said, do you understand?"

Troy spits at Soren, so he throws another punch and repeats the question. All around us, the other players have started fighting in order to keep the refs busy and it's utter chaos.

"Damn, fine I understand. Get the hell off of me." Then and only then does Soren let the refs pull him off of Troy. He heads off of the ice to get cleaned up, and he needs it considering the multiple blows to the face. Soren grabs me and pulls me into a hug, taking me completely off guard.

"I heard him talking shit. I'm sorry he said that stuff."

"Thanks for having my back."

"Always, man."

I receive a two minute penalty, and Soren gets five. As we skate over to the penalty box, I go looking for my girl. The moment we lock eyes she takes in a sharp breath. I can tell she's worried because her shoulders are up towards her ears and Alana has her hand placed on her back, rubbing soothingly. Mia looks less worried and more impressed. I catch her smiling at Soren and I know they're just fine.

I smile at Cami and send her a wink. She mouths the words, "You good?" I nod and she returns the gesture, taking a deep breath and sitting back down. I desperately want to leave the game and go to her, hug her and tell her everything. Suddenly these secrets I've been keeping seem minute in comparison to everything she and I have going on.

I get this overwhelming feeling of wanting her to know me fully and completely, and this high school situation is part of that. I don't want to let it define me and my relationships any more, and I vow to tell her everything. Tonight.

CHAPTER 39

Charlie

WE WON FOUR TO ONE, WHICH WAS A NICE WAY TO END the night after everything that happened. Thankfully, Troy and I didn't have any other contact, and it felt like a weight lifted when the game was over. It'll likely come back the next time we play them, but I'm glad it's over for now.

I head back to the locker room and take a quick shower. As the guys pile in after me and undress, doing the same thing, I take note of the fact that I don't feel as pent up about this situation as I normally would. Typically, I would constantly be watching my back and looking over my shoulder. I used to skip showers after games or use a washcloth to clean up just a little bit before going home and showering there. It was disgusting, but I was terrified.

I know I have Cami and Sophie and their endless encouragement to get closer to my teammates to thank for that. I take a deep breath, relishing in the way the air feels filling my lungs, and finish up before getting dressed. I put on a pair of navy blue track pants, a gray T-shirt, and a Rangers branded athletic jacket. Normally I would throw on a pair of plain sweats and go straight home, but they asked me to do a post game interview tonight. I used to hate press, but I've been trying to embrace it more recently. Tonight though, I just want to go check on Cami and make sure she's okay. Not to mention, I know they're going to ask about the situation with Troy.

I head out to the press box and stand in front of the blue backdrop, then wait for Lydia—our PR manager—to start allowing reporters to ask questions. A few minutes later, Adams takes his place at my side and I settle a little knowing he's out here with me.

"Cade, can you tell me what happened out there tonight with Price? He seemed to really have it out for you." I'm thankful this guy doesn't seem to immediately be painting me in a bad light, I can use that to my advantage, but right before I am about to answer Lydia interjects.

"Let's keep the questions to game play, everyone."

"Actually, I don't mind answering." She looks over at me with wide eyes, probably hoping I would just shut my mouth. I don't want to cause her any trouble, but I do want to stand up for my girl. *But she isn't yours, not really,* my brain supplies. I decide to ignore that and proceed anyway. "Price and I have some history, old history, and usually it doesn't get in the way of the game. Tonight, he decided to bring someone I care about into it and, well, you saw how that turned out."

"But you didn't do most of the fighting, Soren Wright did. How is he involved?"

"Soren is a good guy," Adams says from my left. "And any of us would've stepped in had we been close enough to hear. No one messes with one of us, and Cami is one of us."

I don't bristle at him saying her name, everyone knows who she is because of social media. I do feel somewhat shocked by his claiming of her, though. I never really felt like I was claimed myself, so for them to welcome me as a part of their family and extend that to my girlfriend, well it's not a feeling I'm familiar with. I thought I had that once with my teammates, but I was wholly and completely wrong. I fight the voice that tells me this is the same situation, I know it isn't, and instead I smile at my team-mate and reach over giving him a squeeze on his shoulder.

"Thanks, man. I appreciate that."

"Any time."

After that, the questions move away from relationships and focus back on the game and our strategy. Adams takes those on for a little while and I chime in, trying to be every bit of the old version of me as possible. It's getting easier and easier.

"Charlie!"

I hear her voice and immediately turn in her direction, like a moth to a flame. She's waiting by the doors we usually come out of and has started walking towards me, while Alex and Alana hang back a bit. I didn't expect her to wait, especially because I had to do post game stuff, but I'm happy she's here.

As soon as I turn toward her, she takes off in the cutest little jog towards me. On instinct, I drop my bag and wrap my arms around her middle as she jumps into them. Her arms come up around me, and she buries her face in my neck. I life her up, squeezing her to me, and then set her feet gently back onto the group without letting go of her.

"I was so worried," she whispers into my neck.

"I'm good, baby."

"I know, but it didn't look good. It looked really bad Charlie. What happened?"

"I'll tell you, but not here, okay?"

She pulls back to look into my eyes, and she must be satisfied for now with whatever she finds there. She nods and leans in to press a chaste kiss to my lips. I deepen it just slightly before letting her go and turning towards my sister. She pulls me into a desperate hug and squeezes me three times.

"You scared me out there, you big jerk," she says before she pulls away and shoves my shoulder hard.

"Hey, it wasn't my fault. Everythings good, I promise."

She just rolls her eyes. Alex steps up and clasps my hand in his before pulling me to him and slapping me on the back.

"Good game, man."

"Thanks. You all didn't have to stay."

"Well, Cami wouldn't leave and we weren't going to leave her out here alone."

I swear I see her cheeks flush before she looks down at the ground, but it's dark so I could be imagining things. Soren and Mia come out behind us, he had to stay back a little longer because Coach wanted to talk with him about the fight. I told him I would go in with him, but he declined. He slaps me on the back as he walks up, and Mia goes to hug Cami.

"How'd it go?"

"Fine. I explained the situation. He understood."

"Good, I'm glad to hear that. Thanks."

"Any time," he looks me in the eye and I know he means it. "You doin' okay, Cam?"

"I'm good. Thank you, Soren, for everything. I don't know what was said out on the ice tonight but I know you were stepping in to defend someone and I'm grateful for that."

"Like I said to Cade, any time. You both are family."

Our eyes meet and she smiles at me as if to say, *see how nice it is when you have people to look after you?*

"Don't think we're planning on going out tonight, pretty exhausted," Soren says.

"Yeah us either, I'm wiped. Are you ready?" I ask, looking over to Cami.

"Yep, let's go home."

CHAPTER 40

THE CAR RIDE HOME IS QUIET AND TENSE. CHARLIE doesn't even ask me if I want to go to my place, he knows I would say no. The threat of some kind of danger from paparazzi is long gone at this point; they don't seem interested in my whereabouts right now, but neither of us have talked about me moving back.

His big hand rests on my upper thigh, and mine on top of his. I rub the back of his hand and his forearm gently as we make our way back to his place. Everything in me wants more information, but the air feels fragile. Like if either of us speaks, something might happen. I have desperately wanted more information from him about everything that happened in high school for years. Not just me, but Alana too. We have had many conversations about the way he changed so abruptly since it all happened, but he's been extremely closed off about the whole thing.

I know that whatever happened in the past is related to what happened tonight, because the only thing he would tell us is that we needed to stay away from Troy Price, but other than that I'm completely in the dark. He said he would tell me about it, and I'm grateful, but I can't help but wonder if he's going to keep dancing around the full truth. I hope he'll tell me the whole story starting from his junior year when everything changed.

His phone rings over the bluetooth and his dad's name pops up on the screen. He ignores it, as usual.

As we pull into the parking garage, he sends a soft smile my way that I am sure is meant to be reassuring, and it is somewhat. I know that he's okay—I can tell by his demeanor—but I can also tell he's gearing up for something and it worries me that the truth of his trauma is going to be much worse than I imagined.

If it's not that, there's only one other thing it could be. My first thought is that he's going to stop all of this. I don't know for sure, but I have a hunch that whatever Troy said tonight had something to do with me, and I could see Charlie breaking off our arrangement in order to try and keep me safe. I don't need him to do that, but he's just that kind of guy.

I try not to worry too much until I actually have something to worry about. I know whatever he's got going on in his head, he's going to share it with me. So I gather my things and step out of the car when he holds the door open for me. We walk hand in hand up to the penthouse, no longer caring that we have no one to perform in front of here in the solitude of his home.

"Do you want tea?" I ask as we walk into the kitchen.

"Sure, that would be great. I'm going to put this stuff away and then we can talk in the living room?"

"That sounds good," I say as I turn away from him and towards the counter before pulling down two mugs. He steps up behind me and wraps his arms around my middle, pulling me back into him. He just holds me there for a minute, taking deep breaths.

"I love those mugs," he says over my shoulder.

"I know. This was one of the best trips." He takes one out of my hand and we look at them. We got them on a trip we took with Alana a few summers ago to Florida. We went to a sea turtle conservatory and we were so touched by the story of one of the sea turtles named Gili. All of the purchases we made went towards their efforts, so we each bought two mugs with Gili's picture on them.

He places the mug back down next to the other and spins me around, hugging me close to him. I let my eyes fall shut and bury my face in his chest, then after a few seconds he presses a kiss into my hair and lets me go.

As I turn back around to make the tea, I can't stop thinking about how this silly little routine has become so second nature to us. It must be because we were such close friends before we started all of this, but we went from friends to fake dating to whatever this is now seamlessly. I mean sure, maybe it was a little weird at first, but I don't even second guess the quick innocent kisses or the way his eyes linger on me a little too long when we're alone. It should be scary, but it isn't. I'm not scared of the feeling, but I am scared of losing him. Of losing whatever this thing is that we have between us.

I put the kettle on to brew and as that is heating up, grab two bags of chamomile tea from the cabinet. Charlie started drinking it after games to wind down from the adrenaline. I suggested it a little while ago, back before all of this started when he told me he sometimes couldn't sleep after a game despite being so exhausted. It's always calmed me down, so I figured I would suggest he give it a try. I guess it worked, because I've noticed him drinking it while I've been staying here.

I take the two mugs over to the living room and sit them down on the coffee table, then head to my room to change out of the jersey and into something comfier. I go for a pink set of boxer shorts and a butter soft shirt, then slide on my slippers and go back into the living room. I find him sitting there looking down at his phone, and have to force myself not to stand and stare. He's wearing a pair of gray sweatpants and a plain black T-shirt, which sounds simple but he looks absolutely delicious. I remind myself we have a serious conversation to have, and that helps bring a little clarity back to my mind.

"You look so good in that, but I do miss the jersey dress. I didn't get to appreciate it enough tonight."

"Don't worry, superstar. I'll wear it for you again."

"I'm holding you to that. Come, sit."

I cross the room and sit down on the couch next to him. He grabs my tea and hands it to me. I wrap my hands around it, letting the warmth seep into my fingers and soothe the anxious feelings bubbling up inside me. I'm not entirely sure where this conversation is headed, but he seems far too calm for a breakup so hopefully not in that direction.

Listen to me, *a breakup*. We haven't even made this official and I'm worried about him breaking up with me.

"So, tonight was something," I say before taking a sip.

"Yeah, it was. You deserve an explanation, and I'm going to give you one. But I need you to be patient with me because this is hard for me to talk about. I haven't ever told anyone the stuff I'm about to tell you, and that's scary, so it might take me a minute to get it out."

My heart breaks at the gentle way he is asking for my grace. He looks vulnerable and self-conscious and those are not two descriptors I would ever use for this man. Quiet and reserved, yes, but vulnerable? Never. He has always been the solid rock of our trio, even when things were hard for him he never disappeared or stopped showing up and protecting us.

"You can take all the time you need. I'm here to listen."

He nods his head and takes another drink of his tea before taking a deep breath.

"So, I think I need to start back in high school, when things got weird, for this all to make sense. I know you know something happened, because things changed, and it's honestly silly and I probably blew it way out of proportion but—"

"I'm going to stop you right there," I interrupt and place my hand on his knee. "You can tell me absolutely anything, but don't downplay your emotions or what happened and call them silly.

Whatever went down, no matter what that was or how big or small someone might think it is, it was a big deal to you. That's all that matters."

"You're right. Thanks." He takes another deep breath. "So you know I was captain in high school and had a good amount of buddies on the team. Everyone was always hanging out together and I was always spending time with them, nothing seemed off at all to me. I mean, I'm sure I pissed a few of them off here and there but it was high school and we were playing a sport together so that was bound to happen. Regardless, I felt really secure on that team. I thought I had earned the guys' respect and friendship and I was excited to head into senior year with them."

"I remember. You were always very loud and outgoing and there were people over at your house all the time. You almost never hung out with Alana and I."

His eyes hold a sadness in them and I almost wish I never would have interjected, but I guess no matter what, this story would have brought that out in him.

"Yeah. So one day after practice I was in the locker room alone. I stayed late to run a few drills and brush up on a few things because we heard that there might be a few college coaches attending the next game and I wanted to be prepared. It was rare that they came, so it was important to do well.

"Anyway, I had just finished showering and getting dressed in one of the stalls and I heard this booming. It took me a second to realize it was a group of people running. The noise kept getting louder as they got closer, and I realized they were heading towards where I was. I'm not sure why, but my first instinct was to hide. I backed myself into the corner of the stall and waited for what felt like forever just praying that whoever it was would pass by me. I don't know how I knew it was bad, they were just running, but something in me knew I needed to try and get away."

"That must have been terrifying," I interject and he smiles sadly at me.

"It was. Eventually, they found me and flung the curtain back. At first I was relieved because it was a group of guys from the team headed up by Troy, but when I saw their faces I realized they weren't there to be my buddies. I got to my feet so fast, but they pounced on me and forced me back to the floor."

He stops at this point to take a few deep breaths and run his hand through his hair. I set my tea down and climb into his lap, wanting to be closer. I sit with my legs draped over his lap, and he gathers me in his arms before placing a sweet kiss to my hair and continuing.

"They said a bunch of nasty stuff, stuff I really don't need to repeat, but the gist was that all I had was hockey, I was too showy and prideful and arrogant, and I didn't have any talents beyond what I could do on the ice. They brought my parents into it, saying they only loved me for my hockey ability, and of everything they said I knew that was true."

"Your parents love you, Charlie."

"Yeah, as long as I play a good game and keep bringing in money. They don't care about me or Alana or how we are, all they care about is getting their five minutes of fame and claiming me when I do impressive things. You know how they've treated Lan."

"Yeah, I guess you're right. But still, your teammates had no right to say that stuff to you."

"They were jerks, but they told me that if I didn't step down as captain and recommend Troy they'd make me regret it. Told me I wouldn't be able to skate for any scouts if I was off the ice permanently from a career ending injury."

"They threatened you?"

"Yeah. After the initial shock of that moment in the locker room, I decided I wasn't going to let them push me around. I didn't immediately step down, but they were determined and made my life hell."

"What do you mean?" I ask in a quiet voice, unsure if I really want to know the answer.

"They started messing with me. At first it was small, they'd vandalize my locker or push my lunch off of the table and make a whole scene."

"Wait, that's not small. And why didn't I notice that any of that was happening? You didn't tell anyone?"

"We had different lunch periods, and I was cocky. I thought I could handle it on my own and if I stuck it out they'd eventually give it up. I was wrong though. After a few weeks of stuff like that, they started doing bigger things. Troy ran me off the road once, then scratched my car the next morning. They framed me for cheating and I was suspended for a few games. I knew it was time to give it up when they threatened to mess with Alana."

"Oh, Charlie."

"Yeah." He runs his hands through his hair and breathes out a rough sigh. "Troy told me if I didn't do what they wanted, they'd start doing the same stuff to her. He said they wouldn't stop until she was expelled, and I couldn't let them do that. I walked into the coach's office half an hour later."

"If it was so bad, why not just quit the team?"

"Well, there was no way my dad would have let me quit. Hockey was everything to him, plus I didn't want to leave the team altogether. All I had was hockey and Alana, and eventually you." He smiles down at me. I have a hard time returning it. The churning in my stomach only gets worse by the minute and I have to remind myself that he's here now and he's doing so well and he's okay.

"So, I stepped down and recommended Troy. Coach made him captain the next week and I shut up and put my head down and did my job on the ice. It was like this total one eighty for me because I thought I had all these friends and could trust them, and they just betrayed me like it was nothing. It really messed me up, that's why it's been so hard for me to trust any of my teammates over the years."

"But you're getting better at that," I say as I reach up and swoop back some of his dirty blond hair from his eyes.

"You're helping me."

"You're helping yourself. I am more than happy to be along for the ride, but you're doing the work all on your own."

"Maybe. But you're making it easier for sure," he says and I smile.

"Why didn't you tell anyone? Your parents or Alana or your coach?"

"I was a kid. They said if I told anyone they would make Alana's life hell and I couldn't risk it. I took care of it on my own."

"And you've kept it a secret all these years?"

"I was embarrassed. I had everything—friends, captain, a bright future, a solid social calendar—and just like that it was all gone. I just sort of closed in on myself and didn't want to make anyone else deal with my issues, so I kept them to myself."

"I understand why you felt like you had to handle it alone, but we love you. We want to be there for you, no matter what. The only people who should be embarrassed by this story are the jerks from high school who thought it was cool of them to beat down one of the nicest guys in the world."

"Thanks for saying that," he says with a sad smile.

"You're not alone anymore," I say, taking his hand in mine and squeezing. "You've got me now. Let me carry some of the burden with you."

"Thank you, Cam," he says.

I smile at him. "So what happened with Troy tonight?"

He groans in frustration and shakes his head. "He said some shit about you, basically insinuating that you two were involved back in the day. Got pretty nasty and I got one punch in before Soren pulled me off of him and took over. Told him not to ever speak about you like that."

"Wow, that's really kind of him."

"It was, and I'm glad he did it because if he hadn't I probably would have kept going and I don't know if I would have stopped. After all the shit he pulled in high school and then trying to stir stuff up now, I was beyond frustrated." He hesitates before asking his next question. "Were you two ever involved?"

"Troy and I?" He nods. "No. I don't think I've spoken more than two words to the man. He clearly was trying to get a rise out of you. He's full of bullshit."

"Woah, curse alert."

"I'm serious."

"I know you are. You broke the no cussing rule."

I roll my eyes at him. "I'm sorry he said that and I am so sorry for what those guys said and did to you back in high school. I hate that you've had to hear those words over and over in your head for the past however many years, but I want to tell you that they aren't true. You are more than hockey, you're more than your ability. You are so much more, to all of your real friends and to Alana, and to me."

He stares into my eyes, then lifts his hand and places it on my cheek before sliding it back into my hair and pulling me towards him. He presses his lips to mine in the slowest and most meaningful kiss we've shared. I melt into him and follow his lead, jumping a little when his tongue slips past his lips and presses against mine. I let him deepen the kiss as he pushes me back on the couch so I'm lying beneath him, then in a moment of clarity place my hands on his chest and apply a little pressure to get him to stop. He does immediately and looks down at me quizzically.

"Is this real?" I ask in a quiet voice. I need to know if this is us pretending, or if his actions are genuine and not for some kind of scheme or lie.

"It's real, Cam. I think it's always been real with you."

I stare up at him for a few more seconds, letting the words settle in my mind and heart. I think it's always been real with him too. Smiling, I pull him back down towards me and fall into the moment of being his.

CHAPTER 41
Cami

I WAKE SLOWLY, STRETCH MY ARMS UP ABOVE MY HEAD, and then rub at the sleep in my eyes. It feels like it's pretty early in the morning—the light streaming into the room is still faint and not yet sunny. *Wait*, the light streaming into the room? My room doesn't have a big window near the bed. Where am I?

I startle as I realize there's a body next to me, and in an instant the entire night comes back to me. My conversation with Charlie last night, his story, the kiss, *I think it's always been real with you*.

I squeeze my eyes shut and try to fend off the panic, but I'm not successful. I took things further with my best friend's brother last night, with *my* best friend. I sit up and breathe a sigh of relief when it doesn't wake him. I swing my legs over the side of the bed and place my head in my hands before taking a few deep breaths and trying to calm down.

The last twenty-four hours have felt very real and up until now I have run *very, very* far from anything real.

I am terrified that if I let him in and make him a permanent fixture in my life, I will eventually get bored and want to move on to someone else. The thing is, he's already been a permanent fixture in my life for the last handful of years and I haven't wanted to change that. He's stuck around longer than any man in my life ever has.

I try to push aside the words my family have spoken over me throughout my youth and young adulthood. I never decided getting "bored" of people and things was a personality trait of mine. It's just what my mom has always said, and I've allowed her viewpoint of me to become my reality. I don't want that to be the story here. I want to feel confident in my decision, whether that is to keep things platonic between he and I or whether that is to take this into something serious. I want to make that decision for myself.

About the time I start to get my breathing back in order, two arms wrap around me and pull me back into the middle of the bed. I giggle at the way he manhandles me, but I don't fight it as he places one hand on either side of me and buries his face in my neck placing little kisses there.

"You freaking out on me?"

"Only a little bit."

He stares down at me and tries to bring his head down for a kiss, but I block it and he ends up kissing my palm.

"Morning breath."

He rolls his eyes then sits back beside me.

"Tell me what's going on in that pretty head of yours," he says as he brushes the hair from my face. I turn on my side to face him and prop my head up on my fist. He mirrors the position.

"My mom always says I get bored of things and drop them, and that's why I can't ever hold down a relationship."

"You know I think the stuff your mom says about you is bullshit. I love her, but that's just not true."

"What do you mean?"

"I don't think you get bored, that isn't a fair word to use. That implies that you decide you aren't entertained by someone or something anymore, so you drop it and move on to something flashier. You aren't getting bored, you just know what you want and you refuse to settle for anything less."

The look on my face must communicate that I don't fully understand what he's saying, so he explains further.

"Let's take the last three guys you've dated. First"—he ticks it off on his fingers—"Asshole Asher, way too preppy of a name by the way. That guy didn't pay on your first date, then you gave him a second chance and went on a second one to which he showed up over a half hour late and *still* didn't pay."

"Yeah that sucked."

"Second, douchebag Daniel. All he talked about was politics and he still lived at home. Which isn't a crime in and of itself, but that wasn't what you were looking for in a partner. And finally third, bad breath Benji. Enough said."

I explode in a fit of giggles and he looks pleased with himself.

"All that to say, it's not that you got bored with those guys, you just knew after one or two dates that they were not anywhere near what you were looking for. You don't get bored, you just have standards."

"You sure do pay a lot of attention to the guys I date."

He blushes at that and rolls his eyes. "It's impossible not to, it's all you and Alana talk about."

"Mmmhmm, sure. That may be true for relationships, but my mom seems to think that's true about my entire life, like my hobbies."

"Babe, tell me why it would be a bad thing that you have lots of hobbies? There is absolutely nothing wrong with trying a bunch of different things, or hell even people, until you find something that makes you happy. It is okay to want to find something worth keeping."

"Hmm," is my only response. What he's saying makes sense, but it's hard to break through the words that have been said about me since I was a young girl.

"So the question is, do you think I'm worth keeping?" he asks.

The question breaks me, because how could he ever think he wouldn't be?

"Of course, more than worth it."

"I'm glad to hear that," he says as his face breaks out in a grin. "Can we press play on that conversation we paused before?"

I take a deep breath before replying, "Sure."

"I know this is a weird situation on all fronts. Alana is involved, plus the press, and the fact that this was fake to begin with. It all started a bit rocky, but I'm ready to try it out for real if you are."

"What if it doesn't work?"

"If it doesn't work, we'll figure that out when we get there. There's no way to predict all of the ways this might go, but if we're both honest about how we're feeling and when we need reassurance we can make sure we do it right."

I nod my head, still feeling just a little bit cautious about all of this. I want nothing more than to fall into a permanent and serious relationship with the most stable and respectful man in my life, but the doubts won't fully quiet. I'm sure they never will completely, and I might just have to be okay with that. He must sense my hesitation, because he speaks again.

"How about this, why don't we take the time between now and the trade deadline and try this out for real? We'll take away all of the performing and any pretenses that we might be faking and see how it goes. Then we can re-evaluate when we get to the end of our agreement period and see if we want to keep going."

That sounds reasonable and gives me some small semblance of relief to know we're only making a decision to try until the wedding, then see where things are.

"I think that works. I can do that."

"Okay, good. Now come here," he says, pulling me into him and cuddling close. "I'm not ready to let you get up just yet."

CHAPTER 42

Cami

BESTIE FRIEND

Why aren't you picking up the phone?

ME

OMG sorry I was getting ready for knitting club

BESTIE FRIEND

Oh, fun!

ME

Yeah, I'm excited. I also think we need to get together soon, we probably need to talk about a few things

BESTIE FRIEND

I don't know whether to be excited or nervous.

ME

Maybe a little bit of both

I SHOVE MY KNITTING SUPPLIES INTO MY BAG AND RUN out the door, heading to the subway. I haven't been able to attend knitting club with the ladies in a while, and when I got a call from the retirement home demanding my presence I knew it had been too long.

I am running a few minutes late, and I know I'll be getting some comments from Gladys about it, but I'm almost excited for them at this point. I miss these women when I don't get to spend time with them. I finished my strawberry cardigan the other night while Charlie and I were watching a movie, so it's time to start something new which is always intimidating.

I push through the front door and smile at Shauna before heading to the community room. Four sets of eyes and a heavy silence meet me when I pass through the threshold. They all look equally relieved, happy, and angry. I hesitate when no one speaks, standing near the door but not coming inside. Are they mad at me?

"What are you doing just standing in the door, girl?" Gladys says.

"C-can I come in?"

"Well, of course you can," Linda replies.

"We're just a little shocked to see a celebrity in our midst," Rhonda chimes in.

"What do you mean?" I ask as I move into the room and over to the couches where the women sit.

"Shauna has been keeping us up to date on your romantic escapades," Emery says. "We've been seeing the news articles with you and Charlie and all of your social media posts."

First, I'm shocked that they have had any sort of access to the articles and posts that have been made about Charlie and I. These ladies have always been disconnected from the outside world aside from the few news channels they watch, and news about my relationship is not featured on those channels.

Second, I panic when I realize that they all know that this relationship is fake. They cannot tell anyone about our fake relationship, and I didn't think it would be a big deal when I told them because who would talk to them about it? I guess I didn't think through that one enough.

"Did anyone say anything to Shauna about the ahem, situation, with Charlie and I?"

"You mean that it ain't real?"

"Gladys," Linda exclaims as she swats Gladys on the arm.

"What? She told us it was a secret. No, we haven't said anything."

"Okay, good," I say. "I, um, missed you ladies."

"We missed you, too, sweetheart, these three are just stubborn old hags."

"Well, now I'm more mad at Linda than I was at Cami."

Linda shoots me a wink and I smile at her, falling back into the familiarity of spending time with them. I stand and pass hugs around, and the ice in the room slowly melts. I pull my materials out and get comfy in my seat as they finish up whatever conversation they were having when I arrived. A few minutes later, the interrogation begins.

"So," Emery starts. "Do you care to give us a little update on this whole situation you've got going on?"

"What do you want to know?"

"Everything," Rhonda answers.

"Well, I've been dating Charlie for almost two months."

"Fake dating," Gladys says. It stings a little to even hear her say it, but it's the truth.

"Right, fake dating. It's been going well and the public response has been fantastic, so I think it's helping."

"And with your family? Has it helped there?"

"Well, I haven't really spoken with them much lately. But it will come in handy when the wedding festivities start to happen."

"You just make sure you're getting your end of the deal too," Linda says.

"Oh trust me," I reply. "I am getting plenty out of the deal."

Silence.

"Dear," Rhonda says. "What do you mean by that?"

"A lot has happened."

"You're being very detailed with your answers," Linda jokes.

"Just tell us," Emery says.

"So, things have been going really well. We've been getting closer and a little bit ago I moved into his penthouse."

Gladys chokes on the sip of water she just took.

"What do you mean you *moved in*?" Linda asks as she pats Gladys's back as she coughs violently.

"The paparazzi found out where I lived and he didn't think I would be safe there alone, so he wanted me to stay at his place. We weren't staying in the same room...until last night."

"Okay, I am seriously going to throw you out the window if you do not start telling us the entire story from top to bottom. Do not leave out a detail, do not say some cryptic sentence with no context. I am too old for this," Linda says. I bristle at the directness in her tone, but then I start giggling and I can't stop.

"Oh no, she's clearly drunk on love. This isn't good," Emery says.

"I'm sorry," I say in between laughs. I take a second and gather myself. "Okay, I'll tell the whole story. So we started fake dating and things were good. We established some guidelines of when we could be affectionate and how far that would go and everything was going well, but once I moved into his place the lines blurred."

"Naturally," Gladys says.

"Right. I mean, I tried to hold out but it was like we were playing house. Little by little the kisses only in public started happening in private, too, and cuddling on the couch became the norm."

"I knew this would happen," Rhonda chimes in. I ignore her and keep going.

"I went to his game last night and he played against a high school rival. It got nasty."

"Oh we saw. We've been watching his games," Gladys says.

"Aw, that's nice."

"Yeah, yeah keep going."

"So after the game we had a talk and things...escalated. He shared some big things with me and we connected and one thing led to another..."

"And you banged."

"Oh my gosh, Rhonda, don't put it like that. Ew."

"What, is that not what the kids are saying these days?"

"That's not what *I'm* saying these days," I say with a laugh.

"So are you two just dating for real now? Or still fake but with benefits? What is going on?"

"Honestly, that's a good question. We had a conversation and he suggested we try out being real until the end of our arrangement and re-evaluate things then. I think he was just trying to help me feel better."

"You feeling a little spooked?"

"Just a little. It's a lot and I don't want to ruin anything especially because he's Alana's brother. If something happened and it ended badly it would tear our group apart and might even ruin Alana and I's friendship."

"You know good and well Alana wouldn't let that ruin your friendship," Emery supplies.

"You're right. It just makes me nervous."

"That's understandable. So, you'll do what he suggested and try it out and then see how you feel after the wedding," Linda says.

"Yep, that's the plan."

"When are you going to bring this boy so we can meet him? If it's turning into something a little more serious."

"Well, you know how bingo is happening tomorrow?" They all nod. I can tell they don't really understand where I'm going with this. "He's going to host it."

"Like, he's calling the numbers?"

I nod.

"You better stay close to him, sweetie, these women in here will pounce," Gladys says and I laugh.

"I'll be sure to let anyone who gets close know who he belongs to, don't worry."

"Oh, this is going to be fun."

CHAPTER 43

Charlie

Brookdale Retirement Home is a surprisingly nice facility. I don't know why, but I imagined cobwebs and coughing elderly. What I get, though, is a lively room full of residents who will not stop trying to get my attention. I haven't even gotten ten steps into the event room before they swarm me, and Cami threads her arm through mine and sticks close. It's pretty obvious that she's staking her claim, and I secretly love it. I'll take her cuddled close to me and claiming me as hers any day of the week.

These last twenty-four hours have been surreal, and even though I know she's hesitant, I am on cloud nine. This is going to work between us, I just need to wait for her to get to a place where she's comfortable admitting that fact to herself, and I am willing to wait however long until that happens.

Telling her about my trauma was difficult, but it's brought this lightness that I haven't felt in a long, long time. Having someone else help carry your burdens is a priceless gift that I haven't afforded myself in, well, ever. I thought I might regret telling her and that it would change things between us, that she would feel bad for me and start treating me differently, but I should've known better.

Cami knows me inside and out, and she knows exactly what I need when I need it. She knew I didn't need her pity, and she didn't give it to me. She let me know she was there and made me feel loved and like I wasn't alone. I feel so grateful to have found someone who takes the time to really know me.

"Okay, let him at least get inside the room. Jeepers, you all are like vultures."

"Jeepers?" I whisper to her.

"You seriously can't cuss in a room full of old people. They'll attack."

"But still, I don't feel like jeepers was the right word to use." I laugh. She rolls her eyes and I follow her lead into the room.

There are various rectangle tables set up all around the space with soft cream tablecloths draped over them. Small bunches of four or five roses sit in the center of each one, and a bingo card is placed in front of each of the chairs. At the front of the room, there is a microphone stand and a table with a large cage bowl placed on top. All of the plastic balls that rest inside have different combinations of letters and numbers to call out as you play the game.

When Cami mentioned that she'd have me volunteer here, I assumed I would just help with the dinner rush or something. I didn't imagine some sort of "celebrity" hosted Bingo game. I like Bingo, though, so I'm not complaining about that.

She leads me over to a group of women sitting at one of the tables in the front. There are four of them sitting there, and I realize these must be the people in her knitting club. Two of them look so similar that I know they must be the sisters—Rhonda and Emery. I greet them first, then move to the left to the one with a kind smile and soft eyes. I guess Linda, and I'm right. Finally, I face Gladys and I know it is her by the way Cami described her to me. She told me she'd be hard on me, and it looks like she wasn't joking because the glare she's sending my way could burn.

"Hello, you must be Gladys," I say as I reach out to shake her hand. She stares at it for a second before finally putting me out of my misery and reaching forward to take it in hers.

"Hello, young man. Thanks for coming out today," she says.

"You're quite welcome. Any time I can spend an afternoon with ladies as lovely as you I am all over it."

She lets a small smile escape before she quickly puts her scary mask back on, but I take it as a win.

"You all know Charlie," Cami says.

"We watch you play hockey every time we can," Emery says.

"Well, that's very flattering. Hopefully I don't leave you disappointed."

"Oh, never," Rhonda replies.

"Especially not when you put up that fight for our girl. We liked you even more after that."

I smile over at Cami and she rubs my back. We hear someone from behind tell us it's time to begin the game, so she sits down with the other ladies and I make my way to the table in the front where the organizers tell me how to call the game.

About ten numbers in, the room starts to grow tense. People are glancing over at other people's boards and frantically checking and double checking their own. The prize for this game is a $25 Amazon gift card, so I don't blame them.

"B10...O4...G8."

"BINGO," someone shouts from the back corner of the room. I walk back to where the woman is sitting and check her card.

"It looks like we have a winner."

There are equal amounts of groans and cheers in the room as everyone clears their boards for another round, and after a few more the organizer lets everyone know there is cake and punch being served if anyone would like to stick around. Most people do, and I make my way back over to the table Cami is at.

When I reach her, I lean down and press a kiss to her lips. She smiles up at me and I have to remind myself that it isn't just the two of us here. We are in a room full of people. When I look up at the rest of the women at the table, they're all smiling at us affectionately. It makes me happy to see people who want good things for her.

"Sorry I couldn't rig it for you, Gladys."

"I'll forgive you for it this time," she replies with a wink.

"You're a pretty good caller, you should come do this more often," Rhonda remarks.

"Oh, you just like to stare at him," Cami replies. I feel the blush creep up to my cheeks and the women break out in a fit of giggles.

"Now, Charlie. Are you taking care of our girl here?"

"I'm doing my best, Emery. I hope it's up to her standard."

"She has high ones," Linda says.

"I wouldn't want it any other way," I reply. They seem to be happy with my answer and move on to start asking about hockey and when the next game is.

"We have one against the Capitals in Washington in a few days. Should be a pretty good game."

"Do you ever get nervous before these games?" Linda asks. "I think I would be a mess."

"I used to get pretty nervous, but I don't much anymore. I know my guys have my back."

Cami smiles over at me, the pride clear in her eyes. I feel so grateful for where I am and how far I've come in the last few months, and a huge portion of that is all thanks to her.

We continue to have light conversation until the room begins to clear out and the women announce they need to head back for their afternoon nap. We say our goodbyes and Cami promises to be at the next club meeting before we start heading out through the front door.

"I think you really impressed them."

"Really? I guess that's good."

"It is. I was a little worried they'd really hound you, but they took it easy."

"I was too, but it would have been fine either way. I'm glad you've got people looking out for you."

"Thanks, me too."

We make it to the car and as soon as my phone connects to bluetooth, the car screen lights up with an incoming call. It's my mom, and I hesitate before pressing the button to accept the call. Cami is quiet next to me, and I know she won't say anything. I haven't spoken to either of my parents since this whole thing with her began, and I'm a little nervous about what she's going to say.

"Hey, Mom."

"Charlie. It's nice to hear from you."

"You called me, Mom."

"Well, it's still good to hear your voice."

"How are you?"

"I'm doing alright. Missing my boy, you know. How is hockey?"

I roll my eyes and take an exasperated breath. Most people would think it's kind of their parents to ask how their hockey season is going, especially when they play professionally, and I would feel that way about my mom if this wasn't the only topic we ever talked about. All my parents have ever cared about is hockey.

Even back in high school when Troy and the guys turned on me and I became a shell of the person I was before, they hardly noticed. I don't think either of them asked what was going on or why I all of a sudden stayed home every Friday night and came straight back after games. I kept playing well, so they didn't ask questions.

"Hockey is fine. Did you need something?" She scoffs at my abrasiveness, but honestly I don't care. I love my mom, I really do, but as I've gotten older I have grown more and more resentful of the way she and my dad treated my sister and I. They never ask how she is or check up on her, and the only reason they do it to me is because of my career.

"Well, it's been about a year since we've seen you. I wanted to see if you wouldn't mind coming over for dinner."

"To Florida?" I ask.

"Oh, no. Your father and I have been at the house outside of the city for a few weeks." *A few weeks?* They've been an hour and a half away from my sister and I for a few weeks and they haven't made any attempt to let us know.

My parents bought a small home in Long Island when I signed on with the Rangers. They wanted to have a place to be during the season so they could come to our home games, but clearly that hasn't worked out the way they intended. They're a short distance away and I had no idea.

"No." Cami's head snaps in my direction when I answer, probably because I did so extremely quickly. She widens her eyes at me and I shrug.

"Oh, come on, honey. I miss you so much. I haven't gotten to hug you in, gosh I couldn't even tell you how long."

"Mom, my schedule is really busy right now. Did you see if Alana wanted to go to dinner?" If my sister had already agreed, I would absolutely say yes. I know, though, that she didn't receive the same invite because if she had she would have told me.

"No. Isn't she in Paris for work?"

"She came home. Like a month ago." This just irks me even further and proves my point. They do not care about us, and I'm honestly confused why they even want to have this dinner.

"Oh, well that's good news. I just really miss you sweetheart and I know you're dating Cami." I look over at her and she stares back at me. She grimaces a little, as if to say *uh oh*. I mouth, *it's fine*, and continue on with the conversation.

"I am."

"Why don't you bring her to dinner? We knew her a long time ago, but I'm sure she's changed since then."

"That, and you were never home."

"Speaking of, are you free in the next few weeks? Your dad and I are headed off to the Bahamas soon."

"Of course you are. Mom, I really don't know if—"

"Well, I'll just send you some dates that work and you let me know when you'll come. I love you, honey, bye bye."

The line goes dead before I can even respond, and I look over at Cami in utter disbelief.

"I can't believe she just did that."

"Looks like we're going to dinner with your parents."

February

CHAPTER 44
Cami

COCO

Mom asked me to ask you to bring her a water

ME

I just landed. Does she want me to stop by somewhere? Or does she think I can magically conjure up a bottle of water?

COCO

I don't know, I'm the bride. She just asked for water.

ME

I JUMP ONE, TWO, THREE TIMES AS I TRY TO SHIMMY THE dress over my hips. The dress my sister chose for her bridesmaids is a beautiful forest green, but it's made in this silky material that has zero stretch. Even though this was made specifically to my measurements, getting into it is a struggle.

I finally get it over my hips and pull the sleeves up onto my shoulders. The wedding is later this month, and even though Florida "cold" is only somewhere in the low sixties, we're in long sleeves. I tried to mention that it likely wouldn't be very chilly here, but my mom and sister insisted it would. I didn't fight much after that, I'll just put on plenty of deodorant.

The attendant outside of the dressing room helps me zip up the back, and I walk out to stand in front of my mom and Colette.

"Oh, that looks lovely on you," my mom says. She stands and comes up behind me, pulling at fabric and smoothing down my hair. She places a sweet kiss on my cheek and looks at the two of us in the mirror.

"I love it, Cam. It's going to be perfect. That color is great with your skin tone and blonde hair."

"Thanks, Coco. I really like it, good pick." She smiles at me in the mirror and I smile back, happy to have made my sister happy.

"When do you think we'll get to do something like this for you?" my mom asks as she stares at our reflection. I smile at her and try my hardest not to get defensive. She means well, I know she does, but it's hard to have the same conversation over and over.

"I'm not sure, Mom."

"Well, you and Charlie sure are getting close it seems. You didn't tell us he was the boy you were seeing."

"I didn't want to say names just in case it didn't work out, but yeah it's going well."

"And, this is a real relationship?" my sister asks from the couch behind us. I turn around and furrow my brow, confused how she'd suspect that. Practically no one knows how all of this started.

"What do you mean? Why would you even ask that?"

"That isn't an answer, Cami," she says with a pitying smile.

"Okay, you want an answer, of course it's real, Colette. Why would I lie about that?" We will all just decide to completely ignore the fact that I *was* lying about that at one point.

"Well, you randomly tell us you're seeing someone and that this person is going to come to the wedding, then it ends up being someone you already spend all of your time with and consider a best friend. It's just a little hard to believe that he's all of a sudden your boyfriend."

I close my eyes and take a deep breath, then step off of the platform in front of the mirrors and cross the room to her. I love her to death, but this is honestly such an offensive question. If I was suspicious of someone lying in a situation like this, I would never in a million years ask them outright.

"We've been friends—best friends—for a long time, and after a few different life circumstances brought us closer, we realized we wanted more than friendship." That is *sort of* the truth.

"I'm so happy for you honey," my mom says as she comes to sit with us. My sister gives me a suspicious look, and I can only hope she doesn't pry any further into the details. The truth is, all of this *was* fake until it wasn't and I don't really know when it stopped being fake and started being real.

I mean, sure, we had the discussion only recently that we would try this out for real, but I think we crossed that line a while back and neither of us knows when exactly that happened. All of the small touches and conversations led us here and I can't find it in me to regret any of it.

"Okay," I say as I stand back up and go back to the mirror. "This looks good and I think it fits like a glove. Do you think it needs any additional alterations?"

"I think it looks perfect on you, sweetheart," Mom says.

"As long as you're comfortable, I think it looks great."

I wouldn't use the word comfortable when describing this dress, but it isn't awful. I step down from the mirror and head back into the dressing room to change. When I come back out into the lobby of the store my sister is waiting for me.

"Mom went to get the car. Do you have time to go grab lunch?"

"Yeah, that sounds good. Where are we going?"

"How do you feel about trying something different? There's

this new vegan restaurant that opened pretty close and I've heard great things."

"I'm always down to try something new. What kind of food is it?"

"They have all kinds of stuff. Burgers, nachos, salads, you name it. It's just all vegan."

"Sounds great. My flight doesn't leave until six so as long as I'm headed back to the airport by three-ish I should be good. I'm sorry I couldn't come to stay for longer, work is just crazy right now and I'm taking off for the wedding."

"Well, not to worry. I plan to get your opinion on a million different things in the next few hours," she says as she wraps her arm over my shoulder and pulls me into her.

I laugh and hug her back, thankful that we're on equal footing again. That's the thing about sisters, you can be on weird terms one minute and then a few minutes later you're laughing and talking about going to grab French fries. It's just a sister thing.

"I'm just going to call Charlie really quickly," I say, as I grab my phone from my purse. "He's about to get on a flight for an away game and I want to talk to him before he takes off."

"Okay, I'll let Mom know," she says with a smile.

I turn away and press his name on my phone, waiting for all of five seconds before he picks up on the second ring.

"Hey, baby."

The words make my stomach flip and I smile without even realizing I'm doing it. I used to hate the pet name baby. It felt cheesy and weird, but when Charlie says it to me it's anything but.

"Hey, superstar. You on the plane?"

"Yeah, just boarded. Is the dress fitting over? Thanks for the picture. You looked beautiful."

"Thanks. Yeah, it's over. It went well, although I think Colette may be onto us."

"What do you mean?"

"She asked if we were actually in a real relationship. I sort of freaked a little because there is absolutely no way she knows, but she said she just thought it was weird that we've been best friends for so long and since you've always been around it's hard to believe you're my boyfriend."

"I like hearing you calling me your boyfriend."

"That's seriously all you got from that?"

"No, I'm just saying I like it."

"I didn't hate it," I say with a laugh.

"So how did you respond to her?"

"I told her it was real and I'm sure she could tell I was irritated that she'd think I was lying to her. She backed off and things are fine now."

"That's good. I'm sorry you had to have that conversation. Hopefully it'll be the first and last."

"Hopefully. Who are you sitting by?"

"No one yet, but I'm assuming Soren will sit by me. We've got a thing going."

"By thing, do you mean superstition?"

"We sat together for the first time a few weeks ago and he got a hat trick that night."

"Makes sense. How long is the flight?"

"About an hour and a half, not bad."

"Not at all. Well, have a good flight and text me when you land."

"I will. You text me when you're about to take off and when you land tonight, okay?"

"You got it."

"Are you planning on watching?"

"Already purchased a wifi voucher for the flight so I don't miss anything. You know I'm always watching."

"Thanks, Cam. It means a lot. Have a good time with your mom and sister, and I'll talk to you in a little bit."

"Talk to you soon, superstar."

CHAPTER 45
Charlie

ME

ME

You see?

CAMI

See what? 😉

ME

Don't be smart with me. You know.

CAMI

OH, are you talking about the very subtle kiss you blew to me during post game interviews?

CAMI

No, I must have missed that

TONIGHT'S GAME WAS A ROUGH ONE. WE LOST, AND WE came out to try and lift our spirits but I'm not sure it's helping. My thoughts are elsewhere, on a certain blonde and what she might be doing tonight, and on the dinner we're set to have with my parents when I get back home.

I can't believe I agreed to this. I haven't seen them in a long time, and I have zero desire to. I can handle my mom, but my dad is another story. He still calls after every game—he called about an hour ago—but I continue to ignore it. I don't want to talk to him and I know he doesn't want to hear what I have to say if I was actually honest.

This is how all of our conversations go, or at least how they used to go when I picked up. He'd say hello, I'd say hello, and then he'd jump into a thirty minute unsolicited coaching session. He'd pick on every single mistake I made, like he was running down a list he wrote down. I wouldn't be surprised if he has a little notebook titled 'Charlie's mistakes.'

Then, I'd grunt in acknowledgement, he'd ask if I was even listening, I'd say 'yes, I heard you,' and then he'd say goodbye and hang up. No questions about my life, no conversation about my sister, no talk of what he's up to or how he's doing. These conversations are pure business, and after doing it for far too long I finally stopped picking up.

Cami understands why I don't answer, and she's never tried to pressure me to pick up the phone. I know, through her friendship with Alana, she's seen the way they treat us and it tears her up almost as much as it does us. The three of us, and I guess four now with Alex, are really some of the only family we have.

Soren sits next to me, his head hanging low and the light from his phone reflecting on his face as he stares down at his texts with Mia. They got into an argument before the game and he played like shit because of it. It was one of the many reasons we struggled tonight. He's been texting with her for the past hour because she doesn't want to talk on the phone, and his usual easy going demeanor has all but disappeared.

Theo is across from us, worrying his lip. His kid got sick in the middle of the night last night and his nanny called him freaking out. Apparently their fever broke a little bit ago, but they still aren't feeling very good and the dad guilt he's feeling shows plainly on his face.

It's normal that we each have a few bad nights here and there and that it shows in our game play, but it's not normal that our bad nights all fall on the *same* night.

As if it could get any worse, Josh Murphy, the rookie I can't stand, plops down in the seat next to Theo. The kid didn't do anything specific to make me hate him, but he's never been able to read the room. He constantly makes the worst comments at the worst times and I know I'm going to have to practice an insane amount of self control not to go off on him tonight. The way we're all on edge isn't helping matters.

"Is this the boring table or what? You guys are usually much more lively. Someone's grandma die?" Josh shouts over the music in the bar. I flinch at his harsh tone and loud voice.

"Dude, what if they had?" Theo asks, already done with him.

"Then that would be really effing awkward," he says before reaching over and grabbing my mostly full beer and taking a huge drink. *That* is why I hate him. He says '*effing*' instead of just using the word. He pushes the beer back towards me, and I reach out and push it back at him.

"That's yours now, man. No telling where that mouth has been," I say with a grimace.

He winks at me. "I know that's right."

"That wasn't a compliment," Soren says from my right.

I huff a laugh at him and stand. "Gonna go grab another."

By the time I make it back to the booth, beer in hand, Josh is gone and I breathe a sigh of relief. I can't deal with him tonight and I know if I was around him for too long I would just end up saying something I regret. He's awful, but he's young and imma-ture. I can only hope that with time he grows up a bit and figures it out. If he doesn't do it himself, being a public figure will shape him up real quick.

"Okay, Cade, we know Soren is having lady troubles and I'm worried about my kid, but what's your problem?" Theo asks. "You weren't bad on the ice, but you aren't looking too hot right now. It's clear your mind is somewhere else."

This is another one of those situations where, normally, I would deflect and close off. Actually, I wouldn't have ever put myself in this situation in the first place. I never went out with the guys before, so they never really checked up on me. On the rare occasion they did ask questions, I never answered straight up. I have to make a conscious decision not to fall back into those habits. These two are real friends, and I can trust them. They aren't going to turn on me.

"It's stuff with my parents," I pause and look up at each of them, gauging if they seem like they want me to go on. No one says anything, so I continue. "They basically only care about hockey."

"That's tough," Soren says under his breath.

"Yeah, it sucks. When my sister and I were younger things were okay until I started getting good. Once they realized I might actually be able to take this further than my local team, they stopped paying attention to her and started pushing all of their attention my way. I grew really resentful of that, because I've always been extremely protective of my sister."

"That's good. I'm sure she's glad she had you," Theo says as he reaches over to pat my shoulder.

"Yeah, thanks. We got really close because of all of it, but our parents drew further and further from her, so I drew away from them too. It kind of became us versus them. Eventually when we went to college, they started traveling and were gone all the time. During the holidays we would go home to an empty house with no decorations or warmth. Eventually we started coming up with our own traditions to help with the hurt. Basically, what I'm trying to say is there's a lot of baggage there."

"Sounds like it," Soren says.

"Anyway, my mom called me the other night while I was with Cami. They knew her when we lived at home because she and Alana became friends in high school, not that they cared much to actually get to know her. My mom's calls are the only ones I answer at this point, and I felt guilty that I hadn't seen them in a year and agreed to go to dinner. They asked me to bring her."

"And you haven't seen them in a year?" Theo asks. I shake my head no. "And you haven't spoken to your dad the entire time?" he asks.

"I've spoken to him a handful of times. Every once in a while I feel like I should answer out of obligation, so I've spoken to him but very little and not about anything important."

"So this is going to be quite the reunion. Are you feeling nervous?" Soren asks.

"Yeah, I mean I think so. I feel nervous and I also am so irritated that they have this hold over me. I want to be able to just cut them off and go no contact, but I also love them. My feelings are so complicated and I don't know what to do or how to act."

The table is silent, and I start to get self conscious as I wait to hear what they're going to say. Before I can get too in my head, Theo speaks.

"Have you tried to talk to them and tell them how you're feeling?"

"I haven't. I just didn't feel like I was in a place where I wanted a resolution with them, but I also know that I need to at least try before I completely shut them out."

"Do you think you're at a place now where you might be able to talk to them about all of it?" Soren asks.

I think about his question before I answer. I don't think I've been in a more healthy spot in my life than I am right now. I know a lot of the credit for that goes to Sophie for pushing me and to Cami for helping me to feel safe and actually step out and trust people. I've been opening up to my teammates, and to my girl, and I wonder if my parents might be the next right step.

"Yeah, I actually think I am. I think I owe it to myself and to them to at least try."

"And if it goes poorly and you need to draw a boundary and

stop communicating with them, then you can make that call and feel good about the effort you made," Theo says.

"I should just be coming to you two for weekly therapy sessions," I say as I take a swig of my drink.

"Careful, we'll start billing."

We all break out in laughter and I feel a lightness now that I've talked this through with them. Obviously all of my problems aren't solved. I still have to go to dinner and I still have to face them, and now I also need to have a hard conversation with them, but just talking about it makes me feel better.

I've kept things bottled up for so long, and it's freeing to be able to let some of the pressure off. I convinced myself that talking about it would only make me feel worse, that the people who I share with will only use it against me. I know now, though, that that isn't true.

"Alright, we've solved Cade's problem. Soren, do we need to start helping you type out an apology text?"

"I wouldn't turn down the help."

CHAPTER 46

BESTIE FRIEND

Wear the pink one. My mom likes pink.

ME

Alana, I feel weird about this.

BESTIE FRIEND

Come on, I'm fine. I go to therapy and talk about it there.

ME

Is that supposed to make me feel better?

BESTIE FRIEND

That I go to therapy? Yes. And you should go too.

ME

I made an appointment

BESTIE FRIEND

Omg! When? With Nicole?

ME

Yes, although I feel like it might be a little weird for us to share a therapist

BESTIE FRIEND

Shhh. Good luck tonight. You got this.

I STARE AT MY REFLECTION IN THE MIRROR AND FUSS with my hair for the millionth time. I *have* already met Charlie's parents, but this feels different. I haven't seen them since my senior year of high school, and even then they weren't around us much. They never really cared what Alana did, so we were at my house a lot.

I'm wearing a pink sweater and jeans, which feels a little too casual, but Lan and Charlie both assured me it was fine. I'm trying to clip a bracelet onto my wrist when two hands wrap around me and take the dainty chain from my fingers.

"Let me," he says. He speaks directly into my ear and it causes me to shiver. He laughs at the way I respond to his touch and proximity.

"I'm nervous," I say. Once the bracelet is fastened he drops his hands to my hips and pulls me back into him. I lean against him and lay my head back onto his shoulder. He dips his head and places a soft kiss on my forehead.

"Me too," he says. "I'm not sure how this is going to go, and I don't like you being collateral damage. I'm almost certain they had me bring you because they think it'll keep me from blowing up."

I spin in his arms so I'm facing him now. I lean back against the counter and he keeps his arms around me, slung low on my waist. Pressing up onto my toes I kiss him gently, snaking my arms up and around his neck.

"Well, then they underestimated me. I don't care if you blow up. Actually, if it's warranted I hope you *do* blow up. I'm ten toes behind you, superstar."

"Thanks, baby."

"So do we need a game plan?" I ask, ready to strategize if that's what he needs. I want to ease his discomfort and do what I can to support him. "A code word or a signal or something?"

"A signal?"

"Yeah, like when you make bunny ears or double wink or something like that, I need to make some kind of excuse to get out."

"You are something else, Cami Slate," he says before kissing me again. I push him back and pout.

"I'm serious, I need to know what to do if things go haywire."

"If things get crazy we'll leave and I'll have no problem getting us out. Don't worry about that."

Easier said than done, frankly. Everything in me is screaming to support him and help him, and one of the ways I want to do that is by planning our escape route if needed. I try to push that down though and focus on just being present. That is clearly the way he needs support right now, so I'll do my best to be that for him.

"You ready?" he asks, stepping back and moving towards the door to the bathroom.

"Yeah pretty much, I just need to put perfume on and grab my bag. I'll meet you downstairs."

I grab the perfume Charlie got for me for Christmas, it's Dior, and spray a few times making sure to get my wrists and my neck. Grabbing my bag from where I placed it on the bed, I make my way downstairs. Giovanna is cleaning up from lunch, and I smile at her as I pass through the kitchen.

"Good luck tonight, Ms. Cami."

"Thank you. I will take all the luck I can get."

"Keep an eye on him, yes? They don't treat him right."

I nod, my stomach souring at the idea that things could actually go quite badly tonight. As much as I want everything to go smoothly and for this to turn out perfectly, I can't push away the gut feeling that it isn't going to work out that way.

We climb into his car and start the drive. Their home in Long

Island is about an hour and a half away, so we turn on the music and I settle into my seat. He lets me pick the music and I shuffle a playlist of a few smaller artists I like. It's calming and exactly what I feel like we need before this dinner.

A little while later, we pull up to the house and Charlie puts the car in park. I reach over and squeeze his hand.

"You ready?"

"No, honestly."

My heart twists in my chest and I hesitate on what's best to do here. I don't want to push him, but I also want him to do this if he feels like he needs it. After thinking on it for a few seconds, I determine that I don't need to do anything but stand beside him.

"We don't have to go in. We can turn the car back on and go right back home if you want."

"Thank you," he says as he smiles over at me softly. "Let's just get this over with."

He gets out of the car and comes over to my side, opening the door for me and taking my hand as I climb out. I grab the wine I brought and we make our way to the front door. He rings the bell and after a few moments the door opens and his mom appears behind it.

Mary Cade is a petite woman with short dark brown hair. She's just as I remember her, only with a few more lines on her face. She's wearing an ankle length dress and an apron at her waist, the spitting image of the classic American housewife. Her smile is hesitant, but genuine, as she takes in her son before her.

"Oh, honey, it's so good to see you," she says as she pulls Charlie in for a hug. He stiffens at first, but eventually gives in to the embrace and hugs her back.

"Good to see you, too, Mom."

"Cami, you look just like I remember, only a little bit more mature. Aren't you beautiful?" she says as she places her hands on my shoulders and looks me up and down. She then pulls me in for a hug and I hug her back.

"It's good to see you, too, Mrs. Cade."

"Oh, please call me Mary. Come in, you two, you'll catch a cold."

It's early February, so it is pretty chilly out still. Today's high is somewhere in the forties, and we're climbing back down into the evening temperatures in the thirties.

We step into the small home and I take it in. They've had this house for years, but I haven't ever been here. The outside is navy blue with white accents, and that theme continues inside. The entry hallway breaks off to an office on the left and a half bath on the right, then further in it opens up into the living room and kitchen. It's all one room basically, just an island separating the two. A small round kitchen table sits off to the side, and another hallway in the back corner leads to what I assume is the primary and guest rooms.

Peeking out the windows by the kitchen table, I see Charlie's dad moving around outside.

"George is grilling up some hamburgers for dinner, he should be in shortly. Can I get you anything to drink?"

"Water is fine," he says. "Cami will have tea." I smile over at him, happy to have someone who knows my drink order and who wants to take care of me. It feels unreal, like I need to pinch myself to be sure it's actually happening.

A moment later, Mary hands me my tea and Charlie his water, only there's ice in his. It isn't wrong, necessarily, to put ice in someone's water, but he hasn't liked ice in his water for as long as I've known him. I glance over at him and he sends me a sad smile before taking a sip.

We haven't even been here for ten minutes and I'm ready to give him the bunny ears signal and run. He's been so open, so trusting, lately and I don't want his parents causing him to close back up. I scoot my barstool closer to him and cuddle into his side, showing my support silently. He wraps his arm around my shoulders and rubs circles on my arm.

"Seeing you two like this is something else," his mom says. "I never would have guessed, of all of the people in the world, you'd choose Cami."

"What do you mean?" he asks, and I wish he hadn't.

"Oh, nothing. I just always saw you two as best friends and couldn't imagine you going further than that. I'm glad you've both found someone to settle down with though."

I smile over at her and resist the temptation to say anything else. George waltzes through the back door, saving us from furthering this topic of conversation. Charlie stands and greets his father with a hand shake, which George takes and pulls him in to hug him, slapping him on the back a few times.

"Son, it's good to know you're alive," his dad says with a laugh. "You get a new phone number?" he teases.

"Nope," he responds. I tense at the teasing that is certainly not just teasing. The tension in the room is thick, and I brace myself for the rest of the evening.

"Why don't we make our plates and head to the table," his mom suggests, clearly trying to move to a different topic other than Charlie's dad's unanswered phone calls. "I can make yours, Charlie. Ketchup and mustard?"

"Mustard only," I respond, not giving him the chance to answer for himself. I shrink, a little embarrassed that I interjected, but it was just an instinct. I notice, again, how little his parents actually know him. He leans over and kisses my cheek.

"Thank you, baby," he whispers in my ear. He takes my hand and guides me to the table.

We all take a seat, and dig in. The table is quiet for a moment more than is comfortable, and his dad breaks the silence.

"So, how's hockey going? Last game was a doozy."

I cringe. Not only does Charlie resent the fact that all his dad does is talk to him about hockey, I know he hates when he gives him tips. The last game *was* a doozy, it was a shutout for the other team. Rangers lost three to zero.

"Hockey is fine," he answers in a clipped tone. His dad doesn't pick up on the tension and pushes forward anyways.

"What drills are you running? That coach of yours needs some serious help if he's happy with the way you boys performed out on the ice. It was a shit show."

"George, no need for the language," his mom chides.

"What? Charlie knows I'm right."

I can tell that something is shifting. It almost feels as if the air in the room has changed direction, and I shiver knowing something is about to happen that none of them will be able to come back from easily. I almost jump up and make some excuse to get out, but I'm not fast enough.

"How come you never ask about Alana?"

My heart breaks a little at the mention of my best friend and her broken relationship with her parents. She's done nothing to cause it, but they seem to care very little for her or her wellbeing. It hurts to see her hurt, and it hurts even more to see Charlie hurt in tandem.

His parents bristle at the question, like they're surprised he asked, although I'm not sure why.

"Do you two even know what's going on with her? That she got a promotion? That she's seeing an incredible guy and it's serious?"

"We knew she was in Paris for work," his mom answers.

"Right, because she called and left a voicemail telling you. You wouldn't even pick up to talk to her. What kind of parents don't answer their childrens' phone calls?"

"What kind of children don't answer their parents' phone calls?"

"Oh, yeah. Let me pick the phone up after a game only to get yelled at and told everything I could have done differently."

"You don't want to get better? You don't want to sharpen your skills?"

"You're my dad, not my coach!"

The room quiets at his outburst. He never raises his voice, like ever. He is the one person I can always count on to be even tempered and calm, but he's let go of any pretenses now and I can't help but think he needs this. He needs them to know how he feels. They need to be called out.

"Your sister has always been able to take care of herself," his dad says, ignoring the comment about his coaching.

"She's your daughter. She needed her dad, and you weren't ever there."

"Please, she never needed me. I was busy helping you and if she needed me she should've spoken up or taken up something worthwhile that she could turn into a career. Maybe then we would've had something to pay attention to."

Charlie stares at his father and I can physically see the anger building inside of him. I brace for whatever he's about to say.

"I don't understand what happened to the dad I knew when we were little. Back before hockey and traveling, when things were simple and we were young and you loved us."

His mom reaches up and wipes a tear from her cheek. I feel sad for her. Even though I know she's not been the best parent, I can see in this interaction alone how she follows behind her husband and takes his lead. It's cost her the relationship with her children.

"People change," his dad says with a shrug. He seems so unconcerned with this conversation, it's baffling to me. My parents and sister hound me about my life choices and they aren't always the kindest about it, but they are nowhere near this callous and cruel.

"We're leaving," Charlie says as he stands. He grabs my plate and his, and takes them to the kitchen, careful not to leave a mess behind. I turn and address his mother only.

"Thank you for having us, Mrs. Cade. I'm sorry our visit was cut short," I say as I glare in her husband's direction.

"You have something to say to me?" he sneers. Charlie enters back into the dining area now, pushing me behind him.

"You don't say a word to her, you don't even look at her. As far as we are concerned, you are dead to me. I have no father. You can stop calling because I will never pick up, and I will never speak to you again. If you can't do something as simple as admitting your mistakes and choosing to love your children for exactly who they are, then we are done here."

"Get the hell out of my house!" George yells.

"Gladly. Come on." He takes my hand and I follow him to the front door. His palm is shaking in mine and my heart breaks for him. I can't say I'm surprised, though.

When we reach the front door, Charlie grasps the knob to open it but is stopped by his mom's hand on his arm. He turns to her, sadness in his eyes.

"Sweetie, I'm sorry. He gets worked up and—"

"I love you, Mom, but I will not be around him," he says, cutting her off. "I won't speak to him. If you're really sorry and don't enjoy all of this, why do you let him get away with it? Stop being a passive bystander if you miss us. Take ownership and do something. If you ever want a relationship with me or with Alana, you might want to take that into consideration." He turns, opening the door and stepping out. "You might want to call her, Mom. She misses you and she's got a lot going for her right now. I wouldn't be surprised if she has a big event in the near future that she's going to want her mom around for."

His mom nods, clearly unsure exactly what to say after the evening we've all just experienced, and Charlie continues forward.

He opens my door and I step into the car, sitting down. He reaches for my seatbelt, as if he's going to buckle me in. It's like he's on autopilot, moving through motions even though they don't make much sense.

"I've got it," I say softly. I bring my hand up to his cheek. "Do you want me to drive?"

"No, I need to."

I nod and he closes my door and makes his way around to the driver's side.

As he climbs into the seat beside me, I look over at his profile and something inside of me clicks into place. I have an overwhelming feeling that I am exactly where I'm supposed to be. The surety is something I am extremely unfamiliar with, always feeling the need to move from this thing to that, but this is different.

I might change hobbies and hair styles and nail colors every other week, but my love for the man beside me will never change. My love for him is steady and sure, and I realize that choosing something, or someone, doesn't have to be scary. Life is all about having fun and trying new things, but it's even better when you have someone grounding you while you experience it all.

I know that no matter what crazy activity I want to try, or what hobby I might pick up on whatever given week, Charlie will be by my side for all of it. The permanence in that, and my lack of fear, is a beautiful thing.

CHAPTER 47
Charlie

My grip on the steering wheel is concerning. My knuckles are white and I wouldn't be surprised if there are indentations from my fingers on the leather. We've driven in silence for the last thirty minutes. I think Cami is giving me a second to breathe, but I know I need to check on her and I desperately want her comfort and support.

As if she can read my mind, she reaches over and places her hand on my thigh, rubbing back and forth soothingly. Instinctively, I soften and my grip loosens to something a little more normal. After a few seconds of her touch, she speaks softly.

"Well, that was something."

"Hah," I scoff. "Yeah, you could say that."

She pauses, letting me come to terms with what happened and waiting for me to speak. Cami never speaks too quickly. She's bubbly and bright and silly, but in a serious moment she is the most self aware person. She seems to know exactly what I need, and she never pushes me to talk faster or say more.

"I can't believe he said that stuff about Lan," I say in bewilderment. I knew that, for whatever reason, my parents didn't pay attention to my sister the way they did me, but I never would have imagined the utter lack of care they have.

I keep saying the word they, but after tonight I can't help but wonder if my mom has just been collateral damage in all of this. My dad is a strong man, and while she has free will to make her own decisions, I can absolutely see him telling her not to bother with calling my sister and her listening. I hope after tonight, though, she might start to realize how wrong their actions have been.

Cami sniffles next to me and I whip my head to look at her. She's staring out the window, clearly trying to hide her emotions from me.

"Hey, baby, look at me. Why are you crying?" I grab her chin gently and turn her face towards me.

"I'm sorry, I'm fine, this isn't about me," she says and waves me off. She wipes the tears from her cheeks and takes a deep breath. My attention battles between her and the road, and I'm grateful when we roll up to a red light. I turn towards her.

"Tell me what's wrong."

"It just makes me so sad to hear the way they talked about you and Alana. She's my best friend and she has only ever wanted their love, and you've done all you can to be the best son yet they treat you so poorly. It makes me hate them, and I don't want to feel that way."

My heart softens at her care for my sister. One of my favorite things about Cami is the way she cares for those around her. Alana, me, Mia, the women at her knitting club, and even all of the hockey guys she's met recently. Her love for my sister only draws us closer, because we share that in common.

"I know, it hurts me too. He pushed me over the edge tonight. I don't think we're ever going to be able to come back from that conversation. I won't be able to forgive him, and he doesn't look like he's anywhere near ready to ask for forgiveness or realize he's in the wrong."

"I just don't understand how someone can completely cast aside their child. She did nothing wrong, like literally nothing. And same with you, all he cares about is hockey."

"Hockey and money."

"Have you been giving them money?" she asks. The question has zero judgement behind it, but I tense at it regardless.

"I've sent some to my mom a few times when she's asked, but nothing in the last year. I think he likes that he has access to it if he needs it, but I won't be sending any more."

"I'm so sorry," she says. "I wish we were home so I could cuddle you."

I laugh at the way she phrases it, but I feel all gooey at her desire to comfort me. I begin to think how much things have changed in the last few months. I don't think I've ever been as close to the old version of myself as I am right now, even in the midst of the hurt, and a big portion of that is thanks to the woman sitting next to me.

Opening up to people and letting them in, trusting them, doesn't have to be this big scary thing. Little by little, people earn their place in my life. The more I let in, the more love I get to experience. My life the last handful of years has been a pretty lonely place. I had my sister and I had Cami, but I hadn't completely let either of them in. No one knew the extent of my trauma from the incident in high school, and I didn't want anyone to know.

But day by day, Cami wormed her way into my heart and into my circle of people I can trust, and I am so grateful for it and for her.

"I am so lucky I have you," I say, also wishing we were at home so I could look into her eyes and say this. I don't think I can wait, though. "I am better off because you're in my life and I don't see a future where we aren't *us*. I'm not sure how you're feeling about all of this, but I don't want this to end when we come to the end of our agreement."

She stares at the side of my face, and I heat under her gaze. I'm unsure if that was too much to say all at once, but I need her to know how I feel, how serious I am. I pull up to another red light and the second the car stops, she pulls my face to hers and kisses me passionately.

"I don't want it to end either. I don't think my love for you could ever end," she says, and I bristle at the word. We haven't said those words to each other yet. "I love you, Charlie Cade."

"You do?" I ask, staring into her eyes that slant up at the corners from the huge grin on her face.

"I do. I think I always have, if I'm being honest."

I lean forward and take her lips again, only pausing to pull back and say the words back to her.

"I love you too. I love you so much."

We kiss again, only to be startled by the honk of the car behind us signaling that the light has changed. We both jump apart, then break into giggles as I push on the gas and the car lurches forward.

"I need to talk to Alana," Cami says next to me. "I want to be absolutely certain she's okay with all of this."

"I think that's a good idea. You want me there for that?"

"No, I think it should just be me."

"Whatever you think is best."

She leans her head back on the headrest, turning it to look at me as I drive. We hold hands as she hums along to the music and I've felt more settled in my entire life, than I do with this woman by my side.

CHAPTER 48

Cami

CHARLES 🩶

Let me know how it goes. I'll be in practice for a majority of the day, but if you need me, call.

CHARLES 🩶

I'm giving my phone to the assistant and told him to get me if you call.

> ME
>
> It's your sister. Everything is going to be fine

CHARLES 🩶

She can be scary!

> ME
>
> I'm not worried

CHARLES 🩶

Just tell me you'll call if you need me

> ME
>
> I'll call if I need you. Now go practice.

CHARLES 🩶

I love you

ME

I know

ME

I love you too

WE WALK INTO ANGEL'S AND I SIGH AT THE FAMILIAR atmosphere. Angel's Mexican restaurant is one of our regular spots for dinner, but with Alana being in Paris and everything going on with Charlie and I, it's been a while since we've been.

Sierra, the hostess, seats us in our usual booth in the back and we each grab our menu, acting as if we are going to order something different than the quesadillas we both usually order. A waiter I'm not familiar with comes over and takes our drink order, a Diet Coke for Alana and a Dr. Pepper for me, and leaves us with chips and salsa.

"It's about time we had a bestie date. Our schedules have been insane lately and even though I see you in the office things have been so busy."

"Well, yeah. Now that you're the managing editor and have your own fancy *private* office, I barely see you."

"Whatever, we still eat lunch together almost every day."

"Yeah, us plus one more."

"He always brings chocolates, though," she says with an eyebrow raise.

"You're right, that's a good point. He can stay."

"Whew," she says, wiping her brow in fake relief. "So," she says after a few minutes of light chatting and munching on chips. "Quite the doozy of a dinner with our parents."

"Yeah, Charlie said he talked to you."

"He did."

We pause to place our orders when the waiter comes back over to us.

"I always knew my parents were disconnected and had

favorites between the two of us, but for my dad to put it so plainly really is a punch to the gut."

"It was...a lot."

"I'm sorry you had to be there to witness it. I hate that they dragged you into it."

"I was glad to be there to support Charlie," I say, then reach over to grab her hand on the table. "I'm sorry that they can't be what you deserve. I'm sorry you don't have more support from them."

Her eyes water and she sniffles quietly, clearly trying to hold the tears at bay. I stand and move to her side of the booth, pulling her into a side hug. We stay like that for a few moments before she sits back up and smiles sadly at me.

"Thanks, Cam. I appreciate that." She uses her napkin to dab at the corners of her eyes. "I'm hoping it was a wake up call for my mom and she might finally make a decision that's best for us and for our family and leave him. If he's treating us this way, I can only imagine the way he's treating her."

"Charlie said some of the same things. For your sake, I hope she takes the steps to mend the relationship. I know it would be good for all three of you."

Our food comes, and we both dig in. We have some light conversation about work and a few shoots I have coming up. Things at the magazine are good, and we've entered into a steadier season. The holidays are always hectic, but now we're about to move into spring and things usually settle down some.

Alana has started to ease into her new role, and she's doing fantastic. Everyone in the office respects her immensely, and she's easy to work for.

"I wanted to talk to you about Charlie," I say. My stomach churns with nerves.

"Oh, okay. What about him?" she asks, giving me her full attention.

"I know you said that if something were to happen between the two of us, you would give us your blessing."

"I did say that," she says with a knowing smile on her face.

"I'm sure you can guess where I'm going with this."

"Maybe, but why don't you tell me anyway?"

"Right, well I have feelings for your brother."

We stare at each other for a few seconds, then promptly burst into laughter. Eventually we come down from our giggles, and I speak again.

"This is all so weird, but I want to be sure we're being open with you and I don't want any secrets."

"Some things can remain a secret. Trust me, I don't want to know all of the details."

"Well, I'm not telling you those details," I say, laughing at her.

"So you're saying there are details to share in that department?"

"Lan! We are so not talking about that."

"Okay, fine, fine," she laughs. "Have you two discussed your feelings? I know you were a bit hesitant to make anything official."

"Yeah, we talked about it. I was hesitant, but he shared his thoughts with me and I realized that having something permanent isn't a bad thing. Charlie grounds me in a way that I desperately need. He's steady where I'm wobbly and calm where I'm chaotic. My perfect puzzle piece."

Alana smiles at me, eyes glassy again.

"Lan, if you cry right now I swear I will—"

"I'm sorry, I'm just so happy for the both of you. You two deserve this more than anyone I know."

"Thanks for being so great about this. I was worried it would be awkward."

"Well, it is a little bit awkward. But you've both existed in my life together for so long now that it just makes sense for me. It's an easy transition in my world, plus after finding love myself I don't think I would be a very good sister or best friend if I stood in the way of you two finding what I've found."

"I'm so glad things worked out between you and Alex."

"Me too," she says and her eyes go all gooey. I smile at the love that shines on her face, and feel excited for what's in the future for both of us.

"So, you're still going to the wedding together I assume?"

"Yeah, we leave in a few days. Colette has been blowing up my phone nonstop. I think she's getting anxious and is wanting to make sure everything is perfect."

"That makes sense since it's one of the most important days in her life."

"Yeah, I don't blame her. It *is* going to be perfect, though," I pause, taking a sip of my drink. "Hey, do you think we'll be planning any big important days for you in the near future?"

"Oh gosh, I don't know. We only just got together a little over a month ago," she pauses, smiling down at her lap before looking back up at me. "I do see it heading in that direction, though."

I squeal in happiness and excitement and she laughs. Ever since we were young, awkward girls in high school we have dreamed of these days. We used to plan out our weddings and what dresses we would wear. She always said she'd dance to a Taylor Swift song for her first dance, and I vowed that I would have red velvet cake. It's surreal to be at a place in our lives where we're finally getting all of the things we ever wanted.

Looking at the woman across from me, I have an overwhelming feeling of gratitude. This world is a scary place. It's so big and there are so many possibilities that it can feel paralyzing, but I know with her at my side I can face anything.

CHAPTER 49
Charlie

SOREN

Have fun on vacation

ME

Would you call being bombarded with
questions by my girlfriend's family a vacation?

SOREN

Good luck, soldier

"Can I get you anything to drink?" the flight attendant asks Cami. She's sitting in the window seat and I took the middle. She protested, saying I'm much bigger than she is, but I don't want her to have to sit by some stranger. Turns out the man next to me is an older man who has given the flight attendant one too many weird looks, so I'm glad I insisted.

She also wouldn't let me buy our plane tickets or upgrade us to first class, because this was her part of the deal. She needed me to come with her to the wedding, so she would be paying for the tickets. I only argued for a few minutes before admitting defeat.

"I'll take a Dr. Pepper, please," she says with a smile.

"And you, sir?"

"Water, no ice, please."

"You are crazy for not liking ice in your water. That's disgusting."

"It's easier to drink faster, and I have to stay hydrated."

"Okay, hockey boy." She laughs at me and I roll my eyes at her. To be honest, I just started drinking my water without ice when one of my physical therapists suggested it as a way to get more water down faster a long time ago, and I never stopped. I have no idea if that's really how it works, or if it's a mental thing.

We've been on our flight to Florida for around an hour and a half, which is about half way through the duration. So far, she's been reading a new release from one of her favorite romance authors and I've been playing games on my phone like a third grader.

Now though, she's put her kindle away and is giving me her full attention. She sips her soda and munches on the pretzels the flight attendant handed us, and I can't help but think about how surreal it is that we're on vacation together just the two of us. I mean sure, we're going to a family wedding not a beach vacation, but still this feels like a big step.

"Okay, I need the rundown," I say, turning my body to face hers. "Who all is going to be at this wedding? Who do I need to make sure to impress, and who do I need to avoid at all costs?"

"These are good questions, and I almost wish we would have done some studying before right now but I didn't think about it, so oh well." She takes another sip of her drink and grabs a pad of paper and a pen from the bag under her seat, then starts to make a list.

"So, we have my Aunt Brenda, she's my mom's older sister." As she talks, she adds the people to the list and makes little notes beside them. "She's really nice and shouldn't ask you too many questions. If you are feeling overwhelmed, find her and just stand near her. That should be a good shield."

"Got it, Aunt Brenda equals shield."

"Exactly. Then we have my Uncle Matthew, my dad's brother. He drinks a lot and is pretty rowdy. I'm sure he'll say something inappropriate so you're going to want to work on that poker face around him, not that you need to. You're pretty good at being expressionless."

"Hey," I chide, poking her in the side. "I've been getting better."

"You sure have, superstar," she says and pats me on the shoulder, obviously joking. "So you know my sister, Colette, but you haven't met her fiancé, Derrick. He's really great and a solid guy, not that you'll have much of an opportunity to talk with him since he's the one getting married, but just so you know we approve."

"Glad to know we approve of Derrick."

"Both of my grandmas will absolutely ask you many questions, most of which will be intrusive and not appropriate in the slightest. If you get caught in a conversation with them, just bring up *The Golden Girls*."

"The television show?"

"Yes. They love it and will get into a back and forth, so you should be able to back away slowly and they won't even notice."

"Great tip. Who is going to give me the hardest time?" I ask.

"That would be my parents, most likely."

I've known Miranda and Grant Slate since high school, just like my sister, because of the time we spent hanging out at Cami's. They also were way more involved with their daughter, so they knew where she was and what she was doing at all times. Many of those times she was with me, and my sister of course.

I was a different version of myself back then, though. I had just been through a lot with my friends and was closing in on myself, not opening up to anyone. I'm sure I was growly and cold towards them, and that won't help me now. I'm going to have to work hard to show them the version of me that their daughter has brought out, one that's welcoming and warm and willing to bring people in.

"Any tips?"

"Honestly? No. Just be yourself and be honest; my dad can tell when someone isn't being genuine and he'll call you on it. Don't worry about how he's perceiving you and just be you. He'll appreciate that. My mom will just want to know I'm loved and cared for, and I am," she says with a smile.

"You certainly are. That sounds easy enough."

"You say that now, but I wouldn't be surprised if by the time we are on our way home you're second guessing the decision you made to make this permanent." She says it with humor in her tone, but I can tell this is a real worry for her. She's letting a little bit of her insecurity show, and I'm grateful I've caught it so I can reassure her.

"Cam, I'm not worried about the impression your family is going to leave on me, or the one I'm going to leave on them. There are only two people in this relationship, and they're sitting on this plane right now."

"I knew something was going on with the flight attendant," she teases.

"Shut up and stop deflecting, you goof," I say and she giggles.

"Okay, sorry, you're right."

"Like I was saying, there are only two people in this relationship. Nothing that happens this weekend is going to come in the way of that. You have me."

"Thanks for saying that. I needed to hear it."

"Of course. Now, what are we going to do for the next hour?"

"Oh, we could watch a movie together," she says and bounces in her chair excitedly.

"How would we do that? We can only use one pair of headphones per screen."

"We just pick a movie and push play at the exact same time. What movie should we watch?"

We scroll through the options for a while and land on a recent release. After three tries, we finally push the play button at the exact same time and start the movie. We get part of the way through it before we have to turn it off and prepare for landing.

Once we land in Pensacola, we collect our bags, and grab our rental car, then make our way to the hotel where the wedding is taking place. It's about a thirty minute drive, and the weather is sunny and beautiful. It's a nice break from the cold in New York.

We pull up to the door of the hotel to unload our bags, and Colette is standing there with, who I assume is, her fiancé. Cami practically bursts out of the car and runs towards her sister.

"Coco!" They squeal and jump around in a circle as they embrace, Derrick and I looking on and smiling at their hysterics. I walk up and introduce myself to him, shaking his hand.

"Hi, Charlie, I'm so glad you're here," Colette says as she comes over and gives me a side hug.

"Hey, thanks for letting me come celebrate."

"Well, this one insisted," she says as she hip checks Cami. Her cheeks flush and I smile. "This is such a fun development, the two of you. I was skeptical at first, but I like it."

"Colette, we just got here. Let the man breathe."

"Sorry, sorry, you're right. I'll let you two get checked in and settled. Rehearsal dinner is tonight at seven, the details are in your room."

"That sounds great, can't wait. See you soon."

"Bye," they both say as they turn and Derrick leads her away to wherever they're headed.

"This is going to be interesting," Cami says with a laugh.

CHAPTER 50
Cami

ME

<<one attachment>>

BESTIE FRIEND

OMG you look hot!

BESTIE FRIEND

Has my brother seen you?

ME

LOL, not yet

BESTIE FRIEND

Good luck getting him to separate from you once he does!

BESTIE FRIEND

Have so much fun!

"1...2...3," THE PHOTOGRAPHER COUNTS DOWN AS THE bridesmaids and I prepare to turn around and see my sister in her wedding dress. We all spin on three and cheers break out in the room, all of the girls going crazy at how beautiful she looks.

They all swarm her with hugs and words of encouragement,

but I hang back. My eyes water as I take her in. My little sister is standing in front of me looking like every bit of the woman that she is. Her dress looks even more beautiful on her now than it did a few months ago in the bridal shop, and the added details of her veil and hair style make it even more magical.

Once the girls have had their moment, they split apart and she walks towards me, holding out her arms.

"You look absolutely radiant, Coco," I say as she embraces me. I squeeze her tight and we stay like that for a few moments. It all hits me then, my sister is about to get married.

I'm suddenly overtaken by strange feelings of excitement but also deep sadness. It's always just been my sister and I. We don't have any other siblings, and from a young age we were inseparable. I was so excited for her when she got engaged, but I don't think it clicked for me that she'd belong to someone else now.

Not in a weird way of ownership, but her small moments and silly inside jokes would be shared with someone else and that person isn't me. She will share a bedroom with someone who isn't me, and they'll likely have a laughing fit at one in the morning when neither of them can sleep. I won't be a part of that any more, and that transition is a strange one.

While I am more than excited for her and she deserves every bit of love Derrick is going to offer her, it feels a little bit like I'm being replaced. Someone else gets to be her person, and I have to be okay with that.

I quickly gather myself and my emotions before I pull back, not wanting to burden her with them right before she's supposed to walk down the aisle. The photographer snaps photos of us as we share a moment together, laughing through the tears.

"Are you ready to do this?" I ask.

"More than ever," she says and I squeeze her hand.

We make our way back into the dressing room to touch up the makeup that might have moved around through our tears. Later, all of the bridesmaids go outside with her to take a few photos before the ceremony.

As the photographers are posing some of the bridesmaids for individual shots, I pull my phone out to check on Charlie.

ME

You doing okay?

CHARLES 🩶

Yep, just hanging out with your Aunt Brenda.

ME

Good call. I had them sit you by her for a reason

CHARLES 🩶

My girl is always looking out for me.

ME

I put my phone back into my bag and follow behind the coordinator as she pulls us all into a line to get ready to walk down the aisle. The music starts and nerves begin to bubble in my stomach as our line starts to move forward. I look back and wink at Colette as she joins arms with our dad, then turn and make my way to my place.

As I walk, I look for Charlie. When I find him, he smiles at me and I melt immediately—my broody cold hockey player who turns soft just for me. I love him and I love the way he makes me feel cherished and wanted.

My mind wanders as I make my way closer to where he sits, off to the side. I start to picture what it might be like for me to walk down an aisle to him, but with me in the white dress and him in the tux. The image doesn't scare me, but instead causes me to smile widely.

I love you, I mouth as I pass him. He says it back and we smile knowingly at one another.

We all then turn to watch my vision of a sister float her way down the aisle to her forever.

"Oh, I love this song!" I shout at Charlie over the music. The reception is well under way and I have had the best time dancing with my sister, my family, and Charlie. He's been great, constantly by my side and making sure I don't need anything.

He's gotten a few questions and stares from different family members, but so far it has been surprisingly uneventful. If we can make it out of here unscathed, I will be immensely happy.

We continue dancing through the song, the beat traveling through my toes, up my legs and into my chest. When the song ends, Charlie suggests we take a break outside and I agree, following him to the large yard area with cocktail tables scattered around.

My parents are crowded around one of them, laughing together, and they wave us over.

"Well, I guess now is as good a time as any," he says. I nod at him in encouragement.

"Mr. and Mrs. Slate," he says, shaking their hands. My dad takes it and instead pulls him in for a hug.

"You know you can call us Miranda and Grant, no need for formalities."

"Well, I'm not just the annoying neighbor kid now, so formalities do feel slightly required," Charlie says with a chuckle.

"That's right," my mom says. "Now, you're dating our Cami."

"I am," he says and wraps his arm around my waist, tugging me into him. "I love her very much."

He looks into my eyes as he says the words, as if my parents aren't even there. I get lost in his gaze, forgetting them myself, until I hear my mom's quiet giggle.

"Oh, to be young and in love. I sure do miss those days."

"Our best days are ahead of us," my dad says and kisses her head. I smile at their easy affection after so many years. "Charlie, you're going to look after my girl?"

"With my life, sir."

"Well, then that's all I need to hear. You break her heart, we're going to have more than a conversation. Understand?"

"I understand."

"Good."

"Do you boys mind giving us a moment? I'd like to speak with Cami privately," my mom says. My heart drops into my stomach as I wonder what she would want to speak with me about if she feels the need to dismiss my father and Charlie.

He looks down at me as if to check that I'm okay with him leaving me with my mom. I smile up at him, or at least I hope my face obeys and smiles, and he squeezes me once before letting me go and heading inside with my dad.

"Everything okay?" I ask.

"It's not, but it's nothing you've done."

I breathe a little easier at that, thankful that this isn't turning into another criticism moment. She pulls me in for a hug and squeezes me so tight it hurts.

"I'm sorry," she whispers into my hair. It's so quiet, if she wasn't right by my ear I wouldn't have heard it.

"What for?" I ask as she pulls away. She has tears in her eyes, which automatically makes mine do the same.

"I haven't been fair to you. I know I've been hard on you and I've been overly critical of your choices and I'm just so sorry. Your father and I are so proud of you, and we love you very much. The comments I've made about your choices in boys and activities hasn't been the way a mother should act towards her daughter, and I'm sorry for that."

I take a deep breath, absolutely stunned that the words she just spoke left her lips. This is coming out of nowhere, and I don't really know how to respond.

"What brought this up? Is it Charlie? Now that I'm settled you're happier with me?" I ask. I know it's harsh, but I can't understand how she would just randomly realize the things she's said to me my entire childhood and early adulthood have been completely inappropriate.

"Oh, honey, no. I had a long talk with Colette and she pointed some things out to me. She didn't betray your trust, but she did tell me that she believes you've been hurt by my actions. It took me some time to sit with the things she said, and think about the things I've done. After thinking, I was extremely remorseful. I love you, unconditionally, and whether or not you marry that man or stay single forever, that will never *ever* change."

I start crying then, unable to hold the tears back any longer. Tonight has been an emotional overload, and while I'm so happy my sister is married, and so grateful my mom has recognized her mistakes, I feel overwhelmed.

My mom pulls me into a hug and we stay like that for long moments, cuddled together.

"Let's get back inside, it's cold."

"Mom, it's in the sixties," I laugh.

"Exactly."

She ushers me back inside and I immediately return to Charlie's side.

"Everything okay?" he asks.

I nod and wrap my arms around him.

"Everything is great. I'll tell you about it later. Thank you for coming with me," I say as I cuddle into him. "I'm really glad you're here as my real boyfriend and not my fake one."

"Me too, trust me."

And I do.

March

CHAPTER 51
Cami

BESTIE FRIEND

I'm on my way. How is he?

ME

Just get here. He's being weird

BESTIE FRIEND

What do you mean?

ME

I don't know. He seems okay but I know he isn't. The guys just got here so maybe that will help

ME

Or maybe it'll make it 100 times worse

ME

Lan, I don't know what I'm going to do if he leaves

BESTIE FRIEND

I'm five minutes out.

SOREN AND THEO BURST THROUGH THE FRONT DOOR OF the penthouse, both with worried and somber looks on their faces. They each give me a hug, and when I see Mia it takes everything in me to not burst into tears. She pulls me into a hug and squeezes me tight.

"It's going to be okay," she whispers in my ear.

Last week, Charlie and I got home from Colette's wedding and we were so happy. It's crazy how much can change overnight. We had a great flight home and with the way our relationship has changed over the last few weeks or so it was starting to feel permanent in the best way.

This morning we woke up and Giovanna had the day off, so Charlie made us breakfast and we joked around in the kitchen, making plans for the future, and dreaming about things that are far off, but it was fun. Until I got a notification from a local news network that he was being traded.

We had no idea there was even talk about a trade, everything we had been doing the last few months seemingly paid off. I had honestly forgotten we were approaching the trade deadline with how quiet things had been. Sophie hadn't said anything, and because we were no longer in a fake relationship I think we sort of forgot about all of it.

I expected Charlie to react differently than he did. He has always been anxious about change, and he wasn't completely devoid of anxiety, but it was far better than I was expecting. He normally would shut himself off from everyone, hide out in his room, and let his mind wander to the worst possible scenarios.

This morning, however, he seemed clearly nervous and tense but was very rational about it all. He told me we needed to call Sophie and check to make sure what we were hearing was accurate. There are rumors all the time about this sort of thing, and just because we're hearing it from a random news outlet doesn't mean it's the truth.

I called Sophie and put her on speaker phone. She seemed

absolutely furious and told us she was already on it, and she'd call back when she had more information. We've been waiting since then, and it's almost dinner time now. It's been absolute torture.

"He's in the living room," I tell the guys. Mia and I follow behind them and I watch as they each envelop Charlie in a hug. Mia moves in and does the same, and everyone settles on couches and chairs around the living room. I sit down next to Charlie and snuggle into his side.

"You all didn't have to come over," he says to the group.

"Man, don't even talk like that. We came as soon as we heard. You think they're really talking about a trade?" Theo asks.

"No way in hell. With the publicity you two have gathered lately they'd be stupid to let you go," Soren answers. Mia agrees with a head nod.

"I'm not sure. There's always a chance, that's just how things go."

"I don't know, it still seems far-fetched in my opinion," Soren replies.

"Cam, how are you doing?" Mia asks me. Four pairs of eyes swing my way, and that plus the question seem to unlock the emotional dam I had in place because I burst into tears.

Charlie turns his body to face me and pulls me further into him, and Mia comes to sit on my other side, rubbing my knee.

"Hey, it's going to be okay, Cami. We'll figure it out," he says as he soothingly rubs circles on my back.

"Ugh, I am so sorry," I groan, wiping my face and trying to take deep breaths. "This is so not about me. I'm fine, really, just tired from the trip. Just give me one second, I'll be right back."

I stand abruptly and leave the room, heading for the bathroom in the room Charlie and I now share. I close the door behind me and stare at myself in the mirror, forcing deep breaths into my lungs. Why am I the one reacting like this? He should be the one having a moment, not me. I'm supposed to be holding it all together for him. I'm supposed to be the strong one right now.

A few seconds later, the bathroom door opens and Alana walks through. All of the tension leaves my body at the sight of my best friend. She pulls me into her and hugs me tight, and it feels as if all of our problems will be a little easier to solve now that she's here.

There are certain people in your life that you know will help you keep your head on straight in the middle of a crisis, and Alana is that for me. Any time I'm freaking out, she always calms me down, so having her here now is a relief.

"It really is going to be okay," she says when she pulls back.

"I know. I know that we can do long distance and I can visit and go to his games. Maybe work will let me do some days virtually or something."

"Woah, woah, woah, let's slow down. We don't even know if this is real yet."

"Why would it be out there if it weren't?" I ask. I know, logically, that people put out fake news stories all the time, but I can't imagine why someone would do that to Charlie. There isn't anything for them to gain by doing that.

"There are a number of reasons. It could be someone who wanted to sell a story for some money and fabricated the truth in order to get that. It could be an angry fan from an opposing team. It could be anything, really, and we can't freak out until we know the truth."

"Who are you and what have you done with my bestie? I recall having to talk you down a time or two, but you're sounding very level-headed now. What happened?" I ask, poking fun.

"Therapy. And Alex."

"Well, those are two really good things."

"I am freaking out a little bit. I'm trying to keep it together for you two, but he's my brother. We've always been together."

"I know. But like you said a second ago, we can't freak out until we know the truth."

The door behind her cracks open a bit and Charlie pops his head through.

"I'll give you two a minute," Alana says before turning and walking back out into the rest of the house.

He crosses the bathroom and wraps his arms around me, breathing deeply. He runs his hands down the length of me, to the backs of my thighs, and pulls me up to sit on the counter. He steps between my legs and hugs me close, then pulls back to look at me.

"We're going to figure it out. If I get traded, we will work it out."

"I know," I say, nodding. "I can come and visit and when you have a bye week you could maybe come here."

"Or you could come with me," he says. I look up at him with wide eyes. We just recently made this an *actual* relationship, and now he's talking about us moving to another state together. The idea doesn't scare me like I thought it would.

"You would want that?" I ask.

"Of course I would. I would never ask you to uproot your life, but if you felt like it was the right move for you I would love to have you come with me."

"How are you being so cool about all of this? Isn't this one of your biggest fears? Didn't we do all of the things we've been doing the last few months to prevent this very thing from happening?"

"I'm terrified, Cam," he says with a watery smile.

I haven't ever seen Charlie cry, and while I don't think he's about to burst into tears, he looks awfully close. He takes a deep breath, then leans forward and rests his forehead on my chest. I reach up and play with his hair soothingly.

"What are you scared of?"

"All of it. I finally got to a place with my teammates where I'm not jumping every time someone walks around a corner or racing to make sure I'm never the last one in the locker room. I'm finally opening up, and it feels like that's all being ripped away."

"You've been doing so well," I affirm. "But these guys you've built these relationships with aren't going to just go away. If you move they're still going to be your friends."

"I know. I just don't want to have to do all of that building again with new guys that I don't even know. It took me years with some of them to get to this place."

"I know it's scary to trust new people, but you've learned a lot about yourself over the last few months. I think you're in a much better place now. If you have to start over, you'll be okay."

"And we'll be okay."

"We will."

He hugs me again and takes a deep breath, but the calm bubble around us bursts when we hear shouting from the living room.

CHAPTER 52

Charlie

"CAMI, CHARLIE! SOPHIE IS CALLING!"

I pull her down from the counter and she practically shoves me out of the bathroom. We rush to the living room and Mia meets me in the hallway with my phone, handing it over. I slide my thumb across to answer the call and put it up to my ear.

"Hey, Soph," I say, breathless.

"Hey, Charlie. Are you doing okay?"

"As well as is to be expected, I guess. Do you have news for me?"

"Yeah. Can you come into the office to meet with me?"

"Now?"

"I figured you'd want answers now, unless you want to wait until the morning."

"No, now is fine. You can't tell me over the phone?"

"I'd just rather we discuss it in person," she says and my stomach sinks.

"Come on, just tell me if I'm getting traded. I'd rather not drag it out." Cami places her hand on my arm and squeezes in support.

"You know I wouldn't drag it out if I didn't need to. Just come to the office and I'll explain everything."

I hang up the phone and the room is silent, waiting for me to speak. Cami looks up at me nervously and the rest of the faces surrounding me aren't much different.

I've held it together pretty well today, but if I'm being honest I am an absolute wreck inside. When Cami showed me the news article this morning, I felt like I was going to be sick. Everything I was afraid was going to happen seemed like it was happening despite all the work we put in to prevent it.

She has been a solid rock all day, making lunch for me and offering herself up to hear any thoughts I need to get out, but I haven't really taken her up on her offer. It felt like if I let any of my doubts or fears out, the fragile facade I had in place would shatter. I was on my way to a small breakdown when Sophie called, and considering the fact that she didn't give me much reassurance, I don't feel far off from one right now.

"She wants me to come to the office," I say directly to Cami, even though the rest of them can hear me.

"Did she say why?"

"No, just said she wants to discuss it in person."

"Okay," she says quietly.

"It's going to be okay," I say as I reach my hand out and slip it behind her neck, pulling her towards me and placing a kiss on her forehead.

"Do you want me to go with you?" she asks.

"No, I've got this. I'll come right back."

I hug her and the guys, then squeeze my sister tight before jumping in the car and driving to Sophie's office. The sun is setting outside and I start to think about what my life will be like if I get traded. No more New York City sunsets, no more busy traffic, no more loud streets in the middle of the night—all things someone might complain about, but have become like home to me.

No more Cami, no more Alana, no more Alex or Soren or Theo or Mia. That's the biggest gut punch. After sharing some of my anxiety about my past with Cami, I have felt like I can breathe a little easier. I know that, even if I had to go to another team, that feeling would follow me there.

I'm not saying it wouldn't take me a while to warm up, but I don't think I would be as closed off as I was when I started with the Rangers. I have grown a lot in the last few months, and I feel proud of myself for it. The thing that I was most afraid of, being traded, doesn't seem like nearly as big of a giant as it did back in December.

I remind myself of these things as I enter the building and walk up to Sophie's office. She's already there, sitting behind her desk, but stands and crosses the room to pull me into a hug.

"I am so sorry about all of this. I can't imagine the day you've had."

"It's been pretty sucky, but it happens."

Someone clears their throat behind me and I turn, shocked to see Coach Smith and Michael Montgomery, the owner of the Rangers, at the door to the office. My heart starts beating fast at the sight, because if they're here then this is official. I can't help but think this means they are certainly trading me, and it just got leaked early, but I try not to jump the gun.

"Cade, Sophie," Coach says as he shakes our hands. Michael follows and they both sit down next to me.

"Well, I'm sure you're wondering why we're all here together," Coach starts.

"I am, sir."

"Sophie, why don't you tell him what we've discovered today."

"I'm happy to. This morning, right after you called, I got on the phone with my source at The New York Post and asked them where they got their information. They were, of course, reluctant to share with me, but eventually broke and told me the name."

"Is it someone I know?"

"Troy."

"You're kidding. I can't believe he'd do something like that."

"I know. He's an angry guy, but I didn't think he would stoop this low. Anyways, once I learned who it was I was pretty sure I knew it wasn't the truth, but I had to reach out to Coach Smith to be certain. He and I then met with Michael, and we determined that it was absolutely not true."

The breath leaves my lungs in one big whoosh and I must look visibly relieved, because Coach laughs.

"Boy, do you really think we'd trade you? After the fantastic year you've had so far?"

"I-I wasn't sure," I say, mind reeling and trying to take in everything they're saying.

"Charlie, we really value you as a player and as a person on our team," Coach says. "I would fight for you if they came to me and told me they wanted to trade, but I didn't need to because Michael sees the value in you that I do."

"He's right. Not only are you a beast on the ice, but we've been seeing the work you're putting in with the team. You belong here."

The words settle something within me that I didn't know was out of place. Feeling like I belong on a team is not something I've experienced since that day in high school, and I hadn't even realized that I had started to feel that again with the Rangers until he said it.

I do feel like I belong, and I know those guys are my family. They would stick up for me if I ever needed it, and if I had an emergency I know they'd be by my side in an instant. They have my back and they want good things for me, and I know that with certainty. It feels so good to be able to feel that again with a group of guys.

"We let the Hurricanes' owner know. I'm not sure what they're going to do about it, if anything."

"Thank you all for investigating and figuring out what happened so quickly. It's been eating Cami and I up all day," I say.

"I wish we could have figured it all out faster, but you know how these things go," Sophie says.

"This is all fantastic news, but why did we need to do this in person? Sophie probably could have explained this to me over the phone."

"That's where I come in," Michael says.

CHAPTER 53
Cami

ME

Update?

CHARLES

I just walked in the door.

ME

Have you seen Sophie yet?

CHARLES

Not yet.

ME

Text me as soon as you're done

CHARLES

I will baby.

CHARLES

On my way home.

ME

What happened?

ME

Charlie?

I'VE BEEN PACING THE LENGTH OF THE LIVING ROOM since Charlie left, clutching the phone in my hand waiting for him to text or call or send a carrier pigeon or something. Everyone left about half an hour after he did to give us privacy when he came home, which I appreciated at the time but now I wish Alana or Mia were here.

My brain has been cycling through thought after thought as I've been walking in circles for the last hour and none of them are all that good. If he's traded, how is that going to affect him? Is he going to fall right back into his old patterns and close off again? Isolating in a new location where he knows absolutely no one is not good for him in the slightest.

When he was here and trying to be alone, Alana and I could pull him out of it every once in a while or just drag him to one of our apartments to spend time with him. If he's somewhere where he has no friends, who is going to do that for him? I know he said I could go with him, but we haven't even figured out the logistics of that. What would I do about work?

Not to mention, the fact that we have no idea where he'd end up if he was traded. Hell, he could be going to the Hurricanes for all we know. If that were to happen I don't even want to think about how he would react to that. I could see him retiring early if the Hurricanes were his only choice.

Or what if everyone on his new team is just like his team in high school? What if they hate the way he plays and they hate any amount of confidence he has and instead of being friends with him, they beat him down until he's nothing but a shell of the person he's worked so hard to bring back?

I've certainly thought myself into a spiral, which is about to turn into a full on tornado if he doesn't either a) text me back, or b) walk through that door immediately. I groan in frustration and look down at my phone. Still nothing. He said he was on his way home half an hour ago and it normally doesn't take much longer than that to get here.

Oh no. What if he got into a wreck?

Thankfully, I'm saved from myself when the door opens and Charlie walks in. I take stock of his entire body. He has an easy expression on his face, it's not red from crying or stress. His eyes seem calm and at ease, but that's not enough to assuage the anxiety climbing inside me, so I continue to scan.

His shoulders seem good, they're down and not tensed up. His arms hang leisurely by his side and he isn't fidgeting nervously with his hands like I am likely doing right now. The bottom half of him seems fine, so I scan my way back up searching for anything that is amiss.

"See something you like?" he says and winks.

The man winks at me. At a time like this, while I am on the verge of a breakdown? And he's trying to be playful?

"Charlie, please tell me what's going on. I'm out of my mind nervous right now."

He steps forward and pulls me to him. I go willingly, always happy to be in his arms, and melt into his chest, breathing in his familiar scent. It's become home for me over the last few months.

"Everything is okay," he whispers into my hair.

"They aren't trading you?" I ask, pulling away to look up into his eyes. He's smiling down at me, and I allow myself to take a breath. He doesn't look like he's devastated or delivering bad news.

"They aren't trading me," he says with a smile.

"Oh my gosh, why didn't you call me and tell me that?" I exclaim, and shove his shoulder without any real fire behind it. "I've been pacing around this apartment worried for an hour and a half."

"I'm sorry, I just wanted to tell you everything in person."

"There's more?"

"Yeah, why don't we take a seat and I'll explain it all?"

He makes us both tea and we take a seat back on the loveseat. He pulls my legs into his lap so I'm practically sitting on top of him, and pushes my hair behind my ear lovingly. This feels very familiar to the last time he shared something deep with me.

"So, what did Sophie say?" I ask.

"That's the thing, it wasn't just Sophie. Coach and Matthew Montgomery were there too."

"Matthew Montgomery as in the *owner of the Rangers*?"

"The very one."

"That seems...dramatic. Is it normal that he would attend a last minute meeting like this?" I ask, dread building in my stomach again. Why would he have been there?

"Not at all, I've only seen him at major team events and things like that."

"Okay, so why was he there?"

"Well, Sophie told me that the story was given by someone and was a lie."

"Why would they do that, though?"

"It was Troy," he says. My blood boils as I remember all the things Troy has done to this sweet and kind man.

"I'm going to put glitter in his air vents," I say before turning, setting my tea down, and starting to get up.

Charlie pulls me back to him. "Woah there, tiger. Glitter?"

"Imagine if you turned the air conditioning on in your car and glitter exploded out."

His eyes widen. "That would take forever to get out."

"Exactly," I say, resolute in my idea.

"We will revisit that idea after we discuss everything else, because it isn't a bad one."

"He does live in North Carolina though, so we'll have to work-shop that. But please continue."

"Right, so Troy sold the story to the New York Post and I guess had enough believable evidence that they thought it was true.

Sophie told the Hurricanes management, but who knows if they'll even do anything about it."

"He cannot just get away with that."

"I'm sure he'll get some kind of suspension at the very least, but I couldn't tell you exactly what that would look like."

"Okay, fine. I want to make him suffer, but fine."

"So vicious," he says, pressing his forehead to mine. "I like it."

"You're killing me. I just want to know what happened."

"You're right, I'm sorry. So they told me I wasn't being traded but that still didn't explain why Matthew was there. Until he pulled a stack of papers out of his briefcase."

"He brought a briefcase to an emergency meeting?"

"Well, when you're carrying important things like my contract to re-sign I guess you need one."

"Wait," I say, pressing my hand to his chest. His smile is bright and hopeful and it brings tears to my eyes. "They want to re-sign you? You got a contract?"

"Four more years."

"No way! Charlie, that's perfect. I am so happy for you." I lean forward and press my lips to his. After a few moments he pulls back and smiles at me.

"Thank you, baby. That gives me four more years, and then I can decide about retirement once we get there. It was exactly what I could have hoped for, and I have you to thank for it."

Me? Why would he have me to thank?

"You did all of this on your own. You're out on the ice, not me."

"It's about more than the ice, though, which is why we've been doing everything we've been doing since December. Your help with social media and the list you made brought in so much positive publicity, it's all thanks to you."

"Well, sure that was part of it but you did a lot of the things on that list. I just came up with the ideas."

"And like I said when you showed it to me the first time, you saved the best for last," he says as he pulls the list out from his back pocket. I haven't looked at the actual list since we discussed it back in December. I remember him making that comment about me putting myself last on the list. I didn't believe him when he said it then, but I believe he feels that way about me now.

"You are the best thing that has ever happened to me, Cam." He cups my face in his hands, his tea long forgotten on the coffee table. "This whole idea might have been insane when I first brought it to you, but I couldn't be more grateful Sophie had the idea and you said yes. It brought me the best thing I could have ever asked for."

"Charlie," I say, unable to say much more.

"I love you, Cami."

"I love you," I say, then lean forward and kiss him deeply.

We spend the night tangled together, talking about the future and what things will look like now that we know he's staying in New York.

"You should move in here," he says a little while later as we lay in bed. I push up on my elbow so I can look down at him and gauge how serious he is. He looks pretty serious.

"Really?"

"I mean, only if you want to."

"I want to," I say, faster than is probably acceptable. "Do you mean like, let go of my place?"

"Yeah. You don't need that apartment if you're living in this one."

I smile at him, then lean down and press a kiss to his lips. I flop down in the bed next to him and cuddle close, happy to call this place and this person home.

April

CHAPTER 54
Charlie

SIS

Alex wants to know if he needs to wear a sports coat.

SIS

I told him yes, but apparently he needs your confirmation as well 🙄

ME

Yes, a sports coat.

ALEX

Thanks, man

SIS

This is ridiculous.

WE WALK INTO THE FANCY HOTEL BUILDING IN THE CITY and I marvel at the way they've decorated the entire place. It's late April, still pretty chilly in New York, but the weather is nice today. It's in the sixties and sunny, and Cami chose a gorgeous pink dress to wear so I'm a happy guy.

We made it through to the second round of playoffs before our season came to an end, and I have to say I'm happy with it. Of course, we would have loved to go on and win the Stanley Cup, but I knew our team wasn't quite there yet this year. I have high hopes for next year, though. We've all been working better together lately, and while it was too late to have it together for this season, I think we have a jump on the next.

The end of the season party is tonight, and I have more people than I've ever had attending with me. Alana usually comes to these things, but I haven't ever invited Cami. I didn't ever want her to feel obligated to attend, and she never asked to, until now. She didn't have to ask, she knew she was coming.

Alex and Alana are already sitting at our table when we walk in, and they stand to greet us.

"Hey, man, nice sports coat," I say to Alex, just to piss my sister off. She gives me a death glare and he and I both laugh.

"It was not a good idea to allow you two to become friends," she says, shaking her head in disappointment.

"You know you love it, sunshine," Alex says before pressing a kiss to her temple.

"Yeah, yeah," she replies.

We take our seats, letting the girls sit next to each other and Alex and I on either side of them. A little while later, Soren and Mia show up and sit down with us at the table. Over the last few months, the six of us have become more acquainted with each other and it's turned into a fun group that we let Theo in on as well, even though he doesn't have a girlfriend.

"They really went all out with these decorations," Soren says from across the table.

"I was thinking the same thing," I reply.

The tables all have bunches of red and white flowers on them, arrangements that I know cost an arm and a leg, not to mention the other decorations around the room. There are countless red, white, and blue balloons, more flowers on the stage, and the catering is as fancy as it can be.

We usually have these end of the season parties, and they *are* usually a big deal, but it surprises me every time. I'm not really sure why; I know they can afford it, but it's nice. I don't know if every team has parties like this each season, or if it's just an us thing, but I look forward to them every year. Even when I wasn't super close with my teammates, it felt like an opportunity to close the door on one chapter and open up the next one.

As we eat our dinner, we laugh and talk about memories from the past season. Our friends listen in and Cami smiles affectionately at me as we talk. I know she's thinking about the fact that I wouldn't normally engage like this with my teammates or have anything to contribute to the conversation, and I think we're both grateful that I do this year.

A while later, Coach Smith makes his way onto the stage at the front of the room and taps the mic, getting everyone's attention. He stands tall and proud as he thanks us for another great season and shares that he's excited for the next one. He then moves into awards, which they do every year. They typically do awards like best improved, rockstar rookie, showmanship, things like that. I'm pretty sure it was something our PR person, Olivia, came up with a few years ago. She wanted to be able to post more about the end of season party on social media and gave Coach the idea.

"And lastly, we have one more award. This award is one that the guys voted on this year, and I am happy to present it."

We always vote on the award for Most Valuable Player, and that didn't change this year. What did change was I was able to actually submit a vote that made sense because I knew my players much better this year than in the past. In the past, I used to just vote for whoever had good stats, but the other guys always took it deeper and voted for someone who they felt deserved it for more than just their time on the ice. I voted for Soren this year, for obvious reasons.

"This award is going to a man who has shown himself to be a true team player this season. He's stepped out of his comfort zone and has brought an energy we all needed on the team," Coach pauses and grabs the wooden award on his left. "Charlie Cade, why don't you come up here, son?"

I freeze, unable to move from my seat. I certainly wasn't expecting him to call my name, so my reaction time is quite delayed.

"That's you, superstar," Cami whispers from my side, tears in her eyes.

"What?" I ask, still bewildered.

"You got the award, go up there," Soren says.

I stand, reluctantly, and slowly make my way up as people all around me clap and cheer. Being the center of attention is so far out of my comfort zone, so it feels like an out of body experience as I make my way to the stage. One second, I'm sitting in my chair and the next I'm standing next to Coach. He gives me a firm pat on the back and hands the award to me. Someone snaps a picture and I hear Cami cheering the loudest in the back of the room.

"Charlie, we are so proud of you and the team wants you to know that. They want you to know that they see you as a brother, and that you belong here. There is a place for you on this team and with these guys, and they made that clear to me not only through their votes but also by the number of them that stopped by to tell me how much you deserved this award this year."

I look out into the crowd at the many faces of the men I've grown close to over the last few months. Not only Soren and Theo but a number of others all across the team. Those friendships just started to fall into place once I began to feel more comfortable, and they all smile back at me in encouragement.

I take it all in—the guys looking back at me, Coach standing next to me, Alana crying quietly in her seat, and Cami next to her beaming up at me with the proudest look on her face. I take in the way I feel right now. Solid, sure, confident, any word besides scared or worried. These guys did that for me. Sure, I stepped out and made an effort, but they met me where I was and brought me into the fold and I couldn't be more grateful.

"You want to say a few words?" Coach asks.

"Um, sure." He steps back and I move over to the podium, clearing my throat. "First, I just want to say thank you. Thank you for voting for me, I totally wasn't expecting that. Thank you for being a safe space for me to come to and be myself. I, um, I don't share this much and I won't get into the details, but I had a really bad experience on a team in high school that caused me to close off and not engage with others much. I isolated myself, and I thought that was good enough for me."

Cami smiles at me from the table and Sophie, who arrived during dinner, nods her head in encouragement.

"Until my agent Sophie told me I needed to get my act together." Everyone laughs at that. "And my girlfriend Cami showed me what it was like to be known and to be loved. I had been known in the past, but I hadn't been loved. I hadn't been cherished or cared for or seen as an equal, until her."

I second guess the words as I say them, because my sister sits next to her and she has always shown me love and care, but my eyes shift to her and I see an understanding there. She knows what I mean.

"I am so thankful for you, Cami, and all that you've shown me these past five months. I couldn't do this without you," I say and she mouths *I love you* back at me. "And to all of you, my teammates, thank you again. Thanks for voting for me, for standing up for me, and for making this team a place where I feel comfortable."

Everyone applauds as I make my way back to my seat. I pull Alana into a hug first.

"I'm so proud of you," she whispers in my ear.

I move then to Sophie and shake her hand, which she pulls forward and envelops me in a hug as well. I thank her for all of her help not only this year, but every other one too. Then I move to my girl.

I pull her in and kiss her deeply, not caring when the whoops from the guys around me come.

"Thank you," I tell her.

"I could have said all of that about you too."

"Well, then it seems like we make the perfect pair."

"We definitely do."

CHAPTER 55
Charlie

8 Months Later

TEXAS IS AN INTERESTING PLACE. I HAVE ONLY BEEN here a handful of times for hockey games and things like that, but I never got any free time to explore the cities we were in. This weekend, we're in the small town Alex grew up in, celebrating Christmas.

My mom is with us this year, which is a big change. After the dinner at their house, she had finally had enough and left my dad. She took the house in Long Island so she could be closer to us, and she's been much more involved since then. She has monthly dinners with us and comes to my games when she can. It's been a nice change.

Earlier this week, Cami and I traveled to Florida to spend some time with her family for the holidays, and after a crazy time there with her newly married sister and brother-in-law, we jumped on another flight and met my mom in Texas.

Alex's friend Banks is hosting us in the small inn that his family owns just five minutes away from Alex's mom's house. It's really the perfect setup, and I could see us doing every Christmas here from now on.

Banks's daughter, Halle, is the star of the show today. We have all been opening various gifts from one another, but there's nothing quite like watching the joy of a child as they open their gifts. She's spoiled by not only her father, but also Alex's mom and Alana, plus we got her a few things as well.

"Dad, look at this one," she shouts as she holds up a pair of roller skates and pushes them in Banks's direction.

"Wow, honey, those are really awesome. What do you say to Auntie Alana?"

"Thank you," she sing-songs as she barrels toward Alana and almost takes her down with the force of her hug.

"You're so welcome, sweetie. You have to make sure you wear a helmet, though."

"Oh yeah, gotta stay safe."

"Exactly," her dad says before handing her another.

We go on like this for a while, watching her open various trinkets and toys. Eventually Alana opens a gift from Alex—a box set of Barbie DVDs—and I laugh. Despite the fact that the gift may seem funny, I am so grateful my sister has found someone who knows her so well. They got engaged a few weeks ago, and I am so excited and happy for them. They make a great team.

Cami and I determined we wouldn't do gifts this year, just because of everything we've had going on lately. She moved all of her things into the penthouse in May and I had some time off during the off season. We went on a long vacation to the Bahamas and then came back just in time for preseason things to pick up.

Even though we agreed no presents, I do have a trick up my sleeve. I have a feeling she won't care all that much that I went back on my promise, though.

Once we've opened all of the gifts, I point out a small box that is sitting tucked in between the branches towards the back of the tree.

"Wait, I see one more. Cami, can you grab it?" I ask her.

"Oh, sure." She reaches back into the tree and pulls out the little black box, then reads the name on it. "It looks like this one is for me. I thought we said no gifts?"

"I couldn't help myself, here let me see it." I take the box from her dainty hands and laugh at the confusion on her face. If she didn't understand before, she definitely does now as I move to get down on one knee and open the box to expose a glittering ring inside.

Her hands shoot up to cover her gaping mouth as her eyes dart from me, to the ring, and back again. I wait for her to collect herself, her eyes watery, before I start to speak.

"Cami, this last year has been the craziest ride of my life. From starting something with you that had an expiration date, to having real feelings, to falling in love, I have enjoyed every single minute of it. I am so thankful to have you by my side," I say and she sniffles, reaching up and brushing tears from her cheeks. "I don't want to know what life would be like without you in it. Can you do me a favor and marry me, so I never have to find out?"

She laughs and bends down to kiss me through her tears. She pulls back and looks me in the eyes before saying a very happy yes and I slide the ring onto her finger. She holds it out in front of her and twists her hand from side to side, inspecting it.

"This is absolutely beautiful, Charlie. How did you know the one I wanted?"

"I had a little help," I say, nodding toward my sister. She stands then and pulls Cami into a tight hug.

"Wait, we get to wedding plan together now," Cami says with glee and the two of them sit down together and start to talk about details.

Alex comes over to me and gives me a hug, congratulating me.

"We got lucky with those two," he says.

"We absolutely did," I reply.

Acknowledgments

And just like that, my first duology is complete! When I decided I was going to actually write my first book, Tied Together, I wasn't quite sure where it was going to go. Most people plan out these things, and I will admit that going forward in my author journey I am doing that, but when I got started I did not. I wrote Alex and Alana and as I was writing their story, Cami and Charlie demanded I give them attention immediately. As I was going through editing and releasing Tied Together, there they sat in the back of my mind begging me to open the word doc again. Once it was time to shift my efforts to Best for Last, it flowed like water. These two characters felt so familiar to me and so familiar to each other, and writing that relationship was a gift. I had so much fun with their story, and I sincerely hope you did too.

First, I need to say a huge thank you to all of you, the readers, for the ways you've changed my life in the last half year or so. Your enthusiasm and excitement for my first book and the subsequent excitement for this one have fueled me and pushed me forward when I felt like I was just about done. Thank you for that. Thank you to the advanced readers who read, review, and share about my book on all of the platforms. I would not be here if it were not for you.

Thank you for coming to reader events, book signings, book fairs—you name it —and showing support for me and so many other authors. You have no idea what that means to us. You've given me a quiet confidence I didn't have before and I am forever grateful for that.

To my mom, Michele, and my grandmother, Linda, thank you

for being my biggest cheerleaders. My mom has had one copy of my first book on her TV stand in her living room and one on her bedside table since I handed them to her months ago. She reads a few pages a night on her kindle, despite the fact that she's already read her physical copy. She used the multiple friendship bracelets from my preorder as Christmas tree ornaments last year because she purchased so many copies. She supports me endlessly and I cannot thank her enough.

My grandmother is constantly checking in on me, asking details about my writing process and how things are going. Of everyone I know I think she might be the most excited about reading this book. I hope you loved it.

To my dad, who bought multiple copies of my book without consulting my mom first, only to find that she too had ordered multiple copies. Thank you for your support, for designing my website and helping me keep it updated, and for teaching me how to dream big and make pathways where it seems like there aren't any. You have never *ever* made me feel like anything was impossible for me.

To my sister, Bekah, thank you for honestly everything. I am not me without you and I feel so grateful that we have the relationship that we do. You are an incredible support in my life and I really would be drowning without you. Thanks for always picking up the phone, even with a baby on your hip and one on the way, and being ready to listen to my fears and worries about this book (and everything in life, let's be honest) and talking me down and giving me advice. I love you.

To my new author bestie, Emily Tudor, thank you. Your excitement for this book has certainly gotten me through many many roadblocks. Thank you for always being there to scream about character art, cover design, plot ideas, and every little thing in between. I am *so, so* happy we are friends.

To Lex, my critique partner, October birthday twin, forever book recommender, and friend. You are endlessly supportive and have held my hand through this entire experience from starting Tied Together to now. I can't tell you how grateful I am for your willingness to chat with me when I'm freaking out (from excitement or worry) and the way you communicate so clearly. Maybe a funny thing to be grateful for, the way someone communicates, but it makes all the difference. You are phenomenal. I am so thankful to know you.

To my friends and family that I haven't mentioned by name above, thank you. Every text, phone call, and random check-in, they all mean so much to me. Your support means more than I could ever describe to you. I have the very best community around me.

To my alpha and beta readers: Lex, Emily, Alicia, Kate, Chelsea, and Natasha, thank you for all of the hard work you poured into these pages. We wouldn't have a final product if it weren't for you.

To my phenomenal editor, Kristen. You are extremely kind, considerate, professional, and smart. These books would be a hot mess without the hours and hours of work you have put into them. Working with you for the last year and becoming one of your friends has been a privilege.

To my phenomenal cover designer, Sam, you once again created something so beautiful and I am so honored to get to work with you.

And, if you've made it this far, thank you! Thank you for reading and for taking a chance on my words. I hope I'll get to see you for the next one.

About the Author

Baleigh Jayne is a Texas native who loved to read and write from a very early age. She found herself immersed in worlds outside of her own and in the lives of characters she'd never met, and longed to create ones of her own. Fast forward a few years, and she decided to make her dreams a reality by becoming an author. Now, Baleigh writes contemporary romance that is full of light-hearted fun, swoony kisses, and deep lessons that just about anyone can learn from.

When Baleigh isn't writing or posting on Instagram, you can find her sipping on a Diet Coke and listening to Taylor Swift, or hanging out with her niece Georgia and her nephew Elliott. She also loves cozying up with a good book or spending time with her family.

To learn more, visit her website https://authorbaleighjayne.com/ or follow her on Instagram @authorbaleighjayne.

www.ingramcontent.com/pod-product-compliance
Lightning Source LLC
Chambersburg PA
CBHW030235120726
47903CB00005B/1499